HANNIE RISING

Jeanette Baker

Cover Design and Interior format by The Killion Group
http://thekilliongroupinc.com

ACKNOWLEDGEMENTS

Many thanks to my husband, Tommy O'Callaghan, for his detailed recollections of life inTralee before the European Union, many of which add color to this book. As for the people of Kerry, their wit and charm are unmatched.

A special thanks to Dr. Patrick English of Tralee who described the nuances of Irish emergency medicine.

CHAPTER 1

Mickey

Mickey Enright released a long, slow breath. The stabbing pain that just minutes ago had collapsed his lungs and sent knife-like, jagged thrusts pounding down his left arm and through his chest had disappeared, leaving in its place a euphoric, slightly energized sense of well being. Afraid to trust this new sensation, Mickey kept his limbs perfectly still. Slowly, ever-so-slowly, he opened his eyes. Activity somewhere below distracted him, drawing his attention. Shifting for a better view, he looked down upon a scene of what looked, to him, like professional chaos.

In a small, white-walled room, smelling of antiseptic, five people, one man, the rest women, all dressed in medical scrubs, swarmed about a motionless figure stretched out on a table. Except for the patient, he recognized all of them. Doctor Dougherty lived in the housing estate above Cahirweesheen, not too far from his own house in Ballyard. They didn't move in the same circles but Johannah, Mickey's wife, spoke highly of him and they'd occasionally met while walking.

Molly O'Leary was a nurse and his mother-in-law's neighbor. She kept an eye on Dolly and reported to Johannah when her mother talked to the walls or argued with people dead for decades. Marie Sullivan, another nurse, was called in on child abuse cases. She'd gone to school with Mickey's daughter, and was recently married. He and Johannah had attended the wedding. He remembered thinking she'd been a mousy little thing when she was a girl but that she'd turned out nicely in the end.

Kitty Donohue and Claire Malone were regulars at Betty's Pub on Rock Street. They'd grown up in Kevin Barry's Villas just as Mickey had, one in Number 5, the other in Number 14. Kitty and Claire had gone to nursing school together and still lived in the old neighborhood. He grinned remembering the trouble they'd cooked up on the street and the laughs he'd shared with them.

It occurred to Mickey that he was the only one there who wasn't a medical professional and that his presence in the room was odd. But no one else seemed to mind or even to acknowledge him at all and curiosity had gotten the better of him, so he continued to look.

"No pulse or heartbeat. He's coding." Doctor Dougherty, his voice clear and calm, called out instructions as he positioned one hand over the other on the patient's chest, pushing hard and fast, thirty compressions to two breaths. He stopped to check the rhythm. "Set up an IV, pull up his medical history and charge to 200."

Marie Sullivan left the room. Mickey was sorry to see her go. She really was very attractive.

Kitty handed the doctor the paddles. "Stand clear," he called out, spreading his arms. "Stand clear."

The room emptied. Mickey winced as the patient leaped and buckled under the force of the jump. He wondered if the man's ribs had broken and if he felt any pain.

"Prepare for intubation and one milligram of adrenaline," Dougherty called out, once again pushing down on the man's chest for thirty compressions, leaning in for two breaths, checking rhythm.

Claire Malone plunged a syringe into the man's arm, attached a tube and inserted the other end into a liquid-filled bag which she hung on an IV pole. "One milligram of adrenaline administered." Mickey couldn't see what she was doing with the other tube. "Patient intubated," she continued.

"Prepare three hundred milligrams of amioderone and flush through," the doctor called out, continuing the compression. "Check rhythm and prepare one milligram of adrenaline." Mickey watched while Claire added a syringe of medication to the bag.

The doctor checked the monitor. "No change." He raised his arms. "Stand clear. Stand clear. Charge to 300." His voice had risen. Again the room emptied and, as before, the patient, still unconscious, jumped at the kick of the paddles. "Administer adrenaline and flush through."

Unflaggingly, like machines, the team repeated their rhythm, CPR, shocks, this time to 360, adrenaline, amioderone. Sweat beaded the doctor's brow. "Check his pulse," he ordered, one hand over the other, counting and pumping the unresponsive chest. Finally, he stepped back. "Give him forty units of Vasopressin and keep up the CPR."

Marie Sullivan reentered the room. "No history of heart attack, diabetes or suicide," she reported.

The doctor nodded. "It happens. No internal bleeding either."

The room was silent now as the emergency team labored, a seemingly endless rhythm of shocks, CPR and medication.

Minutes passed, or was it hours? Mickey couldn't be sure. His hands were clenched. Anticipation coated his mouth with a strange metallic taste. How odd for this to bother him so. Did he even know the man?

The saw-toothed line on the monitor had flattened, stretching out, thin and straight. Dougherty looked at the clock. His face was gray. "Stop," he said. "He's gone. I'm calling it. Time of death is 6:17 P.M."

Molly O'Leary dropped her head into her hands and wept. "It isn't fair. Johannah doesn't deserve this."

Kitty was crying, too.

"Your man was always up for a good laugh," Claire said, her face drawn. "The town will miss him."

Mickey frowned. Who would they miss? Why would Molly mention Johannah? His Johannah? Hannie? What had Hannie to do with this man, now a corpse, lying on the table?

Marie Sullivan spoke to the doctor. "The family is waiting. Give us ten minutes to make him presentable. Katie's brought her wee boy."

The family? What family? Katie's wee boy? Were they talking about Evan? Mickey opened his mouth to ask but the words never found voice. He felt air under his limbs, a breeze first and then a wind, a terrible wind, tearing at his hair, stinging his skin, burning his eyes, flinging him back and then forward, his body turning and twisting, tossing and rolling until he was flung senseless into the blackness, the void, and then everything was still.

CHAPTER 2

Johannah

Johannah had read once that when a man marries a woman, it is her hand he will hold in the final moments of his life. She remembered being diverted by the sentiment, by the prophetic and powerful drama of the words, but then she'd read on, conveniently forgetting what had turned out to be a truer prediction of her fate than she'd ever dreamed.

She paused in the action of filing the four remaining death certificates she had no idea what to do with. She'd ordered nine, one for The Building Society, another for the church, the bank, Mickey's life insurance company and their solicitor. At the time, it seemed like a good idea to have a few extra, just in case the utility companies required evidence that she, Hannie, his wife of thirty years, four months, twenty-six days and seven hours, and now his widow was, by default, the responsible party.

She knew now that she'd been overly zealous. Given that the entire town of Tralee had shown up for the viewing, the service at St.

John's and the subsequent wake at the house, she couldn't imagine anyone demanding proof of his demise. The amount of food still in her freezer after three weeks was obscene. She'd sent platters and casseroles home with the children, but even so, she could, without exaggeration, live on the leftovers for months. There were only two solutions she could think of, both of them impossible. She couldn't throw away the food because someone was sure to catch her at the dumpster throwing away the very shepherds' pie or lamb stew they'd brought over weeks earlier. Besides, her sense of frugality wouldn't allow it. She could give it away, but somehow the idea of recycling food after three weeks in her freezer seemed beyond thrifty, more like well on the way to being cheap.

Someone was tapping on her back window. She stood, dusting off the knees of her trousers and pulled back the drape. It was Maura Keane. Thank God. Johannah could use the diversion. She motioned her friend toward the back door and opened it.

Maura shook the rain from her coat and stepped inside. Her freckled cheeks were red-apple cold and her glorious hair, cinnamon-brown and damp from the wet, curled riotously around her face. "Where were you, Hannie? I rang and rang. Where's your head? Didn't you hear the bell?"

"Mind the floor. There's water from your coat all over it. My husband died, in case you forgot."

Maura's hand flew to her mouth. "Oh, God, I didn't mean—I'm an awful fool, love. Forgive me. I'm not thinking clearly. Of course you're at sixes and sevens." She looked around the spare room where Mickey once threw bottle caps at the referees on television when he didn't agree with the call. Now his wife used it as an office. The floor boards shone with the same reverence Maura had seen in the entry hall at the rectory. Not a speck of dust filtered through the still air. Every book was shelved according to color and a distinctive lemon scent rose from the couch cushions. "You need to go back to work, Hannie," she said matter-of-factly. "This place looks like a feckin' undertaker lives here."

Johannah winced, opened her mouth to remind her visitor that she didn't tolerate cursing in her house, not by women anyway, and that she'd had enough of undertakers, but then she decided against it. Maura always did have a mouth that a bar of soap would improve. Johannah had known her since they entered the Convent School together at six years old. She was her first and dearest friend and there would be no changing her. Sometimes, in particularly morbid moments, the thought crossed Johannah's mind that the time would come when one of them would have to face the world without the other. The very idea was so unbearable that she would force herself to change direction, to bury the dreadful possibility with whatever means would ease the moment. She shook off the notion. "Come into the kitchen and I'll put on the kettle. Why aren't you working?"

"Milo is minding the store." Maura unwrapped her scarf, unbuttoned her coat, threw both on the nearest chair and followed Johannah into the kitchen. She sniffed appreciatively. "Something smells good."

"Nan Heaney brought over a coffee cake. Pour yourself a cup of tea. What am I going to do with all this food?"

Maura settled her small form into a chair. "Bring it to work with you. Those cows at the Health Executive never heard of saying no thanks to food."

"That's mean of you, Maura. You sound like my mother and even she wouldn't say such a thing if she wasn't on the way to being completely dotty. They're lovely people with good hearts. Not everyone can weigh seven stone. Besides what does it have to do with you?"

"Not a thing," Maura replied breezily. "Forget I said it. How is your mother?"

Johannah groaned, pulled a knife from the drawer and began slicing the warm coffee cake. "She's desperate. I'm having her bills sent here. Otherwise she'd toss them into the fire or end up sending more than she owes. She shouts at my father at all hours of the night. More than likely her neighbors are after taking up a collection to have her admitted.

"Your father passed away ten years ago."

"Exactly."

"What about Philomena and Kathleen? Are they any help at all?"

"They don't live here."

"Paying bills doesn't require living in Tralee. Do they know you're shopping and cleaning for her, too?"

"They know."

Maura added milk to her tea. "Have you actually told them, Hannie?""It isn't something to just bring up."

"Why not?"

Johannah set a plate of coffee cake in front of her friend. "It sounds as if I'm putting myself forward, as if because I'm doing it all I think I'm better than they are."

"When it comes to caring for your mother you are better."

"Only because they're not here," Johannah argued. "They'd do the same if they lived in town."

Maura shook her head. "That isn't true."

"All right, miss know-everything, what is true?"

"You're a giver, Hannie. Look at what you do for a living. You care for everyone, even when they don't want it. It's people like you who let the takers off the hook. Phil and Kathleen are takers and you're their designated giver."

Johannah picked at her cake. She hadn't had an appetite since they laid Mickey in the ground. Not that she couldn't afford to lose a bit of weight. "What am I supposed to do? She's my mother."

Maura picked out another slice of cake. "Tell your sisters you can't do everything and make them share the work. Just say it out loud, all at once, like."

Johannah shook her head. "Look at you, eating me out of house and home and still thin as a spider's leg."

"Don't change the subject." Maura glanced at Johannah and spoke so as to get the words out as quickly as possible. "Do you think Dolly might be better off in a home?"

"She won't hear of it."

Maura set down her fork. "What will you do, Hannie, when things get worse?"

Johannah forced her mouth to lose its tremble. "She'll have to come here and don't you say another word."

This time it was Maura who changed the subject. "It's Thursday. Are you keeping Evan tomorrow?"

Relieved at the new direction of their conversation, Johannah shook her head. "There's no need. Katie's off this week."

Maura reached across the table and covered her friend's hand. "Can I do anything for you, Hannie?"

Johannah shook her head.

"You know it isn't a bother for me. You'd do the same if anything happened to Milo."

"Bite your tongue, Maura Keane. Don't call down bad luck upon yourself."

Maura sighed and stood. "If you don't need me, I'm off to the Building Society to pay my loan. May God punish them for their outrageous rates."

"Be grateful. With our economy the way it is, you're lucky they loaned you any money at all."

Maura frowned, an expression that raised her short upper lip into a cat-like pout. "You're very good, Hannie. Don't you get tired of always looking on the bright side?"

"Better that than the other." She smiled bracingly. "It's all I can manage at the moment."

Maura nodded, wrapped an arm around Johannah's shoulders for a quick hug and disappeared down the hall. The reassuring click of the dead bolt followed almost immediately. She was gone and once again the house was silent. Johannah, suddenly bereft of energy, couldn't bring herself to move. She attempted a laugh. It failed miserably. *Always looking on the bright side.* Is that what people said about her? It wasn't how she saw herself at all. More like pathetic, lonely and irreparably saddened, a woman crippled by a too early loss, a woman completely unprepared to move forward on her own. Tears sprang into her eyes and rolled down her cheeks. She didn't bother to brush them away. She'd been crying for weeks now. The slightest thing set them off : finding an unexpected picture, Mickey's voice on the answer machine, the memory of a conversation, couples in a restaurant or walking on the road, any sight or scent of two people locked in a world of companionship and she was a weeping mess, no longer coherent.

Johannah hadn't considered the possibility of Mickey dying. Death, grave sites and markers were subjects she thought she had years to sort out. Mickey was so healthy and vital, so youthful, lean and straight and looking years younger than he was. He'd been so proud of his appearance, so carefully casual about relaying an encounter where his remarkable good looks were mentioned. Johannah had long since decided against letting the attentions of other women toward her husband bother her. In the end, Mickey always came home to her …until now.

Now Johannah woke in the morning with the vague uncomfortable feeling that she was alone. But for the briefest of instants, in that gray moment when she was still hazy from sleep, not yet awake but nearly so, when the reason for her discomfort wasn't yet clear, it would hit her all at once, all over again. Mickey was dead. Then the air would leave her lungs in a single gasp. She would lie there hoping it would all be over for her as well, but then her traitorous body would rally, struggling toward survival, sucking in life-giving oxygen, leaving the uncomfortable burn in her chest that no amount of anti-acid medication, fizzy drinks or tap water could completely take away.

It still amazed her how much she missed him. When he was alive there had been times when she'd longed to be alone, when she'd envisioned the luxurious comfort of sleeping in the middle of the bed, of washing only her own clothes, of listening to music she preferred and eating only salad and a boiled egg for tea. She never voiced those sentiments, of course, not even to Maura. But she'd wished for them. Sometimes, in her Catholic background of tangled guilt, she wondered if she'd wished too hard, if God had punished her by giving her what she thought she wanted and then realized, too late, that she didn't want it at all, that she would give anything to wash Mickey's clothes and cook his meals and hear his voice at the other end of her mobile.

It was a silly idea, of course. Johannah wasn't pious enough, nor egocentric enough, to believe that God was overly concerned with the wishes of a middle-aged woman from Kerry. Mickey's heart attack was the result of blocked arteries, a family predisposition, the doctor called it, plaque lining the arteries preventing blood flow to the heart. Smoking and drinking hadn't helped. Neither had the vanillas he regularly consumed. Sick arteries weren't always evident. Who would have thought Mickey Enright with his flat stomach, smooth skin and head full of brown hair was at risk for a heart attack? But he was and now he was gone and she was alone.

CHAPTER 3

Mickey

Mickey was conscious of time passing, but the weight of his eyelids made lifting them too great an attempt. He had no desire to stretch his legs, flex his muscles, even turn his head. He was tired, the kind of bone-weary tired that makes nothing so important as sleep, continual, uninterrupted, effortless sleep. Behind the veil of skin covering his eyes, he saw shadows move, heard voices rise and fall, felt an incredible softness beneath his body coupled with a rocking motion as if he rose, dipped and rose again on a scoop of mashed potatoes.

He was a stranger in a strange land, without Johannah and the children, without anyone familiar. That he knew. Beyond the knowing, he cared not at all. It was wonderful to rest, to feel nothing, to be completely free of stiffness in the knees and back, of cramping in the calves, of the never-ending worry of too many bills and not enough cash, of providing for his family while still keeping back a bit for a pint or two at Betty's or Nancy Miles Pub, of reassuring

Johannah enough to keep her forehead free of the worry line that divided her face with uncanny precision and changed her from the girl he'd married to a woman old before her time.

"Michael Enright." The voice was peremptory, high on expectation, limiting all choice, a voice to be heeded and answered to. With great effort, Mickey opened his eyes.

Standing before him was a small man, olive-skinned, foreign looking, balding except for a carefully cultivated curl falling over eyes so dark they appeared black. He wore a long, loose robe and rough, handmade sandals.

Without thinking, Mickey voiced the question paramount on his mind. "Why aren't you dressed?"

"I am," the man said irritably. "I'm wearing what it is you expect of me." He changed the subject. "You took your time in coming. I'm not accustomed to waiting."

Mickey looked around. Large sand dunes rose and fell all around them. The sky was a brilliant, metallic blue without a hint of cloud. Accustomed to the verdant green and boiling clouds of his homeland, he felt bereft. "Where am I and who are you?"

"I am The Guardian and you are Michael Patrick Enright, although your full name is not as important here as it is where you come from. You may call me Peter."

"I know who I am. It's where I am that puzzles me."

Peter rubbed his chin. "You're not quite where you should be, but if everything goes as planned, we'll have it sorted out in no time at all. The problem is you've a few loose ends to straighten out."

Mickey's eyes narrowed. He wasn't sure about this man, this Peter, with his riddles and his half answers, his bathrobe and those piercing dark eyes that seemed to look into the parts of Mickey's soul that he'd rather not have examined too closely. "Don't be tiptoeing about the bush. Just say it, man, all at once."

"This part is difficult for me," said Peter, scratching the side of his neck and shifting his weight from one foot to the other, the calling card of a man in discomfort. "No matter how often I do this, it doesn't get easier. You're right about one thing. There's no point in mincing words." He drew a deep breath and released it. "You're dead, Mickey Enright, and if you're to end up in a place that's satisfactory to you and to me, there's work to be done. I'll help you, of course, but most of the labor must be yours."

Mickey laughed. This Peter, whoever he was, had swallowed one too many. "Listen lad. I know what ails you. I've been there more times than I care to remember. Why don't you sleep it off and we can talk later."

"I beg your pardon."

"You're drunk," replied Mickey. "You handle it well, better than most, but you're definitely away with the fairies."

Peter sighed. "Drink is not the situation this time, not even for you which is a rare occasion, rare enough to be celebrated. For once in your life try to listen, Mickey Enright, and perhaps you'll understand. You're dead. You had a heart attack while watching the football game on the television. You were shouting at a call when it happened. Johannah found you and rang for an ambulance. It was too late. They couldn't save you."

Mickey began to feel the slightest bit uneasy. "Who couldn't save me?"

"That nice young doctor who lives on your side of town, for one. He tried very hard, as did the nurses. I believe you know them as well. They were very upset. Most people are, of course, when they lose a patient. But it was meant to be. It was your time."

"My time for what?"

"Dying." Peter paused. "Such a harsh word, *dying.* I don't like the sound of it. I suppose we could use *passed away* although that isn't really accurate either. We don't actually pass away. There's no *away* about it. Rather, we move on. *Passed on* is a better phrase, although it could mean a number of things besides leaving one life to start a new one." He looked at Mickey. "That's all there is to it. It's your time to leave your life as you know it and begin again."

Mickey's head was in a muddle. The man was nattering on about passing and dying and starting again. It was outrageous, of course, but there was a small bit Mickey couldn't get out of his head, the part about the nurses he knew and the doctor who lived on his side of town. It was very close to the scene he'd witnessed, too close to be mere coincidence. He decided to test the messenger. "How do I know you're telling the truth?"

Peter looked affronted. "Bearing false witness isn't possible for me."

"You can't blame me for asking. Give me a sign. Tell me what I'm thinking."

"I don't have to be a miracle worker to figure that out," Peter said dryly. "You're not hiding anything, Mickey Enright. You never could. What you're thinking is whatever comes out of your mouth."

"Prove it."

"Excuse me?"

"Prove that you are who you say you are, St. Peter of the pearly gates."

"Surely you know that's a metaphor."

"It's the way I've always heard it. Now, stop changing the subject and tell me something no one else knows except me."

The man's dark eyes were measuring and filled with what could only be pity. "We don't have to do this, you know. I assure you, I'm telling the truth. There is no other alternative here. Yours is the typical reaction of a man such as yourself. Most men who come to us unexpectedly feel just as you do. The adjustment is a bit of a struggle. For some reason women are easier. Nevertheless, you'll become accustomed to your situation, and when you do, we can proceed. Yours isn't a cut-and-dried case by the way. You're hovering on the fence. Now if it were Johannah, we'd have clear sailing. Johannah has led an exemplary life. She's honest, hard-working and unselfish. Her first thought has always been for others, yet another trait females appear to have a handle on. Johannah's destiny is clearly marked."

"What does Johannah have to do with this?" Fear closed around his heart. "You're not thinking of taking *her*?"

"Not at all," Peter replied. "Johannah has a great deal of time left before she's called. Given all she's been through, she deserves some good years." For the first time he smiled at Mickey. "Your concern does you justice. Every little bit helps, you know."

Mickey relaxed. "You've made a mistake."

"Excuse me?"

"You've made a mistake with me," Mickey repeated. "It isn't my time at all."

"My good man," Peter protested. "Mistakes aren't made here."

"Mistakes are made everywhere," countered Mickey. "You sound like an Englishman. Are you English?"

"Certainly not. England didn't exist when I came into my position. I'm an original follower, an apostle, and we don't make mistakes."

"I'd like to speak to a higher authority."

Peter stared at him. "I can't remember orienting anyone quite like you before. There is only one Higher Authority and if you'd done more speaking with Him when you were alive, we wouldn't be having this discussion."

"Am I prohibited from seeing Him?"

"You haven't reached the place where you are able to see Him, although that will come. You may speak with Him, however. Anyone may speak with Him, although the answers you receive may not be the ones you hope for."

Mickey folded his arms against his chest. "I want to see Him."

Peter glared disapprovingly. "You Irish have been falsely credited. You are an impatient and rude people."

"Sorry?"

"You heard me. You have your tea breaks, your pastries and custards and your lovely way of turning a phrase. You've a reputation for politeness. But underneath it all, there's your wit which can be cruel, your vague and twisting replies to direct questions, your unending, merciless, destructive penchant for ugly gossip and, of course, your superior, unquestioning belief that you are the chosen race. You are an arrogant population as well. You have a lovely country, but loveliness isn't unique. You forget the grandeur of the Rockies, the chiseled beauty of the Grand Canyon, the blue glaciers of Alaska. Your tiny scrap of patchwork green, forever surrounded by clouds and inundated by constant, miserable, bone-chilling rain is not what God intended as His model for heaven."

"Why are you telling me this?"

"To point out that you're a stubborn man, Michael Enright."

"All I ask for is a sign."

All at once Peter seemed taller, more forbidding. "Very well, I'll give you a sign. Better yet, I'll show you."

Once again Mickey felt the wind lifting him, stinging his skin, biting into his flesh. It was cold this time, the breath-stealing kind accompanied by a hard rain. Just when he felt the darkness pierce his brain and he could bear no more, it stopped.

Breathing heavily, he looked around. He was behind the wheel of a car, a Viva he'd owned long ago. It was very late, far from the nearest village, and black as pitch. He was stopped by the side of the road and through his rearview mirror he saw a figure walking toward the car. Mickey's hands tightened on the wheel. He remembered the unlocked door and lunged across the seat to engage the lock. Too late. The door opened.

The man slid into the seat. "Thanks for the lift, lad." He reeked of spirits.

Mickey relaxed. "Where can I drop you?"

"Limerick."

Some instinct warned Mickey to keep his destination to himself. "I'm only going as far as the cross at Drumnacurra."

"That'll be grand. There's a caravan park on the way. I'll stop there."

His speech, the small eyes and high sharp bones indicated he was a pavee, an itinerant, one of the travelers barred from the shops and pubs of decent people for their thievery and penchant for brawling. He was also very drunk, a condition Mickey recognized because he was close to the same himself.

The road was narrow and empty with nothing to alleviate the boredom. Mickey, realizing his reflexes weren't what they should be, drove slowly. Eventually the tinker nodded off, his head pressed against the window, oblivious to the dips in the road and the thunk of his head against the glass. His coat hung open and Mickey noticed the pound notes peeking from his shirt pocket. The bulge indicated a significant amount. Where could a drunken pavee have picked up such a wad? Nowhere legitimate, that was certain.

Before a plan had time to root in his brain, Mickey had lifted the money from the tinker's shirt and deposited it inside his own. Heart pounding, he picked up speed and drove the next ten kilometers while his passenger slept soundly. At the fork in the road he stopped and shook the man awake.

"Drumnacurra's less than a mile down the road," he said, pointing out the way. "It won't take you long."

The man rubbed the sleep from his eyes and peered through the window. "There's a serious bite to the air, mate. Would it be too far out of your way to drop me at the caravan park?"

"It would. Sorry lad. There's no rain and the night's clear."

"Right."

Mickey watched the man fumble inside his shirt. His stomach heaved and then righted itself again when he saw the bottle.

Downing a healthy swig, the traveler opened the door and began walking down the road toward the village.

This time the wind didn't feel quite so cold to Mickey. Maybe he was growing accustomed to having his body flung like a bowling ball between earth and somewhere that wasn't quite heaven. When the ringing in his ears stopped, he once again stood before a disapproving St. Peter.

"Do you remember the terrible storm that came in that night, Mickey Enright?"

"I don't. I was very young when the incident occurred."

"How convenient for you." The saint had certainly mastered the art of sarcasm. "Let me refresh your memory. The man you sent away that night, in the wrong direction, fell into a swollen creek and died. Shed no tears for him, Mickey Enright. He was only a tinker."

Mickey appeared older, shrunken and pale, his bravado stripped from him. "All right," he whispered, "you win."

"It's not a matter of winning."

"I'm ashamed."

"Of course you are." Peter's voice warmed. "You have potential. That's why you're here."

"What do you want me to do?"

"It isn't quite that easy. I can't tell you what to do. You must make amends to those you've hurt. In your own way you must decide for yourself to do what is right."

"I don't understand. The man you showed me is long dead. I'm not so bad, you know. I go to Mass on Sundays. I donate a generous amount to the collection plate. I've given up fags and cut down on the drink. I've never seriously looked at another woman." He swallowed. Better to be completely honest. "The incident with Barbara O'Connor when she took off her blouse and sat on my lap meant nothing. Even Johannah never mentioned it, not even once. Ask anyone at all. I'm a man without vice, a clean-living, God-fearing man with responsibilities."

Peter's eyebrows rose. "Say it louder and even you might come to believe it."

Mickey's cheeks reddened. He looked away. "Where shall I begin?"

This time Peter actually smiled. "That's better. Begin at home, Mickey Enright. It all begins at home."

"Is that possible?"

"It's done all the time."

"But I've died. Johannah will have had the wake and buried me. How will I go back?"

"As someone else."

Mickey's head was reeling. "*Someone else?*"

"You'll arrive in Tralee as a stranger. Johannah and your children won't recognize you. If you try to reveal your identity, they won't believe you."

"Is there no other way?"

"I'm afraid not."

"How long will I be there?"

"I don't know."

"I thought you knew everything."

"Who told you that?"

"The nuns at school. The parish priest."

St. Peter shook his head. "Fools, all of them. Don't believe any of it. I'm not the one in charge. All I do is manage the keys."

"But you're the head of the church. You know. 'Upon this rock I will build my church.'"

The saint snorted. "That's always been open to interpretation. Ask any Protestant."

Mickey was rendered speechless. What had the world come to if Saint Peter was calling upon Protestants? "Can you make any decisions at all?"

"A few," Peter concedes. "Most of what will happen depends upon you and Johannah. You may woo your wife, Mickey, as another man. Your time is limited either way, but your stay will be longer if she befriends you. We wouldn't send you back to make her suffer such a loss twice in such a short period of time. But the challenge will be great. You must be in complete agreement for the transformation to take place. If you have the slightest doubt—"

"I want another chance at life. I want to go home, to be a better man. I want to prepare my family, leave something for Johannah and my children. They won't know what to do. Johannah has never been alone. She must be frantic. How is she managing without me?"

"You will be surprised at what Johannah can do," replied Peter.

CHAPTER 4

Johannah

One year later

Stirring raisins into the soda bread batter, Johannah alternated between humming and singing the words, the few she could remember, to the tune, *Whiskey in the Jar.* Mickey had always been the one with the voice. She wouldn't think of Mickey today. Today she was happy and thoroughly content.

The day began as a particularly beautiful Friday. Spring sunlight poured through the windows of her house in Ballyard, warming the oak finish on her dining table and the handmade Irish dresser she'd commissioned from T'os O'Meara, the carpenter whose skill allowed him to pick and choose his projects and to show up when he felt like it, or not.

Johannah was grateful for the circumstances that had given her this home. She and Mickey had moved in when Kate was a baby after her mother-in-law died. They could never have afforded it on their own. Ballyard was where the business owners of Tralee lived behind iron gates in stately homes with names like Ashland House and Faeries Point. On a one acre site, the house, a warm, yellow-gabled, red-trimmed, two-story set back from the road at the end of a long gravel drive bordered by trees, came to her father-in-law from his father. Three of his brothers had never married. That left Mickey, an only child, to inherit the lot.

Because of the weather, Johannah had decided to walk to the Health Service Executive where she worked doing her best to help people qualify for services they needed to make ends meet. They called her a social worker but there was nothing social about it unless endless hours on the telephone setting up meal delivery, home care visits and physical therapy appointments qualified. This morning there was an emergency meeting called by Gerry Fox, her supervisor and nemesis. Johannah had a feeling she knew what it was about.

Stopping in for a take-away coffee at the Daily Grind on Castle Street, she'd noticed a stranger sitting alone at one of the tables. He was a pleasant-looking gentleman, somewhere in his late sixties with thinning gray hair, a belly round enough to stretch the fibers of his cable-knit gansey and friendly eyes. Johannah was fairly sure she'd never seen him before, but he looked up when she walked in and smiled as if he knew her. Tentatively, she smiled back.

He spoke first. "It's quiet here in the morning."

"It usually is before nine," she replied. "Business picks up in the afternoon."

"Do you come here often?"

"Not really, but this morning I need the caffeine. I'm on my way to a meeting at work, one I'm not looking forward to and the coffee will sharpen my wits."

"Tell me about it," he suggested. "Give the caffeine some time to kick in."

And so, without more than a second to think, beyond checking her watch, Johannah did something she'd never done in her fifty years on the planet. She sat down beside a perfect stranger and spent the next twenty minutes drinking coffee and describing what it was like to work at the Health Executive for the likes of penny-pinching Gerry Fox with too little funding and even less time to make an effective difference in the lives of any of the poor souls that were part of her caseload.

Later, upon reflection, she could only attribute her inexplicable and inappropriate self-disclosure, to the odd feeling that he reminded her of someone she knew. While the incident was somewhat embarrassing in retrospect, she couldn't be sorry it happened because of what followed: verbalizing her situation had obviously cleared her mind enough so that when she walked into the meeting and Mr. Kennedy began complaining to the County Council that the land adjacent to the Senior Citizen's facility wasn't needed and should be sold, Johannah had jumped in explaining that the land was definitely needed, cited statistics showing that the demand for additional senior housing was increasing by the hour and that there was even now a waiting list for future sites. Her defense was spirited enough that the County Council voted unanimously to hold on to the property.

The incident had given her such confidence she decided she was up to visiting her mother and picked up a plate of take-away from the local Chinese Restaurant. Dolly had been unusually cooperative, thanking Johannah for thinking of her and not mentioning the short duration of her stay or the fact that both of her sisters had fared better than she had as far as their marriages were concerned.

Then, just as she'd walked in the door, the phone rang. As it turned out, Liam and Kate were coming for dinner, just the two of them. They'd rung separately, Liam first and then Kate. She couldn't remember a time when they were last together, the three of them, without Kate's husband, Dermot, little Evan and whichever supermodel Liam was dating at the time. Johannah hadn't asked how they managed to get away. It was enough that they were coming and she would have them, her precious children, to herself for a few brief hours.

Now, everything was nearly ready. She poured the batter into the pan, opened the oven door and balanced it carefully on the top shelf above the roasting pork loin. Setting the timer, she glanced at her watch. They would be here in less than an hour, just enough time to set the table, pick a bunch of daffodils for the centerpiece and toss the salad.

Kate

The unlucky customers who had the misfortune to shop in Kelliher's Hardware Store that Friday afternoon steered clear of the young woman manning the register until they absolutely found what it was they were looking for and had no alternative but to pay. Then, mumbling inaudible thanks, they beelined for the entrance vowing to take their business elsewhere. The occasional few who had the temerity to greet Kate and inquire as to the nature of her ill humor were quickly routed with a fierce, "Mind yourself. My business is my own."

Kate Kelliher, nee Enright, was angry. She'd been angry for a long time, it felt like years. She'd narrowed down the root of her misery to her marriage. Ever since she'd been mindless enough to marry Dermot Kelliher and set up housekeeping in the tiny apartment over the hardware store his family had owned for generations, happiness had eluded her. The flat was no place to raise a child, not to mention two adults who were constantly banging into each other every time someone wanted a cup of tea or a snack from the cupboard. The bathroom was so cramped there was no need for a lock on the door. All she had to do was sit on the toilet in the natural position. One knee, the left one, and the corresponding forearm would be involuntarily pressed up against the door so tightly there was no possibility of anyone surprising her in the act.

There was a time when Kate had laughed at the inconvenience. That was years ago, before Evan, and long before she realized this would be it, the height of Dermot's ambition, to work in the family store and live, rent free, in this microscopic set of rooms.

She hadn't intended for her life to end up this way. Kate had been to America on an exchange during her third year at university. She'd easily acclimated to automatic transmission, garbage disposals, French toast with maple syrup and mixers that guaranteed water would pour from the tap at the perfect temperature. She wanted frost-free refrigerators and ice makers and coffee shops that opened for breakfast on Sunday mornings and restaurants that weren't bars. She wanted perpetual hot water without having to remember to flip a switch thirty minutes ahead of when she needed it, and heat that turned on and off according to a preset temperature.

She wanted to live in a world that wasn't obsessed by trash, where to store it and where to dispose of it, in the brown, green or white recycler, in the paper and package dumpster, in the compost pile in the garden or, God forbid, surreptitiously into one of the bins opposite a grocery store, strip mall or take-away express.

She wanted to never see another clothesline with flapping drawers and baby nappies. She wanted ranch dressing for her salads, Splenda for her coffee and tall, sweet, sweating glasses of lemon-flavored iced tea on an outdoor patio with a thermometer that read eighty degrees. She wanted checkers in supermarkets to bag her groceries instead of watching with their arms folded while she juggled plastic bags, a coin purse and a baby pram. She wanted plastic bags at no charge when she forgot hers in the car. She wanted to pay three dollars, not six euro for a pastry and a cup of coffee and she wanted to sit in an outdoor café to eat and drink them. She wanted to wake up without thinking about the weather, engage in conversations that had nothing to do with weather and shop for food without taking an umbrella.

America was perfect. So what if no one could brew a decent cup of tea or that the doors in the bathroom stalls only came down as far as a woman's knees which really wasn't very nice at all. So what if white woman never pushed their own babies in their prams or cleaned their own houses? These were small things, hardly significant at all. She wanted it back, the life she left, the entire package.

Most of all, Kate wanted Ritchie O'Shea to divorce his American wife, come back to Ireland and shock all the gossips by walking down Castle street with his arm around her waist. Actually, if she were completely truthful with herself, and she nearly always was, it wasn't Ritchie she wanted. She'd given up on Ritchie long ago, but she did want someone very like him. She wanted all the spiteful women who remembered that she'd been jilted to fall off Fenit Pier in the middle of a very cold rain. She wanted them to know that once upon a time she had a career, not a job, that their deliberate references to her marrying up were rude and boring and that, in another lifetime, she could have bought and sold every one of them ten times over if she'd cared enough.

Coming home had been a mistake. She should have forgotten Ritchie, finished up in Boston and stayed on. Maybe, if she'd pushed a bit, Stuart Walker, the boy she'd dated for nearly six months, would have offered marriage. She didn't love him, but at least she would have been rich. She could be sitting on the deck of his family's cottage in the Hamptons this very minute enjoying one of those odd drinks with the little umbrellas sticking out of the top. Instead she'd come home and ended up with Dermot, his parents and the hardware store.

Kate wanted out, away from Tralee and the town park, from the Stacks, Kevin Barry's, Strand Row, Ballymullen, Cahirweesheen, all the neighborhoods, and Castle Street, The Square, Manor Retail Park, the damn John Mitchell's Football Club, Tesco's Supermarket on Tuesdays, Dunnes in town on the weekend, Garvey's in a pinch, The Tankard, Katie Browne's and the inevitable pubs, Betty's, The Huddle, The Greyhound and what passed for jazz in Tralee on Sundays.

Ever since Ritchie O'Shea threw in the towel, sacked Jimmy Fitzgibbons for passing out during a paid gig, gave out to Johnny Fleming for corruption and boozing, and took himself and his saxophone to the States ten years ago thereby breaking Kate's heart, nothing that met the definition of jazz existed in present day Tralee.

Her father had warned her, not strenuously, mind you. Mickey Enright wasn't one for pointing fingers or sticking his nose into your business. But he'd tried to tell her just the same, right before he'd walked her down the aisle. "Katie, love, we can forget the whole thing if it's what you want. Don't mind the expense or the party. I'll take care of it. Marriage is forever, you know. You don't want to be making a mistake that you can't fix."

God, how she missed Mickey. Twin tears collected in the corners of her eyes. Hurriedly, she brushed them away. How dare he up and die like that, when she desperately needed him, before anything was settled? Nan was no help. She was dotty as a loon and getting worse every day. Liam was only concerned about himself and the latest Miss Ireland he could talk the drawers off of. That left Mom.

Normally, Kate wouldn't have minded asking her mother for anything. Johannah Enright had always been a soft touch. But there were some things her mother steadfastly refused to consider, and one of them was the breaking of a sacrament, particularly the marriage sacrament.

If Kate wasn't at her wits end and so miserable she couldn't even mother Evan properly, much less drag herself out of bed for her job at the Kerry County Council three days a week, she would never consider approaching

Johannah for the huge imposition she was about to ask for. Her mother had been through enough. She was finally standing on her feet and even found the time to mind Evan whenever Kate needed her. It wasn't that she hadn't tried. It was simply that she had nowhere else to turn. What a coincidence that Liam would be there, too. Liam didn't usually show up in the middle of the week. Kate wondered what it was that he wanted.

Liam

Two years ago, Liam Enright had been on top of the world. Now, just eighteen months after the collapse of the building industry and, subsequently, the once lucrative real estate market where he'd plunked all of his proverbial eggs, he was flat broke. He'd resisted as long as he could, managing to pair up last-leg commercial buyers with real estate loans, but when that market dried up completely, he knew there was no alternative but to follow his mother's advice and finish his education.

On the occasions when he was completely honest with himself, Liam admitted that the role of estate agent didn't really suit him. There were those moments when an industry standard seemed nothing short of crooked, such as when he'd talked a reluctant buyer into submitting an offer only for the purpose of waving it in front of another buyer for an even better offer.

Gesumpting they called it. Liam called it snow-balling the innocent. Still, parting an Irishman with his money was no easy task and one needed to make a living.

His mother had warned him of the pitfalls but Liam, blinded by what he thought would be easy money, hadn't listened. At the time he believed there was no alternative. Although he'd done well on his exams, he was tired of school and uninterested in the trades, nor was he particularly handy. The few times he found himself in the position of attempting to help his father, Mickey had shaken his head in exasperation and sent him into the kitchen using the need for a cup of tea as an excuse.

Lord, how he missed his dad. His father understood him as no one else ever could. Liam abhorred physical labor. His one venture into construction consisted of three months on the tools with his dad. It was a nightmare he'd prefer to erase from his memory as well as a lesson in humility. Climbing up and down a ladder countless times, hammering his fingers, working outside exposed to the cold and rain were scenarios he refused to consider as his life's work. Real estate was booming and, for the first time in history, the Irish had money to spend. For five years he'd benefited. He liked working in an office, wearing a suit and tie, interacting on the telephone. He liked the varied pace of his days, the challenge of making a sale, the adrenalin rush of competition.

Then it all crashed. His loans dried up, stocks went down and Fiona, his girlfriend of two years, left him. His mother's words came back to him. *An education is never wasted. No one can take it from you.* He saw the merit in acquiring a body of knowledge necessary enough to society to command a decent income. University called. Marketing was his love, but he would temper it with a body of knowledge like economics, something he could put to good use even when the economy went sour. But he couldn't do it alone. Hence, the phone call to Johannah.

He'd thought long and hard about involving his mother. There was something slightly shameful in expecting his mother to support him. He was twenty-six after all. However, it was only for a short time, two years at the most. Besides, he rationalized, she wouldn't mind having him home again. She was his mother. She was probably lonely. She would welcome the company.

His mother mentioned that Kate would be there tonight, too. Liam frowned. Kate was usually at home during the week cooking for Dermot and Evan. He wondered what it was that she wanted.

CHAPTER 5

Johannah

Johannah sprinkled rosemary over the lamb chops, turned up the flame under the new potatoes and began chopping scallions for the salad. Thank goodness for Tesco Supermarket and the European Union. Not all that long ago food in Ireland was limited to stewed meat and boiled turnips.

"Hi, Mom," Liam's voice called out from the back entrance. "Something smells grand." His familiar form, green-eyed and dark-haired like her people, tall and deep-chested like the Enrights, stood framed in the doorway. He held up a grocery bag. "I stopped at the off-license for wine. Will you have a glass with me?"

Johannah hesitated. Would the combination of alcohol and her children always be difficult for her? It was Mickey, of course, and his excesses. But Mickey wasn't here. She smiled brilliantly and artificially. "I'd love a glass."

He found the Waterford in the cabinet, poured two glasses and handed her one. Johannah kissed his cheek. "You're early."

Liam nodded. "There's something I need to talk with you about and I wanted to do it before the rest of them corralled you."

"There will only be Kate. She's coming alone."

Liam's left eyebrow rose signaling skepticism. "Really?"

Johannah nodded. The wine was really quite nice. She was feeling it already, the consequence of an empty stomach. "She wants to discuss something with me, too. You wouldn't happen to know what it is?"

"I don't, but if it's money, tell her you can't do it. Kate always needs money. She'll bleed you dry."

"That isn't very charitable, Liam. Kate is your sister. She'd do anything for you." Johannah changed the subject. "You're looking well." He wasn't, actually. He looked tired, but there would be no point starting in on that. "What is it you want to talk about?"

She watched the color stain his cheeks and heard the soft, nearly imperceptible catch of his breath. Uh oh, she thought. Another girl gone by the wayside. Johannah couldn't be particularly sad about Fiona. She had never liked her. The girl was too selfish, too phlegmatic, and too infuriatingly thin. Liam was constantly doing for her, with little thanks. But then Liam was always tangled up with some woman. There was the trip to Singapore to meet that girl he found online, the one with the enormous family who lived in huts with lizards running up and down the walls, and the one from some unheard of country in Africa who demanded an Air France ticket and ten thousand euro to bring gold out of the country. Fortunately he hadn't fallen for that, but there *was* a scare involving a Russian girl whose photograph revealed a remarkable resemblance to Catherine Zeta Jones until it became clear that the picture *was* Catherine Zeta Jones. Johannah was about to voice her sentiments when his next sentence stopped her.

"I've decided to take your advice and go back to university."

Johannah's mouth dropped. "Liam," she gasped, "that's wonderful. I couldn't be happier."

His smile was tight. "The thing is, I can't afford it on my own."

"Your marks were high. It shouldn't cost you anything."

"Living expenses aren't covered," he explained.

Johannah sipped her wine and swallowed carefully. The paper cut on her finger from this morning throbbed. "Will you be working at all?"

"There's no work to be had, not where I am anyway. I know you can't help with the money but I thought I might move back here and save on rent and food."

"I see. She set down her wine and turned back to the salad. Mechanically, she began dicing a tomato. Why did children never understand that food cost money? Her mind raced. *Oh God. Why me? Why did other people's children find jobs, move out, marry suitable people, take out mortgages and settle down to raise families? Why were her offspring incapable of managing the business of living? Liam was twenty-six years old.*

Johannah was conscious of the ticking clock and the sound of her silence, proclaiming her feelings louder than words. *Steady, Johannah. Steady now. You don't want to say something you'll regret.* "It sounds as if you've spent some time thinking about this," she managed.

"I have. The housing market has dried up. I'm not getting any younger. I have no trade and no education. I have to do something to make my own way."

Encouraged, Johannah nodded. At least he was thinking clearly. It wouldn't be too dreadful having him home. Certain things would have to change. Gone would be the evenings when she read on the couch through the wee hours with all the lights on and music blaring to counter the insomnia she couldn't shake. Meals would be different, too. She couldn't very well continue her practice of a hard-boiled egg and glass of tomato juice with a child in the house. Her recent haphazard practice of handwashing clothes in the kitchen sink and draping them over the radiators whenever she felt like it would be replaced by her original method of regular laundry days complete with machine and clothing on the line.

Liam would want to lie in on the weekends. She would have to limit her vacuuming to regular hours instead of pulling out the Hoover before work in the morning. Her dream of a craft room where the sewing machine could be left out with bolts of fabric strewn about, magazines open to pages she would get back to when she had the time and books stacked by a deep and comfortable, albeit shabby, chair that should have seen the rubbish heap years ago, was disappearing by the second. She could always change her plans and appropriate Kate's old room, but it was upstairs, not nearly as convenient and right next to the guest room. Maybe Liam could sleep in the room that had once belonged to his sister.

Mentally, Johannah gave herself a shake. This was her son and he needed help. Smiling brightly, she added vinegar and oil to the salad, turned and held out the bowl to Liam. "Well then, you must move back into your old room. I know it will be an adjustment, but we'll manage and it will be lovely for me to have you here."

His smile of relief and grateful thanks shamed her.

He set the bowl on the table, leaned against the worktop and crossed his arms. "There's something else, something you should know."

Johannah's heart sank. "Don't tell me you can't afford your car."

"Nothing like that," he said quickly. "I'm down to the final payments. The rent is due on my apartment and I don't have it, not if I'm to pay off my credit card. I'll need to move in at the end of the week."

"That's not so bad, is it? Johannah asked.

"I just wanted to be sure you're alright with it."

She wasn't alright with it, not at all, but there was nothing left to say. "Clear sailing," as your dad always said."

Johannah had just finished tucking foil around the lamb chops to keep them warm when Kate breezed in a full thirty minutes late.

"Sorry," she said, kissing first her mother's cheek and then the top of her brother's head. "You're too gorgeous for your own good, Liam. It's disgusting and I'm jealous." She smiled at her mother. "Dermot forgot about watching Evan tonight and stopped at the pub. I had to ring around to find him because he didn't hear his mobile. I left as soon as I could. Did I miss anything?"

Liam and Johannah spoke at the same time, their subsequent words mangling the message.

"Not really."

"Liam's moving home."

Kate looked from one to the other. "Sorry?"

Johannah looked at her son.

Liam sighed. "I'm going back to university. I can't afford it on my own. Mom's offered to let me move home while I earn my degree."

Like twin blue windows, Kate's eyes widened. She turned to her mother. "What about your craft room?"

"I'll manage. I can use your room. Would you like a glass of wine?"

"No thanks. I'll have a mineral instead." Avoiding everyone's eyes, Kate unwound her scarf, hung her jacket on the hook in the closet and reached for the oven mitt. "Let's eat. I'm starved." She surveyed the lamb chops. "You didn't add too much salt, did you, Mom? You do remember what I told you about salt?"

Johannah's smile was a bit forced. If only Kate had found a job in her field. Perhaps, if she planned meals during the day, she would be less critical of her family's choices at home. "I remember," was all she said.

Kate served the lamb chops while Liam poured her orange drink and Johannah dished up the potatoes.

Dinner was unusually quiet. "It's lovely having you both here, all to myself," Johannah said, when they were nearly finished. "I feel a bit guilty about Evan and Dermot. Did they have something else to do, Kate?"

Kate shook her head. "I wanted to talk to you alone."

"Shall I leave?" Liam asked.

"Don't be an idiot," his sister retorted. "I meant without Dermot." She bit her lip. "I'm going to say it all at once. The thing is, I'm not happy. I want to come home for awhile. I think it would be good for Dermot and me to take a time out." She glanced at her mother's face and amended hastily. "It wouldn't be too long, just a few weeks, really."

Johannah stared at her daughter. "Precisely, what does 'a time out' mean?"

Kate flushed. Like her brother, the pink stain lit her face with attractive color. "Dermot and I aren't getting along. It's desperate, really." Her voice rose. "I can't do it anymore. I hate living there." Words crowded her throat. She couldn't adequately describe the boredom, the sameness, the gray, dull routine of her life, the sheer effort it took to drag herself out of bed, the lack of intimacy in her marriage, the overwhelming despair she felt when she thought of the never-changing future. She tried to speak and couldn't. Tears spilled over. Kate dropped her head into her hands and wept.

Her mother's voice gentled. "What's happened, Kate? Has Dermot done something?"

Kate wouldn't look up. She shook her head. "No."

"Then, what is it? Tell us."

Liam pushed back his chair. "She's not here to talk to me. I'll check the news and give you time alone."

Johannah waited until he'd left the room. The worst of Kate's breakdown had passed. She pulled a handkerchief from her pocket and tucked it into her daughter's hand.

After a minute, Kate wiped her eyes, blew her nose and met her mother's level gaze. "I'm so miserable, Mom. I can't stand it there anymore in that tiny flat, trying to keep things tidy in a space no bigger than a bathtub, cooking and cleaning and minding Evan, and then working at the hardware when I'm not scheduled at the Council Office. There's never a minute for me. I made a terrible mistake. Nothing was supposed to be like this. I have to leave while I'm still young, or this is all I'll ever have. I want to come home."

Johannah's hand clutched the cloth serviette. She felt the familiar sick heaving of her stomach, her unfortunate and ubiquitous reaction to conflict. "Surely you're not suggesting leaving your husband, the father of your child?"

"I don't love him."

"How convenient."

"That's not fair."

"Fair?" Johannah concentrated on lowering her voice. "I'm not sure we share the same definition of the word. What about Evan?"

"Evan comes with me, of course. I'd never leave Evan."

"I suppose there's no point in reminding you the child has a father who loves him just as much as you do. I can't imagine what Mickey would have done had I announced I was taking the two of you and going to live with my mother."

Kate refrained from reminding her mother that Dolly wasn't the kind of mother anyone would go home to. "Dad would be the first one to tell me not to throw my life away."

"Don't be so sure about that." Johannah looked down at her white knuckles straining at the crumpled serviette. "We thought you'd married too soon. Your father tried to make you wait."

"I know," Kate replied woodenly. "You were right then. You're still right. You're always right and no, there's no point in reminding me."

Johannah didn't want to say it, but she had to. "Please tell me this isn't because Ritchie O'Shea is coming home."

Kate's smooth forehead wrinkled in genuine perplexity. "What are you talking about?"

"You didn't know?"

"No."

Sighing, Johannah stood and began clearing the table. She decided against bringing out the banoffee pie. No one would have an appetite after Kate's announcement. "It's true. I met his mother in Dunne's. She's over the moon." A hint of bitterness edged her words. There was no love lost between her and Kitty O'Shea. "Never mind that half the mothers in Tralee will be in mourning over the news and I'll be one of them."

"I won't pretend to misunderstand you," Kate said evenly, "but you're mistaken. I have no interest in Ritchie O'Shea. It was too long ago to matter and even if it wasn't, he's married."

"Apparently that's not much of an impediment." Johannah clapped her hand over her mouth. Six months ago she never would have said that. What was the matter with her?

"It really is, Mom," Kate said seriously. "He chose someone else. I wish it had gone differently, but it didn't. We can't go back, not any of us."

She sounded resolved and sensible, but so terribly bereft. Johannah's eyes misted. Dermot Kelliher never had a chance. Damn Ritchie O'Shea and his saxophone, his dangerous, blue-eyed charm and that voice that had coaxed the clothes off more than a few women who should have known better. He was the spitting image of his father. Johannah was in a position to know although she would never admit it to anyone but Maura, and then only because the two of them were smack in the middle of the O'Shea fan club nearly a lifetime ago.

Johannah wet the dishtowel with cold water and pressed it against her forehead. Keeping her eyes on the dark line of trees outside her window, she spoke softly allowing nothing of what she felt to reflect itself in her voice. "Of course you must come home. You know I wouldn't turn you away. But don't do something you'll regret, Katie. It's no small thing to dissolve a marriage. You'll never be the same."

From the back, Kate's arms slipped around her waist. "Thank you," she murmured, her lips warm against Johannah's shoulder, and then repeated the words that never failed to call up her mother's laugh. "I'll be very good."

CHAPTER 6

Johannah

"Why don't we have time?" Evan's rosy lower lip trembled. "I have my own money." He opened his hand to reveal two twenty pence coins, their imprint clearly stamped into his palm.

Johannah sighed. "It isn't the money, love. Your daddy's waiting at home. He wants to take you with him. We'll have an ice cream next time."

Evan stopped in the middle of the park footpath, pulling his hand from Johannah's. "I don't like football. I want ice cream, and then I want to go home with you."

Johannah gazed helplessly at the small, dark-haired termagant standing mutinously in the way of foot traffic. She couldn't recall her own children ever behaving this way. Had children changed in twenty years or was she simply out of touch? More to the point, had their ever been an instance when either Kate or Liam preferred her company over the chance to watch a football match with Mickey? She doubted it. More likely, they would have flung themselves on the ground in protest if he'd suggested leaving one of them behind. Mickey had always been the exciting one, the jokester, the playmate. Johannah was the dull one, the second choice, the last resort for both her children.

And yet, they were hers in the beginning, her children, small, sweet-smelling bundles, warm against her chest, fussing when someone different, someone unfamiliar, held them for too long. Perhaps the pulling away had been her fault. Tossing a ball back and forth, endlessly stacking blocks, dressing dolls, fighting make-believe wars, or playing childish card games she found desperately tedious. Mickey was the one for all that. She was good for bandaging skinned knees, helping with schoolwork, reading bedtime stories, bathing, cooking, washing, all the practical, unexciting needs that no one, when all was said and done, appreciated, or even remembered.

Johannah wasn't a woman who enjoyed children's activities. It shamed her to even think such a thing, but it wasn't until Kate and Liam became reasonably conversational, somewhere around age ten, that she actually enjoyed their company. What a dreadful, unnatural woman she was. Glancing at her grandson's stubborn, composed expression, she resolved to change her ways. The first challenge would be to phone her son-in-law. She was tremendously fond of Dermot, but after Kate's confession, he was the last person she wanted to speak with. Until he knew his wife's intentions, it seemed to

Johannah that she was participating in the worst of deceptions. Still, under the circumstances, there was no help for it.

Kneeling on the sidewalk, her eyes level with her grandson's, she coaxed him gently. "Evan, listen to me. I'll call your daddy on the mobile and ask him if we can be a bit late. If he tells me so, I'll take you for an ice cream. But after that, you must agree to go home without an argument. I have an important appointment and I can't bring you with me. Can you accept that?"

"Why can't I go with you?"

"I must go to work. It isn't a place for children."

Evan appeared to consider the matter. He was quite bright for a four-year old. "All right," he said. "Call him now."

"If he tells me to bring you home, I must. I will have no choice. Do you understand?"

"He won't."

Caught between annoyance and amusement, Johannah suppressed a laugh. "How can you possibly be so sure?"

"He doesn't really want to take me to football. It's only because my mommy's working that I must go with him."

Johannah sighed. "Evan, where do you come up with your ideas?" Mustering her courage, she pulled her mobile from her purse and punched in Kate's number.

Dermot answered immediately, remaining silent for several seconds before replying. "Is that really what you want, Hannie? You've had him all day."

"I don't mind a bit," she lied. "If you like I can fix him up with the ice cream and drop him by on my way home."

"That's very good of you. May I speak with him?"

"Of course." Johannah held out the phone.

Evan held the mobile to his ear. "Yes," he said. "I'll come straight away. Nan will bring me." He laughed. "I love you, too, Daddy." He handed the phone back to his grandmother. "He wants to talk to you."

Johannah spoke quickly. "We won't be long, Dermot."

"I don't want him to be a bother, Hannie. You do quite enough for us as it is, and you work very hard."

Guilt smote her. "Nonsense," she said briskly, wishing not for the first time, that she could wring her daughter's neck. "Evan's good company. I'll have him back very soon."

With a foreseeable goal within reach, Evan covered the distance back to the closest vendor serving chocolate-swirled, soft-serve without dawdling. He consumed his treat without any observable soiling of clothing and was handed off to his father with a smile on his face. "Daddy, I have to pee."

"Go along then."

"Do you want to keep me company?"

"If you like."

"I don't have to hold my willy anymore." the child announced.

Hurriedly, Johannah kissed her grandson's cheek, relieved that the excursion and the day, as far as babysitting was concerned, was over. There was no sugar-coating it. Evan wore her out. The child was indulged, the result of a permissive father and an exhausted, apparently resentful mother.

"Would you like a cup of tea, Hannie?" Dermot hovered behind his son, removing his coat and smoothing his curls. He was a large, comfortable man with shaggy hair, fine gray eyes and a long, pleasant face, a good man, satisfied with his life, his work, his child, although perhaps, lately, not his wife. Johannah liked him. She would have liked him even if he hadn't married Kate. She certainly liked him more than Ritchie O'Shea.

"Another time, Dermot. I've an appointment."

"I head that Norah Sullivan's man passed away last night."

Evan pulled at his hand. "Daddy, I have to go."

"He did." Johannah did not discuss the particulars of her cases. I'll be on my way. Say hello to Kate."

"I'll do that. She's working late tonight."

"Is she?" A suspicious thought popped itself into Johannah's mind before it was immediately rejected. Tralee was a small town and Ritchie O'Shea was something of a celebrity. There would be no stepping out without half the population knowing. Surely Kate knew that.

On impulse, Johannah wasn't big on physical demonstrations of affection, she hugged Dermot fiercely and then turned away, hurrying down the street, her handbag hitched over her shoulder, her eyes blind with angry tears.

Ten minutes later, composed again, she knocked on the door of the Sullivan house, a typical, two-story, connected council house, one that looked exactly like a hundred others on the Mary Street side of town.

Mossie Sullivan, the deceased's oldest son, opened the door. He glanced at her briefcase. "They're upstairs preparing him for the viewing."

"Here, in the house?"

Mossie nodded. "Go on up."

Johannah swallowed. The custom of readying the corpse wasn't uncommon in the smaller villages, but Tralee was a town with undertakers enough for all. Tentatively she climbed the stairs toward the sound of women's voices, low and companionable, deep in conversation. The door to the largest bedroom stood open. She peeked inside. Three women stood over the body. She recognized Mrs. Sullivan, her sister, Bridget, and another neighbor on the dole, Sally Malone. Only the two were related, but they all looked the same, tired and faded, older than their years, the result of too many children, too little education and husbands whose priorities ran to drinking their paychecks rather than supporting their families.

"You won't catch me doing this," Bridget said, her hands busy scrubbing the man's fingernails.

"Someone's got to do it," Norah Sullivan replied.

"I'm having Fergus cremated."

"Oh, God, Bridie." Sally Malone looked shocked. "You couldn't."

"I could, Sally. He'll be cremated and I'm keeping his ashes in an hourglass."

Norah Sullivan's hands, busy cutting her husband's hair, stilled. "An hourglass? How do you mean?"

"You know, one of those glass pieces that the sand falls through. You tip it upside down when you're after starting it over again."

"I know the kind, but why?" asked Norah.

"Fergus never worked a day in his life," replied Bridie. "If he's an hourglass, like it or not, I'll feckin' make sure he works 'til the Judgment Day."

The three women burst into laughter.

Johannah stepped behind the door, out of sight and leaned against the wall, her lip caught between her teeth. What was the protocol when women were dressing a corpse? Did one laugh out loud and interrupt them, or come back later? She decided to wait a few more minutes.

One of them spoke again. "There's something wrong, Norah."

"What is it, Sally?"

"Well, look at him, Norah. Look at his willy."

"Sally Malone, the man's dead, God rest his soul," said Bridget. "Besides, he's Norah's husband. You shouldn't be looking at his willy. T'isn't decent."

"But Bridie, I have to look at it if I'm going to wash it, and I'm telling you, there's something wrong."

"What's wrong?"

Mrs. Malone stepped back. "See for yourself."

Johannah couldn't help herself. She had to look.

"I don't see anything," said Bridget.

"It falls over, Bridie." Sally held up the defective organ. "Look. There's no bone in it."

Bridget's mouth dropped. "Are you serious, Sally Malone? You, with a husband and nine children?"

"How do you mean?"

Norah spoke up. "Jesus wouldn't take a man with a bone in his privates, Sally. 'Tis against religion. Men with bones don't go to heaven. Surely the nuns at the convent school taught you that?"

"I wasn't much for schoolin'," Sally admitted. "My mom kept me home."

Once again, laughter filled the room.

Johannah decided it was time to intervene. Knocking on the door, she stepped into the room. "Pardon me," she said. "Mossie told me to come up. Do you have a minute, Mrs. Sullivan?"

"Is that you, Mrs. Enright?"

"It is." Johannah held up her briefcase. "There are a few forms to fill out for your entitlement. It shouldn't be too much of a bother."

Norah wiped her hands on her apron. "No bother at all, Mrs. Enright. I'll be there in a tick." Brushing past Johannah, she leaned over the railing and called down the stairs. "Mossie Sullivan, make yourself useful and put on the kettle for a pot of tea." She smiled at Johannah. "The viewing's set for tonight. Danny was a popular man, like your Mickey, God rest his soul." She crossed herself and pulled out her glasses. "Now, love, let me sign the papers. Dead or not, a few extra quid will be a blessing around here."

CHAPTER 7

Mickey

He watched her as she stood outside *The Daily Grind,* probably debating whether she should stop for a vanilla latte or go straight home. This was the second time he'd seen her in over a year and he noticed more than he had the first time.

It was as if she was the one to come back, a different person in Hannie's body. Her nickname didn't suit her now. "Hannie" was a comfortable name, a name for a mother and grandmother, a woman a bit rounder than she'd like, who preferred ganseys, trousers without waists and sensible shoes. *His* Hannie had disappeared. Johannah was no longer round. She was lean like those meatless girls on the magazine covers. She'd done something to her hair as well. It was loose and longer and when she moved, it swung around her face. She'd replaced the jumpers and loose trousers with slim skirts, tights, tailored blouses and boots. She could almost be called fashionable. The new Johannah disturbed him.

He saw her glance at her watch, start to walk away and then turn about and push open the door. Stepping up to the counter she ordered her usual. "Do you know," she said to the young Polish immigrant manning the counter, "that for the price of a daily latte, a woman can fund a comfortable retirement if she starts early enough?"

The boy shrugged his shoulders. "You only live once and not everyone retires."

"Very true," she replied. "My husband was one of those, who didn't live to retirement, I mean."

"I'm sorry."

"Hello," he interrupted their conversation. "Remember me?"

She turned and smiled. He knew her enough to see that she was already judging the content of what she'd revealed to the young man, thought she'd said too much and was embarrassed by it. There was something about self-disclosure that was always a bit of a chance, especially if the person disclosed to isn't of the same mind.

"Hello, yourself," she said. "Of course, I remember you. Patrick, isn't it? I didn't see you come in."

"I was here already. It's good to see you again."

"Yes," she agreed. "You, too."

"Do you have time to talk while you drink?"

"Not really."

He continued smiling, saying nothing.

"My son has moved home," she hurried to tell him. He's been on his own for some time, but the economy is bad and he's decided to go back to university for a degree. I'm helping him sort things out." She flushed, the color of her cheeks turning a painful red. "Good Lord, did I really say all that? What is it about you that sets my tongue flapping?"

"I understand," he said, smoothing past her questions. "Some other time?"

She didn't move. "Do you come here often?"

"I do."

Once again she checked her watch. "I suppose a few minutes more couldn't hurt. Liam's not a child. I expect he's eaten on his own for quite some time now."

"More than likely." He nodded toward an empty table at the back. "I'm over there."

She sat down across from him. "You see," she said, continuing her conversation, "until now, I've been alone."

He raised one eyebrow and watched the wrinkle between her eyebrows deepen. "My husband died last year and, since then, I've lived alone. But now the children are moving back." She shrugged and considered her drink. "I'm not happy about it, but there's nothing I can do, especially in Liam's case. I can't fix the economy. It's Kate I want to shake and slap."

"I'm sorry," he said, editing out her remarks about the children. "Do you miss your husband?"

"Yes," she said immediately, and then changed her mind. "No, actually, that is—not that much anymore. I did at first, terribly, but then I began to realize that there are compensations."

"Compensations?" he asked carefully.

"Yes. The freedom is lovely." She sipped her latte. "I suppose if someone is going to die well before his time, there should be compensations. Freedom is one of them. Mickey wasn't the easiest man to live with."

He stared at her. Could this woman be Hannie? She looked the same, with thick brown hair minus the flecks of gray he remembered and eyes as cool and green as the slate they pulled from the Valencia mines. But Hannie, his Hannie, would never have said such a thing. What did she mean anyway?

"Is something wrong?"

"You mentioned Kate," he said quickly.

"My daughter, Kate, has a perfectly good husband who, apparently, she finds boring." Johannah's eyes flashed. "What man isn't after a few years?"

His smile faltered. "Hopefully, quite a few."

"But is that reason enough to destroy a family?" she continued as if he hadn't spoken. "I could accept her leaving for a number of other things." She ticked them off on her fingers: infidelity, drinking, unemployment, cruelty." She shook her head. "But boredom? I don't think so. Besides, Dermot isn't boring. He's sweet and kind. Just because he's not—" she stopped. Sanity resurrected himself. She didn't know this man. He could be Ritchie

O'Shea's agent for all she knew. "Do you have children?" she asked.

"Yes," he said. "A boy and a girl."

"I suppose they're grown and on their own."

"They are."

She sighed. "I don't know what I could have done differently."

He leaned forward. "I think you're too hard on yourself. More likely than not, these things resolve themselves. Most of our worries never come to pass."

"I've heard that, but do you think it's true?"

"I do."

"What is your wife like?"

"I no longer have a wife," he said slowly. "But she was lovely. You remind me of her."

Johannah's hand flew to her lips. "She's passed on. I'm so sorry. Here I am, blathering about my own affairs. I suppose it was terribly difficult for you. Men have a harder time than women."

"Is that so?"

"Yes," She nodded. "After the initial horror, I've enjoyed my respite, brief though it was." She sounded forlorn.

"Say no."

Johannah looked at him. "I beg your pardon?"

"Say no to your children."

"I've committed to Liam. How can I say yes to one and no to the other?"

"Would you like some advice, Hannie?"

"Please."

"Liam has good reason. He could be a help to you, contribute his earnings, the adult, able-bodied son that he is. Kate is being self-indulgent. Give her a breather but make it temporary. She's a wife and mother. She has responsibilities outside of herself."

"Liam doesn't plan to work. It's difficult to get work with the way things are in Ireland."

"Are you trying to convince me or yourself?"

"You sound like Mickey."

"Is that a compliment?"

"Yes, of course."

"I wasn't sure."

"He was a very worthy man," she replied, "not a saint, by anyone's measure, but a worthy man. I loved him very much." She smiled and stood. "I'll be off now. Thanks for the listen and the advice. I'll keep what you said in mind."

CHAPTER 8

Johannah

It wasn't until she was nearly past the park and through the lane opposite the parish school did she remember something odd. He'd called her Hannie. No one called her Hannie except for family and close friends.

Maura was sitting on the porch step when she walked up the footpath. "Since when have you taken to locking the door?" her friend asked irritably. "My bum's stone cold."

Johannah pulled out her keys. "I thought Liam would be home. What's so important that you're waiting on my doorstep in the middle of the afternoon? Who's minding the store, and why didn't you let yourself in, you have your own key?"

"I closed up early." Maura followed her inside, "and I forgot the key. I came to tell you that Ritchie O'Shea's back in town."

Johannah sighed, filled the kettle with fresh water and plugged it in. "You're a day late with the news. I ran into his mother last week. You'd think she'd birthed the Messiah."

"Does Kate know?"

"Now she does. I told her."

Maura sat down at the table, clutching her knock-off Gucci handbag to her chest. "Oh, Hannie, do you think that was wise?"

"She was going on about leaving Dermot and coming home to live. I lost my head and asked her if it was because Ritchie was due home. Besides, Tralee is a small town. She would have found out soon enough."

"What did she say?"

Johannah shrugged, poured hot water into the pot and added two tea bags. "She didn't know."

"Do you believe her?"

"I do. Katie tells the truth."

"I suppose it doesn't matter anyway," Maura rationalized. "News like that can't be kept quiet."

"No," Johannah agreed, unable to keep the bitterness from her voice. "More likely it'll be all over the front page of the *Kerry's Eye.*"

"Word has it he's left his wife."

"Half of Ireland has left his wife. It doesn't change anything. He's still married. He'll always be married."

"The church allows annulments, Hannie. This is the twenty-first century."

"Only if your man has money and it won't cause too much of a scandal. Look at Jackie Kennedy and Ari Onassis."

"Times have changed."

Johannah poured tea into two mugs, opened the refrigerator, pushed aside three cartons of yogurt, a block of cheese, the remaining half of the chicken carcass she'd been nibbling on for the last two days, found the milk pitcher, set it on the table and sat down across from her friend. "What are you telling me, Maura?"

Maura Keane poured the milk, added several spoonfuls of sugar, stirred her tea slowly, and drank down half the cup before speaking. "I want you to be prepared, that's all." Her eyes, brown and alert as a robin's, were fixed on Johannah's face. "I couldn't bear it if you suffered any more heartbreak, Hannie, but the truth is, Katie always did have a thing for Ritchie O'Shea, and the only way you'll be changing it is if you tell her what happened with the family thirty years ago. I know it goes against everything you are, but if you could just tell your daughter the truth, she'll be done with the whole lot of them. You really should, you know, before it goes too far."

Johannah stared at her, horrified. "I can't do that."

Maura looked up "Why not?"

"Because everything will change. She won't think of me the same way. Because there are some things that shouldn't be resurrected and the mistakes I've made in my past are among them. I've responsibilities, a job, a house, a mother who requires more and more care every day, interests I'd like to pursue and have little time for. I'm not the same person I was. I have no intention of baring my soul to my daughter."

"I didn't mean it that way."

"I know you didn't. I'm a desperate grouch and it's all because I can't stand up for myself." Johannah's eyes narrowed to thin lines of resentful green. "Do you imagine that I want these new living arrangements?" She hurried on, not allowing Maura to answer. "The truth is, I don't want Kate and Liam home, not either of them. I was beginning to enjoy my life. I don't need to know what time they come in or go to bed. It was a relief to not be their sounding board for problems I can't fix. I'm sick that my house will be taken over, my schedule interrupted and Evan's toys underfoot, but what can I do? The house has empty rooms and they both need help, Kate more so than Liam." She rubbed her forehead. "She cried, Maura. Kate never cries. She argues and pounds her fist and stamps her feet, but she doesn't cry."

"It's your house, Hannie."

Johannah sighed. "They're my children. You wouldn't turn your back on your own, so don't thumb your nose at me."

Maura changed the subject. "I could use a pastry. I haven't eaten since breakfast. A glass of wine wouldn't hurt either."

"Neither will help. As for the pastry, come back next week. With the family home, the larder will be full. I'll be porky again in no time."

"You were never porky, Hannie, and you've never been so negative, even at the worst of times. Has something else happened?"

Johannah rubbed her arms and leaned back in her chair. "Do you ever think that somehow you missed the boat, that you could have done better if only you'd reached a bit further?"

"Every day."

"Why didn't we, Maura? We had everything going for us."

Maura shrugged. "We were in a hurry to grow up. We didn't know any better."

"Exactly." Johannah slapped her hand on the table, hard enough to make the mugs jump. "We skipped over our potential simply to make sure the boat didn't leave without us. That's what happened to Kate. She was going places over there in the States, but all her friends had left school, taken jobs, got married and now juggle working, babies, husbands and whatever else comes their way. Katie, who should have known better, looked around and believed she had no options. Now, she's exactly like them and sorry for it."

"Why are you so angry? How is she different from everyone else's daughter?"

"I must have done something wrong, Maura. She was so smart, leaps above her mates at school. She should have made more of herself. That's what's wrong with us here in Ireland. We tell our children it's enough to have a job. We don't encourage them to follow their dreams."

Maura spoke gently. "Are you talking about Katie or yourself?"

Johannah shrugged. "Maybe I'm angry because she still has time to correct her mistakes, but if she does, it's at the expense of others."

Maura changed the subject. "Who's the man you were talking to at The Grind?"

Johannah frowned. "How did you hear about him?"

"Carmel Roache saw you go in. She was about to follow you when she saw you sitting at a table with him. He's not from the town or Carmel would know him. She knows everyone."

"I don't know much about him. He's a widower with two children, both grown. His name is Patrick." The color rose in her face. "Actually, we talk mostly about me. I don't know what comes over me when I walk in there. He's a good listener."

Maura's eyes twinkled. "You need a man badly, Hannie." She swirled the tea in her cup. "Are you sure you have no wine? The day's turned cold."

"None at all."

"We could walk to the pub."

Johannah shook her head. "I can't. I really should stop in and see my mother. She might need groceries."

Maura stood and shouldered her bag. "I won't offer to go with you, not if you're stopping in at Dolly's. Say hello to her for me and to the kids." She frowned. "Where are they anyway?"

Johannah paused in the act of gathering cups. Her voice lowered. "I don't know. Liam should be home. I thought he might want dinner." She looked stricken. "Maybe he is here and we don't know it. Do you think he heard us?"

Maura walked to the hallway entrance and raised her voice. "Liam," she called out. "Liam Enright, are you home?"

Reassuring silence greeted her. She turned back to Johannah. "All clear. Next time we'll meet at the pub."

Relieved, Johannah smiled.

"Hannie?"

"Yes."

"When next you visit The Grind, find out more about your man."

"Why?"

Maura blew a quick kiss at her friend. "Just do it."

Johannah arrived at her mother's house to find Dolly sitting at the kitchen table, arms crossed against her chest, a mutinous expression twisting her face. She did this more often now, arranging her features in a way that looked nothing like her usual self. No one would ever call Dolly Little a pretty woman, not even when she was young and at her most attractive, but once she'd been pleasant to look at with laughing eyes and a sweet face. Her newest affectation was to push out her bottom teeth and lock her jaw. Johannah, in her private moments, called it grotesque.

An official looking document of several pages was spread out on the table.

"Thank God you've come," Dolly said dramatically. "I could have died with no one finding me for days."

"I came yesterday," Johannah reminded her. "I come every day."

"Philomena came yesterday."

"Philomena lives in Dublin. She hasn't been here for months."

Dolly ignored her. "Look at this." She pushed the papers in Johannah's direction. "It's from a solicitor. I'm being sued."

"What?" Johannah reached for the document. "Why?"

"Because of Seamus. The Costelloe twins said he attacked their mutt."

Johannah couldn't discount the possibility. She was not an admirer of Seamus, her mother's shepherd. Not many were. "Did he?"

"Seamus doesn't bite."

Instinctively Johannah touched the back of her thigh where Seamus's nip had left a significant scar. "Yes, he does."

"Not at all," her mother insisted. "He's a very friendly dog. Those Costelloe lads have it out for me. They were walking their ridiculous little mutt and Seamus ran outside. It was their fault."

"Never mind that. Finish the story."

"He just wanted to play, but the little dog growled and barked. What was Seamus supposed to do?"

Johannah's hands clenched. "What did he do?"

"He defended himself. No one was hurt. I ran outside and one of the Costelloe boys, I never could tell them apart, began shouting and picked up the dog. That's the end of it." She thought a minute. "Do you think the twins could be a bit strange?"

"In what way?"

"They're very feminine, aren't they?"

The Costelloes had been out of the closet for years. "Let me read this." Johannah scanned the document and then reread it more carefully. She moaned. "You have to go to court. They're claiming you owe them fifteen hundred euro for veterinary bills."

Dolly snorted. "Ridiculous. I won't pay it. No one can make me pay such a sum."

"Mom," Johannah explained gently. "If the judge decides for these people, you'll have to pay."

"I won't," her mother insisted. "They're out to get me those Costelloes. I won't pay. It's outrageous. Where would I find such a sum?"

Johannah sighed, mentally deducting the fifteen hundred from her cash account. *Where indeed?*

CHAPTER 9

Kate

It was a typical Irish wake. This time the deceased was Jane O'Grady, Dermot's mother's first cousin, who'd died at the age of ninety-one. First cousins, like brothers and sisters, aunts, uncles and parents, were considered immediate family, the wake, the Rosary prayers and the funeral Mass too important to miss.

Kate, just off from her job, hesitated at the door of Hogan's Funeral Home. She wasn't related to the O'Gradys and she was no longer living with Dermot. Although her attendance wasn't mandatory, she would pay for it if she opted out. She was a Kelliher by marriage and if she didn't at least make the rounds of the family, kneel before the coffin with an obligatory prayer and stay a minute to chat in the adjoining room for a cursory appearance, her name would be bandied about in every household from here to Cork City.

Arranging her features into what she hoped was an expression both mournful and sympathetic, she entered the mortuary and approached the family members seated in a semi-circle around the elaborate coffin. "I'm so sorry. She was a lovely woman," she said, repeating the phrase over and over, making her way through the relatives until she reached Dermot's mother.

Maired Kelliher's mouth, already flat and prune-like, flattened even more. She ignored Kate's outstretched hand. "You've quite a nerve," she hissed against the younger woman's ear. "You should be ashamed of yourself."

"I'm so sorry for your loss," Kate repeated woodenly.

Dermot was next. Reaching for her hand, he kissed her cheek. He kept his voice low, but at a pitch his mother could hear. "Never mind her. How are you, Katie?"

"I'm well, Dermot," she whispered. "Thanks for asking. Will I keep Evan this weekend?"

"Not at all. I'll be around after the service tomorrow to collect him."

Kate's head ached miserably. He was a good man. Why did he have to be so good? It made everything worse. "I'll have him ready."

"Say hello to Liam and your mother."

"I'll do that. Take care, Dermot." Feeling too guilty to remain under the microscope of his family, Kate decided against praying by the coffin and left the room to find her mother.

Johannah, a polite expression on her face, was surrounded by what looked like a tight coven of middle-aged women all speaking at the same time. No matter how awkward she felt,

Kate wasn't about to broach that group. She'd made her appearance, satisfied the conventions. Maybe it would be better if she left immediately. It would give the gossips less to talk about.

"Giving it over to them, Kate? I thought better of you." Her brother's voice, low and mocking, stopped her flight to the door.

She faced him. "I'm not the only subject of their conversation. When they finish with me, they'll start on you, or maybe it will be the other way around and you'll be first."

Liam's eyes gleamed. "Not at all. I'm the one doing the responsible thing, moving back home, helping out, going on to university, enduring the desperate commute to Limerick. You're the devil's temptress, leaving your husband, robbing your child of his dad, taking up with—"

"Stop right there. There's no taking up with anyone. This town isn't big enough to weather that one and I wouldn't act so superior, Liam. You're a grown man living off your mother. You can be sure the gossips will be out in full force over you, too."

Liam lifted an eyebrow. "Are you telling me you didn't know Ritchie O'Shea was back, that all this maneuvering was coincidental? I know you, Katie. Don't expect me to believe that."

"Believe what you want. It's true. You try managing in that tiny little flat, working your life away for nothing."

He stared at her. "What's your game, Kate? Are you trying to pressure Dermot into leaving the business? Because if you are, you're a fool.

It's the biggest hardware store in town, not to mention the auto parts and the electrical. Dermot's the only son. If you put in a bit of time now, you'll have it made in the years to come. I wish I had a family business to take up. Our dad was a great one for the *craic* but providing for his family wasn't his strong point. Without Mom, we'd be scratching to make a living."

Kate frowned. "That isn't a very nice thing to say about your father."

"Maybe not, but there you have it." He flicked her cheek. "I'll say goodbye to Mom and then be on my way. Don't do anything you'll regret. Dermot's a good man."

It was an auspicious time to make an exit. Kate caught her mother's eye and waved, motioning toward the door. She saw Johannah nod and then quickly, so as to avoid anyone else speaking to her, Kate scooted out into the rainy evening. Breathing in the clean, cold air, she stopped to open her umbrella. At first she didn't notice the stream of smoke drifting up, disappearing into the night, or the man standing under it. Then he spoke.

"Hello, Kate."

She knew him at once. His wasn't a voice that Katie Enright would forget. Turning slowly, very slowly, so as to hold the moment, she lifted her eyes to his face. "Hello, Ritchie."

"It's been a long time."

"Yes."

"You're married."

"Yes."

"With a child, a son."

"Yes."

"My mother told me."

Kate swallowed. "Did she?"

He moved out of the shadows and faced her. She tried to fix her eyes on his, to keep her curiosity from showing, to prevent the hunger of her glance while at the same time searching out the changes a decade can make in a man's face and form.

Unfair, was the word that first jumped out at her, unfair, but typical, and just as she expected. He was still desperately handsome, clean-shaven and square-jawed, with heavy-lidded blue eyes and a shaggy head of copper-brown hair that hadn't the slightest intention of thinning. Ritchie O'Shea was born under a lucky star. Nothing had changed. Nothing at all. Her fingers curled into her hands.

He stepped closer. "How are you, Katie?"

She was conscious of the intimate appearance of their encounter, the two of them alone, outlined in the light from the streetlamps. A rush of heat stained her cheeks. "I'm well, thank you. Don't pretend that it matters."

"You're still angry."

"I'd say so."

"Ten years is a long time to carry a grudge."

"Some might agree with you. I don't."

He threw back his head and laughed.

She looked around nervously. "Try to remember this is a wake."

"I might have known you wouldn't spare me, Katie Enright. You'd be the one all right to hold my feet to the fire. What must I do to be forgiven for not taking you up on your offer to run away with me?"

She stared at him. "Is that what this is about, your stalking me here at Mrs. O'Grady's wake? You aren't thinking you can take up where you left off, are you Ritchie? Because, really, you have no business here. If it's forgiving you want, find someone else. You won't be hearing the words from me."

He looked at her for a long minute, one side of his mouth turned up in the old way. Then he dropped his fag and ground it out with his foot. "I'm sorry about your dad."

"Thank you."

"If you think I woke up that morning intending to break your heart, you're wrong. I just never thought of you that way. It wasn't possible. You know that. But people change, Kate. Maybe I've changed my mind."

She folded her arms against her chest. "As you said, it's not possible. Go along now. We've finished our conversation."

"For now. Goodbye, Katie. Remember me to your mother."

She watched him walk away, anger and hurt and something she didn't recognize raging in her chest. For the second time in less than a week, she found herself battling tears.

A man waiting at the bus stop turned around. Embarrassed, Kate pressed her fingers against her eyelids.

"I couldn't help overhearing. Are you sorted out?" he asked.

She nodded.

"Because if you're not," he gestured toward the bench beside him. "There's room here."

She fumbled in her pocket for a handkerchief. "Thank you, but—" She shook her head. What had she sunk to, scrubbing her eyes in front of a stranger? She should run away immediately. But she didn't.

He continued to watch her. Kate wasn't frightened. He was older, somewhere around sixty, with a kind face. It was still early and nothing ever happened this early in Tralee. She was sure she didn't know him, but something about his expression was familiar and strangely compelling.

She sat down beside him. "Are you from the town?"

"I've just arrived." He held out his hand. "My name is Patrick."

She took it. "I'm Kate Enright."

"Enright?"

She flushed. "Actually, it's Kelliher. Enright is my maiden name. It's just that I don't feel married right now."

"I see. I assume that man you were talking with wasn't your husband."

Kate shook her head. "That's Ritchie O'Shea. He's just come back from the States."

"Ritchie O'Shea, the saxophone player?"

"Do you know him?"

"Everyone knows him. It's probably good that he isn't your husband."

"Ten years ago I thought we had potential." She hesitated. "Then something happened and he left me to emigrate. The next thing I heard he was married to an American girl."

"You're married, too, I heard, and you have a child."

"Yes." Kate's hands twisted in her lap. "That isn't working out very well right now."

"Any particular reason?"

Kate shrugged. "It isn't what I expected."

"What isn't?"

"Marriage."

"Ah." He smiled. "Let me guess. You thought the excitement would continue."

She shrugged. "Yes, as well as the romance and prestige. Relief, too, I suppose."

"Relief?"

"Yes. I thought all the worry about finding someone and being wanted and actually beginning my life was over. Never again, I thought, would I have to be out there, looking for someone to love me, worrying that I'd never be chosen."

He looked startled. "But you're a lovely girl. Why on earth would you worry about such things?"

She smiled. "I don't think anyone ever thinks of herself as being lovely enough. Most women don't think they're good enough, smart enough, attractive enough." Her laugh was hollow. "I suppose we have the fashion models to thank for that."

"Good enough for what?"

Kate shook her head. "Anything. Everything."

"What went wrong with your marriage?"

"I'm not sure," she said slowly. "It was all right in the beginning. We had the same dreams, a house in the country, both of us working, a bit of travel now and then. Dermot can be very funny and clever. But Maired, Dermot's mother, wanted him to assume more of the business, we never did anything together anymore and then Evan came along. Not that I regret Evan," she said hastily, but it seemed as if no one ever listened to me. I felt I was missing something." Her eyes welled. "If I knew what it was, I wouldn't be such a mess. The thing is, Dermot is a really good man, but he's a bit myopic when it comes to money and I can't seem to get through to him. I have no influence. Shouldn't a wife have influence?"

"The Kellihers are fine people. Most would say you'd made a good match."

"There's more to a successful marriage than banking on future prospects. Besides, it's Dermot's mother who has the money and she doesn't believe in sharing. Not that she should. It's hers after all." She played with the fringe on her umbrella. "I can't believe I've blabbered like this. You're a total stranger. I apologize for boring you."

"Not at all, but I wasn't talking about money. It's character that's important. Dermot Kelliher has character and he chose you which shows his remarkable good sense." He changed the subject. "I suppose you miss your father."

"Every day."

Minutes passed.

"Do you feel better?" he asked after a bit.

She thought a minute. The frown disappeared from between her eyebrows "I do. I really do." She laughed and stood. "Nothing's changed, but I do feel better. Thank you, Patrick." She held out her hand. "It was very nice meeting you."

He shook it. "My pleasure."

It was only later, after she paid off the babysitter and had tucked Evan into bed that she thought back on that odd conversation. She didn't recall telling him about Mickey, yet he'd asked if she missed her dad.

CHAPTER 10

Johannah

Johannah sat on a bench beside her mother directly outside of the courtroom. She glanced at the clock overhead. Unless things moved along more quickly, she'd never make it to work today.

Dolly looked composed in black trousers and a gray wool coat, her white hair curling in a tight helmet around her head, her jaw set as if she were about to do battle.

"Don't be nervous," Johannah reassured her. "Just explain what happened."

"I'm not nervous. I'm angry."

The Clerk opened the double doors. "You may come in now."

Johannah led her mother to the third row of seats and sat beside her. The Costelloe twins sat on the opposite side of the courtroom. There did not appear to be a lawyer with them.

"All rise for the Magistrate, the Honorable Timothy Dwyer," the Clerk announced.

Johannah stood. Dolly made no move to rise.

"Stand up," Johannah whispered. "You have to stand."

"I don't," replied Dolly, "not for the likes of him. That's Timmy Dwyer, the cheek of him to be sitting up there, presiding over this courtroom. He's Eileen Dwyer's son from the Stacks and a troublemaker if I ever saw one."

White-faced, Johannah slid her hand under her mother's elbow. "Mom, you have to stand. I don't care who he is or how you feel about him. He's the judge and he'll be the one deciding your case."

Dolly folded her arms against her chest. "I won't."

Johannah fought to contain herself. She cleared her throat.

The judge caught her eye. "Is there a problem, Mrs. Enright?"

"May I speak to you privately, Your Honor?"

"Approach the bench, please."

Dolly refused to budge. Climbing over her mother's legs, Johannah made her way to the bench and spoke softly. "Is there another way to do this? My mother suffers from dementia and today isn't a good day."

The Magistrate frowned. "Are there good days?"

"Fewer and fewer," Johannah admitted.

"If it were up to me," he said, flipping through the papers in front of him, "I'd tell you to take her home, but the Costelloe family has suffered damages. I'm sorry, but unless your mother accepts culpability, the issue must be heard in court. Will she agree to that?"

Johannah sighed. "No."

"Then, we will have to proceed."

Johannah took her seat.

The judge nodded at Dolly. "Mrs. Little, please stand."

For some inexplicable reason, she recognized the voice of authority and complied.

"Do you understand the charges against you?"

"They're lying."

"That remains to be seen," replied the judge. "Do you understand that you are being sued for the sum of 1500 euro, a sum equal to the medical bills sustained by the Costelloes for veterinary services performed on their dog after he was attacked by a dog belonging to you?"

Dolly's mouth was set. "Their dog is fine. I saw him just this morning when one of them," she indicated the twins, "took him for a walk."

"Are you aware, Mrs. Little, that the Costelloe family has two dogs? Only one of them was attacked by your—" again he looked at his paperwork, "by Seamus."

"Seamus did not hurt either of their dogs."

"I have the veterinary bill here, Mrs. Little. The charges are specific."

"How do I know it was Seamus and not another dog?"

The Judge's eyebrows rose. "For what purpose? Presumably, if someone else's dog inflicted injuries, he, not you, would be here today answering charges."

"The Costelloes don't like me and they've never liked Seamus."

"It isn't difficult to imagine why," the Judge said under his breath. "Mrs. Little, there is a witness who saw the incident. I have no alternative but to find in favor of the plaintiff. You are hereby ordered to pay the Costelloes 1500 euro. Do you have that amount with you today?"

Dolly turned her back on the bench, folded her arms and stared at the wall.

Johannah spoke up. "She doesn't have that amount with her."

"Do you?

Johannah shook her head. "No."

Judge Dwyer turned to the Costelloe twins. "Is a payment plan acceptable to you?"

Simultaneously they shook their heads. One of them spoke. "We're already out of pocket fifteen hundred euro. We must have the entire amount immediately."

Again, Johannah spoke. "I'll write a personal check today, if that's acceptable."

"Perfectly acceptable," replied the Judge. "Before I dismiss this case, I must issue you a warning, Mrs. Enright. Your mother needs supervision and her dog would be better served by someone who can give him exercise. I don't want to see her in my courtroom again. Is that possible for you?"

"What is he saying, Johannah?" Dolly's whisper could be heard throughout the courtroom.

Judge Dwyer answered for her. "I'm saying that you must no longer live alone, Mrs. Little. If your daughter is unable to have you with her, you must look at an assisted living facility. Do you understand?"

Two identical spots of red appeared on her mother's cheeks. She turned to her daughter, chin up, head held high. "Am I to go into a facility, Johannah?"

Somewhere outside the four walls of the courtroom, the bells of Saint John's Church rang twelve times announcing the lunch hour. A horn blasted. In the too narrow streets, traffic stalled, greetings were called out, conversations began and ended. In the space of a nanosecond, a thousand thoughts circled in and around Johannah's mind culminating in the only conclusion possible. "Of course not. You'll be coming home with me."

"Seamus, too?"

Johannah swallowed. For the first time in two years, the scar on her leg ached. "Seamus, too," she said, hating the miserable, encroaching finality of the words.

"You're joking!" Liam's voice hovered somewhere between laughter and

disbelief when he heard the news. "There isn't room for her. Where will she stay?"

Johannah rinsed the unwashed dishes he'd left in the sink and stacked them in the dishwasher. "That's hardly the issue."

"It bears thinking about."

"We'll sell her house. That will give us enough to add on here."

"You're talking months. What happens until then?"

Johannah sighed and turned to face her son. He was sitting at the table, books and papers spread out before him. Patrick's words came back to her. Liam was a grown man, healthy, able-bodied, attractive and ungrateful. Her voice had an unusual edge. "It doesn't really affect you, Liam. You're gone until quite late every day and when you're here, you're studying. You contribute nothing to this household. It would be gracious of you to be as kind as possible when you and your grandmother are together and it would be a great help to me."

His response was reasonable and removed as if the events of the morning had nothing to do with him. "You know I'll do all I can. But I wonder if you realize how much work Nan can be. She's an incessant talker and she complains constantly when she doesn't get enough attention. I'm here for a purpose, Mom. I don't have time to entertain her."

Johannah didn't answer. She'd stopped listening two sentences before. When did ones child cease to bring on that breathless, dizzy, adoring feeling that made everything he did seem precious and memorable, worthy of marking it down in the baby book or running for the camera? Where did the feeling go? When had she, Johannah Enright, lost it? When did she no longer want to catch him up in her arms and squeeze him close and safe against her chest? When had that warm loving feeling been replaced by a strong desire to slap the smug expression from his face?

Objectively, she looked at her son's long, lean jaw, at the sharp jutting bones and the stubble of hair, two days worth, covering his cheeks and chin, at the sensual mouth that had done God knows what with the loveliest Kerry had to offer. Where had her baby gone? Where was the soft, round, rosy-cheeked cherub who'd shrieked with delight when she'd picked him up after a day at the crèche? It wasn't fair. She wanted him back. Time had passed so quickly, too quickly. This tall, black-haired man who'd spoken of his grandmother, the woman who'd changed his nappies, as if she were an inconvenient stranger wasn't the child Johannah had raised. She struggled to love him. He was her son. There was no alternative but to love him, but should it be a struggle?

"Mom?" Liam waved a hand in front of her eyes. "You're away with the faeries. Are you all right?"

Johannah shook her head, erasing the cobwebs in her brain. "Yes, Liam. I'm fine. To answer your question, I don't know what it will be like having Nan here, but there is no alternative and we'll all have to adjust. I can't do it all myself so, yes, you as well as Kate, and to some degree, Evan, will share in the responsibility. Your schooling is a priority for me as well as you, so I'll accommodate you wherever I can, but I'm human, too. None of this, including having you and your sister back home, has been easy for me. Please take that into consideration while you're complaining." Her smile was forced. "That's it then. I'll go and clear out the study as that's the only spare room left in the house."

CHAPTER 11

Liam

Left on his own, Liam revisited the conversation he'd just had with his mother. Surprised at the tone of her usually soft-spoken voice, he'd watched her leave the room without replying. She seemed different lately. He'd noticed it before but assumed her new independence was a necessity arising from the loss of his father. In retrospect, he wondered why he'd thought any such thing at all. Mickey Enright, beloved by all who knew him, especially his children, was a lightweight compared to Johannah. She was the heart of their family, the rock from where all security came. Mickey's death, although painful emotionally, had not crippled her. If anything, as far as Liam could see, it made her life easier.

Shaken by the unbidden thought, he had a sudden urge to leave his parents' house. Gathering his books, papers and laptop into his arms, he called out, "I'm going to the library to study."

"Collect your Nan on the way home," Johannah replied. "I'm in the middle of doing over the room."

"I don't know when I'll be finished," he said and immediately wished the words back. "Never mind, I'll be back with her in time for tea."

"You're a good boy, Liam," she said which made him feel even worse.

What was it about his mother that made him want to wrap his arms around her and pull her out of the wind? If she'd been the slightest bit pitiful, if she complained or nagged at him or told him he was worthless, he would have laughed and not given it another thought. But she did none of those things. She simply plowed on, doing the right thing, never reminding him that he owed her money or left the toilet seat up, forgot to post the electricity payment or fill the car with petrol. Instead of slagging him about his faulty memory and poor choices, she smiled, opened her door and held out her arms. It was those dark places under her eyes, that fragile determination in the face of whatever life tossed her way, her desire to make everyone around her content if not happy and that desperate optimism that wouldn't fold no matter what adversity fell directly on top of her that made him grind his teeth and kick himself. She was the one sheltering him, and anyone else who came her way. The least he could do, the very least, was to collect his grandmother and bring her home.

The library in Tralee was small by any standards, but it had computers, usually occupied by foreign nationals, wireless Internet service, private cubbies, and except for a few mothers with toddlers and the occasional senior citizen who could see well enough to read print, relatively empty.

He found a spot, flipped open his computer and settled in, resolving to give full attention to his studies for at least two hours before collecting his grandmother.

Liam was well into his first hour when a man with an arm load of books sat down across from him. They made eye contact and the man smiled. For a brief instant, Liam felt as if all the air had been sucked from his chest. He recovered quickly drawing a deep, strangled breath. Whatever was the matter with him?

The man pointed at Liam's laptop. "Convenient, aren't they?"

"They are."

"There's a queue for the library computers."

"Always."

The man extended his hand. "You've the look of your mother. I'm Patrick, a friend of hers."

"Really?" Liam doubted he'd seen the man before in his life, yet there *was* something familiar about him. "How do you know her?"

"She stops in at The Daily Grind before she goes in to work."

"I didn't know that. Are you waiting to use the computer?"

Patrick nodded. "I don't have one of my own. What are you studying?"

"Economics, mostly marketing. I've two years before I earn my degree. I took some time off to work but the economy got in the way." Liam, usually recalcitrant, felt an unusual urge to disclose. "I'm living at home again. It isn't easy. My sister had the same idea."

"Imagine how your mother feels."

Liam frowned. "Has she said anything?"

"It would be normal, don't you think, for a woman accustomed to doing for herself, to feel overwhelmed having her children and grandchild under her roof again?"

"That's not the worst of it," Liam confided. "My grandmother is moving in as well. She's not always clear in the head and while she's not bad in small doses, I can only imagine what living with her will be like."

Patrick appeared to have slipped into deep thought. Liam wanted feedback and for some reason he wanted it from this man, this stranger who knew his mother. "My mom will need help with her."

"Yes," Patrick agreed. "She will. It's fortunate that you and your sister are home to support your mother emotionally and to help with expenses, of course."

"Right." Liam tapped his pen against the cover of his notebook. It was the second time in less than an hour he'd been reminded his mother was supporting him. "The thing is, it's difficult to concentrate at home."

"If I were you I'd be feeling a bit guilty."

Liam nodded. "I know I should be more help, but this is my last chance. You see, I'm twenty-six. If I don't make it now, I never will."

Patrick's lip twitched. "I see."

Eager to make his point, Liam continued. "I lost my job and my apartment. Then my girlfriend left me. It was all due to money, or the lack of it. It's difficult to think of myself as anything but a failure. I have to make a go of it. My mom's always talking about the difference an education makes. She can't want me to waste my time taking care of my grandmother."

"Probably not."

Liam flushed. "It sounds like bollucks, doesn't it?"

"A bit."

"What would you do if you were me?"

"Given your age, the same as you're doing but it isn't what I should have done."

"What *should* I do?"

Patrick smiled. "You already know the answer to that."

"Life is complicated, isn't it?"

Liam was surprised by the bleak look in the man's eyes and even more surprised by his comment.

"Complicated is better than the alternative. In my experience, we can always do more than we think. I'll leave you on your own now. Give my regards to your mother."

He smiled and, again, Liam felt that odd sense of déjà vu.

Dolly pressed her face against the window pane of number fourteen, Kevin Barry's Villas, a neighborhood more than fifty years old and still inhabited by the original families or their descendents. "I'm not buying any today," she said.

Liam, standing outside on the porch step, waved to her. "I'm not selling, Nan. It's me, Liam. I came to collect you. Mom's waiting at home."

"Collect me for what?"

Liam sighed. Either Johannah hadn't explained properly or Dolly had forgotten. More likely the latter. "You're to stay with us."

"I'm not."

"Remember the court case? The judge said you can't live alone anymore."

"He said no such thing."

Liam felt the familiar surge of frustration sweeping through him as it so often did when dealing with his grandmother. "Please let me in, Nan."

She opened the door. "You're sure you're my grandson?"

"Perfectly."

"Mind Seamus. He's feeling out of sorts today."

Liam stepped inside and looked around for the dog. "Where is he?"

She looked around. "He's here somewhere. I won't go without Seamus."

Not in his wildest dreams had he imagined his mother agreeing to live with his grandmother's unpredictable dog. "I'll just ring home for a minute. Mom will explain it all to you again and then we'll be on our way."

Liam stepped into the kitchen and nearly fell over Seamus sprawled on the rug. The dog lifted his head and growled. "Easy, boy," he said placatingly. "Easy does it. No one's going to hurt you." Keeping an eye on the animal, he pulled out his mobile, scrolled down to his home number, pressed the connect button and waited.

Johannah picked up immediately.

"She won't come," he said, keeping his voice low. "She doesn't remember the court case."

His mother's voice was crisp. "Put her on the mobile, Liam."

Liam walked back into the sitting room and handed the phone to his grandmother. "It's for you," he said.

Reluctantly, Dolly held the phone to her ear. "Hello."

Liam watched her face change from wariness to fear and finally understanding. She nodded and handed the phone back. "She said I'm to bring the dog. We'll come back together to collect anything else I need."

Liam spoke into the receiver. "It's me, Mom. Is everything all right?" He lowered his voice. "Does Nan understand what's happening?"

"I have no idea. Just make sure the two of them get into the car."

"Two of them?"

"Your grandmother and that *damn* dog."

In a country where toddlers were weaned on breast milk and the "f" word, Liam could count on one hand the times his mother had used profanity. He wanted to laugh but somehow, under the circumstances, it didn't seem appropriate. "I'll see you straight away," was all he said.

"She's angry," Dolly observed. "Johannah's always angry."

"You can't blame her. She's got a lot on her plate." He eyed Seamus. "Do you think you could coax him into the car?"

"He doesn't want to go. Neither do I. We're two of a kind."

Liam would have given a great deal for a pint of cider. He looked around. "Do you have any spirits, Nan?"

"I have whiskey."

"That'll do. Where is it?"

Dolly's forehead wrinkled. "It's on the—" she stopped.

Liam waited. "Where, Nan?"

"You know, on the thing."

"What thing?"

"On top of the box that makes things cold."

Shocked out of his purpose, Liam stared at her. His grandmother, the queen of prose next to his mother, couldn't remember the word *refrigerator.*

She pointed. "Up there."

Liam reached for the spirits, found a glass and filled it halfway. He handed it to Dolly. "Drink up, Nan. It will relax you."

She drank it quickly, choked and then grimaced. "That's enough of that." She smiled at her grandson. "Will you have one?"

"No, thanks. I'm driving."

"A nacker won't hurt you."

"Another time, Nan. Can you help out with the dog? Mom is holding dinner."

"Just call him. He's a good dog. Really he is."

Liam opened the door to the kitchen. "We're going for a ride, Seamus. C'mon boy." The dog growled, fangs bared. Liam backed away. "He's your dog, Nan. More than likely he'll do what you want."

"Come, Seamus. Come, my love. Liam will take us in his car to Johannah's house. You'll like it there, won't you, my angel? It has a large yard."

Slowly, the dog rose, stretched, and followed Dolly out the door to the car.

Liam found the keys, locked up and followed them outside. "Don't you need your handbag or a suitcase?" he asked, sliding in beside her. The dog, all three-and-a-half stone of him, sat between her legs, his head, chest and forelegs splayed and hanging out the window.

"I don't need anything."

"Are you able to hold him, Nan?" Liam asked, silently praying that the garda would be working the other side of town. "I can close the window. He can sit in the back seat." He sent up a brief, quick prayer that the ripe doggy smell wouldn't kill them off before they made it home.

"I wouldn't think of it, Liam. Seamus is all I have left that is mine."

Chastened, not trusting himself to speak, he set the car into first gear and made his way toward Ballyard.

CHAPTER 12

Johannah

"Nan, Nan," Evan shrieked from the window of his mother's car. "I got a haircut and I didn't cry. I'm to get a fish, a real fish."

Johannah sat back on her heels, stuck the spade into the ground and removed her gardening gloves. She'd taken advantage of the good weather to hang out the laundry and trim the hydrangeas. "My goodness! Aren't you the smart lad?" She watched as Kate unbuckled his seat belt, freeing him to race from the car into her arms. Bracing herself for the full force of his weight, Johannah managed to stay upright as he tackled her. "A fish is it? What kind of fish?"

"A goldfish. I'm to get a goldfish. Mommy promised if I didn't cry, and I didn't."

Kate approached more slowly, stepping around the fuchsia hedge and across the grass. "He was very brave. Now, Evan, remember, the fish was promised if you don't cry the next time either."

Evan's blue eyes widened. "Next time?"

Johannah laughed. "I don't think he's sorted that one out yet." She stood. "Would you like to play on the swings?" She gestured toward the play set that Mickey had built in anticipation of Evan's birth.

He nodded and slipped his hand into hers.

Kate looked around. "Where's Nan?"

"Napping. At least she was when I left her twenty minutes ago. I should probably go check."

"Leave it for a minute, Mom."

Johannah's heart sank. Kate looked preoccupied, even a bit worried. "All right. We'll swing Evan and chat."

Settling her grandson into the swing, Johannah began to gently push him back and forth. He laughed, tilted his head back and attempted to pump the way Johannah had coached him. "Higher, Nan, higher."

"You're high enough, Evan," his mother warned.

Johannah lowered her voice. "Do you have something to say, Kate?"

Kate hesitated and in the space of an instant, between gathering her thoughts and opening her mouth, Seamus rose from a comatose heap on the porch and, at a dead run, headed straight for Evan, teeth bared.

Kate screamed, pulling Evan and the swing after her as she clambered up the slide. At the same time, Johannah deliberately stepped into the path of the dog in an attempt to shield her daughter and grandson.

Ignoring her completely, Seamus altered his route, raced around her and the swings, toward a movement in the grass. Johannah relaxed. Her voice shook slightly. "It's only a rabbit. He was after a rabbit."

"He's a monster." Kate was crying. "He can't stay here. He'll kill one of us for sure."

"He was chasing a rabbit, Katie," her mother said gently. "All dogs chase rabbits."

"I can't believe you're defending him. You saw him. What if he'd hurt Evan?"

She'd climbed down from the side. Evan was clutched tightly in her arms. She kissed his cheeks and then his head. "Are you all right, love? Were you scared?"

The child squirmed in her arms. "Put me down, Mommy. I want to see the rabbit."

"Not until Nan locks the dog in the house."

Sighing, Johannah called the dog. No longer distracted, Seamus came immediately. She gripped his collar and led him into the house, closing the door securely behind him.

"He's an awful dog," Kate repeated when her mother returned.

"You're being unreasonable, Kate. You can't blame Seamus for what you believed he was going to do. He had no intention of hurting you or Evan."

"He nearly killed the Costelloes' dog and don't forget that he bit you."

"That was a long time ago. He wasn't accustomed to me. I imagine he thought I was an intruder."

Kate shuddered, the tears running unchecked down her cheeks. She set Evan on the ground.

His finger crept toward his mouth. "Why are you crying, Mommy?"

She shook her head and brushed the wet away. "I'm not. Go along, now. Check on that rabbit."

Immediately, he struck out toward the side yard where the rabbit had made his escape.

Johannah linked her arm through her daughter's. "Come inside. I'll make a pot of tea."

"Don't leave the yard, Evan," Kate called out.

Deep in the task of digging a tunnel in the flowerbeds, he ignored her.

Eyes at half-mast, Seamus lay splayed in the mudroom blocking the entrance to the kitchen. Johannah and then, more gingerly, Kate, stepped over him.

Kate flicked on the electric kettle, opened the canister and pulled out two tea bags. "I can't imagine why she chose that particular dog."

"I think Seamus chose her," replied Johannah. "Your nan has a soft spot for animals." She refrained from adding *rather than people.*

Kate settled into a chair, her chin in her hands. "How did you know, Mom?"

"Know what?"

"That Da was the one for you? How could you possibly have known that at twenty years old?"

Stalling for time, Johannah took longer than usual to toss the teabags into the pot and add the boiling water. She watched the teapot, imagining the tea steep and the water inside the pot turning a deep golden brown. Then she filled two cups, set them on the table, found the milk in the fridge and sat down across from her daughter. Only then did she speak. "No one knows who to marry at twenty. Your dad and I knew nothing else except to stay together. And we were lucky. That's all there is to it. Were we happy?" She stirred milk into her tea. "Sometimes, and sometimes not. There were the cold times, the times we asked ourselves if someone else wouldn't have made us happier, but what was the point? We'd made our choices. So, we got on with it, made a life, raised you and Liam—" her voice broke.

Kate reached across the table and took her mother's hand. "I'm sorry. I'm an ungrateful brat. I didn't mean to stir things up for you."

Seamus lifted his head, stretched his legs and walked across the kitchen floor to push his nose against Johannah's knee. She laughed.

Reluctantly, Kate joined in.

Dolly's voice startled them. "I told you to wake me, Johannah." She stood in the doorway surveying the scene at the table disapprovingly. "It's nearly tea time and not a child in the house washed."

"There's plenty of time for that," Johannah replied. "Kate just got home. Would you like a cup of tea?"

"How was school, Kate?" Dolly asked.

Kate raised her eyebrows and looked at her mother. Johannah shrugged.

"School was grand, Nan." She patted the chair beside her. "Sit down and have a cup of tea."

Dolly frowned. After a minute she slid into the chair, examining the cup of milky tea Johannah set before her. "Is the water fresh?" she asked.

"Yes," Johannah replied, "and the milk, too."

"You didn't add sugar, did you, Johannah, because I don't take sugar."

"I know you don't, Mom. There's no sugar in your tea." She smiled bracingly at Kate. "Go ahead with what you were saying, love."

"Actually, I think you were the one talking."

"I can't remember."

Dolly rolled her eyes. "Now who's the one being forgetful?"

Kate stood. "I'll wash Evan and then help you with the tea. What are we having anyway?"

"Nothing elaborate, just bacon and cabbage. Take your time."

Dolly watched Kate lead Evan through the kitchen and up the stairs. "He's priceless. Doesn't he look just like Mickey did at that age, pure Enright? You can't tell he's a Kelliher at all."

Exasperated, Johannah's voice was sharp. "You're my mother, not Mickey's. Evan looks like *our* side of the family. You didn't know Mickey when he was a boy."

"I most certainly did. The Enrights were from the Abbey, just like we were. I watched Mickey Enright grow up."

Johannah stared at her. How could she be so sure of some things and so vague about others? "I could use some help with the potatoes."

"Help?"

"Yes. You could peel them or you could set the table."

"Peel the potatoes?" Dolly looked confused.

On second thought, perhaps it wasn't a good idea to give Dolly anything sharp. "Never mind, Mom," she said quickly. "Kate will be down in a minute. Would you like to watch the news?"

"Yes. I'll watch it in the sitting room."

Johannah poured her mother another cup of tea, carried it into the sitting room and turned on the television. Dolly settled herself into a high-backed chair, took the cup Johannah handed her and motioned her daughter away. "Go away now," she said and waved her hand, dismissing Johannah to the kitchen.

Gratefully, she fled.

Mickey

Johannah sat across from him in a skirt and tights that showed off the slim line of her calf, her hands wrapped around a vanilla cinnamon latte with an extra shot of espresso. She was the most beautiful thing he'd ever seen. He wanted nothing more than to reach across the table, hold her hand and tell her just that.

"There I was," she said, "with the dog's nose in my lap and my daughter asking me a question I had no idea how to answer." She smiled ruefully. "I sound like an idiot. You probably have no idea what I'm talking about."

"I might surprise you."

"All right, then, tell me," she challenged him.

"Kate asked if you knew immediately that Mickey was the man you loved beyond all others and whether you were sure you would never love anyone else. Do I have it right?"

"Yes, actually, you do."

He looked down at his newspaper. "What was your answer?"

"I wasn't completely honest, but close enough. Under the circumstances it was the best answer for her."

"How do you mean?"

"I'm not the same person I was at twenty. I had no idea who I was then. I lived in Dublin in university housing. My parents supported me. When I worked, it was for pocket money. I'd never paid a bill, owned a car, managed a bank account. Mickey was handsome and funny, the life of the party. Our chemistry was amazing. What did I know about loving someone, giving up for him, supporting him even when I thought he was wrong, raising children, making meals… making love?" She cleared her throat. "I told Kate that I was completely convinced, but what I think happened was, I was lucky."

He looked startled. "Lucky?"

"Yes. To be part of a marriage that works is really just a roll of the dice, isn't it? I could have married a child abuser, a wife beater, a drunk or a philanderer."

He colored and loosened the top button on his shirt.

"I mean, you can do all the planning you want, read all the books, take all the classes. You can do it all, but until you roll the dice, you won't know if you're a winner or loser. Real love comes later, when you know each other. It comes with sick babies and extra rolls of flesh. It comes with losing jobs and lowering standards and, more than anything, it comes with disappointment, serious disappointment."

He was silent for a long time. She was leaving a great deal out, but he could hardly tell her what he knew.

Johannah looked mortified as if she'd suddenly realized just how much she'd revealed.

"I really should be going," she said, fidgeting inside her bag and pulling out her keys. "They'll wonder where I am."

"I'm sorry," he said simply. "I'm so sorry it was that way for you."

She laughed self-consciously. "Thank you, but it certainly isn't your fault and, anyway, I didn't mean to make it sound desperate. We were very happy, really. You have nothing to apologize for. I'm the one who talked incessantly."

"I enjoy listening to you."

She blushed and bit her lip. "We always talk about me, never you. Why is that?"

"You're much more interesting."

"I doubt that."

"It's true."

"It's also terribly selfish. I'd like to make it up to you. Would you come to dinner one evening this week?"

"I'd like that very much."

"Thursday would work. I'll be home early."

"Thursday it is. What time?"

"Seven o'clock."

"I'll be there."

CHAPTER 13

Mickey

This time he was ready for the stinging wind, the hot gasp of desert air and the turning, twisting weightlessness of his body. Mickey landed, or was it closer to being deposited, on a dusty mountain with a flat plateau. The view was spectacular. Below and to the left, strange trees grew gray leaves and dark smooth pods. To the right verdant fields, tidy and cultivated, offered up a wealth of produce: grapes, lettuce, cabbage, carrots, and olives. Bougainvillea grew wild along the roads, their rich reds and deep purples so lush and brilliant they looked as if they belonged on a movie set. Above it all hung the sun, huge, relentless, scorching. Mickey lifted his arm to wipe his forehead.

The small, dark-eyed man dressed in a tunic the same pale color as the rock, separated himself from the landscape and walked toward him. "I hope the journey was easier on you this time," he said. "It usually comes with practice."

"Hello, Peter."

"Mickey."

"Where are we?"

"It no longer exists. Once, it was called Galilee, my home."

"It's very hot, isn't it?"

"Those coming from countries suffering from perpetual rain might call it hot. I, on the other hand, find the weather extremely comfortable."

"You didn't bring me here to talk about the weather."

"No."

"Then why?"

"Think of this visit as a sort of progress report. I'm your..." he thought a minute, "your probation officer. I want to hear about your impressions. I want to know what you've learned if, indeed, you've learned anything at all."

"To what purpose?"

"For my report. That's my job, to make reports and recommendations."

Mickey rubbed the back of his neck. "It's the heat. Must we have it?"

Peter smiled. "Consider it a sort of desensitization. There are hotter spots. Not that the possibility of your failing ever crossed my mind."

Mickey laughed uneasily. "I'm working very hard."

"I hope so."

He looked around. "Are there any chairs up here?"

"Do you feel the need to sit?"

Mickey thought a minute. "Actually, I don't."

"Then, by all means, proceed."

"I've met them all," he began, "Johannah, Kate, and Liam. It's Johannah I meet regularly. I wait in a café, *The Daily Grind*. She comes in before work and we talk." He frowned. "She's different."

"Different?"

Mickey nodded. "She's lost weight and looks younger, but that's not the real difference. I can't put my finger on it. She seems less tolerant. Johannah was always remarkably tolerant. Forgiving, would be a better word. I don't think she's happy."

"Really? When do you suppose that began?"

"The children have moved back home. She feels it's her duty to help them, but it isn't what she wants."

"Anything else?"

"Her mother has dementia. She's taken her in as well. It's a burden. Everything falls on Johannah. Everything has always fallen on Johannah. She was forever the responsible one. She kept things going when I was out of work."

"That was a regular event, if I recall."

"Yes." Again Mickey frowned. "It's shameful. I don't know why I wasn't more ashamed when it happened."

"Why, indeed?"

"I wish I'd been different."

"There's that, at least."

"I always thought we were happily married," Mickey confessed.

"Were *you?*"

"God, yes." He looked alarmed. "Sorry. That one slipped out."

"Perfectly understandable." Peter smiled. "You've made progress, Michael Enright, more than I'd hoped. You're finally paying attention."

"I haven't told you about Kate or Liam."

"Your relationship with your children and grandchild has never been an issue. Johannah is the important one. You must go back now. I leave you with a word of advice. Be careful with Dolly. The poor woman has enough problems without everyone thinking she's farther gone than she really is."

"I don't understand."

"You will."

With that he was gone, leaving Mickey to brace himself for the onslaught of searing wind and churning stomach and then, gratefully, the lovely familiar sensations of home: wet air, gray skies and green fields.

Johannah

"Hello. Is anyone home?" Maura's voice echoed through the hall into the spare bedroom.

Johannah considered standing to welcome her but gave up the idea immediately. She was too tired and too nearly finished to risk the argument with her knees. "I'm in here," she called out, "in Kate's room."

Maura held up a bottle of champagne. "I bought it at Aldi's. I couldn't resist the price."

"What are we celebrating?"

"Whatever you like. We can even make up something if you need a reason. I'm happy that it's the weekend. Milo and I have tickets for Croke Park."

Johannah looked blank.

"You know. The Munster finals? Kerry versus Dublin? What's the matter with you, Hannie? You were always such a football fan."

"I wasn't anything of the sort. It was Mickey who was the fan. I went along with it because it was important to him." She sat back on her heels. Her mother's clothing was sorted and folded neatly in the chest of drawers. "I went along with a lot of things because it was important to Mickey. I don't have to bother with that anymore. I don't give a flying fig for football or any other sport for that matter."

Maura sat down on the floor and looked around. "This room looks odd."

"Wait until you see it with the furniture and pictures on the walls."

"How do you mean?"

Johannah pointed to the tape marking the spots where pictures would be hung. "She wants her religious paintings all around her."

"What's wrong with that?"

"Nothing, I suppose, unless you can't bear the thought of *Stations of the Cross*, the *Infant of Prague* and *The Virgin of Guadalupe* staring at each other in what was supposed to be your sewing room."

"My goodness!"

"An understatement if I ever heard one."

"I had no idea your mother was so religious."

"She wasn't. If you want my opinion, she's covering her bases."

Maura laughed and stood. "I'm going to find two champagne glasses. You might as well be jolly if you're going to work all night." She hesitated at the door. "I forgot about the dog. Where is he?"

"Outside. He stays out there when Mom naps. She's sleeping quite a bit lately. I wonder if she's depressed."

"Don't think about it. That's what I tell Milo when he starts talking about depression. It's a state of mind."

"Of course it is. That's why they call it depression."

"You know what I mean." Maura looked both ways before stepping into the hall. "I'll be right back."

She returned with two glasses and a towel. Deftly removing the cork from the bottle, she poured the champagne, sat, folded her legs under her and leaned against the wall. "When will the rest of the furniture be here?"

"Liam will collect it tomorrow."

"I suppose it's official, then, the whole moving in business."

Johannah nodded. "Decidedly."

"Are you reconciled to it?"

"At the moment." She swirled her champagne. "I invited him for dinner."

Maura frowned. "Who?"

"Patrick. The man from the café."

"Hannie, you didn't."

"I did and I don't regret it at all. He's very nice. I've come to appreciate him and he's lonely."

"Will anyone else be here?"

"Of course. Mother lives here and so do Kate, Evan and Liam. We'll all be here."

Maura chuckled. "Are you sure you aren't trying to scare him off?"

"It isn't like that, but for future consideration I'll have to give it some thought."

Maura looked at the champagne bubbles rising in her glass. "Are you recovered, then, Hannie?"

"Recovered?"

"From Mickey. Are you ready to try again?"

Johannah closed her eyes briefly. "I'm not sure I can answer that," she said after a minute. "It doesn't work that way. I think recovery has to do with replacement. If someone came along, someone I felt could take Mickey's place in my life, then I would be recovered. Right now there's a gap, a huge, empty, lonely gap. I miss him, Maura. Despite everything, even his sports' fascination. I miss him. I'd give years of my life to have just one more day with him, one lovely, warm summer day walking by the rocks at Fenit, climbing to the shrine for St. Brendan, or strolling along Derrymore Strand to watch rainbows."

"You weren't always happy, Hannie."

"No. We forget those things, don't we?" Johannah smiled. "Thank goodness for that." She looked around. "Not to change the subject, but I'd like to have Mom's belongings in place today. How long can you stay?"

"Until she wakes up."

"Then we'd better hurry."

Dolly

Dolly woke disoriented. Stiff and frightened, she lay on the bed and looked around. Nothing was familiar. Carefully, she eased her legs over the side and sat up. The walls were green. She'd never slept in a green room in her life. As far as she was concerned there was enough green in Ireland to last her ten lifetimes, green and gray. She preferred something bright, yellow or pink would be much better.

Finding her balance, she crossed the room and looked up and down the hall. Where was Seamus? She walked down the stairs, through the hall to the backyard. Whose house was she in and why was no one home?

A familiar whimper reassured her. She opened the door and bent to rub the sensitive spot between Seamus's ears. Good dog, always there when she needed him. "Come, Seamus," she said, crossing the yard to the gate and unlatching it. We'll go home now. I have no lead for you, so you must behave."

Obediently the dog followed her, down the pebbled walkway and out on to the footpath. She stopped confused, but the dog took the initiative, urging her toward the town centre and

Kevin Barry's Villas, her home since the day she stepped inside the doors as a new bride.

Traffic filled the streets. Since when had Tralee become so crowded? There was a time when she'd known everyone coming toward her, when the walk home from town took more than an hour because she would stop and converse along the way. Where had all these strange faces come from? They were clearly not from the town or even from Ireland for that matter. Foreigners with their strange ways and their odd accents frightened her.

Confident the dog was leading her in the right direction, she followed blindly until she recognized the egg-yolk yellow of the O'Sullivan house. For the first time since she'd awakened, her heart resumed a normal rhythm. She was nearly home. Sure enough, she passed the final curve of the street and there it was, her house, black shutters on white, freshly painted, waiting for her. She climbed the brick steps and turned the knob. How odd. The door was never locked, except at night, of course. There was absolutely no reason to do so. The neighbors looked out for each other. Most were original owners or their children. Still, all was not lost. She had a spare key hidden under the porch in the backyard. She kept it for the children when they'd come home late and didn't want to wake her.

Dolly knelt under the back porch and ran her hand under the lip of the top step. Sure enough the key was there. She unlocked the back door.

"Come in, Seamus. We're home, love. Come in."

The dog whimpered but didn't move.

"Come, Seamus. You must be thirsty. Come in."

Slowly, reluctantly, he obeyed. Dolly set the key on the counter, ran the water to wash her hands and reached for the tea towel. It wasn't in its usual place on the towel rack. She opened the drawer to pull out another one and frowned. Empty. Wiping her hands on her trousers, she walked into the dining room. Nothing out of sorts here.

Climbing the stairs on the way to the bathroom, she glanced into her bedroom and froze, horrified. Not a stick of furniture remained. Dear God! She'd been robbed! She must call the garda immediately.

The doorbell rang. Rushing down the stairs, she pulled back the curtain and peered through the glass. A man stood on the porch. Relieved, she threw open the door. "Thank goodness it's you. I've been robbed. My furniture is gone. What shall I do?"

Stunned, he stared at her. "Do you recognize me, Dolly? Do you know who I am?"

"Stop playing games with me, Mickey Enright. You've been married to my daughter for thirty years. Of course I know you."

CHAPTER 14

Dolly

He stepped into the house and looked around. The dining room table and chairs and all the living room furniture except for the recliner were still there. "It doesn't look as if anything has been stolen, Dolly," he said.

"Upstairs," she insisted. "There's nothing left upstairs. Go and look." She followed him to the landing and watched as he checked the rooms.

Only her bedroom had been cleared out. The two smaller rooms remained intact. Descending the stairs, he took her arm, led her into the sitting room and sat down beside her. "Think a minute," he began. "Do you remember that you and Seamus are staying with Johannah?"

"Seamus isn't with Johannah. He's outside in the yard. What does that have to do with my furniture?"

"Johannah felt you would be more comfortable sleeping in your own bed. She had your bedroom furniture delivered to her house."

"The cheek of her."

He frowned. "This is still your home, Dolly," he said gently. "But you need company."

The old woman's chin quivered. "Johannah works all day."

"She's home in the evenings."

"Who will be with me during the day?"

"Is anyone *here* with you during the day?"

She thought a minute. The high bones of her cheeks were flushed. "I suppose not," she grudgingly admitted.

"Johannah will be worried. Shall I walk you back?"

Dolly nodded and then she frowned. "I haven't seen you for quite some time, Mickey Enright. You were in the habit of stopping in for a cup of tea at least once a week. Where have you been?"

He hesitated.

"Never mind," she said, cutting off his explanation. "I suppose you have better things to do."

"I've been away, Dolly, for more than a year. I'm not permitted to tell you where. No one else knows but you."

Her eyes widened. "What about Johannah? Surely she knows."

"No."

"I've never heard of such a thing. Why would you agree to it? What about your family?"

He shrugged helplessly. "I can't tell you that either."

"It sounds as if you can't explain much of anything. Why, I've never heard such foolishness. When will you come out of hiding?"

"I'm not sure, but I do know that, eventually, it will all become clear, sooner for you than most."

"Age does have some advantages, I suppose."

"In a manner of speaking." He smiled. "Call your dog and I'll walk you back to Johannah's."

Ignoring the curious stares of her neighbors, Mickey held her arm until they reached the familiar porch with its border of hydrangeas. "I'll leave you here," he said. "You look tired. It's been a long day for you."

"An unusual one," she admitted.

"Johannah cares about you. Try not to worry her."

"Shall I tell her you were here?"

"That's up to you."

She nodded. "Everything is changing for me. I'm often confused. That isn't the worst part. It's the fear I mind the most. I'm afraid of so many things. Why, do you think, that is?"

"Because you've lived a long time. You've seen more than the rest of us and you're wary. Children are rarely afraid. Fear creeps up on us, a consequence of experience."

"You're different," she said. "I've never spoken to you like this before."

"We're all different. Hurry in, now. Johannah will be frantic."

Dolly snorted. "It would be better for Johannah if I were gone."

Mickey's mouth tightened. "There isn't a selfish bone in your daughter's body. She's not capable of even thinking that way. Appreciate her. I wish I'd done more of that."

Her eyes clouded. "You sound as if you're going away. Are you going away, Mickey?"

"I hope not. I sincerely hope not." He stooped to kiss her cheek. "Go inside now."

She opened the door and watched until he walked away. Then she followed the sound of voices down the hall.

Johannah

Johannah and Maura stood on opposite sides of Dolly's bed, stretching sheets across the mattress, tucking in opposite corners. Pictures that had once adorned her mother's home hung on the walls.

"What on earth—" Dolly began.

Turning at the sound of her voice, Johannah smiled. "You certainly had a long rest. I was just about to check on you."

"These are my things, my bed, my pictures. What are they doing here? What have you done?"

Johannah's smile faded. "I thought you might like to have your own belongings around you. It would seem more like home."

"But I'm not home. This is your home, not mine."

Maura sidled toward the door.

Johannah sighed. "Surely you remember. You agreed to stay here with me."

"I didn't agree, Johannah. I was forced into it by that ridiculous judge, that no-nothing, Timmy Dwyer."

"The result is the same," Johannah explained patiently. "He said you couldn't live alone. You're to live here with me." She smiled bracingly. "It will be lovely seeing each other every day, don't you think?"

"When have we ever seen each other every day?" Dolly snapped. "What makes you think I want to see you every day?"

Johannah recoiled as if she'd been slapped. "I just thought—"

Maura spoke up. "It's been grand seeing you, Johannah. I'll just let myself out."

Johannah waited for the soft click of the door as Maura closed it behind her. Then she spoke to her mother. "If you feel that way about it, we can make other arrangements. Maybe you'd rather be with Philomena or Kathleen."

Dolly crossed her arms. Her voice shook. "I don't want to live with them either. I don't want to live with anyone. I want to go home. Why can't I just go home?"

Johannah's eyes filled. Why did this have to be so difficult? Mentally, she cursed Tim Dwyer. Was her mother really so far gone that she couldn't manage living in the home she'd been comfortable in for more than half a century? How many other women Dolly's age managed quite well as long as they had family to check on them now and then? Who would ever know if Johannah ignored the court order, sent her mother home and stopped in to visit every day? But then there was the dog, the catalyst of their problem. "Are you prepared to give up Seamus?"

"Don't be silly. He protects me. I'm safer having him."

"You might be safer, but no one else is."

Dolly shook her head. "I won't get rid of him."

Johannah drew a deep breath. "Then you'll have to put up with me, Mom. There's no alternative. I'm sorry."

"No, you aren't. Don't say it if you don't mean it."

Heat rose in Johannah's cheeks. Her hands clenched. "Do you think you're the only person affected by all this? Do you have any idea how the rest of us are inconvenienced?" She waved her hand to encompass the room. "This is my house. Until two weeks ago, every room was the way I wanted it. Now, there isn't a spare inch of extra space. You must be monitored all the time. Kate and Liam have arranged their schedules. I have to be home every day at half two, never mind the shopping and errands. All I wanted was to live alone, to have time to myself in my own house." Her voice rose. "You don't understand that. You've never worked a day in your life. When I say I'm sorry things have worked out this way, believe me, I'm sorry."

The line in the middle of Dolly's forehead deepened. "What have you done with Mickey's things?"

"Sorry?"

"Why isn't he living here anymore?"

Johannah sat down on the bed and rubbed her temples. "Oh, Mom. I can't do this. I really can't. It's just too much."

"You aren't thinking about divorce?"

"Of course not."

"I saw him today. He came to the house."

"No, he didn't."

"Don't contradict me, Johannah. He came right into the house when I asked him to check the rooms. I thought I'd been robbed. My furniture was gone."

"Mickey did not come to the house, Mom. You were sleeping. You had a dream."

"He looks desperate, as if he hasn't been sleeping. I think he wants to come home. Men are weak, Johannah. It is our job to forgive them when they are penitent."

Johannah stared at her mother. She'd been raised to respect her elders, never contradict, never speak up much less question or cross. Where did delusionary behavior fit in? Did it harm anyone at all? Was it necessary or even beneficial to correct her mother, her mother whose dementia became more obvious with every passing day? "Mickey and I are fine, Mom," she said wearily. "When he wants to come home, he'll be welcome."

"He said something very odd."

"Did he?"

Dolly nodded. "He said he'd been away for a year and that he couldn't tell me where. He said you didn't know either."

"He's wrong. I know exactly where he is."

Dolly waited expectantly. Johannah stood. "I'll hang the rest of the pictures after tea. Would you like to help me set the table?"

"I'll have it in the sitting room in front of the television where I always do."

Johannah bit her lip. "Are you sure you wouldn't like to sit at the table with the rest of us?"

"Are we expecting someone?"

"Kate, Evan and Liam. They're staying here."

"I don't believe I know Evan."

"Yes, you do, Mom. He's Kate's son, your great-grandson."

"Really?" Dolly looked interested. "I must be very old. Am I old, Johannah?"

Johannah's laugh was nearly a sob. No sane person would believe this conversation. "Not terribly."

"Mickey said I was closer to answers because of my age."

Johannah laughed. "Mom, does that sound like something Mickey would say? I mean, can you remember him repeating anything close to the slightest bit profound?"

Dolly's lips pursed, pulling her mouth into that odd position Johannah found disturbing. "He said it today. I think he's right."

"Okay. I'll leave you alone for a bit while I start our tea. Maybe Mickey will stop in and you can have it together."

"Nothing for me, Johannah," Dolly called after her. "I don't eat in the middle of the day.

Ten pounds too lean is better than having an extra tire around your waist."

Johannah waited until she was in the kitchen with the water pulsing full strength into the sink before she allowed herself to curse.

CHAPTER 15

Kate

Dermot tried to smile but couldn't quite manage it. "I didn't realize you felt this way, Katie. Why did you never tell me?"

Kate smiled sadly. "I did tell you. For years I've complained about how small the apartment is. I've asked you, begged you for a place of our own, away from your parents."

He sighed. "Moving doesn't make sense. We pay nothing to live here. We have no debt. Why can't you understand that? Everything you want will come later. Our retirement will be fabulous."

"Dermot, I'm not even thirty years old. I don't want to think of retirement. What if we don't make retirement? My dad didn't. I want something now. Don't you see how much resentment your way of thinking has caused?"

His voice was strained. "I didn't realize it would come to this. I had no idea you wanted to leave me. You never said you hated the work."

"I've a degree, Dermot. I'm a certified dietician. To be fair, I didn't *always* hate it. It happened slowly. By the time I realized how I felt about this place, I'd already been at it for years. You needed me to help out. It seemed churlish to quit when you couldn't afford the extra help."

"I still can't afford the extra help."

"I can't wait any more, Dermot. It's killing me. Your mother hates me. It's hard coming here, trying to deal with her."

"I didn't realize she was in so often."

Kate stared at her hands, the fingers tight as a tourniquet in her lap. "More now than ever. She wants me to leave. She says she'll take my place until you find someone else."

"She could never do that," he said quickly.

Kate shook back her hair and looked him at him directly for the first time since the beginning of this most difficult conversation. "I think it would be best. We should keep our distance, Dermot. We're separated."

"But not divorced."

"No. Not yet."

"Well then." His smile was forced. "I don't see why we can't be adults and continue as usual. I need the help and you're experienced."

"I need to find a job, Dermot. I need the money. I can't continue living with my mother and not give her anything for food or utilities. You must find someone else, someone whose salary you can afford. We aren't on the same page anymore. I don't want to be here. I want to move on. Do you understand?"

"Whatever you want, Katie. As long as you're happy. That's all that's important."

His eyes were so warm and kind and filled with compassion that she wanted to hit him.

"Don't Dermot."

"Don't what?"

"Don't be so decent. It makes everything harder."

"I can't help that. It's me, Katie. I can't be anything other than myself."

She groaned and headed for the door. "I'll leave you the car but I need it next Tuesday. Is that all right?"

"Of course. I'll pick up Evan for the weekend. Give you a bit of a break."

"Find someone to take my place, Dermot. I won't be back here." Pulling the door closed behind her, she stood in front of the store, under the lintel waiting for the rain to stop, attempting to compose herself. It was after five, nearly dark, and her mother was expecting her for tea. Johannah had invited a friend and she wanted everyone there. Kate had planned on making dessert, contributing her labor since she couldn't contribute anything else. She really had to find a full time job, one that actually paid a decent salary. Evan's knickers were past wearing and he'd outgrown his shoes and trousers. Although it made perfect sense for Dermot to support his son, pride kept her from asking, and she'd die before she approached her mother. But where could she find work in her field in Tralee? She'd have to look in Cork or Dublin. The complications were enormous. An afternoon

shower, heavy and slanted, flooded the footpath.
How could she have left the house without an
umbrella?

She waited for a full five minutes and still
the rain poured down. Just as she was about to
make a run for the taxi idling on the corner, a
blue Yaris pulled up to the curb and a familiar
copper-brown head leaned out the window.
"You'll be drenched in this downpour. Climb in.
I'll drive you home."

For half an instant, Kate considered refusing
him. Then, replacing reservation with
practicality, she climbed in. "Thanks, Ritchie. I
forgot my umbrella. You can drop me at my
mother's."

"No problem."

The air inside the car was warm and dry.
Drops condensed on the window shrouding
them in curtains of fog. Wipers scraped sheets
of water from the windscreen. Ritchie drove
competently, deliberately, making no attempt at
conversation. Slowly, the knots in Kate's
shoulders relaxed and she closed her eyes. Soon,
too soon, he pulled up in front of her family
home just as he'd done so many times in the
past.

"How's the lad?" he asked.

She looked confused. "Sorry?"

"Your son. How is he?"

"Grand. Why do you ask?"

He shook his head. "It's strange thinking of
you as a mother. I don't have children. I feel
like I've missed out."

"It's not as if it couldn't happen. You're still young enough to have a family."

Ritchie shook his head. "Not in this lifetime."

Kate focused on a raindrop zigzagging its way down the windowpane. She wanted to ask the obvious question, but fear of the answer held her back. "I'd invite you in," she said after a minute, "but we're having company for tea."

He grinned. "Would you really?"

"Of course," she lied.

"Your mother never cared much for me."

Kate opened the door and stepped out. "My mother's loyalty has always been appropriate, Ritchie. What did you expect?"

"Nothing else. Goodnight, Kate."

"Thanks for the lift."

"My pleasure."

She ran for the porch and stood under the shelter, watching him drive away, waiting until the car disappeared around the corner, then she opened the door and stepped inside.

Kitchen smells, savory spices and cucumber salad, wafted through the warm air. She sighed with appreciation. Coming home on a rainy night to her mother's cooking was a slice of heaven.

"Mommy," Evan shouted from the top of the stairs. "Guess what?"

Kate held out her arms to catch the warm, propelling weight of her son. Carefully, she unwound the towel he wore attached to his shirt with safety pins from around his neck. "Tell me."

"We're having a guest for tea and I'm allowed to stay up. Nan said."

"What on earth are you wearing, Evan?"

"I'm Superman. I can fly, but not too high."

Kate laughed and kissed his neck. "You smell good," she mumbled.

He squirmed out of her embrace. "Nan says I should wash myself before the guest comes."

"Good idea. We'll wash together." Keeping hold of his hand she started up the stairs.

The door leading to the kitchen opened. "Kate, love, you're home." Her mother's mouth curved into a smile. "How is everything? Did you have a good day?"

Kate opened her mouth to answer but the words stuck in her throat. It was simply too much, the aromatic smells, the warm air, the familiar room, her mother's welcoming words, Evan's moist little hand, trusting and eager. When would she have anything even remotely as lovely and secure to offer him? She sat down on the stairs, pulled him on to her lap and buried her face his neck.

"Kate?" Johannah's voice reflected her concern. "Are you all right? Did something happen?"

Evan struggled out of her lap. "You're wetting me," he complained.

Kate laughed through her tears. "I suppose I am." She wiped her eyes. "I'm sorry. It can't be pleasant with me weeping all over everyone all the time. I don't know what's the matter with me." She forced a smile. "Everything smells delicious and the house looks wonderful. It's so good to be home and yet—"

Johannah rested her hand on her grandson's head. "Mommy's tired, Evan, and I need help with the serviettes. There are six of them on the server. Can you lay one on every plate?"

He nodded, running down the stairs, beating his chest and vowing to save the day.

She sat down beside Kate. "What happened?"

"Nothing at all. It just came over me that I have no plan, no idea for my future. I'm in limbo. I have no home, no particular goal and, as of today, I don't even have a job. I told Dermot I wasn't coming to work any more."

"What about your Council job? Can you ask for more hours?"

"I could, but I don't think that's an option and it isn't what I want to do."

"Which is?"

Kate shrugged. "I'd like to use my degree."

"It isn't as if everything needs to be solved this afternoon."

Kate stood. "Of course, not. I'm being ridiculous and you're having company. I'm sorry I'm late, Mom. I wanted to help you and instead got stuck in stupid conversation with Dermot. I'll wash up and be down in a flash. Send Evan up when he's finished downstairs and don't think about this even for a minute. I'll be fine." She paused on the landing. "Is Liam home?"

"Not yet. Traffic is bad this time of night. I'll try his mobile in a few minutes. Nan is in the sitting room." Johannah hesitated.

"I need to clean up myself and give Evan a bath but I'll keep her company if you have everything else under control."

"That would be a Godsend. I'd really appreciate it."

Upstairs in the bathroom, Kate turned the heat control dial to a higher setting than usual and stood under the spray allowing the blessed warmth to seep into her muscles. Condensation fogged the mirror and wisps of hair curled tightly around her face when she stepped out of the tub. Forgoing everything but a swipe of gloss on her lips, Kate brushed out her hair, stepped into wool trousers and pulled on a knit jersey before running downstairs to find her son. "Evan," she called out. "It's time for a bath."

A draft of cold air flowed down the hall. Kate turned toward the front door. Her brother stood in the entry accompanied by a woman so exotic and striking she could have graced the cover of a fashion magazine. She was also a good twenty years older than Liam.

"Kate," he said, flashing his brilliant smile. "Meet Sheila. I brought her home for dinner."

Kate walked down the hall and extended her hand. "It's a pleasure to meet you, Sheila. My mom didn't mention an extra person would be coming. I thought she set the table for six."

"You know Mom," Liam replied. "There's always room for an extra mouth. Sheila's my partner in economics class. We're supposed to come up with a small business plan."

"Are you now? I'll tell my mom you're here. Maybe you'd like to wait in the sitting room with Nan. Pour Sheila a drink, Liam. I'm in search of my son. He hasn't had his bath yet."

Johannah was leaning over the stove, spooning sauce over the salmon, a sauce that Kate could tell was laced with far too much butter. Evan was kneeling beside the dog alternately feeding him from the length of string cheese and taking bites himself.

"Evan!" Kate shrieked. "What on earth— Mom, do you see what Evan's doing?"

Johannah groaned. "I only took my eyes off him for a minute." She dropped the spoon in the sink, confiscated Evan's cheese and picked him up. Kissing his dirt-smudged cheek, she murmured into his ear. "You're upsetting your mom, love. Run along upstairs and take your bath, will you?"

Evan nodded obediently, tucked his hand inside his mother's and led her toward the door.

"Wait until you see what Liam's brought home," Kate whispered over her shoulder. "This time he's outdone himself."

Johannah's eyes flashed. "Salmon is dear and I bought just enough. I don't care if it's the Pope himself. Liam will have to share his portion."

CHAPTER 16

Mickey

The house looked good, new PVC trim around the windows, bricks edging the concrete footpath, a glass conservatory facing the garden. Johannah had done well on her own. Inside everything looked roomier, less cluttered, less like the home he remembered. She'd welcomed him warmly, drawing him into the sitting room where the family sat, grouped around the fireplace. Dolly, closest to the warmth, dozed in the recliner.

Kate's eyes widened and Liam took a second look when she introduced him.

"You're the man from the library," he said, holding out his hand.

Mickey shook it. "That's right. I believe I mentioned that I knew your mother."

Johannah looked surprised. "You've met?"

Liam nodded. "Briefly. We shared a table at the library."

"You were outside the funeral home when Mrs. Costelloe died," Kate announced. "I couldn't place you at first, but now I remember."

"Right again."

Kate flushed. "It wasn't one of my finest moments. I'm dreadfully embarrassed."

"I won't hold it against you."

"I'm curious," said Johannah, "but I'll play it safe and not ask what the two of you are referring to. I have to finish up in the kitchen. Patrick, if you tell Liam what you're drinking, he'll see if we have it."

"No bother. A club orange will do." He held out a chilled bottle of French burgandy. "I thought you might like this."

She smiled. "Thank you. It will be lovely with dinner. I believe we can offer you the orange. It's Evan's favorite."

Evan looked up from the transformer he was struggling with. "I'll have an orange, too."

"No," said his mother. "No mineral for you. You'll have a glass of milk."

"Killjoy," muttered Liam under his breath.

"But I don't want milk," Evan insisted.

Kate's voice was unnaturally calm. "Did you say something, Liam?"

Her brother improvised quickly. "I was telling Sheila what an obedient boy Evan is, wasn't I, Sheila?"

"Oh, yes," replied the sultry beauty, "very obedient."

"You said another word, Uncle Liam," said Evan, ever truthful. "You said—"

Mickey cut in. "Do you have children, Sheila?"

Pure venom flashed from the woman's eyes. "Certainly not."

Dolly chose that moment to wake from her slumber. Stretching, she looked around her. "My goodness! The room certainly has filled up since I dozed off. Who are all these people?" She fixed her eyes on Sheila. "Who are you, my dear? A friend of Kate's perhaps?"

"I'm Liam's friend."

Dolly's eyebrows rose. "Liam's friend? How can you be Liam's friend? He's a child."

"Nan." Liam crossed the room to sit beside his grandmother. "Sheila is a friend from university." He nodded at Mickey. "And this is Patrick, my mom's friend."

Dolly stared. "What on earth is the matter with you, Liam? He isn't Patrick at all. He's your father. It's Mickey."

Liam's mouth fell open.

Kate gasped. "Good lord, Nan. How could you?" She offered a strangled apology. "I'm so sorry, Patrick. She's a bit confused."

"It's quite all right. I'm flattered."

Johannah appeared in the doorway. "Dinner's ready."

"Not a moment too soon," said Liam under his breath. He held out his hand to Sheila. "The food will be worth everything."

"If you don't mind, Liam," his mother said, when they'd all trooped into the dining room, "I'd like you to sit at the head of the table. Sheila can sit on your right. Mom, you take the place on the other side of Kate. I'll sit beside Evan and Patrick can sit beside me."

"Don't be ridiculous, Johannah," said Dolly. "Mickey should sit at the head of the table. It's his house after all."

After an instant of frozen, embarrassed silence, Liam spoke. "I don't mind. We'll do whatever makes Gran happy."

Johannah looked mortified. "I'm so sorry," she whispered to Patrick, "but if it's all right with you, it would save us a scene."

He looked down into her anxious face and mentally cursed the circumstances that prevented him from shielding her. "It would be my pleasure to sit at the head of your table, Hannie. Think nothing of it."

Unbelievably, Dolly behaved herself for the rest of the meal. Sheila's self-involved comments were remarkably interesting and Evan's table manners had improved greatly over the course of the year. Mickey looked around the table at his family, at the new line between his daughter's eyebrows, at the forced optimism in his son's conversation, at the bewildered expression on his mother-in-law's face and, saving her for last, at his wife, Hannie, a slimmer, edgier Hannie trying to hold everything together, to pretend they were still whole and connected. His heart broke for her. At the same time he felt a deep sense of shame. He hadn't been much help to her over the course of their marriage. He hadn't left her anything she wouldn't already have had except the house. Thank God for the house. Sending up a silent prayer, he asked for enough time to make it up to her in some small way that might make a difference.

She must have noticed his silence. "Are you all right, Patrick?" she asked, her voice low and accessible only to him under the din of conversation. "Should I have invited you when there weren't so many other people?"

"Not at all," he replied. "Your family is lovely. I'm enjoying every minute of it."

"Nan," Evan's voice, high and demanding, captured her attention.

"Yes, love."

"Something happened at school today."

"What was that?"

"Stevie Murphy said the *fuck* word."

"Evan!" snapped his mother. "You know you're not to say that. It's common and very naughty."

"I didn't say it. Stevie Murphy did."

"I don't care who said it. You're not to repeat it." Kate frowned. "For pity's sake, who would have thought a convent school would encourage such language. Maybe I should look for another one."

"Give over, Kate," Liam grinned. "It isn't as if the lad hasn't heard it before."

"Whatever can you mean, Liam?" his sister demanded. "Where else would he have heard it, unless it's from you?"

"Evan, lad, tell your mom who else says the word."

"My mom says it," replied the child. "She says it when she's cross or angry at my dad."

Mickey choked and lifted the serviette to his lips.

Kate's face was a study, all red-cheeked and frozen, her eyes narrow and lazered at her brother. "Thank you very much, Liam Enright, for pointing out my deficiencies as a parent. In future, I'll look to you for a standard as far as parenting goes, you and Sheila, of course."

Evan spooned a healthy portion of pie into his mouth. "My mom's mad," he whispered loudly to Liam. "You better watch it."

Johannah began to laugh and, like a tire with a slow leak, the tension around the table eased. Dolly laughed, too, and then Liam joined in and finally, Kate. Not to be left out of the fun, although it was clear he had no idea why, Evan began to giggle as well.

Mickey relaxed. His family was still together.

Later, after cleaning the kitchen, Liam and Sheila left for the pub, Dolly excused herself for the night and Kate carried Evan upstairs for bed. Mickey and Johannah took their tea into the sitting room. Without thinking he sat in the chair that had always been his. They were silent for a long time.

"Thank you for inviting me," he said. "I haven't had such a lovely family meal in a long time."

"You're very welcome." Johannah tilted her head. "They're very comfortable with you."

"Sorry?"

"Liam and Kate," she explained. "Normally, they're on their guard. They don't warm to strangers easily. Yet they felt comfortable enough to indulge in a spat right in front of you." She looked at him. "I wonder why."

He stared into the fire. "I can't imagine."

"My mother thought you were Mickey."

"Yes." The room was very warm.

"She's ill, of course."

"Yes." He ran his finger under his collar.

"I'm not what you would call superstitious."

"No." Where was this leading?

"I'm not even particularly religious. I don't attend Mass the way I did when the children were small."

"It won't matter."

Eyebrows raised, she stared at him. "How do you know?"

"Common sense," he said emphatically, hoping he was right and that no one with authority was listening. "A woman like you, clearly a good woman, will have no difficulty finding her place in the hereafter."

Johannah sat up. "You're an odd man. Do you know that?"

He laughed. "You're not the first one to say it."

"You called me Hannie."

"It suits you."

"Twice you called me Hannie."

Clearly he was on dangerous ground. "Would you rather I didn't?"

She nodded. "I think so. For the time being, at least."

He smiled. *For the time being* implied she wasn't finished with him. There would be other times. She was very clever, his Hannie. Perhaps she would figure things out on her own. Peter hadn't ruled out that possibility. Mickey would be quite happy if she figured it out on her own.

CHAPTER 17

Mickey

Peter was angry. The jaw of his rough brown face was stiff with tension and his eyes snapped with temper. To make matters worse, on this particular visit, Mickey felt the cold, the kind of numbing cold that seeps into the bones and settles there, the kind he remembered as a child before the advent of electric showers and perpetual hot water, when bath times were torturous ordeals executed before peat fires in large basins that had to alternately be filled with boiling water from an inadequate kettle and cold water from the pump. There was always an excess of cold and never enough of the hot."You're angry," he said, stating the obvious.

Peter's eyebrow rose. "You think so?"

Mickey swallowed. "I know why."

"Brilliant of you."

"I didn't tell her anything."

"You came damnably close."

"Hannie is a clever woman. She arrived at it herself."

Peter came closer, his finger pointed and accusing against Mickey's chest. "You helped her, Mickey Enright. You escorted her mother home. You sat down to dinner with the family at your accustomed place at the table. You called her a pet name that only her close friends and family use."

"You never told me I couldn't," Mickey protested. "You never said she couldn't figure it out herself."

"I told you she wasn't to find out."

"You told me I couldn't tell her. There's a difference."

"Splitting hairs, that's what you're doing."

Mickey frowned and stepped back. "How am I supposed to help her if I'm to stay removed? How will she trust me? They need me. You saw them. They're not doing well without me."

Peter shook his head. "No, lad. Your family's dynamic hasn't changed. You're seeing it objectively for the first time because you've been away. Kate is confused and destructive because she has no purpose. Liam is behaving the only way he knows how, the way you've taught him to behave. Dolly is," he stroked his chin, "well, she's Dolly and can't be held accountable at this stage. A few years ago was another matter entirely, but that isn't my affair. I'm in the business of redemption. Dolly Little will be assigned to someone else. Your grandchild is still too young for me to pass judgment. One can never tell with the young. There you have it, all of them."

"What about Hannie? Don't tell me she's the same."

Peter's face softened the way it did when he spoke of Johannah. "A clever woman, your Hannie. She was nearly out of it, that twisted confusion of relationships that make up her existence. She had nearly seen the light, but then everyone descended on her again, forcing her to resume her old role, peacemaker, diffuser, rescuer, counselor. Once again she's attempting to fix everyone at her own expense and will, of course, fix no one and thereby lose herself."

Mickey was offended. "I assume you're including me in my wife's twisted confusion of relationships."

"You most of all," Peter agreed.

"I only want to help her."

"Do you really?"

"Of course. What else?"

"If you want an answer, I must give you an honest one. I'm not able to do anything else, not even for the sake of kindness."

"God forbid that you should be kind," Mickey muttered.

"Did you say something?"

"Nothing of importance. You were saying?"

"I don't believe you want to help Hannie at all. I think you want your life back exactly as it was. You would be perfectly content to settle into your old ways, when your wife was at your beck and call. It suited you quite well. It would suit anyone with half a conscience."

"You're very hard on me."

"Someone has to be."

"I don't see it that way at all," Mickey said, affronted.

"Of course you don't. That's why I'm here, to show you the way."

"You're not showing me at all. I'm blundering my way through, as you so clearly pointed out."

"I wouldn't call it blundering," replied Saint Peter. "What you're doing is cheating. We had an agreement. You must follow through with it, even when you believe no one is watching." For a brief instant he looked almost sympathetic. "I can't be everywhere you know."

Mickey swallowed. "What am I to do?"

"Step back. Don't attempt to change fate. You'll only waste your time."

"Isn't that what I'm supposed to do? Change fate? Why am I being sent down if it isn't to make life easier for my family?"

Peter's mouth dropped. "Is that what you think you're about, Mickey Enright? To make life easier?"

"Yes."

Peter lifted his hands to the heavens and shouted, "This is what I'm given, a neophyte, an amateur, a beginner, a mere babe in the woods."

Embarrassed, Mickey hung his head. "I apologize," he whispered although he had no idea what he'd done.

Peter shook his head and sighed. "*Easier* isn't the answer, lad. *Easier* doesn't solve anything. I am not in the business of *easy*. You must help them realize that growth comes through challenge, the facing and the overcoming. You must encourage them to do *something*, anything, toward the change that is necessary for personal fulfillment. *Easy* has nothing to do with it. *Easy* is a wastrel's wish. All of them, all your family members, with the exception of your wife, and the child who is not yet responsible, want easier. It is your duty to show them the way. You are not to tempt them with what is easy. You are to show them what is right and in so doing you will redeem yourself."

Despite the cold, beads of sweat formed on Mickey's brow. "I'm not capable," he whispered. "I don't know how. Why must I be the one?"

Peter smiled, a brief turning up of the lips, a crease of the cheek. "Quite simply, Mickey Enright, who better than you?"

Liam

Betty's pub was quiet, even for a Thursday night. People were spending less, holding on to their pennies, buying their liquor at off-licenses and drinking at home for half the price of a pub pint.

Sheila sat on the bar stool, one long slim leg crossed over the other and exhaled. Smoke swirled about her head. She tapped her cigarette against the counter. "Your mother doesn't like me," she said flatly.

Liam frowned. "There's a no smoking ordinance in Ireland, in case you've forgotten."

"No one cares."

"They care," replied Liam, "they just won't say anything."

"That's all right then."

"No. it isn't. Do me a favor and put out the fag."

With a shrug of her shapely shoulder, Sheila dropped her cigarette into her empty glass. "You'll have to order me another."

"No problem." Liam fished in his back pocket for his wallet. At the rate she drank, he'd be out of money and still have four days left in the week before he could collect his stipend again.

"Your mother doesn't like me," Sheila repeated.

"My mother likes everybody."

"Women can tell these things. She sees me as a threat."

Liam stared at her. "What are you talking about? How could you possibly be a threat? She's my mother."

"It's an oedipal thing. Mothers are jealous when their sons bring women home."

"Sheila." Liam had lost patience long ago. "My mother has no reason to be jealous. She's my mother, the only one I'll ever have. I invited you to dinner, I haven't brought you home. Besides, she's accustomed to my bringing friends to the house. She's fine with it."

"Then why doesn't she like me?"

Liam acknowledged the guitar player tuning his instrument in the corner with a wave of his hand and swallowed a healthy portion of his pint before answering. "It could have been because you didn't offer to help clear up, or maybe it was the way you weren't interested in anyone else at the table."

"I was a guest," she said icily, "and in case you didn't notice, I tried joining into the conversation. No one would allow me an opening."

"We're not exactly up on American soaps or where to find the most expensive spa treatments. Seriously, Sheila, you might have tried a bit harder."

"I don't have to try anything." Her voice rose. "I was a guest. You should have tried harder with me."

He stared at her, surprised. "You're really upset."

"Damn right I am." She swung her purse over her shoulder and slid off the stool, exposing all twenty-two inches of long, lean thigh. "It's clear I've made a mistake. I thought you were a gentleman."

"Sheila, don't go," he protested. "It's late. Let me at least see you home."

"Not a chance." She stalked toward the door. "Don't bother ringing me again."

Liam watched her go. He should have followed her, prevailed upon her to accept a ride home. It was too dangerous for an attractive woman with her skirt hiked up to her fanny to walk the streets without an escort. Sighing, he pushed aside his Guinness and reached for his wallet.

"Girlfriend problems?" Ciara McCarthy picked up his glass and gave the bar a quick swipe with her towel.

"She's just a friend," he explained.

"I'm glad to hear it."

"Why is that?"

"You can do better," she said, surprising him. "You *have* done better. That woman is years older than you and her reputation is, shall we say, tarnished?"

He laughed. "You can't be that old-fashioned."

Her eyes twinkled. "Maybe not. But I'm still right. You wait and see. She'll have someone else by tomorrow afternoon."

Liam thought a minute and then slipped his wallet back into his pocket. "How are you, Ciara? The last I heard you were planning on veterinary school."

"I still am, but it takes money and my mom isn't doing well right now."

"I'm sorry. What's wrong with her?"

Ciara shrugged. "The cancer has her for the second time. I'm surprised your mom didn't tell you. She's the social worker on her case."

Liam looked down at his shoes, then he looked back at pretty Ciara McCarthy, at her pouty lips and laughing eyes and wiry red hair. She was younger than he was, working hard behind the bar of a pub, making her plans and caring for her mother without a single complaint. It was more than enough to embarrass a man. "My mom doesn't share the details of her cases with us," he explained. "She feels it's a breach of privacy."

"Good for her," said Ciara. "It's daunting to think everyone knows the details of my family's personal life. Not that I think your mom would spread stories. I know she isn't like that. She's been lovely to us, considering."

The McCarthys were tinkers, itinerants, part of the nomadic population whose ancestors had taken to the roads in carts after they'd been evicted from their lands by Protestant landlords during the penal code years. For decades they'd been looked upon with suspicion by the settled population. Ciara's was of the first generation to hold jobs, to continue their education and make a stab at assimilation. Liam had always liked her, even had a thing for her years ago, before his father cautioned him against her. *Can't be taking up with the likes of them, lad. They'll be coming to your door expecting all sorts of favors and then cheat you blind if you give in to them.*

Liam smiled. "I'll tell her you said that."

She nodded at his glass. "If you're not driving, there's time for another before I close up."

"No, thanks." He looked at his watch. "It's nearly closing time. I'd better go or my mom will be sending out the guards."

Ciara opened her mouth to speak, but hesitated.

"What is it?"

"Since when are you living at home?"

"Since our Celtic Tiger took a dive. I've gone back to university. It's cheaper to live at home."

Ciara laughed. "Easier, too, I imagine, for you."

"How do you mean?"

"Admit it, Liam. You've got your mom cooking and cleaning for you. It can't be easier for her."

Liam frowned. There it was again, the implication that he should be doing more than he was. "I suppose not," he said.

"Well then, I guess I'll be seeing you. Say hello to your mom."

He shrugged into his jacket. "I'll do that."

Outside the streets were empty. Across the pitch-dark sky, a bitter wind chased clouds heavy with impending rain. Ice sheets frosted parked cars, puddles froze, milk rose in their bottles and even the occasional yowling cat gave up the fight and shared heat and whatever shelter it could find with recent enemies.

Hunkering down into the fleece collar of his jacket, Liam fished in his pocket for his keys and headed for the car, thankful for his reprieve after the incident with Sheila, wanting only the clean, kitchen smell of home and then his own bed.

He turned the corner and nearly bumped into a dark human shape heading in the other direction. It took a minute to recognize the man who'd sat across from him at dinner. "Patrick, you're out late."

"That makes two of us."

"Can I offer you a lift?"

"I wouldn't want to impose."

"Not at all," Liam assured him. "Hop in. Tralee isn't exactly London. Wherever you live can't be far."

"I'm staying near the track. You can drop me at the corner of Racecourse Road."

Liam turned down Rock Street. "I'm sorry I didn't get much of a chance to talk with you at dinner."

Patrick grinned. "You were otherwise occupied."

"Sheila's a piece of work, not bad really, just in desperate need of attention. She actually implied that my mom was rude to her because she was jealous. Can you imagine?"

"Some women require a great deal of attention and your mom isn't one of them. Johannah's one of the good ones."

"How long have you known my mom?" Liam asked casually.

"Not long. She's a lovely person. I'm sure your dad was, too."

"Yes." Liam nodded emphatically. "She misses him."

"She's fortunate to have you and your sister."

Once again Liam felt the stirrings of guilt. For the second time tonight he was reminded that he was no help to his mother at all.

"This is my stop," Patrick said not long after they'd left the town center. "Thanks for the lift."

"No trouble at all," replied Liam. Not until he turned the key in his own door did it occur to him that Betty's Pub was an odd choice for a man who lived on Racecourse Road.

CHAPTER 18

Johannah

"But I have ten children, Mrs. Enright. The pension I'm given doesn't allow enough to raise them."

Johannah sighed, set down her briefcase, rolled up the sleeves of her blouse, tucked a towel into her belt and began tackling the mess in Jane Murphy's kitchen. Scraping food into the garbage, she stacked dishes on one side of the worktop, poured liquid soap into the sink, added water, found a sponge and started scrubbing. "Three of your children are adults, Mrs. Murphy. They need to look for work or else apply for services on their own."

"My oldest isn't more than twenty and where would my boys be finding work, with half the country on the dole." Reluctantly, she picked up a towel that wasn't quite as filthy as the rest and began wiping the dishes dry. "You don't want to be doing my work, Mrs. Enright. Mind your clothes."

Johannah was tired of side-stepping. "Someone has to do it," she said bluntly. "This place isn't suitable. You're in danger, Mrs. Murphy. If you can't care for your children, Social Services will take them. I'm sure you don't want that."

"Not a bit," agreed the woman. "But with so little coming in, sometimes I have to leave them."

"You're being paid, quite generously, to stay with them."

"My man needs the money. He's on the road, you know."

Johannah understood this to be a reference to her common-law husband, a man who showed up infrequently, just long enough to leave her pregnant with yet another mouth to feed. "Maybe he should stay on the road and allow you to keep your money for the children."

"You're scrubbing a hole in that pot, Mrs. Enright. A woman gets lonely."

Johannah's lips tightened. Why not say what she felt? Who else would tell the woman, not that Johannah believed for a minute that Mrs. Murphy didn't already know the measure of the man she'd chosen. "Not that lonely. He isn't a good husband, nor is he a father to your children. What do you see in him anyway?"

"He's attractive to women."

Johannah stopped scrubbing. Her mouth dropped. "You're not serious." A picture of Gerard Flynn formed in her mind, unshaven jaw, broken blood vessels marking his nose and cheeks, stomach swollen from the drink, thinning hair and missing teeth.

"I'm no beauty myself, Mrs. Enright. Gerard still wants me. I'm grateful for it and I'll not be judged."

Johannah pulled the plug, keeping her focus on the water draining down the sink, purposely avoiding the missing cabinet doors, the water-stained walls, the curling edges of linoleum floor and the boarded window pane. Her small contribution weighed in at next to nothing. Like a thousand others, this woman's life wouldn't change.

She dried her hands on the towel and pulled it from around her waist. "Tell your two oldest sons to find another place to live. I can't authorize your current allowance while they continue to use this house as their address."

"How will I live until then?"

Johannah hesitated, taking her time to sort through her briefcase and lay two applications on the only clean patch of table. "Get someone you know to verify their new address. Do it today and I'll authorize two more weeks for you."

The beady dark eyes narrowed even further. "You know about the racing money."

Johannah faced her squarely. "I do. May I remind you that dog racing is illegal without a permit. That source will dry up. I'm angry, Mrs. Murphy. The least those big louts you're feeding could do is spare you some cash, enough so you don't have to leave your children alone."

"You're a saint, Mrs. Enright."

"Don't misunderstand me, Mrs. Murphy. I won't have your twelve-year-old daughter missing school to mind the six young ones. Brendan and Stephen have two weeks to file a new address, preferably somewhere outside of Mitchell's Terrace."

"Bless you, Mrs. Enright. Everything will be done exactly as you say. Don't worry about a thing. Tonight is the last night my boys will sleep in this house. They'll be gone tomorrow, I swear it. My word is good, Mrs. Enright. Ask anyone and they'll tell you when Joan Murphy makes a promise, she keeps it."

"I'm glad to hear it."

"Will you be stopping in next week, Mrs. Enright?"

"I will."

"That'll be lovely. If you tell me when, I'll buy some vanillas to have with our tea."

"That won't be necessary, Mrs. Murphy," Johannah replied crisply. "I'll buy the vanillas."

Flushed with energy over her confrontation with the most gifted and outrageous liar inhabiting the close, incestuous world of the Bull Ring, she crossed the road and made her way past the vocational offices and the wrought iron gates enclosing St. John's Parish Church, her destination the rose garden, the town square and her car.

Deciding against The Daily Grind, she headed west on the N21 toward the quiet solitude of the Ballyseedy Woods, an under-utilized recreation spot, a primeval forest with lovely walking paths and strategically placed benches regularly maintained by the County Council.

Normally she avoided the forest. It was the picturesque farmland surrounding the woods that appealed to Johannah. She preferred the gentle relief of tilled fields with their light-touched, lime-colored grass, their even patchwork of dark and light green, harvest yellow, the fallow meadows, cows munching peacefully, bulls butting heads, the orderly neatness of rolling land bordered by hedges, flat expanses broken by broccoli-headed trees, the peace and calm, the beauty and safety, the exposed openness of it.

Today was an exception. Today she would breach the woods. It called to her, the dark, close wildness, the thickness of fern and birch, Irish oak, pine and ash, the deep, dense greenness of it, the smoke-brown branches, the trunks strangled by vines of twisted, prickly, predatory holly, the ground moist and dank with wet, mildewed leaves, the smells of sage and garlic, onion and rosemary, all heavy and shadowed and private, all quivering and buzzing with teeming, hidden life.

A single car was parked in the lot. Slipping inside the gate, Johannah ignored the signpost and struck out for the bridge. There was no sign of another human and almost immediately she felt the sensation of having been pulled back into an earlier time, the Ireland of five centuries before when the air was rich with oxygen, the hum of insects, the scent of wild spice.

Walking briskly into the canopied darkness, she barely noticed the bench just off the path, occupied by two people, a man and a woman. She would have missed it entirely if it wasn't for the bird, a particularly large crow unexpectedly rising from the rose bushes carrying something in its mouth. Her eyes followed the bird's flight and her glance happened to settle on the woman. She narrowed her eyes, rubbed them and looked again. Sure enough. It was Kate, and with her, sitting much too close for Johannah's comfort level, was Ritchie O'Shea.

Frozen into immobility, Johannah stood in place for nearly a minute before mustering her senses enough to retreat, backing away slowly and then nearly running back to her car.

Kate

"We should have met in town," Kate pleated the fabric of her skirt.

"Nervous, Kate?"

"It looks as if we're doing something wrong. If we'd met at Heatons or Manor, there might be a few raised eyebrows, but no one can hang a person for talking in front of the entire town."

"That's all we're doing here, talking."

"Why did we come here, Ritchie? What is it you have to say to me?"

He took her hand. She pulled it away. "I'd like to start over, Katie. We had something once. It's wrong to throw away friendship."

"What exactly do you mean by friendship?"

"Let's start by not avoiding each other. There's no shame in having a coffee together occasionally or visiting now and then."

She looked at him skeptically. "Is that it?"

He looked away. "Do you know you haven't changed? You're still so beautiful I can't stop staring at you."

"This conversation is pointless. *We* aren't a possibility. You know that."

"We always come back to that, don't we?"

She didn't answer.

"I'd like to get to know you again," he continued, "but you're skittish. We haven't exchanged more than a sentence since I've come back. What's happened to you? You've never been one to run from the gossips."

Kate shook her head. "I have a child to think of, Ritchie. I live with my mom. There's more to think of than just you and me."

"Give it a try," he coaxed her. "Who will it hurt?"

Reluctantly, she laughed. "You can't be that naïve, Ritchie O'Shea. It will hurt Dermot and his family and it could hurt mine as well. Evan loves his father. Dermot and I have a civilized relationship. I don't know what would happen if he thought we were seeing each other. He might even think I'd left him because you'd come home. Ridiculous, isn't it? All I need to do is tell him the truth about us."

"Why don't you?"

Kate stood and looked down at him, at the thin, honed symmetry of his face, the blue, blue eyes and bright coppery hair, at the wide, squared off fingers and strong hands. Her heart twisted. She couldn't go there. She wouldn't go there. "Don't flatter yourself. It's because of my mother. And even if there was something between us, ten years is a long time and I'm not a child anymore. Let's go, Ritchie. God forbid that anyone should see us here alone in the woods."

He walked easily beside her, their pace well-matched and comfortable. "I won't be staying here forever, you know."

"Where will you go?"

"Back to the States."

She bit her lip wishing she didn't care about asking the question or, more to the point, learning the answer. "Why?"

"It's difficult here, smaller somehow, narrower. You must know what I mean. You've been away from Tralee, from Ireland. There's not much here to hold a man, or a woman for that matter. It's like turning my back on opportunity. Do you know what I'm saying, Kate?"

She nodded, suddenly wanting to clear her head and vent on a subject that tormented her too often to ever be comfortable. "Sometimes it makes me scream. Here, everyone thinks the world is divided by football clubs, Mitchel's green and gold, The Rock's black and amber, Strand Road's blue and white. God forbid should anyone poach on either side of the divide. For those poor souls it's a lifetime of whispered gossip 'a bit of the Mitchel's comin' out, like,' or 'pure Rock Street your man there is.' It's a nightmare, a desperate nightmare with no end in sight unless it's driving off Fenit Pier."

He stared at her. "You're very bitter, Kate. You're not one of those thinking of driving off Fenit Pier? Because if you are, you'd better come away with me today, even if all I am to you is a means to an end. There isn't anything worth staying for if the staying makes you feel like that."

She shrugged. "Sometimes I feel that way, not always, of course. There's Evan to think of and my mom. My dad's only been gone a year."

"Your mother will survive. She won't expect you to live your life for her. As for Evan, bring him with you. He'll be glad you did when he's old enough to know anything. For Christ sake, Kate, you're a trained dietician. You have a degree in nutrition. What are you doing in Tralee? You should be in Cork or Dublin or back in the States where you could actually work in your field. Doesn't that appeal to you?"

They'd reached the entrance to the woods. Kate stopped to look directly at him. "It's not that simple. Evan has a father. You might not think that's important, but it is."

"People divorce, even in Ireland." Again he reached for her hand. Again she pulled it away. "There's something else, isn't there. Say it."

Nausea cramped her stomach. She swallowed. It was best to just get it out, even though it was no longer satisfying to hurt him. "The thing is, I don't trust you, Ritchie. That won't change. I'll never trust you again. You played with me. You believed there could never be anything between us and yet you let me think there was."

"But all impediments are gone. We could begin again. The past is over. It doesn't matter."

Her eyes, the clear light-filled blue particular to her father's family, were narrow and dark with contempt. "It matters to me, Ritchie, and shame on you for not knowing that."

CHAPTER 19

Liam

Liam switched the bag of take-away Chinese from his right arm to his left and opened the door. "Anyone home?" he called. "I've picked up food for tea. Mom, Nan, are you here?"

A movement on the stairs caught his attention. "Hello, Evan, my man. What are you up to?"

The boy shrugged. "Nothing."

Liam frowned. Evan, normally so exuberant, sounded rather dismal. "Where's your mom?"

"On the computer."

"I've brought home Chinese. Would you like an egg roll?"

"Not so much."

Liam abandoned his bag on the side table and sat down beside his nephew on the stair. "You sound forlorn, lad. Is anything wrong?"

Evan's eyes, round and blue like his mother's, met his. "What's forlorn?"

"It means sad or out of sorts."

Evan nodded. "I feel forlorn." He lost the "l", pronouncing it "forworn."

"Tell me about it."

The child sighed. "I want to go home. I want my dad."

Liam was silent for a minute. "I know how you feel, Evan. I miss my dad, too."

For a moment the child looked interested. "But you're big and you don't have a dad."

"I had him for a very long time. Just because I'm big doesn't mean I can't miss him. You remember Grandad, don't you?"

Evan nodded. "He made my swing set." Then he changed the subject. "Do you know when we're going home?"

Liam hesitated. How much information could a four-year-old take in? "I'm not sure lad. But it isn't so bad here, is it? You have your mom and Nan, your gran and me. You even have Seamus. You like Seamus, don't you?"

"Yes."

"We have a garden here. You like having a large garden, don't you?"

"I do, but I'd rather go home."

Liam was stymied. The poor little bloke really did look miserable. He wondered if Kate knew the extent of her son's unhappiness. "I'll tell you what, Evan. I'm not sure when you'll be going home, but what if we worked on something together to show your dad when you see him next?"

Evan looked skeptical. "What will we work on, Uncle Liam?"

"How would you like to learn a tune on the tin whistle?"

"I don't know how to play the tin whistle."

"I'll teach you."

"Really?"

"Absolutely. You'll be a regular whistle player by the next weekend. How about that? Will you give it a go?"

A smile lifted the corners of the small mouth. "I will, Uncle Liam. I'll try and try until I'm the best whistle player in Tralee and my dad will be proud of me."

"That's the spirit. We'll have our tea and tomorrow after school we'll buy your very own tin whistle. Will you help me serve up the food?"

Evan nodded. Slipping his hand inside his uncle's, he appeared deep in thought. "Will it be easy for me to learn?"

Liam pretended to consider the matter carefully. He stroked his chin, mindful of the small hand in his. "Well, Evan, my lad, I'll tell you this: practice is the key. At first it will be difficult, but if you practice every day, the easier it will be. Anything worth having takes time and effort."

"Nan says that all the time," replied Evan.

Liam laughed. "I suppose she does." Standing, he lifted Evan to his shoulder and picked up the bag of food, heading into the kitchen. "Mind your head, lad. Today, the men are taking over the kitchen."

Giggling, Evan clutched his hair. "You're funny, Uncle Liam. What's Chinese food?"

"The same as Irish food, pork, chicken, fish and vegetables, only the sauces are more interesting."

"Are there potatoes?"

Liam frowned and swung his nephew from his shoulder to the worktop. "There you have me, Evan. I don't think the Chinese eat potatoes." He handed Evan a fork, opened the bag and began removing boxes. "Open one of those and tell me if you recognize any vegetables. Feel free to sample anything that looks good."

A tiny wrinkle appeared between the child's eyes.

Liam laughed and rephrased his words. "If something looks tasty, you may eat it."

The wrinkle disappeared and soon a myriad of open boxes lined the worktop. "I like Chinese food, Uncle Liam," the boy announced.

"You have exceptional taste, lad. I'm pleased to be the one to introduce it to you. Is there enough left, do you think, for the rest of the family?"

Kate appeared in the doorway. "Something smells good."

Evan held up his fork. "I'm eating Chinese."

"I can see that," replied his mother. "What do you think of it?"

"I like it. Uncle Liam is going to teach me to play the tin whistle."

Kate's eyebrows rose. "Is he now?"

Evan nodded happily, all signs of his recent pout laid to rest. "I'm going to show my dad after I've learned."

Kate found a plate in the cupboard and began spooning rice into it. "You might have asked me, Liam. It might make him sick."

"Which one, Kate, the tin whistle or the food?"

"Don't be nasty."

"I won't if you won't."

"It's just that he doesn't eat spicy food."

"Evan's tough," replied her brother, "aren't you, lad?"

"Yes, I'm very tough." Evan held out his arm. "Look at my muscles, Mommy."

Kate smiled and lifted him from the worktop, setting him on the floor. "Impressive. If you're finished eating, go wash your hands. I'll help you."

"No," he said. "I can do it. I'm tough."

She laughed. "Run along. Call me if you need help." Waiting until she heard his footsteps on the stairs, she turned on her brother. "What are you doing, Liam? Since when have you taken an interest in your nephew?"

Liam looked at her steadily. "I admit I haven't been the best of uncles, but it isn't too late to start. The boy needs a man's influence, Kate. He misses his father. I found him sitting on the stairs nearly in tears talking about wanting to go home. He believes it's only a matter of time before the two of you go back. When are you planning to tell him?"

"Nothing is decided yet."

"Why can't Dermot see him more often?"

"I'm not keeping Dermot from Evan."

"Then what's the problem?"

Kate bit her lip. "It's hard on Dermot. I don't want to hurt him."

"It's harder on Evan. He's four years old. He doesn't understand. The two of you should put your own feelings aside and think of your son. Besides, when did you start to care about Dermot's feelings."

"That's not fair. I do care about Dermot. He's a good man, better than I deserve. When did you become the expert? You're not a parent."

"I'm not a fool either." He stood. "Divorce isn't good for children. Think about that while you're reinventing yourself." He set his fork in the sink and changed the subject. "Where's Mom and Nan?"

"I'm not sure. They weren't here when I got home." Kate's mouth trembled. "You can be very cruel, Liam."

"I suppose it's easier to judge others than to look at yourself." He turned on the spigot, thought better of it and turned it off. "Help yourself to the food. I bought it. You can clean up." With that he walked out of the room.

Kate called after him. "It's very nice of you, Liam. Thank you."

Upstairs, Liam poked his head into the bathroom and grinned. Evan was examining his muscles. "Brush your teeth, lad. You don't want a mouthful of false ones by the time you're thirty."

Evan spat his toothpaste into the sink. "I'm tough, Uncle Liam. Look at my muscles."

"Right," he agreed. "You don't see muscles like those every day."

Evan beamed. "I'm *very* tough."

CHAPTER 20

Johannah

She was late coming to Aine's. Tralee was uncomfortably crowded in the summer with tourists flocking in for the festival and European Union buses parked at the museum. Maura had already ordered for both of them, coffee for two, her pert nose deep inside *The Kerry's Eye*.

Johannah slid into the opposite chair. "That's a rag, you know. There's not a word of truth in the whole paper. Have you been waiting long?"

"As a matter of fact, I have." Maura surfaced and folded the paper. "What kept you?"

"I've been arguing with Gerry Fox again. County employees are considering a strike. Two representatives of the union must go to Dublin and, apparently, I've been elected, along with Billy Roache."

"So, what's the problem?"

"He's threatening to dock our salaries. He doesn't understand that he's required to comply with the bylaws and allow us the days with full compensation."

"Surely that's a matter easily verified?"

Johannah sighed. "One would think, but I'm dealing with Gerry Fox."

Maura stirred her coffee. "What about your mother? Who will look after her?"

"I left a message with Kathleen."

Maura snorted. "She'll never ring you back. You haven't a prayer of a chance. You'll have better luck asking the Pope to house-sit for your mom."

Johannah laughed. "You're dreadful, Maura. I don't even know why I bother to tell you anything."

"You bother because you know I won't spare you. I tell you the truth and because I do, you're prepared when it actually happens. Good Lord, Johannah, think what it would be like if you actually had expectations of Kathleen stepping up to the plate. How disappointed you would be when you couldn't go at the last minute." She cocked her head, brown eyes sparkling with curiosity. "I assume the holiday is all expenses paid?"

"It isn't a holiday. It's a business trip."

"All expenses paid?"

"Yes."

"Will you and Billy drive down together?"

"No. He'll leave early with his wife. They've a daughter in Dublin and will stay with her."

Maura reached over to lay her hand on Johannah's. "If the worst happens, and it will, and you have no one, and you won't, I'll take your mother."

Johannah lifted her chin and spoke carefully. "That's very kind of you, Maura, but there's no need. Kathleen will step in. I know she will."

"Suit yourself, but the offer stands." She held out the paper to Johannah. "Look at this. Ritchie O'Shea is playing tonight at the Meadowlands Hotel. Shall we go?"

"Certainly not. I can't imagine anything he'd do would be of interest to me. Besides, it's disloyal to Dermot."

"Your son-in-law? What's he got to do with anything?"

"Kate wants to divorce him."

Maura's eyes widened. "You can't be serious. Who gets a divorce a Tralee?"

"My point exactly. It's desperate."

"You mistake my meaning, Hannie. Half the town is living with someone other than the man or woman they stood up with. Why bother with divorce? It's expensive, not to mention scandalous. Kate will be the talk of the town for ages."

Johannah tapped her forefinger on the table. "I don't care about that. I care that a very good man will be hurt for a whim and that whim is Ritchie O'Shea. What does she see in him anyway?"

"You can't be serious?"

"He's no better looking than Dermot and he's certainly not as plump in the pocket."

"He *is* better looking than Dermot. He's better looking than everyone and then there's his music. Money doesn't matter all that much to someone Kate's age. It's romance that counts.

Besides, Ritchie's hardly poor. How do you know all of this anyway? Surely she isn't daft enough to tell you."

"I saw her in Ballyseedy woods sitting on the bench with him.""You didn't?" Maura's eyes sparkled. "What were they doing?"

"Nothing at all, just talking."

"Oh." Maura drew back disappointed. "You can't exactly hang her for that, can you Hannie? There's no crime in talking."

"If talking was what they were after, they could have gone to Galley's or Manor or the Grand. Why would they sneak off to the woods?"

"I have no idea but I can tell you this: Kate isn't the sneaking around sort. Why not come out and ask her?"

Johannah didn't answer.

Maura sighed. "Ok. But that doesn't explain why you're against seeing Ritchie perform."

"I want him to go away."

"If you do, I do, too," Maura said loyally, "but first I want to see him play." She leaned forward again. "Aren't you the slightest bit curious? He's made a name for himself in the States where there's far more competition than here in Ireland. He's got to be good. What can I do to convince you to come with me?"

Johannah thought a minute. Perhaps she *was* being ridiculous. It would do her good to get out. At least it would satisfy her curiosity. If Ritchie was anywhere near as good as he'd been years ago when the offer from California came, the evening would be worthwhile. Besides, maybe she would gain some insight into Kate's long-lasting obsession. "All right. I'll go with you. But I have to be sure Kate will be home for Evan."

Maura's mouth dropped. "Of course she'll be home. She's his mother for pity's sake. You must stop this, Johannah. You're job isn't to be Evan's mother. He already has one. Step back and stop making everyone else feel incompetent."

"Is that what you think I'm doing?"

"I know it. Now, stop all this and drink your coffee. It's probably cold by now. You haven't asked me about the store or Milo in ages. He's drinking more than ever and I'm thinking of leaving him."

Johannah froze. "You can't be serious?"

"No," Maura confessed, "not a bit, but you're so unavailable, I had to say something to shock you."

"Milo isn't drinking?"

"He is, but he isn't exactly an alcoholic. He just likes his pint or two or three. I'm accustomed to it and have no intention of throwing him out. Can you imagine the talk? I'd be the one everyone in town would blame."

"Do you care?"

Maura refilled her coffee cup. "I shouldn't, but I do. I like to slag the biddies and their gossip, but I don't want to be the one they're gossiping about. " She changed the subject. "Tell me about the strike."

"It's dreadful, Maura. They're talking about cutting our wages but not our hours."

"Why would they do that?"

"The economy. There isn't enough to keep up the current level of home care."

"I'll bet the town council isn't taking a pay cut, nor is anyone else connected with the administration. If they cut your salary, theirs should be cut as well. Are you seriously considering a strike?"

"It looks that way."

"Why must you go to Dublin?"

"Jack Rafferty is there. He's the guru of binding arbitration. He'll tell us what's legal, what to do first and then so on."

Maura looked at her in awe. "And you've been selected. What an honor, Johannah. Obviously you're highly respected."

"More than likely, it isn't personal at all. I've been employed for a long time. Nearly everyone else is younger than me."

"Don't minimize your influence. I'm proud of you. You go to Dublin and knock old Gerry Fox's socks off. Shame on him for cutting geriatric benefits. He'll be there himself some day. I wonder how he'd like it if he could only get oxygen for his emphysema every other Wednesday."

Johannah smiled at her friend fondly. "You're a love, Maura. You always say the right thing. What would I do without you?"

"We're a long way from having to worry about that, God willing." She crossed herself. "Now, gather yourself and call your sister. Tell her you have no choice and that you'll be putting Dolly on the train."

"She could never manage a train on her own."

"I know that and you know that, but Kathleen doesn't. Put the fear of God into the woman and then have Liam drop his grandmother on her porch."

"You're wicked, Maura."

"I'm taking that as a compliment." She gathered her belongings. "I've got to run. Milo's minding the store. I'll meet you at half eight."

Reluctant to go home just yet, Johannah decided to stop at the cemetery. She bought flowers at the stand on Castle Street, once again marveling at the variety of fresh food and flowers available any season of the year since Ireland's admittance into the European Union.

Pulling out into the perpetual traffic jam that choked the streets of Tralee from noon until late evening, Johannah drove slowly but persistently down the Boherbui Road to Rathass and parked across from the town cemetery. Struggling with her umbrella and sheltering her daffodils against the wind, she walked tentatively down the gravel path leading to her husband's grave. The heels of her shoes sank into the rain-soaked soil. "Damn," she swore softly.

A voice spoke behind her. "Can I be of help?"

She peeked out from under her umbrella. "Patrick! What are you doing here?"

"I was looking for someone who lived here in Tralee. She died recently."

"Who would that be?" Johannah asked. "Maybe I know her."

"Jane O'Grady."

"Of course. She's a relative of sorts, by marriage. I attended the wake some weeks ago. How are you connected?"

"Like you, by marriage."

"Did you know her well?"

"Not really. Why?"

Color rose in Johannah's cheeks. "I'm sorry. I didn't mean to pry. It's none of my business."

"I'm not offended."

"It's just that most people don't comb cemeteries of this size in the rain looking for someone they barely know."

Patrick smiled. "I have the time."

"Of course. Jane is on the other side of the cemetery where the Rock Street crowd are buried." She hurried to explain. "Like most towns, Tralee is separated by its clubs, John Mitchels, The Rock, Strand Road and Na`gael. We bury each other that way as well."

"I know something about town rivalries."

Johannah nodded. "Sometimes it's difficult to move about when you've grown up in a certain area. But it isn't as bad as someone new altogether. Those poor souls are 'blow-ins' even if they've lived here for fifty years. It's not fair, really, but it's a fact." Lord, she did prattle on. Better to keep silent than to risk appearing even more foolish.

Without speaking, they walked past graves both elaborate and mean, tasteful and garish. Kate stopped at her husband's gravesite, bending to lay the flowers in front of the stone.

"Mikey and I never discussed dying. I suppose it's because the subject is so unpleasant."

"Either that or you thought you would have more time. He wasn't very old."

"No, he wasn't. It's a shame, really. I didn't know what to do. The children thought he should be here, in Tralee, where it's easy to visit, but I don't know if they bother. I wouldn't ask them, of course. We avoid emotional subjects in order to avoid emotional scenes. The Enrights aren't comfortable with drama."

"That's not such a bad thing."

"Oh, yes, it is," she said emphatically. "It's terrible. I'd love to be one of those families who argue by shouting and throwing plates and then hugging and kissing when it's all over."

"Surely you can't mean that, the shouting and throwing plates part."

"I certainly do. It's healthy and cleansing. We just walk about with our chins up and shoulders back, but inside we're in dreadful pain."

"I've heard that awareness is the first step toward recovery."

She looked up at him, realizing for the first time that he was a head taller and that his eyes were clear and light and fine. Why hadn't she noticed before?

"What are you thinking?" he asked.

"Nothing of any importance."

"Tell me," he coaxed her. "I want to know."

"All right." The rain slowed to an annoying drizzle. She snapped shut her umbrella. "I was thinking about how much I hate graves."

He looked startled. "Really?"

"Yes. Imagine how wet and miserable it is to be buried under the ground in this wet. I mean, it isn't Florida, is it? When I go, I want to be burned and sit in a vase on Kate's mantle, all cozy and warm and cared for."

"Not Liam's? You could divide the ashes and give half to each."

She tilted her head. "I hadn't thought of that. It would depend on whom he married. Think of the potential problems an absent-minded daughter-in-law could cause."

He threw back his head and laughed.

"What's so funny?"

"You are. Have you always been this way?"

She looked puzzled. "I don't know what *this way* means, but I don't think I've changed much. Personalities develop in the first few years of life. At least that's what the experts tell us."

His eyes looked very bright. "I wouldn't know," he said softly. "I'm not one for paying close attention when it's important. It's a fault of mine."

"Now is as good a time as any to start." She smiled. "That's what my mother always told me."

"I've met your mother and know better than to argue with her."

"Smart man." She checked her watch. "I must run now. I've an engagement this evening and then I'm off to Dublin for a few days. I shall miss you. You're wonderful to talk with, Patrick."

"The feeling is mutual. Goodbye, Johannah."

CHAPTER 20

Mickey

A man could become accustomed to almost anything, Mickey reflected, scooping up a handful of smooth white sand as he stared at the clear waters of what must certainly be some island in the Pacific. He hadn't traveled much. It had never been a priority. Johannah would have loved to travel, but with the children, the house and money always so tight, the opportunity hadn't come.

Peter, he noticed, always chose a different destination for their meetings. He'd offered no explanation for his preference for diverse locations, but Mickey was sure there was a lesson somewhere. He knew it as surely as he knew the color of his daughter's eyes. Peter did nothing without a reason.

Sensing a presence, he scanned the horizon and then turned to gaze upon the cool green promise of the palm-studded hills. Sure enough, a dark speck on the white sand approached. Mickey stood in anticipation.

"How are you, lad?" Peter asked when they faced each other.

"She's leaving for Dublin. She wants to be cremated," Mickey blurted out.

"Yes." Peter shifted his gaze to the sea. "An unforeseen complication, but irrelevant to your mission."

"Which one?"

"The cremation part. It doesn't matter what they do to our bodies. They are vessels, nothing more. The complication is Dublin."

"I don't understand."

Peter locked his hands behind his back. "Walk with me. I must prepare you for the next portion of this mission you've undertaken."

Mickey fell in beside him, curious, yet concerned. For a small man, Peter's stride was long, his pace swift. "I'll remind you that I didn't choose to undertake anything. I was coerced."

Peter stopped in mid-stride. "You wanted another chance. I didn't misunderstand, did I?"

"What I *wanted* was to rewind time. I wanted my life back the way it was."

"Do you still want that?"

Mickey hesitated. *What exactly did he want?* To return to the life he thought he had with Hannie and his family? He'd come to realize that his former life, the self-centered, indulgent life he'd bull-dozed through without regard to others never existed, or if it did, it was only in his own imagination. The rest of them, Kate, Liam, Dolly, they had their own versions of reality and priorities that no longer included him… if they ever did. "I don't know what I want," he said at last.

Peter nodded. "That's the first intelligent answer you've given me. You're learning, Mickey Enright. I'm pleased with you. Now, listen closely. When Johannah returns from Dublin, you will be tested. The temptation to reveal yourself will be strong, but you must resist. Remember, whether it appears so or not, everything is proceeding according to plan. Fall back on that thought when you need it."

Mickey looked alarmed. "Can't you tell me more than that?"

"There's no point. Trust me." With that, Peter resumed his pace, leaving Mickey, confused and more than a little alarmed.

Johannah

She'd pinned her hair into a messy bun at the back of her head, securing it with a rhinestone clip, brushed her teeth, changed her clothes and was finishing a container of soy yogurt when the key turned in the lock.

Kate opened the door. "Come along, Evan," she said over her shoulder. "We'll have our tea and then you can visit with Rory." She looked surprised to see Johannah. "I didn't think you'd be home."

Johannah, the image in Ballyseedy Woods still fresh in her mind, was unusually short. "I live here. Why wouldn't I be home?" She smiled at Evan. "Hello, love. How was school?"

"Grand." Evan held out a large piece of drawing paper with an unidentifiable figure filling the page. "I made this for you."

"Did you?" Johannah reached for it. "My goodness. Isn't it remarkable?"

"It's a panda bear. They live in China. We're learning about them in school. His name is Ted."

"What an excellent name. Shall I tack him up right here on the refrigerator?"

Evan nodded. "Yes. We can look at him whenever we like."

Kate interrupted. "I called and no one answered." She looked around. "Where's Nan?"

"In the sitting room reading the paper. She might like some tea as well."

"Are you going out?"

"Yes." Johannah rinsed her spoon and left it in the sink. Turning around, she spoke deliberately. "I'm meeting Maura at The Meadowlands. Apparently, Ritchie O'Shea is playing there tonight. I hear he's very good…as a musician, that is."

Kate nodded. She looked tired, but that was all. "Yes. I imagine he's even better than he was before he left for the States. I'll take care of Nan. Have a good time."

Filled with remorse, Johannah kissed Evan and hurried out the door. What had she expected? Flaming cheeks, stammering, obvious guilt? What she really wanted was an explanation but that wasn't likely to happen. The Enrights always were a close-mouthed bunch. And so, apparently, were the Littles as evidenced by her own behavior. Maura was right. She should simply ask Kate a direct question.

The hotel carpark was nearly full, but she managed to squeeze into a space between two large utility vehicles. Deciding against her umbrella, Johannah left it in the car, hitched her bag over her shoulder and headed for the door. Inside the pub, she looked around for Maura, hesitating between choosing a seat at the bar or a table in the back. She preferred the table but it was too far from the stage, something Maura wouldn't appreciate. Still, she wasn't here and the seats were filling quickly.

Taking the initiative, Johannah slid into the long booth facing the door and set her purse on the chair opposite, waiting for her friend to arrive. Shrouded in the dim light, she looked around recognizing most, but not all of the patrons. There was a time when she knew everyone in Tralee, but no longer. The influx of foreigners and increased tourism had erased its insular, small town feel.

The band was nowhere to be seen but they had already set up, with three microphones out front and a complete set of drums. Ritchie O'Shea would never go begging for backup in Tralee.

Maura appeared in the doorway. She waved, made her way through the tables, pulled out a chair and sat down across from Johannah. "Sorry I'm late. Milo wanted to come. I had to convince him he'd be bored to tears. Jazz isn't his thing anyway. Have you been here long? I suppose not since you haven't a drink."

Johannah, struggling with her own thoughts, ignored the question and asked her own. "What is it about the Irish that they all must prove themselves musicians? Where are the lads who want to be doctors and lawyers, teachers and accountants? Surely it's more difficult to become proficient on an instrument than it is to be a barrister. A musician needs not only the theory, but an ear, talent, good fortune and the ability to tolerate starvation, while acquiring the law asks nothing more than a motivation to study."

Maura stared at her. "What are you talking about, Hannie?"

"Doctors and barristers make enormous money. Musicians make nothing."

"Sorry?"

"What's the matter with young people? Why do all the lads want to play in front of an audience and why are young girls so taken with musicians?"

"Is this about Kate?"

Johannah bit her lip. "A bit."

Maura leaned forward. "I can't answer your question about musicians, Hannie. We were there once, too. But I can tell you this. Kate would have run after Ritchie if he'd been the postman. The way the two would look at each other made me want to reach for a newspaper and fold it into a fan. Now, I'm going to the bar. What can I get for you?""A glass of wine and some ice."

She'd finished her glass and started on another when the stage began to fill, first Georgie Lynch on the bass and Ambrose Smith behind the keyboard, then Donal O'Sullivan on the drums, Jimmy Duggan and his guitar and finally, the acknowledged lure of the evening, Ritchie O'Shea carrying his famous Mark VI saxophone, the one he'd bought in America and smuggled home in his mother's suitcase to avoid the VAT.

Maura raised her eyebrows. "He was always handsome, but then I'm partial to red hair."

Johannah ignored her and leaned forward. The first notes of rich, smoky music filled the room, evoking images of a world she'd only read about, a world of sizzling bayou nights, sugary drinks, skimpily-dressed women with carmine-stained lips pressed into the shoulders of dark, sweat-slicked men in loose pants, men born with tango steps in their blood. No matter what she thought of him as a person, there were few who could match Ritchie O'Shea when it came to jazz, no one she could afford to see live anyway.

It was seductive, this world of music, and the men and women who succumbed to its call. By day they were ordinary beings, too short or too round with sagging jowls and receding hairlines. At night, on stage, they were a breed apart, entertainers, musicians, and the sultry tunes pouring from their instruments and their throats were sung to every hopeful, lonely soul harboring even the slightest hint of imagination. Johannah closed her eyes, grateful that Maura, a music-lover to the bone, required nothing in the way of conversation.

Too soon, the band announced their break. Johannah opened her eyes. "You were right," she said to Maura. "He's exceptional. I'm glad you talked me into coming."

"You can tell that to the band leader. He's coming this way now."

"No. I don't want—" But it was too late. She found herself pasting a false smile on her lips waiting the last few seconds before Ritchie O'Shea made his way to her table.

"Nice to see you again, Mrs. Enright, and you, too, Mrs. Keane."

"Don't be calling me Mrs., Ritchie O'Shea," said Maura. "The years pass by quickly enough. You'll have me thinking I'm old as my mother, God rest her soul."

He laughed and for a brief enlightening instant, Johannah knew what it was Kate saw in him.

"Do you mind if I sit down?" he asked, pulling up a chair and seating himself before either woman could object, not that they would with the manners drilled into them from birth. "I didn't know you were jazz fans."

"We aren't particular," Maura explained. "We'll come out for whoever's good."

"Thank you." His eyes rested on Johannah, cool and speculating. "How is Kate?"

Johannah's eyebrows rose. She wouldn't have brought up the subject of her daughter, but now that he had… "Don't you know?"

"We don't run in the same circles."

"Really? Not even yesterday?"

He stood and smiled. "Good night, Mrs. Enright. Enjoy the evening."

"Well," Maura said, tipping her glass for the last of the wine. "I don't think he'll be back."

"I'll live."

Maura sighed. "Couldn't you have tried to be the tiniest bit polite? He was only trying to be nice."

"He knows I don't like him. I've never liked him, and in case you've forgotten, he's the one who brought up Kate's name in the first place. I wasn't going to say a word. Imagine lying so blatantly when I almost ran into them."

"He didn't exactly lie, Hannie. Besides, are you sure it was him?"

"Positive."

Maura nodded. "I suppose you'd know better than anyone. He's the image of his father."

"The apple doesn't fall far from the tree."

A woman passing by their table stopped. "Mrs. Enright? It is Mrs. Enright, isn't it?"

Johannah forced herself to smile. "Sheila. How are you?"

"I've been better. That sorry son of yours broke it off with me."

Johannah stiffened. "I'm sure he realized you wouldn't suit."

"I'm over it."

"Smart girl. Possibly it's for the best."

"I really cared for him."

"But you don't anymore, not after the way he's treated you." Her voice dripped with sarcasm.

"I was wondering if you could do me a favor?"

"Of course," Johannah lied.

"Tell him I've moved."

"Have you?"

"Yes. I'm living in Currow with my sister." Sheila reached into the pocket of her impossibly snug denims and pulled out a piece of paper, handing it to Johannah. "This is my new number. Would you ask Liam to ring me?"

Maura leaned over to look at the numbers. "You had it already written down. How did you know we would be here?"

Sheila shrugged. "It pays to be prepared. Lovely seeing you."

Johannah watched her go.

"She's gorgeous," said Maura.

"Yes."

"A bit old for Liam, don't you think?"

"Yes."

Maura shook her head and looked at Johannah. "You can't possibly want your son to attach himself to the likes of her?"

"No."

She laughed, grabbed the slip of paper from Johannah's fingers, tore it up and fed it piece by piece into the candle flame. "Well then, that's that," she said when the last of it was nothing more than charred carbon.

Johannah's expression didn't change. "If only it were so simple."

"What are you talking about? It's very simple. The problem is solved."

"In the end, people do what they want, Maura, no matter how hard we try to convince them otherwise. Sheila and Liam will meet on the street or in a pub and if he wants to, he'll continue seeing her, just like Kate and Ritchie have continued it."

Maura frowned. "Johannah…" She hesitated.

"Go on."

"Have you considered seeing someone professionally?"

"What on earth for?"

"You're obviously depressed. I've never heard you like this, so fatalistic and negative, not even after Mickey died."

Johannah stared at her.

"An objective listener might be all you need. You have a lot to be grateful for," Maura continued, "a good job, healthy children, a beautiful grandchild, even a possible love interest."

"Who might that be?"

"Patrick."

Johannah laughed. "Don't be ridiculous. I told you there's nothing there. However, you're right about the rest of it. I do have a great deal to be grateful for and I know you disapprove, but I have to tell Liam about Sheila. The time is long past when I can make decisions about his personal life." She picked up her bag and slid out from the booth, leaned over and kissed Maura's cheek. "I've had enough music for the night. I'm going to think about what you said while I'm in Dublin."

CHAPTER 21

Kate

Kate waited until she heard the front door close behind her mother before she ran downstairs to the kitchen. Evan needed his breakfast and she was due at her job at the Council Office, but she didn't want to risk being interrogated about Ritchie. It had taken enormous effort to maintain a neutral expression when her mother mentioned she and Maura were going to watch him play last night. Pulling the Wheatabix box from the cupboard, she broke one into a bowl and had reached for a banana when the door opened and Johannah walked back in.

"Good morning," her mother said cordially. "I bought sausage. Maybe Evan would like some."

"Cereal is fine. I'd rather he not eat so much saturated fat."

Johannah nodded. "I suppose you're right." She changed the subject. "I forgot to call your Aunt Kathleen. Is Nan awake?"

"I haven't seen her."

Johannah sighed and reached for the phone. "She's sleeping longer and longer every day."

"Depression?" suggested Kate.

"Possibly, although what she has to be depressed about, I have no idea."

Kate continued to chop the banana. "No one knows why someone else would be depressed. Nan is away from the home she's lived in all her life. Everything is new to her. When life doesn't turn out as we expect, people get depressed."

"If that were the case, everyone would be depressed."

"I suppose to a small degree, everyone is." Rinsing her hands, she pulled a dishtowel from the drawer. "Have you fed the dog?"

Johannah nodded and turned her attention to the phone. "Hello, Kathleen? No. It's me, Johannah. I'm grand, thank you. I have a favor to ask. I'm on my way to Dublin for my job. I need someone to stay with Mom. Liam can drive her up."

Kate poured herself a cup of tea and left the kitchen to wake Evan. When she returned her mother was seated at the table, staring at the phone. She sat down beside her. "Is everything all right?" she asked.

Johannah shook her head. "Not really."

"What's the matter?"

"I can't go to Dublin. Kathleen won't take Nan."

"Why not?"

"She has no room for her."

"That's impossible. Her house is huge."

Johannah spoke carefully. "She doesn't want to. It would disrupt her routine, curtail her freedom." She replaced the phone.

"It isn't the end of the world, Mom. I'll take care of her."

"What about the Council job? You can't stand them up after they've given you more hours."

"Liam and I will work it out. Just go and don't worry."

"Are you sure, Kate?"

"Absolutely," she lied. "Don't even think about it."

"What about Liam? He might have other plans."

"He'll have to change them. It's little enough we do for you, Mom. In fact it's a bit of a relief to be able to pay you back for all you've done for us. Liam won't mind at all." She was determined to threaten her brother to within an inch of his life if he showed even the slightest bit of reluctance.

Johannah breathed a sigh of relief. "Thank you very much, Katie. It would solve everything. I'll just say goodbye to Evan, check on Nan and be on my way."

"Are you driving?"

"I am."

Dolly appeared in the kitchen in a bathrobe and slippers on the wrong feet. "Did I hear my name?"

"We were just saying you should be down about now," Kate said. "What can I give you for breakfast?"

"The usual. A cup of tea and toast."

Johannah sighed with exasperation. "Have something more than that, Mom. You're too thin."

Saying nothing, Kate pulled a carton of eggs from the refrigerator. Deliberately keeping her back to her mother, she cracked one into the bowl and then, separating the whites from yolks, added the whites to the whole egg, beating them slightly before pouring them into the heated skillet. Then she toasted two slices of bread and quartered a tomato, slid the egg mixture onto a plate and presented it to her grandmother with a flourish. "There you go, Nan, just the way you like it."

Dolly smiled and tucked into her meal. "Thank you, love."

Johannah threw up her hands. Who was it that said personality traits skipped a generation? Evan's footsteps pounded on the stairs seconds before he appeared in the kitchen. "I'm hungry," he shouted. "I want sausage and bacon."

"It's cereal and bananas," his mother replied cheerfully. "Say goodbye to your Nan and then sit down and keep Gran company. Here's your breakfast."

"Where are you going, Nan?"

"To Dublin." Johannah pointed to her cheek. "Kiss me goodbye and I'll bring you home something."

Evan offered his lips. "When will you be back?"

"I'll be home before you know it."

"How will we do things?"

"You'll have your mom and Liam and Gran."
He looked doubtful.

Kate laughed and shook her head. "Isn't it amazing how quickly he's forgotten how we managed in our own home for most of his life?" She watched her mother hug Evan fiercely, wave goodbye to Dolly and rush out the door to her life, a life as far away from children and breakfast dishes and marital squabbles and personal doubts as her own was full of them.

Kate placed a cup of tea in front of her grandmother. "I must drop Evan at school, Nan," said Kate. "Will you wait here or dress and ride with us?"

"I'll wait here and have another cup of tea with Seamus." She looked around. "Where is he?"

"In the yard." Kate refilled the milk pitcher. "If you're finished, Evan, brush your teeth. It's time for school."

Evan beamed. "I like school. Mrs. Mahoney lets me erase the board and pass the crayons."

Dolly nodded. "Good boy," she called after him as he climbed the stairs. "An education is never wasted. That's what I always told the children. No one can take it from you. I never had any but the basics myself. We didn't in my time, but your nan had a good education and so did your mother."

Kate's expression was bitter. "It isn't doing me much good right now, is it, Gran?"

"I suppose that's your fault, Katie. We make our own decisions, don't we? I recall no one could tell you much of anything although your mother certainly tried."

Kate turned her back and gave another swipe to the already immaculate worktop. It would be too much to expect sympathy from her taciturn grandmother. If there was one thing she could say about Dolly, it was her penchant for zeroing in on the truth. How odd that she could remember details from years past when she couldn't remember her own address or how to sew on a button.

"She was always a good girl, Johannah was," Dolly continued, "not as good as Philomena or Kathleen, but a good girl all the same."

Suddenly Kate was angry for her mother. "You might remember that it's my mom who's taken you in, Nan. Neither Phil nor Kathleen has offered one penny on your behalf."

"Why should they?" returned Dolly. "I didn't ask to come here."

Kate gave up. "I'll be back as soon as I drop Evan at school. Think about what you'd like to do this morning."

"What about your job?"

"I've decided to skip work today."

Dolly opened the newspaper. "Take your time. I'm in no rush."

Evan didn't want to hold Kate's hand. "I'm big now," he reminded her when she tried to guide him across the street.

"I know that, love, but sometimes mommies need to hold on to something, too. It makes me happy. So, how about it?"

With a sigh of resignation, Evan slipped his hand inside his mother's. "What did you put in my lunch box?"

"Ham sandwich, an apple and crisps."

He nodded, happy with her selection. "You didn't cut the crust off, did you?"

"Not a one."

"Good, because only girls have the crusts cut off."

"I'll keep that in mind." She waited while he aimed his toe at a stone and then kicked it. "Your dad will come for you at the end of the day."

"Is it his turn?"

"Yes."

"Are you mad at Daddy?"

"Of course not, Evan. Daddy never does anything for me to be mad at."

"Then why are we living with Nan?"

Kate hesitated. How did one explain to a child the web of complexity that renders a successful marriage? Should she even try? "I need to find work that makes me happy, Evan. It's not possible to do that and live with Daddy."

"Why not?"

"There isn't time. I'm very busy there." She had no hope of his understanding but she had to try.

Unbelievably, Evan had no more questions. Kate kissed him goodbye at the entrance to his school. "I love you," she whispered.

"I know," he said, and walked across the yard. Turning one more time he waved goodbye at the door and disappeared from view.

With a sigh of relief, Kate turned toward home. She would take Dolly for a walk in the park and stop for a coffee at the museum café. The walk would do her grandmother good as well as tire her out, enough for a nap. With luck, Liam would be home and Kate would have the rest of the day to look at employment opportunities on the Internet. Ritchie's words hit home. She should be looking in Dublin and Cork, even America.

The house was unusually quiet when she unlocked the door. The dishes had been dried and put away, *The Irish Times* neatly folded. "Nan," she called out. "I'm home. Are you ready to go?"

No answer. Climbing the stairs, Kate peeked into the bathroom. Empty. Walking quickly to her grandmother's room, she opened the door. Empty as well. Just to be sure, she checked the closet and then opened the window, scanning the yard. No Nan and no Seamus. "Nan, if you're home, please answer me."

At this point she had no hope of an answer. Where should she look for Dolly? She was completely nonplussed. Liam. She would call Liam. Hopefully his mobile would be turned on.

He answered immediately. Never had she been so grateful to hear his voice. "Liam, it's Kate. Nan's missing."

"What?"

"She's gone. I was supposed to be minding her but she didn't want to go with me to drop Evan at school. I came back and she's gone."

"Is the dog gone, too?"

"Yes."

"I'm on the way home. Give me fifteen minutes. Meanwhile, call the garda."

"You're not serious? They won't do anything."

"For God's sake, she's an old lady who doesn't always remember things, hardly a criminal case. It shouldn't tax them."

"All right. I'll try. Please hurry."

"I'll be there shortly. She can't have gone far."

"Thanks, Liam. I take back every awful thing I've ever said about you."

He laughed and hung up.

CHAPTER 22

Dolly

Dolly had waited until Kate and Evan rounded the bend at the bottom of the road. Then she'd folded the paper neatly, washed up in the bathroom, dressed carefully in her blue print dress with the matching wool jacket, found an umbrella, called Seamus and marched out the door. She had no money in her bag but her credit was good anywhere in Tralee, not in the take-away shops, of course, but she'd never purchased food in one of those dreadful little holes anyway. She would go to the Grand or to the Munster Bar. They had lovely sandwiches and a proper tea. Maybe she would have soup as well. Then she would walk back to Kevin Barry's and drop in at the Fitzgeralds or the Hennesseys. Later, she would stop at St. John's, light a candle for those members of her family who had already passed on and then make her way over to the cemetery.

Filled with purpose, she quickened her pace. The day was cold and cloudy, but her spirits were light. She had a mission. She was in control. What day of the week was it anyway? She had no idea. For a moment she was bothered by the lapse but then she discarded it. People forgot things all the time, especially when they got older. It meant nothing at all.

"Hello there, Dolly." Frank Malloy tipped his hat and stopped in the footpath, preventing her from continuing.

"Good morning, Frank. How are you?" Seamus settled at her feet.

"Fine weather we're having for this time of year."

"A bit cold for me."

"Lovely day for a walk."

"It is."

"We haven't seen you in Kevin Barry's for awhile. Where are you off to?"

"I've been visiting Johannah for a while, but I'll be home soon. I've a few errands in town first."

"How is Johannah?"

"She's well, thank you."

"A terrible thing it was, her losing Mickey that way. How long has it been now?"

"Sorry?"

"How long has it been since Mickey passed?"

"I have no idea what you're talking about, Frank Malloy. The idea of Mickey passing. Why I saw him only a few days ago."

He stared at her. "I wouldn't mistake a matter like that that, Dolly. Mickey was a friend of mine. He was a friend to all of us. Nearly everyone in town attended the funeral Mass."

Dolly drew herself up. "Go away now, Frank. I have errands to run. Don't you be spreading gossip about Mickey Enright passing on. I can't imagine why you would say such a thing." She brushed passed him, disregarding his presence and his words as if they'd never happened. "Come along, Seamus."

The Grand was crowded but she didn't mind waiting and soon her favorite table in front of the window opened up. Sighing with relief, she leaned back into her chair, tucking her umbrella and bag into the corner. "I'll have a pot of tea and a toasted sandwich special," she said to the waitress, obviously a blow-in from one of those Eastern European countries she'd never learned to pronounce. Dolly could tell from her accent and that golden skin tone that was definitely not Irish. It didn't matter, as long as the girl didn't confuse her order. Some of these people were quite competent even though it wasn't like the old days when the children were in school and she would meet Bridie or Carmel at the Munster Warehouse. Bridie was gone now and Carmel had moved to the States long ago. She didn't begrudge Carmel her good fortune. The way Dolly looked at it was she'd landed squarely in the middle of her two friends, neither the worst nor the best of the lot. Settling back into her chair, she relaxed her fists and looked out the window. On a day like this she could almost forget the fear that never seemed to leave her as well as the circumstances that led to her living in her daughter's home.

"Sorry, lady." The girl had brought her tea. "Sorry, but dogs must wait outside."

"My dog won't hurt anyone."

The girl shook her head. "No dogs inside."

Dolly's cheeks flushed. "Young woman, you may not speak to me that way. I would like to see the person in charge."

People began to stare. Once more the girl shook her head. She opened her mouth again but before she could speak, a smooth voice interrupted. "Thank you, Sonja, I'll handle this." Dick Boyle, manager of the hotel, smiled. "Hello, Mrs. Little. How are you this afternoon?"

"Quite well, until now."

He sat down beside her. "You see, Mrs. Little, it's this way: there are new regulations regarding the operation of food establishments. Animals are prohibited from areas where food is prepared and served, with the exception of those who aid the handicapped. You aren't handicapped are you, Mrs. Little?"

"Most definitely not."

"Well then, I suggest we tie your dog outside the building. He'll be waiting for you when you're finished."

"But I want him with me."

"That isn't possible."

Seamus growled and bared his teeth. Dolly folded her arms. "Seamus stays with me."

Boyle sighed. "They said you were loony, but you're obstinate as well. I'll have to call Johannah."

"Johannah is in Dublin."

"Let her stay," someone called out. "There's no need to abuse an old lady. Let the dog stay, too."

"I can't," asserted the manager. "Please, Mrs. Little. I don't want to call the garda."

"You wouldn't dare. I'll tell your mother, Richard Boyle, that you've the manners of a pig."

"That's it." Boyle stood. "I've tried to be accommodating but you leave me no choice. Finish your tea, Mrs. Little. It's on the house, but I'm calling the garda."

Liam

He had no idea where to look. Liam was frustrated. He'd never bothered to wonder what Dolly did with her time. How could she have left that way, tying them all up with worry? And then there was his mother on her way to Dublin, a first class hotel and restaurants. She should be here, looking after Nan. She was *her* mother after all. He had better things to do than mind an old lady. Instantly, he felt the sting of his own selfishness. Johannah looked after everyone. She deserved a break, even when the reason for the trip was business related.

Parking the car on Castle Street, he fished in his pocket hoping to find change for the meter when someone tapped on the window. It was Ciara McCarthy. He rolled it down. "Hello, there."

"Shopping?"

"Not exactly. I'm looking for my grandmother."

"Is she lost?"

"I'm afraid so. She took off some time this morning. She could be anywhere."

Ciara's wing-shaped eyebrows drew together. "Have you contacted her friends?"

"I don't know them."

"Where does she go when she has free time?"

Liam looked sheepish. "I don't know that either. I'm afraid to say that we haven't spent much time together since I left home. I suppose it's my fault. I've been busy."

"Shame on you, Liam." Ciara smiled sunnily. "It's never too late to change. I'll help you."

He laughed. "You'll help me change?"

"No. I'll help you find your grandmother."

He looked surprised. "That's kind of you."

A soulful howl rooted all pedestrian traffic. Ciara pointed toward the Grand Hotel. "I have a strong feeling she might be easier to find than you think."

Liam's gaze followed the direction of her finger. A police vehicle was pulled up in front of the hotel while one of the guards cautiously circled some sort of howling beast. Another two guards pulled a cuffed and struggling woman from the hotel toward the vehicle. Liam recognized the woman immediately. "Stay here," he said, leaving Ciara with the car.

Cursing, he raced down the street, arriving at the same time Seamus had found an opening and, teeth bared, hurled himself at the officer attempting to seat Dolly in the back seat of the car.

"Wait," Liam shouted, pushing aside the guard who had momentarily released his prisoner in an attempt to kick aside the dog attached to his trouser leg. "What are you doing? This is my grandmother. She's eighty years old for Christ sake."

"I'm not eighty, Liam. I'm seventy-six," Dolly announced, "and that man," she pointed to the hotel manager hovering nervously at the entrance to the Grand, "that man refused to serve me."

"I was happy to serve her," Dick Boyle said. "I *am* happy to serve her, but not her dog. We can't have dogs in eating establishments. We'll be closed down."

Liam was furious. Ignoring Boyle completely, he appealed to the guard who was now restraining Seamus. "She's an old woman. Haven't you crimes to solve? What are you doing abusing an old woman?"

"We had a report," the guard with the ripped trousers replied. "Someone reported she was disturbing the peace."

"Are you out of your mind? Look at her wrists." Liam pointed to the metal circles even now raising angry welts on Dolly's skin. "Take these off immediately."

"I can't be responsible for that, now. She resisted arrest."

"You'll be responsible all right, when we file a law suit against your department."

A crowd had formed. "Shame on you," a bystander shouted. "Let her go. You, give it to 'em, Dolly."

"Don't back down now, Liam," someone else called out. "They're worthless, never there when you want them and now this."

"What's going on here?"

Liam turned. Patrick, his mother's friend, stood beside him.

"They've handcuffed my grandmother."

Patrick nodded at Dolly. "That seems a bit extreme."

"It certainly is," a woman behind them said.

"Lovely to see you, Mickey," Dolly said. "My wrists are hurting. Can you help me?"

Patrick looked at the older guard. "These gentlemen seem like reasonable sorts. I'm sure they understand the situation. Am I right, lads?"

Liam had his arm around his grandmother. The younger of the two guards was fumbling in his pocket. Retrieving the key, he removed the cuffs. The crowd cheered.

"C'mon, Nan," Liam said gently. "The car is down the street." He whistled at the now subdued dog. "Let's go, Seamus."

"What about Mickey? Why isn't he coming with us?"

"Hush, Nan," Liam said under his breath. "Patrick has things to do."

"I didn't mean any harm, Liam," Dick Boyle called out. "Remember me to your mother."

Liam ignored him and led his grandmother, the dog following, up the street to the car. Just then, Kate rounded the corner of Castle Street, sighing with relief when she saw her brother and grandmother. "Liam, thank God you found her."

"You missed the excitement. Dick Boyle called the guards on her because of the damn dog." Liam could barely get the words out. "They cuffed her, sons-of-bitches. Look at her wrists. She needs a doctor."

Kate's eyes filled. "Oh, my God. Mom will kill me. I was supposed to look after her."

"Don't cry, Katie," Dolly soothed her. "I don't need a doctor. Mickey took care of the guards and Liam will drive us home."

Kate groaned. "Nan, please don't say things like that. Dad's dead. People won't understand."

Dolly shook her head. "I see him, Kate. I see him all the time."

"*All the time?*"

Dolly considered. "No, I suppose not. I saw him three times. At Kevin Barry's, at your mother's dinner, and just now, on the street."

Kate bit her lip. "How did he take care of the guards?"

"Never mind all that now," Liam said. "For some reason she's got it in her head that Patrick is Dad. I have to admit, he's been more than kind to us. We'll go home and think no more about it."

Kate narrowed her eyes and stared at the woman sitting in the driver's seat of Liam's car. "Is that Ciara McCarthy in your car?"

"I was asking if she'd seen Nan when the commotion started. She's probably waiting to hear what happened."

"Ciara McCarthy?"

Liam bristled. "Why not? Do I interrogate you about your friends?"

"No, of course not. It's just that I didn't know you were friends."

"I don't tell you everything, Kate. You're my sister, not my priest."

"No need to be so touchy, Liam. I only asked." Kate slipped her arm around her grandmother's shoulders. "Are you hungry, Nan? Did you have your tea?"

"No, I didn't," replied Dolly. "You must remind me to tell Annie Boyle that her son is a pig."

"Maybe we should forget all about this, Nan," suggested Liam, "and next time you want to go out, tell one of us. We'll be happy to take you."

Dolly looked skeptical. "Will you really, Liam?"

"Absolutely."

"I suppose I could do that, if you promise."

"I promise, and Kate does, too." He challenged his sister. "You do promise, don't you, Kate?"

Kate shuddered. "I certainly do."

CHAPTER 23

Johannah

Johannah edged over to the side of the narrow road, considered the space available for passing traffic, and forced her left tires up over the curb. Then she consulted her map. This clearly wasn't the bypass road. Driving through the town centre of Naas, Ireland's horse capital, would take more than twenty minutes and eliminate any hope of freshening up at the hotel before her meeting.

A knock on the window startled her.

"Are you lost?" a man shouted through the glass.

Johannah nodded and opened the window. "I'm looking for the bypass road to Dublin."

"You missed the turn."

"I didn't see a sign."

"There is one but it's down," he explained, pointing to a spot down the road. "If you look in the grass about thirty spades from the road, you'll see it."

"In the grass?" Johannah repeated. "I'm supposed to look in the grass?"

He nodded. "You would have seen it straight away."

She pointed to the cross in the road she'd recently passed. "If I take the left fork, will that get me there?"

"You might but it would take you by way of Kinsale."

"Kinsale? I don't want to go to Kinsale. That's on the other side of the country."

"That's where the left fork will take you."

Fighting back a headache, Johannah forced herself to speak calmly. "Is it the right fork I should take at the cross?"

"That would be the one."

"Let me be clear. Is that the one to get me straight there?"

"If it's Dublin you want."

"It is."

He leaned against the window and stroked his chin. "I can't think why. T'is an unpleasant place, Dublin is. But there's no accounting for tastes. I suppose there are reasons aplenty for traveling to Dublin."

"I'm going to a meeting," Johannah volunteered, "to prevent a salary cut."

He straightened and held out his hand. Johannah took it. "God bless you, lass. You're working for all of us." He stepped back. "Now go along and mind you, take the left fork."

"The left one. I thought you said that led to Kinsale?"

"I was having a bit of fun with you. T'is the left fork after all."

Johannah sighed. She'd never get to Dublin at this rate. "Now I don't know whether to trust you."

"There's none better." He laughed. "My mother was a Tralee lass just like yourself. I can't mistake the speech. Be off with you now and take the left fork. I wouldn't steer you wrong."

As it was, she was already late by the time she parked in the hotel carpark. Foregoing check-in until a later time, she made her way to the conference room and cautiously opened the door.

Jack Rafferty stood at the head of a long, oval table, his back to the door, referring to a power point presentation visible on the overhead screen. His voice was low and confident with an accent that did not belong in the Republic. Johannah stiffened. She knew nothing about the union organizer except by reputation. Although his name was Irish, his accent was from Belfast. If she was sent here to learn negotiation methods from an Orangeman, she would just as soon leave now.

Then he turned, nodded at her and, without skipping a beat, continued speaking. Johannah's relief was palpable. Despite his cultured accent, impeccable haircut and tailor-made suit, his eyes, even from where she stood, shone clear like blue glass, and the fine lines at the corners of his mouth could only have come from a lifetime of laughter. This man was definitely one of their own.

Billy Roache caught her eye and motioned to the empty seat beside him. Carefully stepping over an obstacle course of legs, Johannah made her way to the far corner of the room, sat down, and attempted to concentrate on the message.

"The good news is," Rafferty said, "Ireland is a country with a long history of social service. Now that we're part of the EU, certain basic necessities for our elderly, our children and our unemployed must be maintained. The bad news is that we're a people accustomed to subjugation, to suffering, to doing without. We've had enough of upheaval and rioting." He paused.

Nods and scattered whispers broke the silence. He held up his hand. "With that, I must tell you it's time to get over the distaste for public spectacle. You must put your reservations aside. You are not alone. Talk to each other. Nearly every county in The Republic is represented. Protests, marches, and public gatherings, especially in large numbers, are resources that many of you find tawdry, but are necessary for successful arbitration and resolution. The public will support you. A good percentage of our population collect public benefits. You're not asking for salary and benefit increases. You're asking to maintain what you have, which isn't unreasonable. It certainly won't make anyone here wealthy."

He smiled and, once again, subdued laughter lowered the tension level in the room. "Strike is a last resort," he reassured them. "Rarely does it come to that." He closed his notebook. "With that, I'll leave you to your tea. We'll meet again this evening and discuss specifics for your region. Thank you, ladies and gentlemen." He held up a legal notepad. "Don't forget to sign in."

Billy Roache turned to Johannah. "Go along now and check off your name. Then we'll talk about our tea."

"If you don't mind, Billy, I'll just go up to my room. I took a wrong turn and got held up. I need a few minutes to clean up and rest."

"Not a bit. Take your time. I'll stop off at the bar and have a few pints." He winked. "Ellie won't mind, especially if she doesn't know."

Johannah hesitated. Her inclination was to warn him they had another meeting this evening but good manners and natural reserve stopped her. He already knew that. Experience told her she could no more prevent him from indulging than his wife could. Besides, it was none of her business. "I'll see you later, then." Hooking the strap of her briefcase over her shoulder, she picked up her handbag and made her way around the table to the sign-in sheet.

Jack Rafferty handed her a pen. "Mrs. Enright, is it?"

"Yes." Johannah scribbled her name and returned the pen. "How did you know?"

"Your name wasn't checked off. It was the only one."

"Sorry about that. I don't get out much."

"It was an observation, not a criticism."

She raised her eyebrows. "You can't imagine how relieved I am to hear that. I was trembling in my pumps all the way over here."

For an instant he looked surprised. Then he threw back his head and laughed.

She waited until he'd finished. "Did you want to tell me something, Mr. Rafferty, or may I go up to my room now? It's been a long day."

"I'd much rather you let me buy you a drink in the bar."

"Actually, that's another thing I don't do much of. But thank you for the offer just the same."

His smile faded. "Have you taken a dislike to me, Mrs. Enright?"

"Not at all. I'm just very tired."

He looked unconvinced.

She relented. "To prove it to you, I'm going to insist that you give up the *Mrs. Enright* and call me Johannah. I'm on a first name basis with all my friends."

"Thanks. I'll do that. Get some rest, Johannah. I'll see you at half eight."

"Ring me if I'm not down. I never can figure out how to manage hotel alarm clocks. They either don't go off altogether or they shout me awake in the middle of the night."

"I'll do that if you'll give me your room number."

She paused at the door. "Call the desk. They'll connect you."

Her room overlooked the square. Seated in a high-backed chair, a hot cup of tea in her hand, she thought back over their conversation. Could he possibly have been flirting with her? It had been so long she couldn't be sure. Did people actually fence with words anymore, or did they simply lay their cards on the table and exchange room keys? Jack Rafferty was appealing in a refined, articulate sort of way, not at all like Mickey.

Sex was something Johannah didn't think about. There was no point. She'd relegated the subject of intimacy with a man to the think-about-it-later part of her mind, due to lack of opportunity rather than disinterest. It saddened her to think of that part of her life as permanently over. She would have liked to invite Jack Rafferty to her room, if only to satisfy her curiosity but, according to Maura, most men expected repeat performances and Johannah wasn't the least bit interested in that either. She was fifty years old and no longer willing to compromise. Women always compromised, pretending they were less capable, less intelligent, their work less important. Sex was responsible. For a woman, sex led to love and love made her sappy. Johannah considered herself a prime example. She would have done anything for love of Mickey Enright. She *had* done anything and put up with everything because she loved him, and before that she'd felt the same about Francie O'Shea. She wouldn't necessarily have changed it, but she was older now. That part of her was finished and she certainly wasn't going to walk in blindly again.

Pulling back the curtain, Johannah looked out over the bustle of Dublin. A Viking town was Dublin, then an English town and now, an Irish City. She sipped her tea and reached for the phone. It was past time to ring Kate.

CHAPTER 24

Kate

Kate, in the middle of a phone conversation with her mother, forced herself to sound light-hearted and in full command. "Everything's fine, Mom. Nan decided to go for a walk the day you left, but Liam found her. There was no harm done."

"I'm glad Liam stepped in to help you, Katie. You shouldn't have to do everything on your own. Maura will help, too, you know."

Kate felt her heart pound. There was no way her mother wouldn't find out about the fiasco at the Grand Hotel, but she hoped it wouldn't be until after she was home. "Nan seems to have taken to your friend Patrick. He's spending some time with her. What a lovely man he is. Where did you meet him anyway?"

"I thought I told you. We met at The Daily Grind on Castle Street. He doesn't seem like a stranger at all, even though he's new in town. I shall have to thank him when I get back."

"How is it going with you?" asked Kate.

"Well enough. I've enough information to fill up a notebook. "

"What do you make of Jack Rafferty?"

"How do you mean?"

"He has quite a reputation. I've heard he's planning to go into politics."

"I wouldn't know anything about that. He's all business here and that's fine with me." Johannah changed the subject. "How's Evan?"

"Grand. He's not long asleep." Kate hesitated. "I miss you. The nights are long when you're not here."

"You should be home, Kate. How's Dermot?"

"I don't know. We don't talk."

The silence on the other end of the line was palpable. Finally, Johannah spoke. "What's happening, Kate?"

"I don't know."

"All right, then. What do you want to happen?"

Kate sighed. "The impossible. I want my life to have taken a different turn. I want to be young again with all the choices ahead. I want Dermot to be the way he used to be when we first got married. I want him to think that what I want is as important as what his mother wants. What does that make me, Mom? A terrible person?"

Johannah's laugh held little humor. "No, love. It makes you normal. There's not a woman alive who hasn't wished that at least once during her marriage."

"Even you?"

"Especially me."

"Do you wish you'd thrown in the towel?"

"Is that an American expression?"

"I suppose. Do you know what I mean?"

"I do. The answer to your question is, no. That was never an option, not in my world anyway."

"What would you do if you were me?"

"Would it make a difference to you, whatever I said?"

"Possibly."

"How can I answer that? It depends on so many things."

"What things?"

She heard her mother sigh into the phone and bit her lip. Just once, she'd like for Johannah to approve of her.

"We'll talk when I get home. Perhaps you'd better just concentrate on Nan and Evan. Remember that I love you. Tell Maura to call me on my mobile."

Kate said goodbye and settled the phone into its cradle, poured herself a cup of tea and stared into the distorted reflection of the metal teapot. Did mothers ever approve of their daughters? Sally O'Brien's mother did, but then her A levels had been over the top and she ended up a barrister in private practice in London. Still, Charlotte O'Brien probably confided to her friends that money and position didn't make up for grandchildren.

Dolly walked into the kitchen. "Any hope for a cup of tea?"

Kate jumped up. "Sit down, Nan. I just made a new pot."

Settled into the chair beside the radiator, Dolly stirred milk into her cup. "You're looking blue."

"I have some uncomfortable decisions to make."

"Dermot?"

Kate looked surprised. "Right. I didn't think you knew."

"I'm not dead, Katie. You're here with the child and Dermot's at your house. It doesn't take a genius to put two and two together. Too bad, it is, but then these things happen. Not in my day, of course. We had no divorce in Ireland in my day, more's the pity. The queue gathered from here to Dublin when our government came to its senses and finally allowed it. Thank God that's ended."

Kate stared at her grandmother, wide-eyed. "Do you believe in divorce, Nan?"

"I believe that people shouldn't live in misery, whatever that means."

"Do you think I'm living in misery?"

Dolly sipped her tea. "Without a doubt."

Kate posed the same question she'd asked her mother. "If you were me, would you divorce Dermot?"

"It depends."

"On what?"

"Did you ever love Dermot? Are you attracted to him? Do you respect him? If the answer to all three is no, then there's no hope at all. If you respect him but aren't attracted to him, there's still no hope. If you're attracted to him, there's always hope even if you don't think you love him and even if you don't respect him. In a nutshell, attraction is the key. If you can't imagine what you ever saw in him, it's over." The wrinkles in Dolly's forehead deepened. "Does any of that help?"

Kate was silent for a good thirty seconds, stunned at her grandmother's lucidity. "You surprise me, Nan," she said at last. "I wouldn't have thought you had it in you to say any of those things, especially to me."

"You haven't answered any of my questions."

"I'll have to think about them."

"Thinking is good. There's always hope if you need to think."

"Mom says hello. That was her on the phone."

"Your mother is a good person," Dolly stated matter-of-factly, "even if she is wrong about me."

"How is she wrong?"

"I should be in my own home. Even if I have lost brain cells, I still have more than most people are born with. I'm certainly smart enough to live on my own. Even slow people, retarded people, manage to live on their own."

Kate poured her grandmother another cup of tea. "You might have a point there, Nan. Still, there's plenty of room and you're with your family. Most people would give their eye teeth to be home with people who want them."

"Does anyone really want me?"

"Of course we do."

"You never came to see me much when I lived in Kevin Barry's."

"Because it's out of the way and we're busy. This is much nicer, having you here every day."

"I feel like an obligation to you and Liam, as well as your mother."

"You're not at all, Nan. We're happy to have you. Really we are."

Dolly's voice softened. "You're a good girl, Katie. Your mother raised you right. I'm a difficult old woman who should keep her mouth shut." She looked around. "Where is your father?"

Kate blinked, unprepared for the question. Their conversation had seemed so normal. She found her voice. "He's not here, Nan. Would you like to go for a walk? Liam should be home soon and it won't be dark for quite some time."

"I'd like to see Mickey."

"You can't."

"Why not?"

Kate set her cup down on the table, hard. She watched the crack make its way across the porcelain. "He's dead. He died over a year ago."

"Nonsense. Why does everyone persist in telling me this? I've seen him, talked to him."

Kate stood and began clearing the dishes from the table. "Let's change the subject. I'll make you a sandwich and then you can go upstairs and get ready for a walk. We'll go round to Kevin Barry's and visit some of your friends."

A knock sounded on the door. Grateful for the reprieve, Kate walked through the hall and peeked through the glass. Her mother's friend, Patrick, waved at her. She opened the door. "Hello, Patrick. How lovely to see you. Mom is still in Dublin."

"I know. I'm here for your grandmother. I thought she might like to take a walk with me and stop somewhere for tea." He pointed to his watch. "It's that time."

Was he a magician to appear at the exact moment he was needed? Kate stepped aside. "I'm sure she'd love it. Please, come in."

Dolly stood in the hall. "Mickey, it's you. Tell this ridiculous child that you're still in the land of the living."

Kate looked imploringly at Patrick. "I'm sorry," she whispered, "but she won't give up the idea that you're my dad."

"I've been called much worse. From what I've heard, Mickey Enright wasn't a bad bloke."

Kate laughed. "You won't get an argument from me."

"I've come to take you out for tea, Dolly. Will you spare me an hour or two?"

"Yes, I will. Give me ten minutes and I'll be ready to go."

"This is really very kind of you," Kate said when her grandmother had disappeared from view.

"Your mother asked me to look in on you and help wherever I could."

"Did she really?"

"Yes."

"That's funny. She didn't mention anything about it when she phoned today."

"I'm sure she has a great deal on her mind."

Kate nodded. "That's probably it. I'll help Nan get ready. Make yourself comfortable in the sitting room."

Dolly was in process of inserting a hat pin into the back of her wool beret when Kate knocked on the door and stepped inside. "Is this all right?" she asked, turning her head to the side.

"You look grand, Nan. It's just a light tea. You know what they say, better to be under dressed than over."

"I've never heard that, nor do I believe it. It sounds like something one of your generation would make up. How many pairs of denims do you own anyway?"

"Quite a few, I suppose."

"You have a nice figure, Katie, but no one would ever know with those trousers down around your hips and the shapeless blouses that are all the rage. Whatever happened to hats anyway?"

Kate laughed. "I don't know what happened to hats, but I won't argue with you about any of that. I think the clothes women wore fifty years ago were beautiful. Tell me where I can find them and I'll buy some." She stood behind her grandmother and fluffed out the thick white hair. "You have such beautiful hair, Nan. I wish you hadn't cut it."

"It's easier to wash and comb."

"Easy is the rage, is it?"

Dolly looked surprised. "I suppose it is. Point taken. You're a good girl, Katie."

"So you've said. Be kind to Patrick, Nan. Remember, he's Mom's friend and a very nice man."

Dolly hands, the skin as fine and dry as parchment, clasped Kate's. "He looks different, but he's Mickey. I promise you that."

"How can you be so sure, Nan?"

"He knows things."

Kate frowned. The air had suddenly gone cold. "What things?"

For a moment Dolly looked confused. Then she shrugged her shoulders and moved toward the door. "Things, that's all. Feed Seamus for me, will you, or shall I bring him along?" She stopped a minute. "Do you remember the door I had closed in when I rented rooms during the Rose of Tralee Festival?"

"Yes."

"He knew exactly where it was. He told me he could open it up again if I wanted. Now who but Mickey would know that?"

"Half of Tralee, that's who. The houses in Kevin Barry's are all the same."

"He doesn't live in Kevin Barry's. If he's a stranger, a blow-in, how would he know about my door? I haven't had it for fifteen years."

How would he know such a thing? Someone must have mentioned it, probably Dolly herself. Shrugging off the odd chill creeping along her spine, Kate followed her grandmother down the stairs. Patrick stood near the mantel examining the framed pictures of the family. He looked so trustworthy in his khaki trousers and wool pullover. "Where did you say you were going?" Kate asked.

"Galley's is close and the food is good. Is that acceptable, Dolly?"

"It is."

"Will you be home straight away?" Kate flushed. "I was only asking because Mom might call again. Nan wouldn't want to miss her twice."

Patrick's eyes twinkled. "She'll be here at half-eight unless you'd like her back sooner."

"No, not at all," she stammered, sure she was so sounding like an idiot. "Half-eight is fine."

CHAPTER 25

Johannah

They sat in the lobby of the Grafton, sated after the hotel's spectacular late afternoon tea. Jack Rafferty leaned back in the over-stuffed chair, his gaze speculative, curious. "I've never been to Tralee. I've heard it's beautiful."

Johannah laughed. "Tralee? I can't imagine who would have told you that. The Ring of Kerry is lovely but only if you avoid tourist season."

"But that's not really Tralee, is it?"

"No."

"Describe it."

"Sorry?"

"Describe the town, the countryside, your favorite places." He waved his hand. "What is it like? Why do you stay there?"

Why did she stay in Tralee? Why did anyone stay in the town where she was born and raised? "It's my home," she began slowly. "My mother and children live there. I have friends and a grandson. My husband is buried in the town cemetery. I'm comfortable knowing my way." She tried to put herself in his place, to see her, Johannah Enright, the person, through his eyes. Her reasons were normal and sound, but did she sound weak? A woman whose choices were made for her, a woman who succumbed to her circumstances instead of choosing them? Suddenly she was annoyed. Who was he to ask such a question?

"You don't look old enough to have a grandson."

Her look was level, cool, slightly mocking. "Please, Mr. Rafferty. Don't be predictable."

He nodded. "All right. Did you grow up in Tralee?"

Johannah nodded. "I did."

His eyes never left her face. "Tell me about it. I want to see it as you do."

Johannah was feeling definitely uncomfortable. It had been a lifetime since she'd been the object of a man's undivided attention. "I'm not sure where I should begin."

He waited, saying nothing, allowing her to find her own way.

"The town is well enough, I suppose, although the sense of community isn't the same as when I was a girl. There are so many strangers, mostly from other countries within the EU. I live on the edge of the town, not quite in the country, but enough out of the way to avoid the gossips, not too far that I can't run across the road and pick up a liter of milk or a loaf of bread when I run short." She warmed to her subject. "My house isn't in an estate. The lot is big and the family beside me owns cows. The neighbors second next door have a pig."

"A pig, in the town?"

"It isn't a very large pig," she explained. "Once it got out, ran between our two gates and ended up in the cow pasture. A cow had just given birth. She was terribly protective of her calf and nearly went crazy when she saw the pig. My neighbors, and half the town, fearful she'd harm her own calf, chased after the pig, bumping into each other, falling down, cursing. One of the recruits even pulled out a lasso. Imagine lassoing a pig as if he were John Wayne. No one ever did catch it. Somehow, the pig knew when to go home. It was hysterical to see everyone, covered in mud and cow dung walking home completely disgusted with themselves."

He looked incredulous rather than amused. Johannah was embarrassed. What was she doing describing pigs and cows to this man who oozed of sophistication? She lifted her chin. "What about you, Mr. Rafferty? Where do you live?"

"Call me Jack. I don't actually live anywhere, but I was born in Belfast."

So, she wasn't wrong about his accent.

"My brothers live in the States and my sister immigrated to Australia with her husband twenty years ago. My father died when I was a child and my mother passed on five years ago. I rent a flat in London but it's not much of a home. I'm rarely there."

"Have you no wife or children?"

"No."

She should have felt pity for one so removed from family and friends, but there was something about Jack Rafferty that wouldn't allow it. Still, Johannah felt an obligation to respond. "Do you enjoy that sort of life?"

"It suits me."

She looked away.

"You're thinking it's a lonely existence."

She was thinking exactly that, but to pass judgment on someone else's habits was beyond rude. She smiled. "It wouldn't suit me, but that's what makes the world interesting, isn't it?"

He changed the subject. "How did you get involved in this collective bargaining situation, Johannah? I wouldn't have thought a woman like you would be in a place like this."

"There you go, assuming when you don't even know me."

"Am I wrong?"

She laughed. "Not really. I was nominated by default. The others all have dependents who can't live without them."

"It sounds to me as if you have those things as well."

"No one is so indispensable that she can't be replaced, especially not for a few days."

He looked thoughtful. "I suppose not."

Johannah glanced at her watch. "My goodness. I didn't realize how late it is. I've a meeting and then a dinner engagement, although how I'll manage a bite after this feast I'm not sure. Do people here really eat this much?"

"Only on special occasions. Must you go so soon?"

"I'm afraid so." She stood. "Thank you very much. The tea was lovely."

He reached out to stop her. "May I see you again?"

She froze. He couldn't mean what she thought. Recovering quickly, she smiled. "Of course. You'll be coming to Tralee."

He looked at her steadily. "I meant in a social capacity."

Johannah hesitated. There was no doubting his sincerity and for the moment she was flattered. Jack Rafferty was attractive and educated, more sophisticated than anyone she'd met before and certainly more worldly. That he might be interested in her was a certainly a feather in her cap. But she was also wise enough to know the benefits of staying with her own kind. "I'm not sure that would be a good idea," she said gently.

"Will you consider it?" He smiled an attractive, craggy smile designed to wear down the defenses of any woman, never mind a vulnerable one who'd recently lost a husband and had no hope of starting over in a town where everyone knew his neighbor's business.

Johannah relented. "I will."

"Then I'll ask again. Don't forget the rally tomorrow."

She had no intention of attending the rally. Kate and Liam had been on their own with their grandmother long enough and she had what she'd come for, perhaps a bit more. "Good night, Jack. Thanks again for the tea and the company."

Early the next morning, before dawn, she drove home through Kildare and Naas, the tree-lined roads of Ireland's horse country, past white fences and lime-rich grass, gracious, ivy-shrouded estates, their chimneys breathing white smoke into gray skies, and playful foals with burnished coats, their legs so impossibly thin it appeared an act of courage to lope across the meadowlands.

Johannah replayed her conversation with Jack Rafferty. She was surprised at the tiny tug of pleasure his attention brought her. Twelve hours later, the thrill, the rush of satisfaction, the surge of power that comes to a woman when she learns a man finds her attractive after she'd long ago relegated that part of life into the distant past, still lingered. Still, she didn't intend to dwell on it for very long and she didn't regret refusing his advance.

Advance. She considered the word, wondering if it was too strong, sounding it out loud, rolling the syllables off her tongue into the silent, heated air of her car. Yes, she decided. It was definitely an advance, subtle, noncommittal, but well within the range of the definition. She chuckled at the idea of Jack Rafferty in Tralee, keeping her company, sitting beside her at Mass, walking with her in the evening. Anyone she brought home would raise eyebrows, but Jack Rafferty in the flesh, a man so unlike Mickey Enright he could be a different species, would render her family as silent as door posts.

The humor of the potential situation faded. Johannah, all alone in her small car with hours of travel ahead, allowed herself to be completely honest. She didn't want another marriage like her last one. In fact, she was quite sure she didn't want another marriage at all. It was much more comfortable living alone. At least she thought it would be, given her limited experience. She didn't suffer from headaches anymore, nor did she talk to herself in the mirror, imagining conversations she would never have the nerve to engage in. It wasn't Mickey's fault. He wasn't a brute or even unreasonable. The worst that could be said of him was that he was a bit selfish, but then what man wasn't? Johannah blamed herself for overreacting. It was her own nature that was lacking. She was a woman uncomfortable with conflict. Even the slightest hint of it would send her into maneuvers designed to bring on the inevitable aching head and clenched jaw. Why would she put herself through that again if it could be avoided? *Because you're fifty years old and the possibility of climbing into bed all alone for another three decades is too sad to think about.*

Forcing herself to relax her grip on the wheel, Johannah slowed to a stop at the roundabout and looked to the right. She mustn't feel sorry for herself. That led to depression and one depressed female in her house was enough.

More than that, she mustn't make foolish decisions based on emotions that weren't real.

Pulling out into the line of traffic, she indicated her exit, moving smoothly toward the Tralee Road for the three hour drive home. It was only half eight when she turned down Oakpark Road, made a left on Racecourse, a right on Clash and stopped at the station crossing. The gate was closed. She looked both ways. Not a train in site. The gate was still manually maintained by the Mahoneys who lived in the small house off to the side. Their shades were pulled.

Irritated, Johannah was about to turn around, retrace her route and drive home from the other side of town when suddenly the thought of another twenty-five minutes in the car, after climbing out of bed before dawn and driving the better part of four hours, was too much. Paddy Mahoney was paid to man the station. He could catch his sleep on someone else's watch. What would Kate do? Was this what she meant by the Irish accepting a level of discomfort that wouldn't be tolerated elsewhere?

Pressing the horn, Johannah relished the piercing, dissonant beep. Then she waited. Still no sign of life from the house. Once again she pressed down on the horn, harder this time, releasing and pressing again and again, until the front door of the gatehouse opened.

Mrs. Mahoney, clumsily tying the sash of her robe, ran out. "Have you lost yer mind, Hannie Enright? T'is eight o'clock in the mornin'."

Johannah rolled down the window. "The gate's closed and there's no train."

"Would it be too much for yer ladyship to go around? We've been up half the night."

"I've been driving since before dawn, and yes, it would be too much."

Open-mouthed, Lizzie Mahoney stared. "What's gotten into you, Hannie? Is something wrong?"

"Not at all, Lizzie. I expect you to do your job, that's all."

"The night was a long one."

"It happens to all of us. But this is your job. You're blocking the road. What if an ambulance needed access?"

"I don't see flashing lights, Hannie."

Johannah gave up and rolled up the window. "Maybe automation wouldn't be such a bad thing," she muttered.

At the roundabout heading toward Kilorglin, she inhaled deeply and smelled the salt-laced air of the open Atlantic. Her mood lifted. No matter what, it was always a grand feeling to come home.

Mickey

Once again it was hot, too hot for comfort, but the view was lovely, palm trees and white sand and water so clear and pale a blue it looked like the water in the Aquadome in Tralee. Peter was already there before him, a small white-clad figure sitting on the sand gazing out at the sea.

Mickey sat down. "Where are we this time?"

"Maui. It's one of the Hawaiian Islands."

Mickey shaded his eyes. "I know that."

Peter looked surprised. "Really? I didn't. When I was alive, there wasn't much world to know about. We're on the northeastern shore. Not too many tourists here. I wonder what it was like when it was new."

Mickey looked around at the pristine loneliness, the jagged, lava-rock shoreline, the white foam on the blue water, the rutted, twisting road that dropped off beyond the cliffs. "Probably not much different than this."

"Maybe so." Peter shrugged. "I thought you might like it."

Alarm bells rang in Mickey's brain. Since when had Peter ever taken his preferences into consideration? "Why?" he asked warily.

"I beg your pardon?"

"Why does it matter that I like it?"

Peter looked affronted. "You're insulting me. Everything I do is for your own good. This entire endeavor is for you."

Mickey was not to be placated. "It's a reasonable question."

"I suppose it is." Peter stood, brushing the sand from his robe. "Walk with me."

Side by side, without speaking, they walked the length of the beach, the only sound the drum of waves against the shore.

"It would be best if you simply told me," Mickey said at last. "I'm imagining the worst."

Peter stopped and studied the horizon. At last he spoke. "You've done well, better than I expected."

Mickey shook his head. "Nothing has changed. Kate is confused. Liam seems well enough, but then he always manages to land on his feet. Dolly isn't happy either."

Peter looked at him. "You haven't mentioned Johannah."

"No." Mickey smiled sadly. "I suppose that's because I don't know her anymore. She isn't the Hannie I remember."

"Are you giving up?"

"Let's just say that my goal has changed."

Peter breathed a sigh of relief. "I'm delighted to hear it, my boy. I was beginning to be worried."

Mickey's eyes twinkled. "If I didn't know better I'd say you've grown fond of me."

"Not at all. I never become personally involved in my projects. It isn't encouraged."

Mickey changed the subject. "I've a few things left to do."

"I can give you a bit longer. We're not quite out of time." He hesitated.

"What is it?"

"Advice isn't something I normally indulge in."

Mickey smiled. "You're making an exception?"

"Just this once." Peter clasped his hands behind his back. He chose his words carefully. "You must remember that everything moves forward as it is intended. There are no random acts, no impulsive decisions, no changing of fate. It will help you bear whatever comes, no matter what it is." His black eyes blazed with passion. "Remember our Savior and His sacrifice."

"You don't often invoke religion. Why is that, I wonder?"

"Would you consider yourself a religious man?"

"No."

"More's the pity." Peter's face relaxed. "You have your answer."

"How long do I have?"

"Long enough."

Mickey held out his hand. "*Slán anois.*"

Peter gripped it. "*Go dtí go gcasfar le chéile sinn arís.*"

Mickey's laugh echoed through the pristine air. "You know more than you'll admit, my friend."

CHAPTER 26

Johannah

"Hello," Johannah called out. "Anybody home?"

"We're in the sitting room." Book in hand, Liam rose from his chair and kissed his mother's cheek. "Nan and I are keeping ourselves company. You're home early."

"I finished up and saw no need to stay longer." She rested her hand on her mother's shoulder. "How are things, Mom?"

Dolly glanced up from her knitting. "I have no complaints."

Johannah's eyes widened. "That's wonderful."

"Except that you keep this house very cold, Johannah. If you pulled the curtains it would stay warmer."

"Maybe, but then we would need more light, wouldn't we? Can I find your jumper?"

"I'm all right with the blanket on my knees. What trouble did you stir up in Dublin?"

"Let me change and make some tea for all of us. Then I'll be right in to tell you everything. Where's Kate?"

"Working."

"That sounds promising. Where?"

Liam settled back in the chair. "She's at Kelliher's, but don't get your hopes up, Mom. She's still determined to teach Dermot a lesson."

Johannah stopped at the door, turning back to look at her son. "Is that what you think she wants, to teach him a lesson?"

"What else?"

"She might want to be done with him."

Dolly dropped her knitting. "What kind of language is that? She wants nothing of the sort."

Liam nodded. "I agree with Nan. It doesn't sound like Kate. She's not that cold."

Was everyone blind? Ten minutes ago Johannah had been hungry for the sight of her family. Now, already, she was annoyed with them. "We'll see," was all she said.

Upstairs, in her own bedroom in front of the long mirror she kept tilted at a twenty-five degree angle because it took off two stone, she stripped off her bracelet, set it on the chest and stepped out of her skirt. She caught sight of her reflection in the mirror and her hand stilled on the top button of her blouse. In the shadowed half-light of late morning, the lines around her eyes blurred. She looked young, very young, nearly as young as Kate. Kate, who at this very moment might be planning a life with Ritchie O'Shea, just as Johannah had once hoped to have with his father. *Hoped* in such a context was an understatement. Such a sad little word. It had been so much more than that. The bans had been read, the arrangements made, the families united in anticipation of the day when Johannah Little and Francis O'Shea would be wed in St. John's Parish Church.

Sighing, she lay down on the bed. Just for a few minutes she would close her eyes and rest.

The double ring of the phone woke her. Groggily, she rolled over and picked it up. "Hello."

"You're home." Maura's no-nonsense voice flowed through the wires.

"Just."

"Are you up for a drink, or is it too soon?"

"Isn't it a bit early?" Johannah thought of Liam, deep in grandmother duty, attempting to study. "Can we make it later?"

"How late? It's already half nine."

"You can't be serious." Johannah sat up, struggling to clear her mind. "I've slept away the entire day. I need to get my mother into bed."

"No problem. I'll give Milo his supper and be over at nine. Shall I bring the wine?"

"If you want more than tea."

"Red or white?"

Johannah laughed. "Whichever you prefer."

"I missed you."

Johannah was touched. Maura didn't run to sentimentality. "I wasn't gone long."

"It's not the distance, although knowing you're five minutes away is comforting. It's that you were unavailable."

Johannah frowned. "Is something bothering you, Maura?"

"I was thinking what it would be like if you weren't around. Who would I talk to?"

"You have Milo."

"Don't be daft, Hannie. He's my husband. I can't talk to him. He's the one I talk about."

It was a ridiculous statement and Johannah should have laughed. Normally, she would have, but this time it struck her differently. It wasn't at all funny. It was sad. "Don't be maudlin. I'm not going anywhere."

"Thank God," Maura replied. "I'll see you at nine."

Maura opened the door without knocking and tiptoed through the hall into the kitchen. "Is everyone out of the way?" she whispered.

"There's no need to whisper. Liam's out and my mother's sleeping."

"Is this her usual time?"

"Like clockwork."

Maura found two wine glasses in the cupboard and settled into a chair. "She closes up a bit early doesn't she?"

"You would, too, if you were up at four in the morning."

Maura groaned. "My God, Hannie, how do you do it?"

Johannah applied the corkscrew to the wine bottle. "I have a good friend who brings wine and conversation."

Maura lifted her glass. "Fill it to the brim. I walked over."

"I can't offer you a bed but the couch is available."

"Milo would have a coronary."

Johannah opened the glass doors of the hutch and replaced the wine goblets Maura had chosen with the Waterford. Then, filling both goblets, she sat down across from her friend.

"Mmm." Maura nodded approvingly. "Nice touch. I'm honored."

"We deserve the best. Besides, who am I saving them for?"

"Kate, or Liam's wife, maybe."

Johannah tried not to sound bitter. "I'll be dead before Liam matures enough to settle down and it's clear that Kate has no interest in preserving tradition." She smiled. "I didn't mean that. I love them dearly. You don't look sixteen with your hair tied up like that. How is it that you never change?"

"You're trying to distract me."

"Maybe, just a bit."

"Tell me about Dublin."

Johannah felt the heat in her cheeks. "Everything went as expected."

"Are you sure, Hannie?"

"Quite sure." She looked up, her eyes meeting Maura's. "What have you heard?"

"That Jack Rafferty couldn't take his eyes off you, that he wined and dined you and barely spared a word for anyone else."

Johannah's mouth dropped open. "You're not serious?"

Relenting, Maura laughed. "Not entirely. But the word is out there might have been some interest on his part."

"If there was, I'm sure it didn't last until I was out of the carpark and on the way home."

"Why would you say such a thing? You're a lovely woman. You have an education and a job. You own your home and your children are grown."

"My children may be grown but they live with me, as does my grandson and my confused mother. Can you imagine someone putting up with that if he didn't have to?"

"Mickey did."

"Mickey and I were a lifetime married. The children were his. He *had* to put up with everything. It's the bargain he made when he stood beside me in church and made promises."

"He did a great deal more than that and you know it."

Johannah was silent. She did know it. Mickey's heart had always been in the right place. Because of it, she'd forgiven him countless times.

Maura pressed on. "Are you not the least bit interested in Jack Rafferty?"

"I wouldn't say that."

"What would you say?"

"He's handsome and brilliant and interesting, and no one I'd ever be comfortable with. Why are you asking all these questions? Is this what you meant when you wondered what it would be like if I wasn't around?"

"You're not old. It's possible you might start again and there's no one new in Tralee."

"Maybe I'll find someone old from Tralee."

"Like Patrick?"

"No," Johannah said quickly. "There's nothing for me there. Besides, it's been just a year. I'm not ready for that yet."

Maura poured another glass of wine and changed the subject. "What's happening with Kate?"

"I don't know. Liam thinks she won't actually divorce Dermot. He said she's teaching him a lesson."

"Do you agree?"

Johannah rubbed her forehead. "I think she'll leave him, especially if she finds a job in Cork or Dublin."

Maura sat up, her brown eyes wide and troubled. "Is she looking?"

"Apparently."

"Because of Ritchie O'Shea."

Johannah's fingers slid up and down the stem of the wine glass, appreciating the delicate etching, the heavy crystal, the contrast of fragile stem and heavy goblet. "I don't know."

"You must tell her, Hannie, before this goes any further."

Johannah formed her words carefully. "What is it you think I should say?"

"Tell her the truth."

"What version would that be?"

Maura leaned across the table and covered Johannah's hand with hers. "Give her some credit."

"Katie always did favor Mickey."

"She loves you. That won't change. You've been a brilliant mother. Besides, Mickey never held any of it against you."

"Didn't he? I've been an adequate mother, Maura, at times a distracted mother, nothing more than that."

"How is that any different from the rest of us?"

Johannah shook her head as if to rid herself of troubling thoughts. "You called me. Tell me what's new with you?"

Maura leaned back in her chair. "Milo wants to retire."

Johannah waited.

"Did you hear me, Hannie Enright? My husband wants to retire."

"Is that bad?"

"It's terrible. He'll be home all the time, in my business, leaning over my shoulder. I won't have a moment's peace." Maura looked stricken.

"You work together now. How will it be different?"

"We share the work. When he's at the store, I'm home. The house is my own, quiet, peaceful, just the way I like it. Now, he'll always be there."

"He must have plans. People retire because they want to do something else."

"Don't be ridiculous, Hannie. People retire so they can sleep late, watch football on the telly and visit the pub anytime they please."

"If that's so, you shouldn't complain. You'll still have the house to yourself."

Maura rolled her eyes. "I can see I'll get no sympathy here."

"You're making this much worse than it is. Milo has lived here all his life. He'll be busy. It's not as if you need the money." Without warning, her throat closed, a sign the tears were very close. When she spoke her voice sounded thick and foggy. "Be grateful you have someone who cares if you come home."

Maura's hand flew to her mouth. "I'm so sorry, Hannie. I don't know what's come over me. I'm a witch. Forgive me?"

Johannah laughed. The tears receded. "If you're not careful I'll make you take your wine home. It's making me pathetic. Besides, all I need is for my mother to come down and see us teary-eyed over a bottle of wine."

"Wouldn't that be desperate?" Maura's chuckled wickedly. "It'll be just like old times."

CHAPTER 27

Johannah

Mrs. Litchfield was old, old enough to have experienced, in a country slow to change, the leftover practices from the days of the Protestant ascendency when money and religion gave her class privileges most hadn't a prayer of enjoying. Despite the fact she hadn't a penny to her name and lived in council housing, her manner was the haughty, patronizing affectation of the lady born.

Johannah, one of the generation born and raised from birth in the Irish Republic, had no patience with her attitude although she tried to remain professional when she visited the woman. "How are you feeling?" she asked, flipping through her notes.

"Well enough, I suppose. The woman who delivers the food is impertinent. I asked her to step inside instead of delivering it on the porch. She refused."

"That doesn't sound like Brigid. Perhaps she was in a hurry."

"Every day?"

Johannah frowned and took a good look at Edwina Litchfield, noting the pallor of her cheeks and the tight clench of her fist on the handle of her cane. "Why do you need it delivered inside?"

"It isn't mannerly to leave food on the steps as if I were a dog."

"No. I suppose it isn't." Johannah pulled out a chair. "Please sit down, Mrs. Litchfied. Would you like a cup of tea?"

"I would."

Johannah filled the kettle and plugged it in. She opened the cupboard, looked at the mugs and hesitated. She could use a cup herself, but it hadn't been offered. Edwina Litchfield probably considered her to be hired help. Selecting a single beaker, she set it on the counter and waited for the water to boil. "Has your clergyman stopped in, Mrs. Litchfield?"

"I don't remember if it was this week or last."

Johannah found the teabags, dropped one into the teapot and added boiling water. "Is your hip bothering you?"

"Not too badly." She pointed a shaking finger at the mug. "Please fill it all the way, Mrs. Enright."

Johannah filled the cup, poured milk into the mug and set it in front of her client. "The doctor's office said you asked for pain pills."

"I thought that kind of information was confidential."

"Apparently not."

"I only need them at night. I think too much and when I think I hurt."

Despite herself Johannah laughed. "It's not the thinking that hurts you. Will you do something for me?"

"If I can."

"Rate your pain, with ten being the worst and one being the least."

"Seven."

"That's not good."

"It's seven," the woman said emphatically. "I'm old. Old people frequently have aches and pains. I'm accustomed to it. You'll notice I don't complain."

Johannah filtered out the editorial, focusing on the issue. "The hip isn't healing, Mrs. Litchfield. You need to have it looked at. I'll arrange the transportation."

The woman's lip trembled. "I won't go into hospital again. I just can't bear it. All I need is the food brought into my kitchen."

Johannah spoke gently. "I'll make sure Brigid brings it into the kitchen if you'll agree to visit the doctor. I'll make an appointment for you."

"Will you be there?"

"Not necessarily, but I assure you, someone will be there with you."

"What about that nice woman who cleans my house?"

"A medical professional would be best."

"She's very kind. First she cleans and then I make the tea and we drink it together. It can be terribly lonely living by oneself." She frowned.

"You recently lost your husband, I believe. I read about it in *Kerry's Eye*."

"Yes. He passed last year."

"I'm sorry."

"Thank you. Who is it that cleans your house? Does she have any medical training at all?"

"Mrs. O'Shea is her name."

Johannah froze. "Kitty O'Shea?"

"Do you know her?"

"I do."

Mrs. Litchfield brightened. "Will you recommend her?"

"I'm afraid not."

"Why not? Have you taken a dislike to her?"

"Kitty O'Shea is not trained in health care. However, that shouldn't stop you from enjoying her company." She picked up her bag. "I'll fill your prescription, ring the doctor and find someone to take you to his office. You'll be feeling better in no time."

"You're very good, Mrs. Enright."

"It's my job."

Edwina Litchfield looked like a small bird perched on her chair with her head tilted at an angle. "Yes and you chose it. Not many do. It speaks highly of you. That's why I must ask you if you don't care for Kitty O'Shea because of her husband?"

Johannah was sure she hadn't heard correctly. This woman, this little woman, this blow-in, who was not a native of Tralee, who worshipped at a colonial church, who had not a single family member who cared whether she lived or died and who knew absolutely nothing about the people of this town could not possibly presume to go where not even Johannah's closest friends would dare. "I beg your pardon?"

"I asked you if your personal feelings about Mr. O'Shea have interfered with your professional judgment regarding his wife."

Johannah stared at her, too shocked to register the emotion rising in her throat. Seconds slipped by. A lorry passed in the street, its brakes squeaking. A woman called her children in for tea. Raindrops pelted the corrugated tin roof on an outdoor shed. Johannah heard none of them. "My dear Mrs. Litchfield," she said at last, drawing out her words slowly. "Despite what you may believe, your age and frailty do not give you the right to meddle in business that doesn't concern you. Please remember that I am responsible for requesting services covered by your benefits. If the government is to cover your medical expenses, you are obliged to use government screened providers. Kitty O'Shea is not one of them. Now, if you'll excuse me, I'll be leaving."

"When will I hear from you? I'm in a great deal of pain."

Johannah didn't turn around. "Some time tomorrow."

"Goodbye, Mrs. Enright."

Pretending not to hear, Johannah closed the door behind her and walked to her car. Fumbling in her handbag for her keys, she unlocked the door, popped open the boot and threw her briefcase inside. Still shaking, she contemplated her next move. The rain had stopped. A milky sun struggled to break through the clouds. Still unsure of her destination, she hooked her bag over her shoulder and walked in the direction of Castle Street and The Daily Grind. Perhaps Patrick would be there. She had a strong desire to confide in someone impartial, someone unfamiliar with the events that happened thirty years ago, steeping her family and the O'Sheas into the kind of scandal abhorred by private people. Not that the O'Sheas were all that private. Every one of them had taken to the stage, playing in bands throughout the country. But it wasn't until Ritchie that any one of them had achieved real fame. *Ritchie,* the son Kitty had used as leverage to lure Francis away, the man who threatened Kate's marriage. Perhaps that wasn't fair. Perhaps Kate's marriage had been wrong from the start and wouldn't have survived anyway.

Johannah willed herself to be fair for a full ten seconds and then gave up. She didn't want to give the O'Sheas the benefit of the doubt. She hated each and every one of them beginning with Francis and then Kitty, filtering down to Ritchie and the five sisters who followed him. Six children. How dare he have six children with a woman who, according to him, meant nothing?

She pushed open the door of the café and looked around. Patrick wasn't there. Suddenly, all the energy that had spirited her out the door of Mrs. Litchfield's house and through the streets deserted her. She sat down at a small table and dropped her head into her hands. If she didn't get a grip on herself fairly soon she'd be in tears and the whole town would hear Edwina Litchfield's version of what had happened that afternoon and, worse, remember the unspeakable events of thirty years ago.

A concerned voice broke into her thoughts. "Are you all right, Johannah?"

She turned. Patrick, looking comfortable and safe, stood over her. "Patrick, thank God you're here."

Pulling out a chair, he sat down. "Tell me what's gotten you into such a state."

"Is it obvious?"

He hesitated. She could see him struggle between diplomacy and the truth. "You're very kind, Patrick. It wasn't a serious question."

He relaxed. "You look as if something is troubling you."

She sighed. "How long do you have?"

"As long as you need. Would you like a coffee first?"

"A latte, please. Make it a large one."

Ten minutes later, buoyed by a fruit scone and a chai latte, Johannah attempted to explain. "I've had a voice from the past resurrected, which isn't all that unusual except that I wasn't prepared. It's been coming on for a long time, but I've ignored it and now it's right here." She held a hand up in front of her face.

"I don't understand, but I'm willing to learn if you care to tell me about it."

She looked at him, at the concern in his eyes, at the dear familiar normalcy of him, at the reasonableness of his responses and wondered why she couldn't have fallen in love with someone like him. "It goes back a long time," she began, "more than thirty years."

He nodded. "I'm listening."

She breathed in and out for several seconds, attempting to slow the erratic beating of her heart. "I was engaged to someone before my husband," she began. "The banns were posted in the church. Two weeks before the wedding a woman came forward claiming she carried my fiancé's child. I think he was as surprised as anyone. Naturally our engagement was broken and he married her."

Patrick's eyes were on her face, waiting, expectant.

"That's it," she said.

"You're quite sure?"

"I am."

"Your story is as old as time, Johannah. You've done nothing to be ashamed of. I fail to see why, after all these years, it still worries you."

She turned the cup around several times, marking the shine of the laminated table. "One of the ladies I check in with mentioned it today. She's become friendly with my former fiancé's wife and wants her to assume responsibilities for which the woman isn't trained. When I tried to explain that this would never be approved by the council, she accused me of partiality because of my past."

"Clearly, she doesn't know you."

Johannah smiled. "Thank you for that."

"How did you leave it?"

"With a few choice words on my part and an early departure." She pushed away her pastry. "I want someone else to take her off my hands. I was so angry I didn't trust myself."

Patrick frowned. "You didn't answer my question."

"What is it?"

"Why should this bother you after all these years?"

"Because of my daughter's fascination with Ritchie O'Shea."

He nodded. "I see."

"No, you don't. You couldn't possibly because you're not from the town. Ritchie O'Shea is his son. He's the boy who was born seven months after Kitty announced she was pregnant with my fiancé's child."

"So," Patrick began carefully, "if I understand you, the idea of having your daughter involved with this lad would be a blow to your pride?"

Johannah opened her mouth to clear up the confusion, to expose the real problem, the basic ugly truth of it, the reason that Katie Enright Kelliher could never in ten million years be the wife, mate, no, not even the friend of Ritchie O'Shea. But the words died in her throat. She hadn't the courage. "Yes," she said shortly. "I suppose that's it."

"Did you love this man very much?"

"Desperately."

"And your husband?"

"I loved him much more than that. We had a lifetime together."

She watched him. He was clearly laboring under some strong emotion.

"Did you love him *desperately*?"

Suddenly she couldn't bear it. Mickey didn't deserve this, the clinical exposure, the calculated analyzing of the reasons for their life together. He wasn't a perfect husband but neither, God help her, had she been a perfect wife. She stood. "I appreciate the coffee, Patrick and the listen. But I must be on my way. I've said too much."

He was standing, too, watching her with grave eyes. "It stays only with me, Hannie. You know that."

She nodded, picked up her bag and walked through the door without looking back. Good Lord, what had come over her, and hadn't she already told him not to call her Hannie?

CHAPTER 28

Liam

Liam slid into a booth facing the entrance to the shopping mall and looked around. The place was full up with mothers and babies. Shifting uncomfortably, he looked at his watch. It was earlier than he thought. Ciara would be another five minutes at least. He considered approaching the counter and ordering a coffee but the queue forming at the door discouraged him. His location was prime and he dared not give it up. Out of his element, Liam wondered why she'd chosen this place instead of The Greyhound or The Munster Warehouse.

Five minutes ticked by slowly. He ignored the telling looks thrown at him by those waiting for a seat. Finally, he spied Ciara's distinctive red curls weaving their way through the crowd. Smiling she sat down opposite him.

"What are you having?" she asked. "I'll buy."

Immediately he stood. "Not a chance. I've a pocketful of change and I'm jiggy from sitting."

She looked surprised. "I'm on time. Have you been waiting long?"

"I came a bit early."

"In that case, I'll have a cappuccino with cream instead of froth, and a cinnamon- streusel muffin." She dug into the huge bag sitting beside her, pulled out a five euro note and handed it to him. "The last time we met you were unemployed. I don't want to take advantage."

Dazed by the unexpected offer, he found himself in the queue waiting to order, attempting to make some sense of what had just happened. *Ciara McCarthy was paying for herself.* Having no experience with women who offered up money, he didn't know whether to be offended or grateful. Deciding he would wait and see what the rest of the day offered, he managed to place his order without mishap and carry it back to the table where Ciara waited.

She cut the muffin in two and offered him half. "I can never eat a whole one," she explained. "They're delicious. Try it."

Liam bit into the pastry, washing it down with a cup of coffee.

"Well?" She smiled, sure of his response.

"You're right. They're terrific." He looked around at the dark paneled walls, the floor-to-ceiling glass window facing the carpark, the espresso machines gushing steam and the case filled with confectionary. "How did you find this place?"

"It's the only coffee house in Manor, other than the cafeteria upstairs. Everyone comes here."

"I'd never heard of it."

She laughed. "How often do you shop at Manor?"

He acknowledged the hit. "Not too much, I guess."

"How's your gran?"

Liam laughed. "Giving us all a run for our money. I don't think my mom had any idea what she was getting into by asking her to move in with us. But it's done."

Ciara's level gaze was disconcerting. "Your mom is a social worker. She knows better than anyone. She probably had no choice."

Liam wanted to change the subject. He couldn't explain his reasons for wanting to see Ciara McCarthy outside the pub, but here he was and he didn't intend to spend the time discussing his relatives. "I thought we'd take a drive to Killorglin and see the first day of Puck Fair."

She sipped her cappuccino, carefully patting the cream from her lips with a napkin. "You want to see my people first hand? Isn't it enough that you have to put up with their drunken brawls in the pubs? Does it make you feel good to compare yourself to them?"

He realized his mistake. "I didn't mean it like that."

"What *did* you mean?"

"I like the excitement of the fair. I like the horses and the bartering. It reminds me of what

Ireland must have been like years ago. The travelers are undiluted Irish, the descendents of people whose homes were razed during the famine years."

She wouldn't be diverted. "You have no animosity towards them, the ones who steal you blind the minute your back is turned?"

"Are you for or against them, Ciara?"

"I'm a realist, Liam, but neither am I ashamed for what I can't control. I was born into the culture. That I can't help, but I don't have to be pulled down by a way of life I want no part of."

"How does your family feel about that?"

She sighed. "We don't always get on, but they're my family, aren't they?"

Liam nodded. "So, what's it to be? Puck Fair, or a drive to Dingle over Connor Pass?"

"Do you think your gran might like to see the fair? Your mom could probably use a day to herself."

His mouth dropped. "Are you serious?"

"Absolutely."

The last thing he wanted to do was to take his grandmother on what he hoped would become an actual date with this unusual girl. Then, unbidden, he found himself remembering something his mother's friend, Patrick had said. *It would be normal, don't you think, for a woman like your mother, accustomed to doing for herself, to feel overwhelmed having her children and grandchild under her roof again.*

Swallowing the last of his coffee, Liam stood and held out his hand. "This should be interesting."

Together they left the shop and headed toward his car.

Johannah looked bewildered. "You want to take Nan to Puck Fair?"

"Yes." Liam held his mother's gaze. "It was Ciara's idea."

"I see." She turned her smile on Ciara. "That's lovely of you, dear, but are you sure you want to spend your time looking after my mother?"

Ciara nodded. "I do."

Johannah was uncharacteristically blunt. "Why?"

"My mom says it's a good judge of character to see how a man treats his family."

"Really?" Johannah looked at her son, an unreadable expression on her face. He stared back without blinking.

"Nan's out in the yard," said his mother. "I can't imagine she wouldn't want to go. I'll find her jumper, some wellies in case it rains, and an umbrella."

Dolly sat in a lawn chair, her slight frame supported by the straight back, her eyes closed against the sunlight. She sat completely still, almost at peace and for a moment, Liam imagined her laid out to rest in her coffin. His chest tightened. He wasn't ready for that. He knelt down and took her hand.

Her eyes opened. "Liam. What are you doing here?"

"I live here."

"Have you moved in?"

"Yes." He nodded at Ciara. "Do you remember Ciara McCarthy?"

Dolly shaded her eyes with her hand and studied Ciara. "Are you Des McCarthy's daughter?"

The girl flushed. "I am."

"Your father sharpens my knives." Dolly frowned. "I haven't seen him for some time. Why is that?"

Liam remembered that Des McCarthy hadn't sharpened knives in years. "He's in a new line of work, Nan. We've come to take you to Puck Fair with us, if you're willing."

Dolly clapped her hands. "Will we bring Seamus? He loves the animals."

Visions of his grandmother's dog attacking sheep and nipping at the heels of horses flitted through his mind. "I think not. There isn't room enough."

"I haven't been to the fair since I was a girl."

Shamed that it was Ciara who'd thought of his grandmother rather than himself, Liam squeezed her hand. "In that case, let's not lose any more time."

Dolly insisted on sitting in the back of the car. "I like being chauffeured," she said. "It makes me feel important. Wave goodbye to your mother, lad. She looks worried." Frowning, Dolly asked, "Should there be reason for worry? You do have your driving license, Liam?"

"I do, Nan. I've had it for years."

"That's all right then." She stuck her head between the front seats, squinting at Ciara. "Who are you, my dear? I don't think I've met you before."

"I'm Ciara McCarthy, Mrs. Little. My dad sharpened your knives, remember?"

"Des McCarthy, the tinker?"

Ciara reddened. "Yes, that's the one."

"You don't look like a tinker."

"Some of us don't. Times have changed."

"I fell in love with a tinker, once," she reminisced, settling back in her seat. "I wasn't much more than a child. Lord, he was a handsome devil. He came to mend the fences and mended me right along with them. His name was—"

"Nan!" Liam said sharply. "We don't need his name. Besides, that's no way to talk. Don't mind her," he said to Ciara who was having a hard time keeping a straight face. "She doesn't remember all that well anymore."

"Shame on you, Liam Enright. There's nothing wrong with my memory."

"We have a guest in the car. What will she think of you?"

"If she's a tinker, she's heard worse." Again she insinuated her head between the two front bucket seats. "You've heard worse, haven't you, dear?"

"Much worse," Ciara agreed.

"There. You see, Liam. I'm not shocking anyone. Besides, I'm old. If I can't shock people at my age, I'll never do it."

Mentally, Liam counted to ten before he spoke. "Do you have your belt buckled, Nan?"

"I don't like seatbelts."

"It's the law. Buckle your belt or the garda will ticket me."

"The garda," she said scornfully. "Where are they when we need them?"

"Please, Nan."

"All right," she grumbled. "I'll do it, but only for you."

"I warned you," Liam said, his voice low. "We could have actually been enjoying this trip."

"Oh, I am enjoying it," Ciara said, "more than you can possibly imagine."

Liam maneuvered the car onto the N70, through Milltown and Castlemaine. He found a coveted parking spot near the town center and, with Dolly on one side and Ciara on the other, hiked across the bridge, past the revelers and the famous goat sculpture, into the picturesque river town of Killorglin.

The Gathering was in full swing. Teeming with caravans pulling horses, travelers from every corner of Ireland had set up shop to barter jewelry, trinkets, t-shirts, posters, watches, cds, food and, of course, the animals they were most associated with, horses.

"I wonder if you know," Ciara began conversationally, "that Irish travelers can be traced back thousands of years to central

Romania and the Steppes of Russia and that horses are everything to them, including a rite of passage."

Liam noticed the tell-tale *them*, a clear-cut disassociation with her race.

She directed her conversation at Dolly, but Liam felt as if he was the one she intended to educate. "When a boy reaches the age of twelve or thirteen he is given his first horse."

"I didn't know that," answered Dolly. "How interesting."

"Long before that," Ciara continued, "he is taught to ride barefoot and bareback using only his voice and the reins." She pointed to a group of children on a nearby hill. "Look."

Intrigued, Liam watched the pavee children, sharp-cheeked, dirty, spewing bold language, their eyes like blue glass, moving as one with their yearlings in a kind of loose-hipped, fluid grace that made professional jockeys look awkward.

He glanced at his grandmother and was surprised to find her cheeks wet with tears.

"They're lovely," Dolly whispered. "Why do we dislike them so?"

Ciara sighed. "Because they're taught at their mothers' knees to lie, cheat and steal the knickers from your clothesline, and they won't hesitate to do so." She pointed to a man with a filthy, horizontal-striped sweater stretched over a healthy stomach and the traditional tweed cap pulled low over his brow. "Do you remember him, Mrs. Little?"

Dolly frowned. "I don't think so." She stared. "There's something about his voice. Good God, is that Des McCarthy?"

"In the flesh. Would you like to meet him?"

"I would."

"Step carefully. The ground is disgusting and those wellies look new."

Liam followed, minding the animal dung, the stinging flies and the wriggling animals, trying to catch snippets of the barely intelligible, sing-song dialect of the Irish Pavee, wondering if and when his grandmother, exhausted from their excursion, would expose her disease.

"Ciara, me love." Des McCarthy bussed his daughter's cheek. "I'm after walkin' away with nothin'. Last year me profit was five times as much." His flinty eyes took in Dolly and Liam. "Who have ye brought me today?"

"This is Dolly Little and her grandson, Liam Enright. We're doing the fair today."

The man stared. "Dolly Little, you say? I know Mrs. Little. Dolly, you haven't changed a bit."

"I can't say the same for you, Des McCarthy," Dolly said flatly. "You're fat as a pig and you still owe me sixty pounds for the tools you stole from my husband's barn." She held out her hand. "Give over."

Liam groaned and looked around, praying that if he was forced into a brawl he'd come away with all his teeth. "I'm sorry, Mr. McCarthy. Sometimes she's not herself."

Des McCarthy stroked his grizzled chin. "T'is herself for sure. She always did have a memory like an elephant. I do owe her." Reaching his hand into his pocket, he pulled out three twenty euro notes. "This should do it, Dolly. Never say Des McCarthy doesn't pay his debts."

She folded the money. "It certainly took you long enough."

Liam linked his arm firmly through his grandmother's and threw a look at Ciara. "It was a pleasure meeting you, sir. We'll be on our way now."

Her face wreathed in smiles, Dolly took his arm. "That went well, I think. What's next?"

CHAPTER 29

Kate

"I thought you had a computer at home." Ritchie O'Shea peeked over the dividing wall of the library cubicle.

Kate shrugged and continued to stare at the monitor. "The server is too slow at home."

"Find anything interesting?"

"A few look promising."

"Where?" Ritchie walked around to her side of the row of computers and pulled up a chair.

"Mostly Dublin."

"Ah, Katie, you've got it all wrong. You should be looking across the water. America is the future."

"It doesn't look so promising," she snapped. "Their stock market is jumping up and down and most of their college graduates are working at Starbucks."

"That'll change."

"Not soon enough for me."

He reached across her to type something on the keyboard. A picture of the Hollywood Bowl appeared on the screen.

Kate felt her chest tighten.

"Do you remember what it's like, Katie, to sit in a bowl under the stars with eighteen thousand people, to listen to entertainers so famous that tickets sell out the day the show is announced?"

"I do," she whispered.

"There's nothing like that in Ireland."

"Except The Point."

He laughed softly. "Not even close."

"There's more to life than entertainment."

"Are you trying to convince me or yourself? I know you miss it, Kate. I know you regret coming home."

She looked at him, at the Celtic tilt of his blue, blue eyes and the stubborn square of his chin. Once, she thought the sun rose with the lifting of a copper-brown eyebrow, but no longer. He was still Ritchie O'Shea, but something inside her had changed. What was it her mother's friend, Patrick, had said? *It's probably a good thing he isn't your husband.*

Kate turned off the computer. "I must collect Evan. We're planning his birthday."

"Am I invited?"

"Probably not. See you later, Ritchie." Conscious of the question in his eyes, she gathered her belongings and walked out the door.

Maneuvering the aisles of Kelliher's Hardware was a gauntlet in itself. Gritting her teeth, Kate pushed open the door and instantly breathed in the scent of varnish and wood-shavings. Cautiously, she made her way through crowded aisles, past metal teapots, ceramic tableware, pots and pans, vases and lampshades, all, in her opinion, tasteless, turning where the small appliances, sinks and toilets, priced twice what Guiney's in the square offered, sat beside nails, fittings, screws, tools, batteries and machinery that someone, somewhere, perhaps someday, might need.

She'd deliberately chosen a time when her mother-in-law, whose laser-sharp gaze had the power to wound, worked on the books behind closed doors. Had Maired Kelliher always hated her, or had it come later, after Kate so clearly expressed her desire to separate from the tiny flat and family store?

"Mommy!" Evan's voice pierced the mote-filled air. So much for anonymity. She turned and caught him in her arms.

"My goodness, what a welcome." Kate buried her face in the sweet muskiness of his shoulder. "Did you miss me?"

He thought a minute. "Not too much. Dad took me to the caves."

"The Crag Caves in Castle Island?"

"Yes."

Kate considered her son. Brutally honest, children had a way of humbling a parent. If ever there was the inkling or hope that one was special, a child's candor erased all of that. "Where is your dad?"

"Cutting wood for Mr. O'Dowd."

Keeping a firm hold on Evan's hand, Kate stood. "Let's find him, shall we?"

Dermot stood in front of a power saw examining two freshly cut planks. "They're right as rain, T'os. Someone will take care of you at the counter."

"If they're not right, I'll bring them back."

Dermot shook his head. "You gave me the measurements. I'm afraid they're not returnable this time."

"I'm not so good with a measuring tape."

"Call me if the fit isn't right. We'll make it work."

T'os O'Dowd grinned, showing a mouth with missing teeth. "That's the stuff."

Kate waited until Dermot replaced the saw and dusted off his hands. Then she exploded. "Aren't you the least bit worried that your son might have stepped on a nail or had his finger cut off? For God's sake, Dermot, this is a hardware store. You're supposed to watch him."

He looked at her steadily, waiting until she finished. "You're underestimating Evan. He's grown up here." Dermot smiled. "Nice to see you, Katie. We've been waiting for you. Do you want to come up?"

She flushed and nodded. Once again she sounded like a shrew around him. Why was he so bloody reasonable all the time?

The flat looked different, roomier somehow. She looked around. "Have you rearranged the furniture?"

Dermot busied himself in the kitchen making tea. "It looks that way because I'm the only one who lives here now."

Kate closed her eyes.

"Are you sick, Mommy?"

She opened them quickly. "Not a bit. Sit here and tell me about the caves."

Evan climbed into her lap. "It was very dark and the stagtites were very big."

"I think the word is stalactites."

He frowned. "That's what I said, stagtites."

"What else?"

"It was cold and I had to wee. Dad said I should wait but I couldn't, so all the people came to the toilet with me. Some went in, too, 'cause they had to wee. Then the man said I should go home."

Dermot carried in the tea tray. "I hope you still like vanillas. There was a special at the bakery."

"Evan was just telling me about Crag Craves."

Her husband laughed. "It was quite an experience. I think we'll stick to the park playground for awhile."

Disarmed, comfortable for the first time in a very long time and imagining the ridiculous scene, Kate laughed, too. She struggled to maintain, couldn't and gave herself up to laughter, cheeks red, breathing labored, tears streaking her face. "I'm sorry," she gasped after a minute. "It's just that it's too funny."

Dermot's eyes twinkled. "Now I see the humor in it, but it wasn't at all funny when it happened. You should have been there."

Suddenly the laughter was gone. Kate looked stricken.

"I didn't mean it that way," Dermot said quickly.

"I know you didn't. You're not capable of trying to wound me."

He sat down beside her. "Poor Kate. You don't know what you want, do you?"

"I beg your pardon?"

He shook his head. "Never mind. Have your tea and we'll talk about Evan's party."

Kate opened the door keeping a firm hold on Evan's hand and nearly fell over the dog. She nudged him with her foot. "Move, Seamus."

He opened one eye, rolled it forward and back and then closed it again.

Using the heel of her shoe, Kate slid him out of the way. "You lazy old thing. Some watchdog you turned out to be." She walked down the hall into the kitchen. "Hello, anybody home?"

Her grandmother sat at the table reading the paper oblivious to the black smoke rising in pungent swirls from the toaster.

"What on earth—?" Reacting quickly, Kate pulled the plug and opened the window.

Dolly looked up from her paper. "You're home. I was beginning to wonder." She folded the paper and held out her arms. "Come to Gran, Evan. I've missed you."

Evan walked into her embrace, allowing himself to be hugged and kissed. "Will you read me a story?" he asked.

"I certainly will." She took his hand. "Lead the way to your room, young man." At the door, she turned back to whisper, "I don't know what's come over your mother, leaving the toast to burn that way. It isn't at all like her. I must watch her more carefully."

Fearing another bout of helpless laughter, Kate nodded, waved them away and looked out the window. Johannah was gathering laundry from the line and attempting to fold it, huge sheets that caught the wind from the west and billowed around her slight frame. Kate frowned. She'd never thought of her mother as thin but that's what she was, definitely thin, and quite pretty, even in those trousers that were too large for her and one of Kate's castoff, hooded shirts.

Buttoning her pullover against the morning chill, Kate opened the door and crossed the lawn to help her mother battle the sheets. "Give me an end. This wind is impossible."

"Thanks, love." Johannah surrendered one side of the sheet and, together, they managed a credible fold.

"I was thinking about Evan's birthday," Kate began.

"It's getting close, isn't it?"

"Yes."

"Will we plan a party?"

Kate nodded and drew in a gulping breath. "He'd like that."

Johannah looked at her daughter. "Is something wrong?"

Kate finished folding a pillow case. "It's complicated."

"How so?"

"Oh, you know. Shall we invite Dermot and the Kellihers? What about people other than family? Under the circumstances, will we be asking our friends to take sides if they come and Dermot and the Kellihers aren't invited?

Johannah took the laundry from her daughter's arms. "This calls for a pot of tea. You put away the laundry. By the time you're done, I'll have it ready."

While the tea was drawing, Johannah sliced raisin bread, Kate's favorite, and unwrapped a stick of fresh butter.

"You didn't have to go to all this trouble, Mom."

"It's no trouble. What's Nan doing?"

"You mean besides burning toast?"

Johannah frowned.

"Never mind," said Kate. "She's reading a story to Evan upstairs."

"That's a relief. We can have a reasonable conversation. God forgive me for saying such a terrible thing about my own mother, but it's true." Johannah sat down. "Have a snack with me and we'll talk about Evan's party. Dermot and the Kellihers will, of course, be invited. Evan has Kelliher relatives. You'll have to come to terms with that, Kate."

"I know. It's just that if we have it here, it won't be at a neutral place."

"This isn't a neutral place?"

"It's my home, Mom. It's my place."

Johannah looked mystified. "Are you at war with the Kellihers?

"Of course not. It's just that they might not feel comfortable."

"Why not? They've been here hundreds of times."

Kate gritted her teeth and uttered the words she knew were tantamount to drawing a line in the sand. "All right, Mom. I'm the one who won't be comfortable.

Johannah's eyes, normally as cool and green as a slate quarry, turned angry. "You can't be thinking clearly. If you're worried about people's comfort levels, you would have thought this entire situation through more carefully. Why didn't you talk to Dermot or try counseling before you left? People who divorce suffer a great deal of discomfort." Placing both hands on the table in a splayed position, she drew a deep breath. "I said I wouldn't ask you, but I have to know. What is your relationship with Ritchie O'Shea?"

Kate's surprise was sincere. "We don't have a relationship."

"I've seen you together, Kate. If nothing's going on, why do you tolerate him?"

Kate struggled to answer. She didn't actually like Ritchie, but she didn't dislike him either. "He's interesting," she said slowly. "He thinks and articulates clearly. He's not afraid or embarrassed to express himself."

Johannah stared at her. "It can't happen, Kate. I'm sorry you set your sights on that one, but it's impossible."

Kate's cheeks flamed. She shook her head. "I wish you would understand. All that's over. I fancied him when I was a schoolgirl. I admit that I thought it might be possible when he first came home, but I know better now. I don't think of him like that. Ritchie is the only one who can talk about the things I remember. He wasn't satisfied staying here in Tralee, just as I wasn't." She waited a moment. "Just as I'm not."

"You didn't have to come back."

"I know that. Neither did he. But we're here and we're two of a kind, strangers in our own land. I suppose, in a way, I feel sorry for him."

"What does that mean?"

"We don't fit."

Johannah picked up her spoon and slowly, slowly, began stirring her tea. "Explain yourself, Katie Enright, because, at the moment, you could be speaking a foreign language."

Kate rested her chin on both hands. "Have you ever seen pictures of the Hollywood Bowl?"

Johannah thought a minute. "Yes, actually."

Kate continued as if her mother hadn't spoken. "Imagine a massive theater, enough for a crowd of eighteen thousand, set in the round, amidst hills tall as our mountains, the Hollywood sign cut into the land, the air warm as summer and thousands of people all around you."

She caught Johannah staring. Kate pointed her finger at her mother. "I know that look. You're asking yourself how you could have given birth to a child so unlike you. You're probably thinking you brought home the wrong baby. But, that's ridiculous because we do look alike and even if we didn't, hospitals are very careful about those wristbands infants are manacled with as soon as they pop out of the womb." Her mouth turned up in a half smile. "Am I right? Is that what you're thinking?"

"Not at all," her mother replied. "I'm imagining summer air and eighteen thousand people just as you told me to."

"It's a magical scene," Kate said dreamily. "There's nothing like it here, nothing even close."

Johannah sighed. "Life isn't a concert, Katie. It's getting up every morning, plugging in the kettle and spooning porridge into bowls. It's about family and friends and what's comfortable and who'll take you in when you need a handout. California may be a lovely place with their Insinkerators and Hollywood, no rain and all those children with straight teeth, but it isn't your home. You have no one there. Do you want Evan to grow up not knowing his family? You made your choice, love. If Dublin is where you find your life's work, so be it. Dublin is a four hour train ride. But California is impossible. You've more than just yourself to consider."

"Are you saying I don't count, that I must set aside my own needs for Evan? Won't he be better off if he has a happy mother?"

"He will not and giving up is part of raising children. It's what every mother does from the moment she learns she's pregnant until she draws her final breath. You should have known that. I regret not making it clear enough while you were growing up."

The still, comfortable air of her mother's kitchen was thick with silence. Kate looked everywhere but into her mother's eyes. Her owned burned with the effort not to burst into tears, not for herself but for Johannah who clearly resented spending a lifetime denying herself for her family. It was so sad, so terribly sad. "How did you bear it?" she whispered at last.

"What?"

"The day in and day out misery."

"What on earth are you talking about?"

"How could you manage for all those years doing for everyone else, denying yourself?"

"I did nothing of the sort," her mother retorted. "I loved it. Knowing my family was happy and tended was tremendously satisfying. It still is. That's why you, Evan, Liam and Nan are here. I wouldn't have it any other way. Your needs are mine. That's the way it works."

"Didn't you ever wonder or wish it could have been more, or at least different?"

"Do you mean did I ever wish I could float down a canal in a gondola with a hot sun overhead and a dark-eyed man whispering in my ear? Of course, I did. That's what the library is for." She stood. "It's still there, Katie. Think about it. Now, I must meet Maura. We're walking to Ballyseedy. Friends are very important as well. You should look up a few of them."

Kate watched her walk upstairs wondering why it had taken nearly thirty years to have this kind of conversation with her mother.

CHAPTER 30

Liam

Kate challenged him, tapping her finger against his chest. "Dermot needs help at the shop. But maybe working behind the counter at a hardware store isn't good enough for you."

Liam swallowed his temper. "Give over, Kate. I never said anything of the sort and, please, lower your voice." They were having lunch on the second floor of what used to be the Munster Warehouse and the tables were close enough to swap cutlery.

She looked around, adjusted her volume marginally and continued. "But you're not jumping at it, are you?"

"I've only just heard of it. For pity's sake, give me a chance to soak it in."

"Mom would never tell you, but she could use a bit of help with the groceries, especially if there's a strike."

Liam barely heard her. Voices inside his head drowned out her words. First his sister, *You're a grown man living off your mother. You can be sure the gossips will be out in full force over you, too.* Then Patrick, *"You and your sister must be a great help to her.* Finally, Ciara's rebuke the night Sheila walked out on him: *Admit it, Liam. You've got your mom cooking and cleaning for you. It can't be easier for her.*

"You're right," he said slowly. "Mom could use some help. I'll talk to Dermot."

"It wouldn't kill you, Liam. I mean—" she stopped. "Really? You can't mean it."

Liam frowned. "Is Dermot looking for help or isn't he?"

"He is, of course. I never thought you'd be interested." She smiled. "It would be great, Liam and such a favor to all of us, even me."

His eyes twinkled. "Don't go trying to talk me out of it."

She punched his arm. "Go see Dermot today. I know the strain is doing him in."

Liam nodded at her water glass. "Are you drinking water or may I have it?"

"Go ahead. I'm not fond of warm water."

"America spoiled you, Katie."

"Stop or I won't buy your lunch."

He held up his hands. "I'll say no more, except this: Dermot is a very good person. Is there no hope for the two of you?"

"He's tied to his mother's leading strings."

"I know the feeling."

Kate shook her head. "It isn't the same at all. You don't really want to be home. He does."

"He can't very well leave his mother altogether," Liam maintained reasonably.

"People don't do that. Imagine someone telling us to leave our mother. Maired Kelliher is old and Dermot's an only child."

"Our mother is completely different. I'm not suggesting we abandon Maired. We could move out of town into a bigger house. If we weren't falling all over each other, maybe she and I would get on better."

"Have you talked about it?"

"All the time." She shook her head "I want to work in my field, Liam."

"Which one would you rather have?"

"Sorry?"

"If you had to choose, which one would you rather have, a larger house or a job in your profession?"

"The job," she said immediately. "I worked hard for my certificate."

"You shouldn't have come back to Tralee. There's nothing here."

"My point exactly."

"You should have figured that out before you married Dermot and definitely before you had Evan. "He reached into his pocket, pulled out a twenty euro note and pushed it across the table, toward her. "Never say I don't pay my share."

"Are you leaving already?"

"I'm off to see Dermot, striking when it's hot."

"I wanted to talk to you about Mom's friend, Patrick."

"Save it and we'll talk tonight." He checked himself. "Is it your turn to take Gran to Bingo or mine?"

Kate sighed. "I'll take her, Liam. You know very well it's my turn."

He grinned and stood. "Don't let her cheat. She nearly blew the roof off St. John's Church when Brigid O'Connor found out she didn't have Bingo after all."

"Old biddies," Kate muttered after he left. "They're not so holy either."

Liam drove into the carpark shared by Kelliher's Hardware and Garvey's Grocery, kept to the left and drove through the gate and into the hardware's private lot, the lot that closed from 1:00 until 2:00 in the afternoon, a holdover from an era when everyone went home in the afternoon for a proper tea.

An unusual emptiness settled in his chest when he entered the shop through the back door. He couldn't remember a time he hadn't come into the shop without Mickey by his side, shaking hands, greeting acquaintances, steering him to the hardware aisle, explaining the difference between an over mount and under mount sink and the right amount of water to mix with grout to ensure a stable consistency. Mickey tried to interest him but Liam never paid attention. He was all thumbs when it came to the trades and when his father veered in that direction it bored him. What he wouldn't give now for an hour of his father's company no matter what Mickey chose to gander on about.

"Liam." A hand came down heavily on his shoulder. "How's it goin,' lad?"

Liam nodded. Sean Cronin was Richie O'Shea's backup at the Greyhound on Sunday. He played the drums badly but he was so good-natured no one had the heart to tell him. "Grand, Sean, and you?"

"Couldn't be better. Now that Richie's home the gigs are rollin' in. We don't have enough days in the week. I hear you're back in Ballyard."

"I am."

"Given up on the estate business, have you?"

Liam sighed. It would be too much to hope that he wouldn't get stuck sharing his recent history. "For now," he said, extricating himself from Sean's grip. "I'm here to see Dermot."

Sean whistled. "I heard the beautiful Kate is over the moon because Richie's home. Poor Dermot."

Liam stiffened. "I can't imagine who would tell you such a thing, but you've been misinformed. Richie O'Shea has nothing to do with the matter and I wouldn't be spreading gossip if I were you." He brushed Sean's hand from his shoulder. "I've business with Dermot and must be on my way."

Somewhere between the lamp shades and the tea kettles his rage subsided. Damn Kate, her selfishness and her quest for personal happiness. Who was happy? There was a bit of fun at times and a general satisfaction with the world when things were on the upswing, but actual happiness? Who sat around and measured his degree of happiness? Kate, that's who. And in so doing she'd come up short, acted on it and consequently messed up the lives of her family. Liam was honest enough to admit that he was the least of her victims despite chancers like Sean Cronin. It was Dermot who was most affected, then Evan and then Johannah.

Dermot sat in his office staring down at the paperwork strewn across his desk. Absentmindedly, he tapped a pencil on the blotter.

Liam could tell from the slant of his focus that he wasn't concentrating. He cleared his throat. "Hello, Dermot."

Dermot looked up. "Liam. It's grand to see you. What brings you here?"

Liam hesitated. He desperately wanted to say he'd come merely to check in, say hello and shoot the breeze, but Dermot would see through the lie and pretend he hadn't. "I came because Kate said you might need some help in the store and I'm in need of work."

"Kate sent you." Dermot looked incredulous.

"She said you could use a body to man the desk."

Dermot nodded. "I could at that, but the job doesn't pay much. Did she tell you that?"

"As a matter of fact she did. I don't need much as long as you don't mind me cracking the books during slow periods."

Dermot stood and held out his hand. "Done. Can you start on Monday?"

Relieved that it had gone so easily, Liam shook his brother-in-law's hand vigorously. "I can. What time?"

"What time do you start school?"

"I'm free all day except for Tuesdays and Thursdays."

"Perfect. Do you have time for a cup of tea?"

Liam smiled, pulled a fold-up chair from the corner and sat down. "How are you holding up?"

Sighing, Dermot flipped the switch on the electric kettle and shook his head. "I'm afraid I don't understand your sister, Liam. She won't tell me straight away what it is she wants. Oh, she mumbles about a house and her schooling and wanting to find a job that suits her, all right, but are those reasons enough for breaking up a marriage? Is she really that unhappy?"

Liam frowned. "They sound like good reasons, Dermot. It can't be comfortable living with a child in those rooms above the store. Kate comes from Ballyard. She's accustomed to a certain level of comfort."

"She knew where I lived when she married me."

"I think she believed you would move to larger quarters when Evan was born. You've been married six years. Children need a garden to play in."

Dermot raked his fingers through his wavy, too-long hair. "I suppose I could see my way to buying something larger, a place with some land, maybe. But what about the job? No one in Tralee would pay good money to see a dietician.

Who would hire her?" He poured a cup of tea, added milk and handed it across the desk to his brother-in-law.

Liam was beginning to feel a small degree of sympathy for Kate. "She mentioned something about starting a business for people who need specialized diets."

Dermot's eyebrows shot up. "Really? She never said anything to me." He thought a minute. "I like it. It's a good idea."

"It might take a bit of investment," Liam said cautiously.

"If it's what she wants we could work out a business plan." He looked at Liam. "You could help us. That's your expertise, isn't it, investing money?"

"In a manner of speaking." Liam gulped down a scalding mouthful of tea. "What about your mom? Do you think she'll see her way past the money?"

"It doesn't matter. I have money of my own." Dermot slapped his knee. "Good for Kate. Who would have thought?"

Liam took his time walking up the hill to Ballyard, wondering how he was going to broach the idea of starting up a special diets business to his sister who, he was quite sure, would never in her wildest dreams consider such a plan, no matter how sound the scheme was.

Liam wasn't ready to discuss Dermot's proposition with Kate. He took the keys from her hand and set them on the kitchen counter. "I'll collect Evan from the crèche. I promised him we'd buy a tin whistle."

"He hasn't been in a crèche for years, Liam. He's in school."

"He hasn't been *alive* for years. He's four."

Kate reached for the keys. "You know what I mean."

Liam tried a different approach. "I'm sure you could use a few hours for yourself, do something you'd like to do."

Kate hesitated. She was in the middle of an online application and she did want to finish it. "If you're sure."

"Completely."

"He's at the Montessori School across from the library near St. John's Church. I'll ring and tell them you'll pick him up. Otherwise they won't let you take him."

"Do that." Liam grinned. "I'll have him back in time for tea."

"Make sure he wears his seat belt," she called after him. "It's the law."

He saluted, backed out of the driveway and headed toward Ballymullen. Traffic was already heavy and it wasn't yet late afternoon. Parking in an empty space in the library carpark, he crossed the street to collect Evan who was already waiting for him. Kate was ever reliable. The child was puffed up over the idea that his uncle had come to take him on an errand.

"Will we drive in your car, Uncle Liam?" Evan asked after he'd taken enough time buttoning his jumper to assure that everyone in the vicinity had managed an eyeful of his magnificent relative.

"We will, but first we'll walk through the park, find your whistle and then we'll drive home. If you like we can buy an ice cream at Garvey's."

Evan raised hopeful eyes to his uncle's face. "Before I've had my tea?"

Liam realized his mistake. "I suppose it isn't a good idea. Your mom wouldn't like it."

"She wouldn't mind, Uncle Liam. Really, she wouldn't."

"I think she would, lad."

Evan drew a deep breath. "Will we tell her?"

Liam managed to control his laughter. Taking his nephew's hand, he crossed the street, choosing the close beside the Christian Brothers' School and shook his head. "Let me give you some advice, Evan. It's no good hiding things from your mother. She'll find out. They always do. If you want your ice cream and you're sure it won't spoil your tea, come right out with it. Take your medicine like a man. Besides, what's the worst she can do to you?"

"She doesn't do anything to me."

"Then what's the problem?"

Evan shrugged. "I can't remember. Where are we going?"

"To Chris Larkin's music store in the square. We're picking up a tin whistle."

"I know that. But which *way* are we going?"

Liam was perplexed. How many routes into town would a four-year-old be familiar with? "Which way would you like to go?"

"The long way."

He had no idea what Evan was talking about but decided to humor him. "The long way it is," he said and kept walking down the path through the rose garden, through the gate to Denny's Street.

"Is this the longest way, Uncle Liam?"

"It is, lad."

"My daddy's store is this way," Evan confided.

"So it is."

"I go there every Sunday."

"Do you now?"

Evan nodded. "Garvey's is next door and it has ice cream."

Liam laughed, scooped the child into his arms and set him on his shoulders. "You little scamp. Your mind was set on ice cream all along, wasn't it?"

"I came right out and said it, just like you told me to."

"Yes, you did. If anyone deserves ice cream, it's you. Shall we find your tin whistle first?"

"Yes."

Later, in the music store, after rejecting several whistles of the green and gold variety, Liam settled on an original Clark's, black with gold lettering. "This is the one, Evan. Look, the holes are small enough for your fingers. It's important that you're able to cover the hole completely or the note won't be true." He demonstrated with a quick slide up and down the scale.

"May I try, Uncle Liam?"

"What about your ice cream?"

"First I want to try the tin whistle."

"That's the spirit." He led Evan out of the store to a stone bench near the center of the square. "You'll have your first lesson straight away. Watch me."

For the next fifteen minutes Liam blew into the mouthpiece while he coaxed the small fingers over each hole.

"When can I blow, Uncle Liam?"

"When you feel comfortable with the notes."

"I want to blow now."

Liam handed over the tin whistle and watched Evan alternately fingering and blowing, occasionally managing the two at the same time. "You're a master, Evan, the most talented four-year-old tin whistle player on the planet."

Evan beamed.

"Hello, there." Ciara McCarthy in a gauzy blouse and short denim skirt materialized out of nowhere.

Liam clapped Evan on the shoulder. "Ciara, this is my nephew, Evan Kelliher. He's learning to play the tin whistle."

"I can see that. How many lessons have you had?"

"Just one," replied Evan. "Uncle Liam bought me this whistle." He held out the instrument. "Do you want to hold it?"

"I certainly do." Ciara accepted the child's offering, inspecting it carefully. "Lovely. Probably the loveliest one I've seen. What are the holes for?"

"You press your fingers down and blow into the top," Evan explained.

Ciara blew into the whistle. "Like this?"

Evan nodded. "You're squeaking. Hold your fingers over the holes."

Ciara handed it back to him. "It's harder than it looks, isn't it?"

"Uncle Liam says I'm talented."

"I'm sure he's right."

"What does talented mean?"

Ciara laughed. "It means you've great potential."

Evan looked confused.

"It means you'll be very good very soon."

The frown cleared from between Evan's brows. He nodded solemnly. "I think so, too."

"Ciara," a harsh voice called out from the shadowed entrance of the hardware store. "We're goin' now."

She sighed. "I've got to go. Nice meeting you, Evan."

Liam stood. "Don't leave. I'll give you a lift home."

"No," she replied quickly. "It isn't necessary. I'm here with my brothers."

"Tell them you're staying."

"No." She sounded almost desperate. "It's fine. I'll see you later."

"Ciara—" Liam reached for her arm.

"Please, Liam," she pleaded. "Don't cause any trouble."

"Why should there be trouble? I'll take you home. There's no harm in that."

Two thick, masculine figures separated themselves from the shadows and walked toward them. Liam recognized the McCarthy brothers, Anselom and Paddy, from the Crescent. He stood his ground.

Paddy's thick hand circled his sister's arm. "Didn't you hear me? I said we're goin' now."

She jerked her arm away. "I'm coming."

Liam straightened to his full height. "I'll drive Ciara home."

Anselom pointed a stubby finger at his chest. "Mind your own business. This is a family matter."

"She doesn't want to go," replied Liam. "I'll drive her home."

Evan slid off the bench and slipped his free hand inside Liam's. "I want to go home, Uncle Liam."

"Listen to the lad," said Anselom. "Take care of your own family and leave us to ours."

Liam's eyes narrowed.

"I'll be fine, Liam," Ciara said quickly. "I don't want any trouble. Take the boy home."

Evan pressed against Liam's legs. "Please." His voice was a whisper.

Torn between a contrary streak in his temperament, Ciara's obvious embarrassment and Evan's plea, he stepped back. Sanity told him to think of the child. More than likely Kate would never allow him out with her son again if he created a scene. He squeezed Evan's hand. "We'll go home now, lad, and show the whistle to your mom and Nan. Say goodbye to Ciara." He deliberately ignored the McCarthy men.

"Goodbye," said Evan obediently.

Ciara smiled. "Enjoy your whistle," she said before walking quickly across the square.

"Don't be sniffing around my sister," warned Anselom, "or we'll come after you."

Liam leaned in close to the thick-featured face. "Fuck you, McCarthy," he said, his voice no more than a whisper.

Anselom McCarthy's fists balled but Liam stood his ground.

Ciara, hands on her hips, called out from the entrance to the square. "Are you coming or not?"

Paddy stepped in front of his brother. "Leave it. The peelers will be pullin' you in, not him."

"We're not finished, Enright," Anselom growled.

Liam, still holding Evan's hand, walked back through the park toward his car. Absorbed in his own thoughts, he didn't feel the resistance pulling at his hand.

"You're walking too fast, Uncle Liam," Evan complained.

Immediately, Liam slowed down. "Sorry. Is this better?

Evan nodded. "I don't like those men."

"It's probably better that you don't."

"Do you like Ciara, Uncle Liam?"

Liam shrugged. "I thought I did. This isn't the best time to answer your question."

Again Evan nodded. "It's probably better that you don't."

He laughed. "I think it's time we found you an ice cream."

CHAPTER 31

Mickey

He'd nearly given up and decided to leave when she appeared at the door of the café with Maura Keane. Mildly annoyed that his conversation with her would be curtailed by the presence of her closest friend, yet realizing how absurd his feelings were, he smiled and gestured to the two nearest chairs. "Will you join me? Coffee is always better with company."

Without the slightest hesitation, Maura pulled the chair up to his small table and sat down. "How are you, Patrick, and where do you keep yourself all day? I don't see you about in town."

"I suppose we don't move in the same circles."

Maura's bright brown eyes probed. "That's a good one." She glanced up and accepted the coffee Johannah held out to her. "What circles do we move in, Hannie?"

"Sorry?"

"Mickey says we don't move in the same circles."

Johannah stared at her. "You called him Mickey."

Maura's brow wrinkled. "Did I?"

He nodded. "I heard it, too."

"I can't think why I would do such a thing."

"Never mind." Johannah handed her a napkin. "What were you saying?"

"I don't remember." Maura held her hand against her forehead. "Yes, I do. I wondered where Patrick kept himself all day. I never see him in town. Do you see him, Hannie?"

"All the time," replied Johannah. "I can't take more than a step without bumping into him. He's become a regular nuisance." She winked at Patrick.

He laughed. "What have you ladies been up to today?"

"Walking," replied Johannah, "in Ballyseedy Woods. We started from Ballyard and walked along the Killorglin Road."

"That's quite a hike and the road is narrow."

"Hannie knows that road like the back of her hand. She would walk that way with Mickey when she was young, as well as others." Maura lifted her eyebrows meaningfully.

He looked at Johannah, waiting for her to divert the conversation, but she didn't. There was nothing he could do but express interest. "Is that so?"

Johannah explained. "She's talking about a romance I had long ago with a man in town. I told you about him. It was over thirty years ago, before I married Mickey."

"It wouldn't have been if he hadn't left you at the altar," Maura added.

He frowned. "Surely not."

Johannah shook her head. "There was never an altar. It was over long before that."

Not so long before, he recalled.

Maura echoed his thoughts. "Not that long."

"That's enough, Maura." Johannah's tone was firm. "It's ancient history and no one is interested."

He watched Maura sip her coffee and wondered what her game was. Once again he changed the subject, addressing Johannah. "How's that grandson of yours?"

"Nearly another year older. We're having a party for him and it looks as if we're inviting the town. Consider yourself officially invited, Patrick."

Maura looked surprised. "You haven't invited me."

Johannah stared at her. "It goes without saying. You've been to every party I've ever given. Of course you're invited."

Mollified, Maura finished her coffee and stood. "I'm off. I have inventory to check in." She kissed Johannah's cheek. "Look after yourself, Hannie. Goodbye, Patrick."

Johannah waited until she'd gone. "I apologize. Sometimes she can be a bit much."

"She's always been quite a character."

Johannah frowned. "Excuse me?"

He rallied. "Is something wrong, Johannah? You look bothered."

Johannah rubbed out the crease between her eyebrows and smiled. "How do you always know how I'm feeling?"

For some reason, speaking became difficult. He swallowed. "I feel as if I've known you for a very long time."

Impulsively, she reached across the table and touched his hand. "You've become a very good friend, Patrick. I feel fortunate to have met you."

"So," he said, after an uncomfortable silence, "tell me what's wrong."

She sighed. "It's Kate. She's so unhappy. It breaks my heart."

"Has she ever been happy?"

Johannah shook her head. "I don't think so. I wouldn't say she's been depressed or miserable, but when I look back it seems as if she's never satisfied."

He could feel her thinking. "Do you feel guilty?"

"I suppose, and in so doing, I've reacted the wrong way. I've tried to make her smile even when it wasn't the best for our family. Kate's smiles, because they're so rare, come at a price. I start out with every intention of being firm, but she wears me down. I give in more than I should and now she's an adult who can't cope with disappointment." Her eyes were very bright. "Yes, I feel guilty. I certainly had a part in creating the person she's become. I'd hoped she would have sorted it out by now."

"What about her father?"

Johannah shrugged. "Mickey indulged her, too, but not in the same way. He left Kate to me." She looked down at her hands. "He preferred Liam. I suppose that's natural."

"Why would you think that?"

She flushed. "Don't all men prefer sons?"

"Not necessarily."

Abruptly she stood. "I must go. It was lovely talking to you, Patrick. Evan's birthday is next Saturday at one o'clock. Please come."

"I'll do that." With a thoughtful look on his face, he watched her leave the café.

Johannah

She turned right on Castle Street and left on Denny's Street, walked quickly past the Grand and Imperial Hotels and turned left into the town park toward the rose gardens. Roses soothed her. Ireland and summer roses, the two went hand in hand. The English boasted of their roses, but until one saw the lovely clustering array and variety of Irish roses, from butterscotch gold and deep purple to the purest white, one had not yet experienced the top tier of the species.

Finding her favorite wrought iron bench, beneath heavy trees, enough removed from the footpaths to be sheltered from view, Johannah sat down and considered her predicament. Why, after thirty years of disinterest, had the whole Francis O'Shea mess come up again? She hadn't far to go for the answer. It was Ritchie and the fever in his blood to be different, to want something more, to go against the flow. It was bred in him, that restlessness of spirit, the risk-taking, wild yearning that simmered and boiled and overflowed in half the population of Ireland, depositing them on distant shores in search of a way of life that made it impossible to ever return to the gray skies and green patchwork fields of their homeland.

It simmered in Kate, too. Why wouldn't it? She was part of it, a fey child, all eyes and limbs and air-light bones and streaming hair, always looking to the West, drawn to the sunlight, such as it was. When she'd left for America, Johannah hadn't expected her to return, except for visits. She welcomed the idea believing that Ritchie O'Shea would be banished from her daughter's mind forever. She wanted Kate to find someone wonderful in America, in that continent of dense population, that diversity of nationalities and gene pools, someone far removed from Ireland and Kerry and Tralee. But instead, Kate came home, settled in, married Dermot, produced Evan.

Foolishly, Johannah believed the wanderlust had left her, that she was content. Honesty forced her to examine her conscience. Had she really expected Kate with all her expectations and the rich potential of her mind to be happy living above a hardware store, filling in at the counter, working in the council offices? Dermot was a lovely man, but was worthiness strong enough to replace excitement? Could dependable, gentle Dermot Kelliher replace the charismatic excitement of Ritchie O'Shea? Kate said she was no longer infatuated. If that were true, the closely guarded secrets of Johannah's past could remain her own. If not.... She rubbed her arms. Lord, she missed Mickey. He would have laughed at her, just as he had years ago when the possibility of Kate and Ritchie had first risen. Once again she felt the burn in her chest that she recognized as anger. How dare he leave her alone like this, when there was so much of life to get through, before everything was sorted out?

CHAPTER 32

Liam

Johannah, busy at the cooker, looked up and smiled. "I'd almost given you up. Did you find the tin whistle?"

Evan held it up. "Ciara said I'm going to be very good, didn't she, Liam?"

Liam nodded. "She did."

His mother's eyebrows rose. "Ciara?"

"We met her in the square." Liam's reply was terse, a clear sign he wasn't interested in continuing the conversation.

Kate was pulling folded serviettes from the sideboard. "I hope you're hungry, Evan. Nan's making shepherd's pie."

"Not too hungry," replied Evan. "I ate—" he stopped, flushed, and looked at Liam.

"I bought him an ice cream," Liam confessed. "It was small enough and he deserved one." He rested his hand on his nephew's head. "We walked from the library into town and he never complained."

Evan beamed proudly. "Uncle Liam nearly had a row with Ciara's brothers."

"What?" Kate and Johannah spoke in unison.

Liam sighed. "Is there any hope of a cup of tea?"

"As soon as you explain yourself," replied his mother.

"It wouldn't have come to anything, not with Evan there."

Kate's cheeks were very pink. "I certainly hope not."

Silently, Liam found a mug in the cupboard, set it on the table and filled the kettle. "I told you, Evan was never in any danger. Anselom McCarthy and I had words. That's all."

"What words?" asked Johannah.

Liam gritted his teeth. His chest felt tight and the blood pounded in his temples. "It's my business. I know I'm dependent on your hospitality but I'm still an adult. I don't have to share everything."

"You most certainly do." Johannah's voice rose. "Especially when it concerns all of us."

"It doesn't."

"Evan," said Kate, "run upstairs and practice your whistle. When you're ready, I'll have a listen." Obediently, he left the room. Without speaking, she picked up the kettle, filled the teapot and added two bags of tea. "Are you all right, Liam?" she asked, her voice low and calm.

"I'm fine," he replied, and then changed his mind. "No, I'm not. I offered to take her home and she left with *them*." He spat out the pronoun. "Anselom and Paddy were itching for a row, making threats and she still refused my offer and went with them. *Don't cause any trouble,* she said. The trouble is with them. It's always that way with those people." He stopped, suddenly aware of his words. "I didn't mean that," he said quickly. "She's not like that."

"No," replied Johannah, "but they are. And they won't change. You know that, Liam. No one has to tell you."

Kate poured tea into the mug and handed it to him. "You never told me how you got on with Dermot."

"Not now, Kate."

"Ok. Whenever you're ready."

Her acquiescence shamed him. "I'm sorry. It's just that I'm not in the mood. We'll talk later."

"No problem. It'll wait."

Grateful for the reprieve, Liam escaped upstairs.

Betty's Pub didn't fill up until after ten. Liam unzipped his jacket, shook the rain from his hair and looked around. Ciara was deep in conversation with one of the regulars. She glanced his way and waved him over but he ignored her, choosing instead to greet Patrick who stood at the other end of the bar, an untouched pint in his hand. "Patrick, you look like you need company."

Patrick laughed. "How are you, Liam? Can I buy you a pint?"

"I wouldn't say no."

Patrick held up his forefinger. "I wouldn't have thought it."

Out of the corner of his eye, Liam saw Ciara reach for a glass. "Why not?" he asked.

"Yours isn't what I would call a drinking family," observed Patrick.

"You've never met my dad."

"No."

Ciara set the pint in front of him and left without speaking. "He was a drinker, I suppose, but then no more than anyone else." He frowned. "I never gave it much thought. No one has ever asked me that question before but now that I think about it, my Dad liked his drink. I never noticed it affecting him, but then work wasn't always steady. Maybe that's the reason." He paused briefly. "If ever there is a reason."

Patrick nodded.

"I don't remember it being an issue between my parents," Liam continued, his tongue unusually loose tonight. "My mother never mentioned it. She keeps things to herself which is why I can't properly answer your question." He grinned.

Again Patrick smiled. "It isn't a requirement." He nodded in Ciara's direction. "Now, tell me, did you have a falling out with that very attractive young publican?"

Liam's grin faded. He looked at Ciara and then looked away. "How did you know?"

"Neither of you has said a word to the other."

Liam shrugged. "I misjudged her, that's all. It doesn't matter."

"It doesn't matter and yet with all the pubs in town you just happened to wander into this one, did you?"

"I was hoping to find you."

Patrick looked surprised. "Really? Here, in Betty's Pub?"

"This is where I met you once before, after you came to dinner. I gave you a lift to Racecourse Road."

"I remember. How can I help you, Liam?"

"You probably have better things to do than listen to my troubles."

"Not at all. I have all the time in the world."

"It isn't something I want to advertise."

"I understand."

Liam lifted the pint to his lips, changed his mind and set it down. He stared into the dark, foamy liquid. "I may have made an error in judgment. I brought my nephew, Evan, to the square to buy a tin whistle. Ciara and her brothers were there."

"Ah, the McCarthy lads."

Diverted, Liam looked up. "Do you know them?"

"I do. Together, they're a force to be reckoned with. I wouldn't want to come upon them one dark night."

"I don't care about that," replied Liam. "They're blow-hards, more bark than bite."

"What's the problem, then?"

"Today, in the square, Ciara was very like them. I couldn't separate her from the two of them. They didn't want her around me. When I offered to take her home, she refused and left with them."

"I see."

"Do you? Because I don't. I thought I could care for her, but the idea of her going home to where they live is more than I can stomach. Why is that?"

"You've been brought up to believe they're not like the rest of us, a clan apart, so to speak, second class citizens. They're not accepted in most establishments because of their behavior and reputation. Ciara is climbing out of that. She's working and trying to educate herself but she's close to where she comes from, with a foot in both camps. Enough time hasn't passed for the likes of them and us to mix freely. They're still travelers. Until they settle into housing estates and give up the roaming, the stealing and brawling, the division remains."

Liam was silent for a long moment. "My mother said the same thing, in different words."

"It doesn't mean people can't cross over, lad."

Liam's laugh held little humor. "Family's important and life's hard enough. I can't see myself sharing a pint with Anselom and Paddy McCarthy and as far as Des McCarthy sharing Sunday dinner with Kate and my mother..." He shook his head. "It won't happen."

For the first time that night, Patrick tasted his pint, taking time to savor the yeasty flavor before setting it aside. "If that's so, I hope it hasn't gone far enough for either of you to be too disappointed."

"I am disappointed," Liam replied, "but I've made no promises."

Patrick's level gaze held a question for which words were unnecessary.

"I've done nothing I regret," Liam hurried to assure him. For some reason it was important that this man approve of him.

Patrick relaxed. "You're a good lad, Liam. Your father would be proud of you."

Liam laughed. "My father would have warned me to get out before it began."

"Don't be so sure. Ciara is a lovely girl and your dad sounds like a reasonable type."

Raised voices at the door interrupted Liam's reply. He turned to see Ciara and two burly men in the throes of a public disagreement. "Speak of the devil," Liam muttered.

Patrick turned around. "She looks like she's handling her own."

Liam nodded. "For now. If they have drink taken, she hasn't a chance."

"Will you involve yourself?"

Liam kept his eyes on Ciara and her brothers. "Only if I'm provoked, or if they lay a hand on her."

"Half the men in this room will be on them if they do."

"I'll be one of them."

Just then, Anselom McCathy spied Liam. Pointing him out, he shouted. "Your boyfriend's here, slut. Why not us?"

Liam stood.

"Shut your mouth, dirty tinker," a slurred voice called out from the shadows.

"Fuck you." Anselom tore off his jacket. "I'll kill you."

His brother laid a warning hand on his shoulder. Anselom shrugged it off.

"You and who else?" the anonymous voice answered.

Four men separated themselves from the bar and surrounded the McCarthys. "Go home, lad," one of them said. "No one will serve you here."

Ignoring the warning and unable to identify the source of the taunts, Anselom focused his rage on the man he recognized. "Come outside, Enright," he shouted. "I'll be waitin' for you."

Crossing the wide-planked wooden floor, Liam stood in front of his attacker. "I've no quarrel with you, Anselom," he said quietly, "and I won't fight you."

He strained at the arms that held him. "You're fuckin' my sister, you bastard."

"No, I'm not," replied Liam, "but if I was, it's Ciara's business and your father's, not yours. Go home and sleep off your drink."

Anselom sneered. "You're afraid of me, aren't you, pretty boy? You're afraid I'll mess up your face."

Liam grinned. "I'd be a fool if I wasn't. You're three stone heavier than me."

Anselom jerked his thumb in his brother's direction. "Paddy'll fight you."

"That might work, but I've no quarrel with Paddy either."

"I'm not fightin'," Paddy McCarthy interjected. "All I came for was a pint or two."

Furious, Anselom turned on his brother. "You won't be getting' that in here, either. Didn't you hear her?" He pointed at their sister. "She won't be servin' the likes of us. We're tinkers." He drew out the word. "She's forgettin' where she came from."

"I'm not forgetting anything." Ciara tapped a fearless finger against Anselom's chest. "I won't serve anyone who's drunk and making a nuisance of himself. You're spoiling for a fight and the drink is making you brave. Go home and mind yourself. Mam has enough troubles without bringing more down on her. You should be ashamed of yourself, Anselom McCarthy, embarrassing me in front of everyone."

Anselom ignored her. He challenged Liam. "I'm goin' but first I want you to say you won't fight me. I want everyone to hear it."

Liam nodded. Turning he faced the bar where the regulars hung on every word. "I refuse to fight Anselom McCarthy," he said, his voice carrying to the four corners. "You are witnesses." He turned back to Anselom. "Will that do it?"

"Aye. That'll do it." Anselom shrugged away from the now lax grip of the men holding him.

"One more thing." Liam lowered his voice so that only those immediately around could hear him. "Don't come here again bringing trouble on your sister, not unless you want her sacked. If that happens it'll be you who's responsible for bringing the groceries home to Mitchell's Crescent."

Anselom threw him one last look of loathing before disappearing out the door with Paddy, a silent shadow behind him.

Like the sun peeping from behind a dark cloud, the mood in the pub lifted and conversation resumed. Ciara smiled shyly. "Thanks, Liam."

"You were managing on your own until Anselom saw me. I did nothing."

"Yes, you did." She turned to resume her position behind the bar.

Liam spoke quickly, before his nerve deserted him. "What happened this afternoon?"

She turned back, ever direct, not misunderstanding his meaning. "Evan was with you. Sometimes, people have to put aside what they want in the interests of good judgment. Anselom isn't predictable. What if he'd provoked you? I didn't want the child to be frightened or, worse, watch you hurt. Who would have helped you? Who would have watched over Evan if you couldn't?" She sighed. "Tonight was different. You know everyone here. I really like you, Liam. I'm sorry if you misunderstood, but if it happened again, I'd do the same thing." She sighed. "I'm from the Crescent, Liam. Things are different for me than for you. I can't afford to be foolish for a principle. I'm working very hard to escape my roots but it takes everything I have. I won't let you disapprove of me."

He couldn't deny it. He had disapproved of her. "How do you live with them?"

"They aren't home much. Our paths rarely cross. I have to get back to work." She smiled. "I hope you'll ring, but if you don't, it won't damage me. I've been hurt before and no doubt will be again."

He watched her fill two pints, set them in front of her customers, return a teasing jibe, make change and wipe down the bar before he remembered he'd left Patrick in the middle of a conversation. Crossing the room, he apologized.

"Don't even think about it," replied Patrick. "I enjoyed the show." He pulled a twenty euro note from his wallet and handed it to Liam. "You're a fine young man, Liam Enright. I'll be on my way now. Your pint's on me. Take what's left and buy the lady a cup of coffee."

CHAPTER 33

Dolly

"Who are all these people anyway?" Dolly stood at the foot of the stairs, her hands on her hips, a frown on her face. "They're scaring Seamus. He won't come out from under the porch."

Johannah, balancing food-laden platters on both hands, stopped briefly on her way to the dining room. "It's Evan's birthday. We've invited people from town. Seamus will be fine. If he so much as bares his teeth at anyone, he'll spend the rest of the night in the tool shed."

"I don't like your tone, Johannah. It sounds as if you're threatening me."

"I'm threatening Seamus, not you." She disappeared around the corner. Dolly considered going after her, remembered all the people in the house and decided against it. Johannah never did like confrontations. Instead, she sat down on the stairs and rested her chin in her hand. It seemed as if she'd been here forever and she didn't like it. Who in the hell was Evan anyway?

A shadow appeared at the door, followed by a large, male body. "Hello. Is that you, Dolly?"

She breathed a sigh of relief. "It is. Come in, Mickey. I'm feeling very low just now."

He stepped inside. She noted the wrapped package in his hands. "I suppose you're here for Evan's birthday, whoever he is. There are strange people all over the house."

He sat down beside her. "He's your grandson. Why are you feeling low?"

She thought a minute. "I'm no longer necessary."

"How do you mean?"

"If I wasn't here, not a single thing would change." She frowned fiercely. "Don't you dare tell me it isn't true."

"I wouldn't dream of it." He shifted and stretched out his legs as if to stay a while. "I was thinking how liberating that could be."

"*Liberating*? To be unnecessary? How did you come up with that?"

"Think about it, Dolly. All your life you've been responsible to your children, your husband, your home. I can only imagine the pressure you were under." He smiled. "But now that's over. You can enjoy your life. Let other people be responsible. Let them cook and clean, plan parties and write thank you cards. You, on the other hand, have nothing to do but look lovely, smile graciously and do exactly as you please. If guests stay late, you can excuse yourself and go to bed. With any luck, everything will be cleaned up by the time you come down in the morning. As far as I'm concerned that's a pretty good trade for a lifetime of caring for others."

She stared at him. He'd always been a lovely man, but sometimes his head was a bit skewed. "There is satisfaction in doing for others, Mickey Enright."

"There is satisfaction to be found in all of life's stages, Dolly Little."

She wouldn't beat around the bush. "Even in yours?"

He nodded. "Even in mine."

"Will you be here long?"

"Not too much longer, I think. Something will happen soon. I'd thought to do more good, to make it easier on everyone. Instead I've learned patience as well as a bit of acceptance. In fact, now that I think of it, this whole endeavor was more than likely for my benefit, not the others."

"I have no idea what you're talking about."

"No. I suppose not."

Dolly reached over and touched his arm. "You've done more than you think. Johannah always was independent, but not particularly strong. She's strong now. Liam is a good boy. He's a quick one, Liam is. You don't have to say anything twice."

"What about Kate?"

"Kate is…searching. She might search her entire life. Some women do."

He sighed. "I worry about Kate. I'm not sure she realizes how much she has to lose."

"I always liked you, Mickey, but you've changed."

"Have I?"

"Aye. You've a kindness to you, a sort of softness I never saw before."

"Before?"

"You know, before you came back to us."

Patrick stared at her, amazed. "You're a remarkable woman, Dolly. You've the advantage. But will you keep this talk to yourself? I've made a promise, you see."

"Who would believe me?"

"That could be an advantage."

"If you say so." She bit her lip. "When you go, Mickey, I'd like to come with you."

He nodded. "I wish it were possible, Dolly. I really do, but the decision isn't yours, or mine, to make." He stood and held out his hand. "Shall we join the others?"

She shook her head. "You go ahead. I'm manning the door. You can expect a few surprises today. Hannie has invited half the town and Kate the other half. It should be interesting."

"If you're sure. I don't like to leave you here."

She waved him away. "Come back if it suits you. I'll be here."

Dolly watched him disappear through the door to join the party. It was a shame, really, that he'd been taken so early. She'd liked Mickey Enright from the beginning, liked him more than that first young man Hannie brought home. There was something about Francis

O'Shea and that family of his that didn't ring true. Dolly had no proof but she'd always believed he hadn't done right by Johannah. Luck was with them all when she called off their engagement and married Mickey. The whole thing had happened so quickly, too quickly for respectability as far as Dolly as concerned, but she would have given more than a little respectability to be rid of Francis O'Shea. There were a few tense moments when Kate seemed caught up in the O'Shea drama with that handsome son who emigrated to America, but then she married Dermot. There was nothing wrong with Dermot Kelliher and a great deal to appreciate, even if he did have that stuffy mother. Speaking of parents, she probably should make an effort to socialize and help Johannah.

She pulled herself to her feet and was nearly into the other room when she heard the bell ring. No one ever rang the bell. People knocked, announced themselves and walked right in. It was customary in Tralee to welcome neighbors, to leave doors unlocked or, at best, to attach a house key to a string and leave it dangle through the post drop so guests could wait in comfort inside. Keys were never lost that way. The system worked quite well except when the occasional traveler caravan showed up in the town. Entire households attending weddings and funerals had been wiped clean by tinkers who read the news.

Dolly looked through the glass. This man was definitely not a tinker. She opened the door and waited.

"Hello," he said.

"Hello," she replied. "If you're comin' in, mind the mud. The floors are just washed."

Carefully, he scraped the mud from his shoes. "I'm sorry to disturb you, but I have a bit of a problem. I've hit a cow crossing the road. It came out of nowhere. I wonder if I might use your phone?"

Dolly's eyebrows lifted. "A cow did you say?"

"I did."

"Was it a cow or a bull?"

He looked nonplussed. "I'm not sure."

"Where did you hit this cow?"

"Sorry?"

"Did you hit the cow in the head?"

"No." He looked confused for a moment. "At least I don't think I did. Why do you ask?"

"If you hit the cow in the head and he lost his teeth, you might be liable, you see, because the cow wouldn't be able to eat."

Realization dawned. "Is that so?"

She saw the twinkle in his eye. He wasn't slow.

"I'm sure my insurance will take care of the cow."

She persisted. "What kind of coverage would you have?"

"I really need to use your phone."

Dolly crossed her arms. "What business do you have here in Tralee?"

He held out his hand. "My name is Jack
Rafferty. I'm here to see Johannah Enright.
Would you know her?"

Dolly ignored the gesture. She didn't trust
men in expensive suits and posh accents. "What
do you want with her?"

For a fraction of a second he hesitated before
answering. "We met in Dublin. She told me to
stop in when I came to Tralee."

"This is Johannah's house. We're having a
birthday party. Can you come back tomorrow?"

"Yes," he said after a slight hesitation. "I'll
do that. Will you tell her I stopped in?"

Just then Johannah opened the kitchen door.
Her initial look of surprise turned to pleasure.
"Jack, how are you? I see you've met my
mother." Gently, she nudged Dolly aside.
"Please come in. My grandson is having a
birthday party. I hope you'll join us."

"I don't want to impose but I really need a
phone. My mobile is dead. I didn't realize this
was your house. I've hit a cow, you see."

She laughed. "You can't be serious."

"I'm afraid I am."

"Then you'd better come in. The phone is in
the hall. You can call your insurance company
from there. When you've sorted things out,
you're very welcome to join us." She squeezed
her mother's shoulder. "Isn't he, Mom?"

Dolly sniffed. "Whatever you say, Johannah.
T'is your house after all."

Johannah

Johannah was surprised at the shock of pleasure she felt at Jack Rafferty's unexpected appearance. Leading him into the sitting room after his phone call, she looked around for the most likely person to introduce him to, someone intelligent and worldly, someone interesting who would talk about more than the weather forecast or a pig let loose in the cow pasture. As far away from her in-laws as possible, Kate stood near the door talking with Patrick. Of course, Kate and Patrick. Perfect.

"Let me introduce you to my daughter." She hooked her arm through Jack's and made her way through the crowd to the other side of the room. "Katie, Patrick, this is Jack Rafferty, a friend I met in Dublin when I was there recently. He's with the union," she explained hurriedly, anxious that Kate wouldn't assume what wasn't there.

Patrick held out his hand. "How are you, Jack? Staying long in Tralee?"

"Not too long, a few weeks at the most. I'm here to mediate between civil servants and management. Hopefully we can avoid a strike."

Kate smiled. "You don't sound like you're from Dublin, Mr. Rafferty."

Jack Rafferty smiled. "I'm originally from Belfast, but now my base is in London, such as it is. I'm not there all that much."

"Are you an instigator?"

"Kate!" Johannah's eyebrows rose.

This time he laughed, the small lines around his eyes deepening, making him, Johannah thought, even more attractive. "I try to sort out a situation, not enflame it."

"Is there a future in that?" asked Kate.

"Definitely." He regarded her speculatively. "I'd say you're a bit of an instigator yourself, Kate."

She looked surprised. "How do you mean?"

"You say what's on your mind."

Patrick chuckled. "That's our Kate."

"It certainly is," agreed Johannah.

Rafferty turned his level blue gaze on Patrick. "Have you known the family long?"

"Not really, although it seems so. Can I bring you a drink, Jack?"

"I'll have a mineral, an orange bitter, if you have it."

"So, Kate," Jack continued after Patrick left the group, "your mother tells me you were educated in the States."

"Yes, although it hasn't done me much good here. I'm thinking of relocating to Dublin or, possibly, London."

"But not the U.S."

"No. I don't think I'd go back to America, but one never knows. I suppose they need dieticians everywhere."

"They do, even here in Tralee."

"Those positions are long taken," Kate explained. "A hospital might have one or two. Believe me, I've tried."

He nodded. "I suppose people must do whatever is necessary to find work."

Patrick returned with an orange squash. Jack thanked him and redirected his attention. "What brought you to Tralee, Patrick?"

"Retirement and the weather."

Jack's eyebrows rose. "The weather? In Ireland?"

"Aye. The air is warmer here."

"Where is your home?"

"In the Northwest."

"A Connemara man. I know it well."

"How's that?"

"My mother's family is from Inishmore. I have family on the island. Do you know the Horans of Kilronen?"

"I've never been to the islands."

Once again Jack Rafferty raised his silver eyebrows. "But you've kept up with your Irish."

"Of course." Patrick appeared distracted. Then he smiled. "I must say hello to Liam. A pleasure meeting you, Jack. I hope to see you again."

Jack Rafferty lifted his glass. "I'll make a point of it."

Johannah stared after Patrick's retreating figure. She considered him a close friend, she'd confided personal details of her family life, had coffee with him at least twice a week and yet she knew very little about him. Never once in all the months she'd known him had she considered asking any of the questions Jack had asked him in less than ten minutes. Their relationship was based completely on her, her emotions, her family, her difficulties. Suddenly, Johannah was ashamed.

CHAPTER 34

Johannah

Maura found her in the kitchen positioning four candles in the center of Evan's birthday cake. "Who is that gorgeous man with your daughter?"

"I thought you knew. It's Jack Rafferty."

"My God, Hannie, that's the man who asked you to have dinner with him in Dublin?"

"Himself, in the flesh."

Maura's mouth dropped. "What's the matter with you? He's terribly good looking."

Johannah stepped back to survey her handiwork. "Yes, he is. What do you think of the candles, Maura? Are they too close together?"

"Are you daft? Piss on the candles, Hannie. Who cares about candles? That man is a keeper. If it wasn't for Milo I'd fight you for him. I might even do that anyway."

Johannah poured two cups of tea, added milk and handed one to Maura. "Calm down, Maura. Jack Rafferty is a very likeable man. He's a good-looking man and an intelligent man. But we have no idea if he's a keeper. Milo is a keeper. Mickey was a keeper. Patrick is a keeper."

Maura set down her cup of tea, found a goblet and poured herself a healthy glass of wine. "You're insane, Hannie Enright. You can't compare Patrick to that man. Next you'll be telling me you and Patrick will be posting the banns."

"No, I won't. Patrick is a dear man and a wonderful friend, much more so to me than I am to him. But that's all. There will be no posting of the banns. As for Jack Rafferty, I barely know him. I admit," she continued earnestly, "it's flattering for a man like that to show up at my door and have everyone sit up and take notice that it's Hannie Enright who's pulled in a big one, but if I let myself go beyond that, and I do because I'm a reasonable woman, I realize he's just passing time. He knows nothing about me. He lied about not knowing this was my house. No one turns up this street by accident, halfway up the hill into Ballyard and manages to stumble on the right house. I don't like that. Why not just say he was looking for me?"

"Give him a chance, Hannie. He's here. He's interested. Do you want to spend your life alone?"

"No. But I don't want to be dazzled by someone I can't talk to after the introductions are over. It's Kate we should be pushing on him. She's the one who wants to live in London, see the world, acquire wealth."

"Speak for yourself. I wouldn't mind acquiring a little wealth myself, just enough so that the bank account is never empty. Still, the Kate idea isn't bad. May-December romances work out so long as both parties know what they want. Unfortunately, I don't think it's Kate he came across the country to visit."

"Poor Dermot. We're disregarding him like he was yesterday's cabbage."

"Don't be concerned about Dermot Kelliher. He'll be fine. There's more than one smart young woman in Tralee who's willing to wait for Maired to meet her maker, God forgive me."

"What an awful thing to say."

"I blessed myself. Didn't you hear me? Don't pretend to be shocked, Hannie. You know yourself if it wasn't for Maired, those two young people might have had a chance." She opened the door to peek out at the guests. "Isn't it the oddest thing that children's birthday parties turn into entertainment for the nosies? Kate's still talking to Mr. Rafferty. She's laughing. He's actually made her laugh. Could be you're on to something, Hannie. The only other time I've seen Katie enjoy herself is with Ritchie O'Shea."

"Let's hope he doesn't show up," Johannah muttered. She picked up the cake. "Bring the matches and the ice cream. Tell Kate to find Evan and the rest of the children. We'll get this over as soon as possible."

"You do throw the best parties, Hannie."

"You're not helping me, Maura Keane. I need them for the cake cutting. Then we can open gifts and send everyone away."

"You're kidding yourself. Short of throwing them out on the street, you'll get rid of no one until nightfall, and not even then if you're serving spirits."

"Those with children will go home."

"They aren't the ones worrying you."

"Open the door. I'm coming through." Johannah carried the cake into the sitting room. "Everyone gather in the garden," she called out. "We're cutting the cake."

Patrick materialized and held open the door. "You look anxious."

"I am, a bit." She spoke through her teeth. "Kate and Maired Kelliher aren't speaking. I suppose I can't blame Maired. After all, Kate's the one who left."

He took the cake from her arms and carried it to the picnic table. "It isn't your responsibility, Hannie. This is Kate's doing. She's the one who'll handle the fall out. Try not to think about it and enjoy yourself for Evan's sake. He's a grand wee lad and he deserves a happy grandmother."

For a long moment, Johannah caught up in her personal embarrassment, grappled to understand the content of his words. When she did, a sense of calm rose in her chest. She looked at Patrick, relief and affection in her eyes. "You're very good. Thank you, Patrick. I bless the day I met you."

From across the yard, Evan caught sight of his cake and ran to her. "Nan, Nan, is it time for my candles?"

She stooped to kiss his nose. "It is, my love."

"Then can we have the egg race?"

"We'll use potatoes instead."

"Can Owen help me blow them out?"

Johannah mentally about-faced. Candles. He was back with the candles again. Over the child's head, her eyes met Patrick's. "Today you may have anything you want. It's your birthday."

Later, when all but the last few remaining guests had left, Jack Rafferty found her in the kitchen, scraping potato salad into the garbage. "I always wondered why Insinkerators never took hold Ireland."

She looked up at him. "Where have they taken hold other than America?"

He shrugged. "Canada, maybe."

"Canada doesn't count. Canadians are Americans, too."

"I suppose they are, although they don't like to admit it."

Johannah smiled. "Have you been everywhere, Jack?"

"No, not even close. My dream is to settle down in one place and never use a map again."

"Really? That wasn't my impression the last time we talked." She filled the sink with water. "You did a fine job of managing the hoards."

"Everyone was friendly."

She corrected him. "Everyone was curious."

"Who was the man with the wool cap who went on about losing his pension?"

Johannah sighed. "He's Robbie Kelliher, my son-in-law's uncle. We have to invite him, you see. He's Evan's family."

"I don't understand. Why wouldn't you invite him?"

Johannah handed him a dishtowel. "Make yourself useful." She watched approvingly as he picked up a plate and began wiping the surface. "He robbed the post office," she explained. "The government doesn't look kindly on civil servants who help themselves to the till. He was turned off and his pension revoked. It's an embarrassment for him, but more so for his family, I think, because he brings it up every time he drinks."

Rafferty whistled. "I don't think I'll ever forget this day."

"I'm sure you won't."

He regarded her curiously. "What about you? Does he embarrass you?"

She rinsed the last dish, picked up a towel and began to dry the pots and pans. "Not a bit. He's nothing to do with me."

He changed the subject. "Your mother is a character."

"My mother has Alzheimer's. She's not herself."

He frowned. "I never would have known. I'm sorry."

Johannah smiled. "No, I'm sorry. The subject is a sore one. You see, my mother is an intelligent woman, which make it worse. Unless you know her, you wouldn't think she's ill at all. It makes things difficult. People allow for illness. They don't allow for eccentricity, not even here in the backwoods of Ireland."

"Is that what you think this is, the backwoods?"

"It certainly isn't Dublin."

"We've only five cities in the entire country. That puts all of Ireland in the backwoods category."

"Point taken." She hung the damp towel over the back of a chair. "Tell me why you're here, Jack."

"You have an employment crisis here in Tralee, Johannah. A civil servants' strike is a serious matter. I'm here to negotiate terms between your union and management."

She looked at him, at the quality clothing, the expensive haircut, the hands that had lost all evidence of manual labor. "That's your official version, but that isn't what I meant. Why are you here, at my house?"

"Ah." The blue eyes lit with laughter. "You do get to the point, don't you?"

"I don't have time to waste. Are you interested in me, I mean beyond friendship?"

"Yes."

Blood rose in her cheeks. "I don't think I'm the one for you."

"Why not?"

"That should be obvious. Look around you. There's no place for the likes of you here, and I'm not going anywhere else. I don't *want* to go anywhere else."

"You have a lovely home, charming, intelligent children and a professional occupation. I don't know what you mean by obvious."

She shook her head.

He folded the towel and set it on the counter. "Look. I'm going to be here for a few weeks. Can we take it slowly and see how things go? That's all I'm asking."

"Tralee is a small town."

"Are you afraid of the gossips?"

"Certainly not," she replied firmly.

"Well?"

"I suppose it can't hurt. A few weeks should make everything quite clear."

"Done." He held out his hand.

She took it. "This isn't a contract, you know."

He laughed. "For a minute there, it felt like one. I'll be leaving before you change your mind."

Maura poked her head in the door. "Do you need help, Hannie?"

"As a matter of fact I do. Would you mind seeing Jack to the door? He's had a long day."

Maura's eyes brightened. "Not at all. Come along, Jack. Between here and the door, I'll tell you everything you need to know about Tralee."

"Leave me out of it, Maura," Johannah warned.

She winked. "My lips are sealed."

CHAPTER 35

Kate

Dermot looked around curiously. "I've never been here before. It's been open about three years, has it?" He pronounced the three without the *h*, *tree, tree years*.

It grated on her nerves. All the *dese, dem* and *dis*, instead of these, them and this, all the *Katerines* and *Katleens*. Where had they learned to speak English? Didn't they watch American television, listen to American music? "At least three years," she replied, curving her tongue, placing it between her teeth, emphasizing the *th* sound. "Parking is easy here at Manor, the coffee is good and it isn't a pub."

"It's not much for food, is it?"

"No. People come for snacks and coffee drinks."

"*Gloria Jeans*. The name is odd. Where does it come from?"

Kate shifted impatiently. "I believe it's a chain."

"An American chain?"

"Yes."

"I see." Dermot looked down at this coffee. "Why are we here, Kate?"

She drew a deep breath and dove in. "I'm interviewing for a position as a dietician in a Dublin clinic. If I get it, I'll be using my degree. I wanted to tell you because it means I'll be moving away. If I don't get this job, I'll look for another, somewhere else, somewhere away from Tralee. I wanted to know your feelings about sharing custody."

He stared at her, his eyes glazed with shock. "You're really serious," he said at last.

"I am."

"What does your mother say about your plans?"

"I haven't told her. I wanted you to be the first to know."

"Have you thought of Evan?"

"How do you mean?"

"He'll be away from his family, his friends, everything familiar."

"He's five years old, Dermot. He'll adjust. It will mean opportunity for him as well. Dublin is a city with history and culture, good schools, interesting people."

"Is Ritchie O'Shea going with you?"

Kate stared at him. "Not you, too, Dermot. I can't believe you asked that question."

"Is he? Spell it out, Kate. Yes or no."

"No. There is nothing between Ritchie and me beyond an old friendship. If I don't get this job, I'll look elsewhere, in Cork, Limerick, even London."

"America?"

"No. As much as I'd like to, I won't go there. It's too far away. I want you to see Evan regularly."

"Have you given up on opening your own business, the special diets' idea?"

"Sorry?" She looked genuinely baffled.

He sighed and rubbed his forehead. "I suppose Liam got it wrong. All right, then. You've told me. Aren't you putting the cart before the horse? You might not get this one."

"Thanks for the vote of confidence. Whether I do or not, I wanted to prepare you. Even if this position doesn't come through, I'll get something, Dermot. I want to use my knowledge. I want my mind to be challenged. I don't want to work behind the counter of a hardware store or behind a desk at the council office. I want Evan to see me reach my potential. I want to teach him to follow his dreams, not to settle into a job because it makes sense for his family."

Bitterness colored his words. "You're talking about me."

"It's a way of life around here. You're not alone. It's the way we live. Leave school, get a job, any job to survive until retirement, collect your pension, sit back and be grateful you don't have to work anymore."

His face was flushed. He stood. "I don't want to argue with you, Katie. Consider your message delivered. When you secure a position somewhere, we'll talk about a schedule for Evan. I have to go back to work, mundane as it is."

"Dermot—"

He held up his hand. "You've said enough."

She watched him walk out of the shop and cross the street. Stirring her coffee, she waited, resigned, for the familiar guilt to wash over her. One minute ticked by and then another. She felt sorrow and regret and a fresh, clean feeling she remembered from her college days, a feeling of progress. Then she frowned. What had Dermot meant about starting her own business? She must ask Liam."

A movement distracted her. She heard a familiar voice. "Kate. Are you waiting on anyone?"

She looked up and smiled. "Patrick. How nice to see you. I was meeting Dermot, but he's gone home. Would you care to join me?"

"I'd like that. Can I get you anything? Another coffee or a scone?"

"Actually I'm having a latte. I'd love another."

"Like your mother. I'll be back in a flash."

I'll be back in a flash. He sounded just like her father. In fact, he reminded her of Mickey. Not that he looked anything like him, but the mannerisms and the way he phrased his speech. Nan called him Mickey, but then how dependable was she?

Carrying two lattes, he set them on the table and pulled up a chair. "How are things?"

Her eyes sparkled. "Quite well, actually. I have an interview in Dublin at a clinic. They need a dietician. I've never used my degree, but they're willing to start someone in an entry level position."

"That's quite a bit of news, Kate. What does your mother say?"

Kate flushed. "I haven't told her yet. The truth is, I'm afraid."

"Of your mother?" He looked astonished.

"It was always easier to talk with my dad," admitted Kate.

"You must miss him."

"Every day." Her eyes were very bright.

"You're not giving your mother credit."

She frowned. "Sorry?"

"Your mother will be pleased that you've taken this initiative. Any mother would be proud of you, but your mother has gone to great lengths to give you an education. She would want you to use it, if that's what you really want. Dublin is a four hour train ride. You can come home every weekend if you like. She knows that."

"She'll miss Evan."

"She'll miss you even more, but look at you, cheeks rosy, eyes bright, a smile on your lips. She'll be thrilled and proud that you're following your dream, even though it will be a period of adjustment for all of you."

"How do you mean?"

"You'll have to find someone to care for Evan when he's not in school and you're working."

Kate bit her lip. "He's never been around strangers, not without one of his family nearby.

He loves the crèche, but he didn't in the beginning."

"You're accustomed to having your mother nearby as well. I know you went to America when you were in school, but you didn't have a small child. It's difficult without friends and family. But, you're a smart girl. I'm sure everything will be fine…eventually, as long as you're following your dream."

"It's funny you should say that. Those are the exact words I used with Dermot, following my dream." She laughed. "Actually, you've been an inspiration."

"Me?" He looked skeptical. "How?"

"You're not a young man and yet you've come to Tralee, a stranger, and started again, spoken to strangers, made friends, taken chances. I think you're very brave."

"Do you?"

"Yes. You remind me of my father."

"Really?"

Kate nodded. "Mostly it's because you're easy to talk with. Ask anyone. Mickey Enright was a great one for conversation."

"What would he say about moving to Dublin?"

She hesitated. "I don't know. My dad wasn't one for moving around. He liked our family to stay together. He didn't want me to marry Dermot but once I did, he embraced him as one of the family. I think he'd approve if he knew how unhappy I am here. Even the Kerry accent makes me want to explode."

"But you lived in America. Did that bother you?"

"No. Why should it?"

"They speak a different kind of English over there in America?"

She shrugged defensively. "In a manner of speaking."

"What about your dad? Did he have a Kerry accent?"

Kate looked at him, finally realizing where his questions were leading. "Yes, he did. What are you trying to say, Patrick?"

"Nothing very profound. Sometimes the things that bother us are due to a state of mind. This is your home and it isn't all bad. You'll want to come back for Evan's sake and your own. You both have roots here. Someday, you'll have reason to appreciate them."

He finished his coffee and stood. "I'll be off now."

She caught up with him at the door. "I'll walk you to your car."

"Thanks very much, but I walked."

"Then I'll give you a lift, wherever you're going."

"Actually, I was on my way home and I need the exercise. It isn't that I don't appreciate the offer."

"If you're sure."

"Completely. Say hello to your mother for me."

"Patrick?"

"Yes."

She hung back, suddenly self-conscious. He was a comforting man, solid, level and kind.

"What is it, Kate?"

"I don't know. I'm not sure. It's just that I have the oddest feeling."

He waited.

"I will see you again, won't I?"

He smiled. "That you can be sure of."

CHAPTER 36

Johannah

Jack Rafferty turned the key in the ignition and allowed the car to idle in the circular gravel driveway leading to Johannah's front porch. "I'm mystified. You said to wear something very casual and to eat first. Where are we going?"

Johannah glanced at his navy cashmere sweater and creased wool trousers, then at her own denims and sweatshirt. "I had something else in mind when I said casual."

"Am I overdressed?

"Never mind. Have you heard of the Sean McCarthy ballad competition?"

"I have. He was a songwriter from Listowel, wasn't he?"

"Actually, he's from a small village near Listowel called Finuge. Quite a few writers have come out of Listowel because of Bryan MacMahon."

"Ah, the Master."

"You've heard of him?" She looked surprised.

"We're not totally devoid of Irish culture in Belfast, Johannah."

"Really?"

He looked amused. "Really."

"Do you speak Irish?"

"No. Do you?"

"I do. I work for the government. All of us are proficient in Irish. It's a requirement. Do you play an instrument, step dance, sing? Do you have a party piece?"

"No to all of the above. Do you?"

"Of course. What about Irish history? Do they teach you Irish history in Belfast schools?"

"No, again."

"Well then." A small satisfied smile played at the corners of her mouth. "You have a lot to learn." She pointed to the sign at the roundabout. "Turn here. We'll take Racecourse Road and avoid the town."

"I do know Bryan MacMahon, John B. Keane and Sean McCarthy. Don't forget, we have Seamus Heaney."

"Yes, you do."

"He pales beside your Yeats and Wilde."

"They were Protestants. I don't count them."

"They were sympathetic to the cause for Irish freedom."

"They didn't write about the Irish experience. I don't blame them. They couldn't."

He smiled. "There's a lesson in this somewhere. I'm trying to figure out what it is."

"Not at all. I wouldn't presume such a thing."

"Are you always this opinionated?"

"Heavens, no. I spent most of my life stifling my opinions. I don't intend to any longer, however, so beware."

"Warning taken." He looked out the window at the patchwork beauty of the tilled fields, cows stretched out in sated contentment, sheep knee deep in grass, and gilt-edged clouds settling over the mountains. "This is beautiful country, heaven on earth."

"It is," Johannah agreed. "Kerry is one of the *do not miss* stops for tourists. I've lived here all my life and I still appreciate our scenery. We're nearly there. Pull up onto the footpath behind the other cars. It's only a short walk." She nodded at his tasseled loafers. "I hope your shoes survive the journey. This is sheep country."

She led him to a whitewashed structure with a thatched roof. A round, full-faced woman with a great deal of missing teeth stood at the door. "That'll be ten euro each," she said.

Jack reached into his pocket but Johannah stopped him, pulled out her own wallet and a twenty euro note. "I invited you."

The room was set up with folding chairs in rows and risers to the side, all facing a make-shift stage. A single light bulb hung suspended from the ceiling. People, well-dressed and otherwise, sat in small groups chatting companionably. Johannah chose a seat close to the door. "In case we have to make a quick escape," she whispered.

"Have faith," Jack replied and took his seat.

Soon, a large man with a mop of white hair wearing a sport coat with frayed sleeves stood, a signal that the entertainment would begin. Johannah opened her program. Fourteen ballads and their artists were in competition with each other for the thousand dollar prize. "These are all originals," she said in a low voice. "Are you prepared?"

"More than that. I'm intrigued."

She smiled. "Right answer. Try to remember your questions and, if I can, I'll answer them when it's over."

For two hours, men and a few women from Galway to Wexford, Dublin to Tralee, sang and played their tunes for three judges who listened, rubbed their chins and wrote not a single note. In the end, Pete Gilroy, who sang of the changes in Galway took the prize.

"Lovely music," Jack remarked when they were in the car on the way back to Tralee.

"A bit rough," replied Johannah, "but sincere."

"What's Jimmy Dennihan's connection?"

"He's from the area. Do you know him?"

"I follow football to a small extent. But I also know him professionally. I had no idea he was a music lover."

"It's more a matter of preservation of the arts," explained Johannah. "Ireland is suffering from a loss of population and reduced social contact. Small businesses are dying and the Internet has taken the place of gathering at the local shop and pub. Not that we have a lack of pubs, but a festival is a good way of keeping people together. Tralee is an exception. We're a town, not a village, and filled with European Union expatriots. Few of us know everyone anymore. I suppose it's the price of progress. Did you enjoy the evening?"

"I did. Does that surprise you?"

She nodded. "A bit."

"Why is that?"

She hesitated. "I really don't know how to say this."

He waited, expertly maneuvering the narrow country roads.

"You seem very worldly, very sophisticated. I wanted to show you how I live, where I live. These are my roots."

The high beams of a car in the distance blinded her for an instant before the driver flicked them off.

Jack glanced at her and then turned his attention back to the road. "Where do you imagine I come from, Johannah?"

"How do you mean?"

"I was born in 1957 into a Catholic family in West Belfast, the seventh child in a family of ten. We lived in the Divas Flats on the Ormeau Road. Before that we lived in a row house where the toilet was outside in the yard and nine families shared the one. I grew up with violence all around, the RUC and British Army on one side and the IRA on the other. It was expected that once we came of age we would join. The riots, the marches, the checkpoints and the burnings saw to it that we would."

"Did you?"

"No. I bolted. I took the ferry to London and never looked back. What you see before you is a man who reinvented himself through manual labor, schooling and falling into the right company at the right time. So, you see, I may be bereft of Irish culture as far as language and music, but I know my history and I've paid a price. My parents are dead and the rest of my family doesn't speak to me."

She waited a long minute before answering. "I'm sorry," she said at last. "I had no idea."

He pulled into her driveway. "You've a lovely home here. You've done well for yourself."

"The house belonged to Mickey's parents. It came to him without a mortgage, and then to me when he died. Neither of us really earned it."

"But you're maintaining it."

"Yes."

"I had a lovely evening." He leaned over and kissed her cheek. "Good night, Johannah."

"Would you care for a cup of tea before you go?"

He hesitated and then grinned. "Thanks. The invitation is tempting, but I've an early day tomorrow and a report still to go over tonight."

"Another time, perhaps?"

"I look forward to it."

He waited until she was inside the house before driving away. Without turning on the light, she watched from the window until his tail lights disappeared beyond the bend. Jack Rafferty was not what she'd expected. There was more to him than she'd imagined. She'd wanted him to come inside for a cup of tea. In fact, if she was completely honest with herself, she'd wanted quite a bit more. Quite rapidly, he was stripping away her defenses and it scared her.

CHAPTER 37

Kate

Kate fastened the middle button of her jacket and turned to the side evaluating, in the ladies' mirror, whether she should go for the more professional silhouette or stick with the casual. She'd pulled her hair back and twisted it into a low knot at the back of her neck, fastening it with a clip from her bag. Her white blouse under the navy jacket was pressed and crisp and her gray skirt was both flattering and practical. Professional, she decided, was more appropriate. She would keep the jacket buttoned. The heels were nice, too. It never hurt to dress up and the black pumps added just enough height. She breathed deeply, smiled at her reflection in the mirror and exited the room in search of a lift.

The woman at the desk smiled warmly and picked up the phone. "Welcome, Mrs. Kelliher. Don't bother sitting down. I'll tell Mr. Cleary you're here. He'll see you immediately."

Less than a minute later, she was seated across from the hospital administrator she'd spoken with on the phone. "Thank you for making the journey, Mrs. Kelliher," he said. " Did you fly or take the train?"

"I flew Ryan Air from Farranfore. It's less than a forty minute flight. I'll do a bit of shopping and return later today."

He came right to the point. "I've looked over your application. Your marks are impressive, as are your recommendations."

"Thank you."

"May I ask why you waited so long to seek employment?"

Kate's heart pounded. She smoothed her skirt. "I married shortly after coming home and had a child. My husband and I worked together in his family's business. I never planned on that becoming a permanent condition. I always wanted to use my education and now that my son is of school age, it's possible."

"We don't get many applicants from Tralee. You understand that the position is in Dublin."

"Yes."

"Is your husband willing to relocate?"

"We're separated."

"I see."

Kate leaned forward. "Half of Ireland is separated, Mr. Cleary. I have an education. I'm qualified for this position. I must work to support myself and my son. I would much rather be gainfully employed than on the dole. From the description on your website, you have a problem. You need my services."

James Cleary formed a pyramid with his hands and rocked back and forth in his chair, something he did when he was thinking deeply. Finally he spoke. "We're a senior center. The difficulty is transitioning elderly patients into healthy meals after they've eaten white bread, black pudding and sausages for seventy years. Most think it's absurd to consider such a change given our residents' advanced ages, but heart attack is a painful death and even when it can be avoided the surgeries are more uncomfortable as well as expensive. Do you have any ideas, Mrs. Kelliher?"

She scooted the chair closer to his desk. "The caloric requirements for the elderly are quite low. The key is small portions and presentation. Egg-white omelets with low-fat cheese, tomatoes and mushrooms are appealing as well as beans, turkey sausage in small amounts, a variety of vegetables, fish, sauces made with low sodium broth, herbs and fat-free yogurt. Chicken can be prepared so that it's delicious, served with brown rice and boiled potatoes. There are endless substitutes for salad crème, eggs and cooking oil." She ticked them off on her fingers. "Frozen yogurt, sorbets and ice cream can replace pastries. Bread and milk are difficult but I've found that if the transition is gradual, the change can be made. That leaves room for a treat now and then, birthday cake or a scone with jam. Seniors have difficulty with too many vegetables and dairy. That must be taken into account as well."

"You've kept up, despite the lapse in your work history."

"Changes are always being made. I'm interested in food as well as health. There is a dramatic link between protein and cancer. I don't expect seventy-year-olds to give up meat, but there are ways to make attractive, tasty meals without an excess of protein."

"It would help our budget as well.""Yes, that, too."

He reached across the table to shake her hand. "You've made a very favorable impression, Mrs. Kelliher. I'm convinced. However, I must go over your qualifications with our board of directors. I'll be contacting you either way within the week."

She stood. "Thank you, Mr. Cleary. I look forward to hearing from you and hope the news is positive."

Kate bubbled with excitement. Standing in line at the Ryan Air gate and filled with new purpose, she desperately wanted to confide in someone. Pulling out her mobile, she scrolled through her contact list until her mother's number appeared in the window. Then she hesitated. Johannah would pretend to be pleased but her heart wouldn't be in it. She was against the split with Dermot and would miss Evan terribly. There was no point in upsetting her until Mr. Cleary confirmed that Kate had the job.

The line was moving. Slipping her mobile back into her bag, she handed her boarding pass to the attendant and walked across the tarmac to the plane, considering her options. Liam felt as Johannah did. She wouldn't call Liam. Nor would she call any of her friends. The girlfriends of her school days had become casual acquaintances after marriage and motherhood and wouldn't be more than mildly interested. That left Ritchie O'Shea and Dermot. Ritchie would be happy for her. He always encouraged her to leave Tralee, think for herself and use her education. She would call Ritchie as soon as the plane landed.

Within minutes of her call, he was there. Leaning across the seat he opened the passenger door for her and kissed her cheek. "I'm glad you called. Where have you been?"

"In Dublin." Her eyes shone. "Can we stop for a coffee? I have to tell someone."

"Of course. Do you have a preference?"

"Not at all. I've news, Ritchie. I had an interview in Dublin at a senior center. They need a dietician. It went well, very well. Nothing is confirmed, yet. The board of directors has to approve, but I think I have the position."

"In Dublin?"

"Yes. Isn't wonderful? I'll be away from Tralee and I'll be doing something useful. I don't know what the salary is, but it's a start."

"I didn't realize you were set on Dublin."

"Of course you did. We discussed it in the library."

"I thought we'd settled on America."

She focused on the raindrops streaking the windscreen and considered whether correcting him was worth an argument. What was Ritchie

O'Shea to her anyway? Certainly not significant enough to change her mind, but he was an old friend, enough of a friend to collect her when she needed a lift home. "You misunderstood," she said. "There is no *we*. I thought I made it clear that I would never take Evan away from his family."

"There is opportunity in America that isn't here, Kate."

"That's why I went to Dublin. I found what I need there." She shook her head. "I thought you'd be happy for me."

"That's short-sighted, isn't it? Why should I be happy about a decision that eliminates any possibility of seeing you? I'm off to America."

"And when might that be?"

"I've a few ends to tie up, but probably next month."

She didn't reply. The silence stretched out between them until they turned on to the Tralee Road. Then she spoke. "I don't think I want that coffee after all."

"Suit yourself. Where shall I drop you?" he asked.

"Ballyard. My mother's house. Thanks for coming for me, Ritchie."

"My pleasure." He pulled into the driveway.

Kate climbed out of the car. "If I don't see you before you go, good luck."

"It's like that, is it?"

"I think so. Goodbye, Ritchie. God Bless." She didn't bother waiting for him to leave before walking into the house. Her grandmother was in the sitting room drinking a cup of tea. "Hi, Nan. How are you?"

Dolly looked up and smiled. "I'm grand, Katie. Where have you been?"

Kate sat down on the couch. "I went to Dublin to see about a job."

"Any luck?"

"I won't know for a few days."

"Dublin is quite a drive, isn't it?"

"Not too bad any more with the train and the airport." The house was very quiet. "Where's my mom?"

"I believe she's napping. Your mother works very hard, you know. Shall I wake her for you?"

"No. Let her sleep. My news can wait."

Johannah appeared in the doorway. "I thought I heard a car. Welcome home, Kate. How did it go?"

"It looks promising but I won't have confirmation until the board of directors approves. I think I made a good impression and they definitely need someone."

Johannah's smile disappeared. She looked stricken. "Then you'll be leaving soon."

"I think so, if I get the job."

"Are you sure about this, Kate? Dublin can be very lonely without family and friends."

Kate stood. Naturally her mother would feel this way. What had she expected? "It will give you and Nan an excuse to visit and I'll be home often. Don't forget, I'll be bringing Evan to see Dermot."

"Have you told Dermot?"

"I don't have the job yet, Mom. I didn't want to tell you until I was sure. I knew you wouldn't be pleased."

Johannah crossed her arms and leaned against the doorjamb. "It isn't that I'm not pleased, Kate. I'm very proud of you. I just wish that you could have found something closer to home." She straightened and smiled brightly. "Still, it could be worse. You'll still be in Ireland. I'm very pleased about that."

Laughing, Kate crossed the room and embraced her mother. "Thank you. Where's Evan?"

"Dermot has him. I told him you would be over after the plane landed. I'm sure he's anxious to hear how it went."

Kate bit her lip. Dermot would have to be told about her decision but she'd hoped she wouldn't have to see him until her move was secure.

Johannah looked anxious. "Would you rather stay with Nan and I'll pick up Evan?"

She was tempted, but the image of Johannah trying to evade Dermot's questions was simply not palatable. Mustering her courage, Kate shook her head. "No. I'll tell him exactly what I told you. It looks good, but nothing's certain yet."

Her mother smiled. "Good girl. Take the car. It's supposed to rain for what's left of the day."

Taking advantage of having transportation, Kate drove through the Manor round-about and parked outside of the chemist near Tesco. She needed shampoo and hand lotion but first she would treat herself to a cup of tea and a scone at the café upstairs. Bypassing the line of customers waiting for a late lunch, she chose the fruit scone and a small pot of tea, and paid the cashier. Carrying her tray, she headed toward the seating area and froze. Seated in the barrel chairs near the window were her husband, her son and a young, blond woman she didn't recognize. *Dermot, laughing and talking, with another woman.*

Blindly she turned around, tray still in hand, and headed in the opposite direction. Where were the stairs and where could she rid herself of the tray and disappear? Her handbag slid off her shoulder to her forearm, spilling her tea. She stopped to adjust it and her vision cleared. Reason set in. Manor was a public place. She had every right to enjoy her tea just as Dermot had every right to entertain whomever he pleased. *But not with Evan.* Her teeth clenched and her steps slowed. At the nearest empty table she sat down, mechanically buttering her scone, adding milk and sugar to her tea. She would take her time, breathe deeply and enjoy her food. She would pretend everything was the same as it was ten minutes ago. She would do as she'd intended, visit the chemist, phone Dermot, tell him she was coming. Then he would invite her to join him and introduce her to the woman. There was probably a very good explanation. Kate relaxed. Dermot would never begin seeing someone while he was still married. Dermot was responsible and settled. From the very beginning of their relationship, he'd never shown the slightest interest in anyone else. The woman was probably someone he knew from the store, someone he'd run into by chance here in the café. That was it. He wouldn't fancy someone like that anyway. She was definitely attractive, but flashy. Dermot had never been impressed with flashy.

Her package from the chemist tucked under one arm, Kate stood at the foot of the stairs, pulled out her phone and scrolled down to Dermot's mobile number. He answered immediately. "Kate?"

She struggled to speak, the rush of emotion at hearing his voice unnerved her.

"Kate? Are you there?"

"Yes. I'm home. Is it a good time to collect Evan?"

"Of course. I can drop him by if you like. I'm at Manor, at the cafe."

"I'm at Manor, too. Shall we meet upstairs?"

"I'm already there. Come up."

Kate disconnected and quickly climbed the stairs. She pretended to look around for her husband and son, waving at Evan when he spotted her. Taking her time, she made her way through the tables. The woman was gone. "Hello, Dermot." She kissed Evan on the cheek. "Did you have a good time with Daddy?"

Evan nodded. "I had soup and jello."

"That sounds yummy." Kate sat down. "Did anything else happen?"

Evan's brow furrowed. "No."

Dermot interrupted. "How are you, Kate? How did the interview go?"

"Well, I think. I won't know for a week, but it looks promising. It's a good job, Dermot. Be happy for me."

He nodded. "If it's what's you want, I am happy for you. But I want you to know that you have choices."

"What do you mean?"

"Liam mentioned you were thinking about starting your own business, a special nutrition business for people who need a particular diet. He said he could help you."

"Where would I get the financing?"

Dermot colored. "From the business."

"Your mother wouldn't approve of that."

He looked at her steadily. "My mother doesn't have to approve. I'm the primary shareholder in the business and you are my wife. Everything that's mine is yours. You have a right to it. For Christ's sake you've worked hard enough behind that desk."

Evan slid off his chair and climbed into her lap. "Can I have a toy?"

Kate settled him into the crook of her arm. "Not now love. We'll be going home soon." She turned her attention back to Dermot. "What are you saying, Dermot?"

"I'm trying to apologize. I've been self-centered, thinking only of the future and retirement. I've disregarded your needs, your education and your desire for a home of your own."

"That's very kind of you, Dermot," she said slowly. He still hadn't explained the woman.

"But?"

"I think it might be too late."

He sighed. "I want you to be happy, Katie. I'm proud of you. I want you to know that."

Kate could no longer speak. Why didn't he argue with her? She nodded, set Evan on his feet, took his hand and walked quickly toward the stairs.

CHAPTER 38

Liam

He pulled into the driveway. His mother's car wasn't in her usual spot. Liam breathed a sigh of relief and was immediately ashamed. Johannah wasn't a bigot and she'd never interfered when it came to his friends.

Ciara McCarthy looked at him. "Are we going to sit here or go inside the house?"

"Sorry." Liam laughed. "I'm surprised that we're the only ones here, that's all. I wonder if they've left Nan alone."

"She's all right as long as it's just for a bit, Liam. Most of the time she remembers what she needs to." Ciara's voice was calm and reassuring, completely without drama, a quality he'd come to appreciate.

"Kate found her in the kitchen with her toast on fire."

"There are appliances that automatically turn off when the food is finished cooking." She hooked her bag over her shoulder. "Come on. Let's go in and face the worst."

Liam opened the door and stepped inside. Ciara followed him. "Hello," he said, "anyone home?"

No answer. The house was quiet. "It looks like it's just us."

Ciara raised her eyebrows. "Now, that's an invitation. What mischief can we get into before the grownups arrive home?"

He laughed. "More likely Evan will run up the stairs and surprise us in the act. Closed doors mean nothing to him."

"In that case, let's start dinner. I bought enough chicken for everyone."

"You didn't have to do that, Ciara. I have no idea what my family's dinner plans are."

She began pulling food out of her bags. "Then you'll have leftovers coming out of your ears."

"I can ring my mom."

"Do that or she'll be horrified that I've taken over her kitchen."

A car pulled up in the driveway. Liam looked out the window. "She's here and Nan is with her." He opened the door and waited for his mother and grandmother to climb out of the car. "We're cooking dinner." He reached out his hand. "Careful of the steps, Nan."

"You're a good boy, Liam. Is there time for me to nap? I'm wrecked. Your mother doesn't know when to stop."

"I think so. We've only just started."

Johannah rolled her eyes. "Who's we?"

"Ciara's here with me."

She smiled. "How nice of you and Ciara. Is there enough for everyone?"

Liam relaxed. "Apparently so."

"Nan and I have been shopping. I'll put these bags away, settle her in for a nap and be down to help you."

"No need for that, Mrs. Enright," Ciara said, her head appearing behind Liam's shoulder. "Liam and I have it under control."

Johannah looked at her son. "Somehow I don't think it's Liam who has it under control.

"He can make you a cup of tea."

"That would be heavenly. Liam, your nan might be better for one as well. You can carry it upstairs to her." She called after her mother. "How does that sound, Mom?"

Dolly fluttered her hand, a gesture Liam presumed meant acceptance, and continued up the stairs. Johannah followed her.

Ciara handed Liam a box. "I bought crème cakes for dessert. Put one on your nan's tea tray. A rose in the bud vase wouldn't hurt either."

"They'll know I never thought of this on my own. A mug with milk and sugar is the most they'll expect."

"Next time you'll know better," she promised, turning back to the chicken.

Liam's steps sounded loudly on the stairs. He balanced a tea tray complete with not only the requisite milky tea, but a proper pot, cup, saucer and spoon, a crème cake and vase complete with a fresh flower. Johannah met him on the landing and raised her eyebrows. "How lovely. And to think you thought of all this yourself."

He looked embarrassed. "You know I didn't."

"I see."

Her long level glance unnerved him.

"What?" He knew he sounded defensive.

"Take your offering in to Nan and then come to my room. I want to talk with you about something."

Mentally, he groaned and walked down the hall.

His grandmother's door was open. She sat on the bed staring at the window.

Liam set the tray on the small writing desk. "What are you looking at, Nan?"

She put her forefinger against her lip. "Shhh. T'is a bird bathing in the bath. Look at how she preens herself."

Liam looked over her shoulder and smiled. A robin, fluffed and wet, sat in the birdbath, her feathers silver with drops. "I haven't seen a robin yet this year."

"Is that what she is?"

Liam frowned. His grandmother knew the name of every bird native to Ireland. He sat down on the bed and took her hand. "I've brought your tea, Nan, and a crème cake."

She smiled and touched his cheek. "You're a good boy, Liam. Leave it here. I want to watch the robin for a bit."

"Shall I stay with you?"

She appeared to consider it and then shook her head. "No, not this time. I'm very tired, you see."

"I'll check on you later. If you're not up for tea, I'll have Ciara save you a plate."

Her forehead wrinkled. "Ciara?"

"Never mind, Nan. Get some rest." He closed the door behind him, looked at the floor for a moment and then made his way to his mother's room. She stood at the sink washing her hands.

"Sit down, Liam. This won't take long but you may as well be comfortable. How's Nan? Did she drink her tea?"

Liam sat in the chair with the high back, the story chair where his mother had read him a million children's books. "She's watching a robin and said she'd drink it later."

Johannah sat on the bed across from him. "What's going on with Ciara?"

Liam felt like laughing. Trust his mother to come right out with it, no beating around the bush, no prelude, no nice conversation to soften the telling question. He wanted to tell her it was none of her business but he couldn't say such a thing to his mother. It was just a question after all, one any normal mother would think of asking even if she wouldn't come out and actually say it. "We're seeing each other."

"As in romantically?"

"God, Mom, is there any other way?"

"Of course there is. You could be friends."

"We are friends but it's more than that. She's nice and smart and pretty. She has goals. I'm attracted to her. She's attracted to me."

"I'm sure that's true."

He ran his hands through his hair, a gesture he resorted to when he was frustrated or uncomfortable. "That isn't such a given, you know, a girl being attracted to me. Not any more. I'm not exactly a catch. I'm in college, without a penny to my name and I live with my mother."

She stared at him for a moment and then she laughed. "I suppose when you put it that way, you have a point."

He relaxed and then stiffened again with her next comment.

"She's a traveler, Liam. They no longer roam the way they once did but they think differently. It's in their blood. They're very inbred."

"What's that supposed to mean?"

"They pass down genetic mutations. Their life spans are short. It's difficult for them to settle down, to stay in one place, to follow through with obligations. It's a way of life, one they embrace and want to keep." She lifted her hands. "They aren't accepted, at least not yet. They won't accept you."

"I know all that."

"Then tell me what you're doing."

He looked at her. "I'm seeing a girl, a nice girl. That's all. We don't talk about the future. We both have plans. Hers, I might add, don't include roaming the country in a caravan. She's motivated, Mom. I'm disappointed in you. I didn't think you were a bigot."

She sighed. "Liam, I like Ciara. But these things don't work. Her father and brothers aren't served in the pubs. Her mother and sisters can't read a newspaper without help. It isn't just the two of you. There's a world out there that must be lived in. I'm not a bigot, I'm a mother and you're my child. More than anyone, I have your interests at heart." She stood. "Now go downstairs and help the girl with our tea. Please don't tell me she paid for it."

Quickly, Liam escaped, without responding to her last comment which of course announced his guilt more than if he'd simply come out with the truth. Once more, he wished that his father were alive. Mickey would understand. Men weren't judgmental. They accepted people for who they were, themselves, not their whole bleeding family.

He stopped on the landing to tie his shoe when it occurred to him that he'd like to hear Patrick's thoughts on the matter. How odd that he should think of him just now, and yet, not really. Patrick would be the perfect person to confide in. He was not family and yet he knew Johannah and he'd met Ciara. Patrick could be counted on to offer up impartial advice.

CHAPTER 39

Mickey

Mickey checked his watch from his seat in front of the fiction section. He kept one eye on the entrance to the library while at the same time attempting to read his newspaper. He'd been waiting for the better part of an hour. Just as he was about to give up, the familiar lanky figure he was expecting walked through the door.

Pretending interest in the paper, he didn't look up until Liam stood before him.

"Hello, Patrick. I hoped I'd find you here. I have no idea where you live."

"Liam, how are things?"

Liam sat down and lowered his voice. "A bit confusing at the moment. Do you have time for a coffee? I'm buying."

He folded his paper, stood and tucked it under his arm. "Who could refuse an offer like that? Where did you have in mind?"

"Anywhere will do. Quinlins, I suppose, or the Greyhound."

"Those are pubs. You did say coffee?"

"I did. I'll go anywhere except The Grind."

"Why is that?"

"My mother is sure to stop in and just now I'd rather not run into her."

Mickey looked at the tall young man, his dark hair, the sharp blade of his chin, the eyes so like Johannah's…his son. His heart hurt. "Are you in trouble, Liam?"

"No, not a bit. I'd just like your opinion on something. I already know what my mother thinks and I wanted someone else, someone not connected to my family, to give me an unbiased opinion."

"That sounds reasonable. We'll go to Aine's in The Square and I'll buy."

The weather was unusually balmy and every seat in the small outdoor patio of the restaurant was filled with smokers. Deciding against an inside table, they carried their coffees to a bench in The Square.

"Now, tell me what's on your mind."

"You've met Ciara."

"I have.

"What do you think of her?"

"She's a lovely girl. Why do you ask?"

Liam stared into his coffee cup, a dark expression on his face. "My mother doesn't approve. She said relationships with the itinerants are doomed." He looked up. "What do you think?"

"I think it depends upon the relationship."

"How do you mean?"

"You're young, Liam, and you're schooling isn't complete. You haven't much experience.

Your mother may have the impression you're thinking of making this relationship permanent."

Liam's brow furrowed. "Why should she? I never have before."

"As children age, the possibility increases."

"I suppose so. But that isn't the point, is it? What if I did want to marry Ciara? Why should anyone disapprove? She's a worthy person."

The day was a lovely one for the season, bright and cool. Mickey appreciated days like these when once he wouldn't have given them a thought. There was so much he wanted to share with Liam, now that he no longer could. "When you prove yourself, your mother will come around."

"Sorry?"

"When you achieve your goals, when time has passed, when you've shown Johannah that your mind is made up and you know what you want, she'll accept your decisions. Your mother is afraid that you'll find yourself in a situation you're unhappy with and can't escape."

"Divorce is legal in Ireland."

"It still isn't easy and going into a marriage with the idea that you can divorce isn't a wise move."

"I didn't mean that," replied Liam hastily.

"I'm sure you didn't."

Liam looked at the older man. "You're very accommodating. Thank you for talking with me."

"I'm honored."

Liam laughed and shrugged. "I know this sounds ridiculous but, the thing is, you're easy to talk to. In that way you remind me of my dad."

"Thank you, Liam. That means a great deal to me."

"How long have you lived in Tralee?"

"Not long."

"Are you happy here?"

"For now."

"Does that mean you might relocate?"

"There is that possibility."

Liam hesitated, then spoke quickly, slightly embarrassed. "You will let us know where you end up?"

Mickey looked into his coffee and then up at the sky, anywhere but into the sincere face of his child, the son whose future, he now knew, he would have no part in. "Of course."

Later, as he walked the lonely strand of Derrymore, heedless of the thick ropy circles of kelp rotting on the wet sand, he looked up at the sky. "How much longer do I have?" he asked out loud. "They feel it, Kate and Liam. Somehow, they know my time is limited." He closed his fist and struck his palm with it. "I want no more surprises, Peter. I must know when this will finish. I've never asked you to come. Now I'm asking. Come now."

He walked for nearly an hour before he saw a dark speck in the distance. Hurrying toward it, his footsteps heavy with the effort of moving across sand, he fell, righted himself and began to run. When he was close enough to recognize the familiar white-robed figure, he slowed, panting, until the saint reached him.

Peter spoke. "You're in a hurry this morning."

Mickey's breathing normalized. "I need to know when my time is up."

"I can't give you a time and date. You've made great progress so far, better than I'd hoped."

"My children know something. They feel I'm leaving them."

"Yes." A simple comment uttered without explanation, for no reason other than to fill a silence.

"What's happening, Peter?"

"In your own fashion, you're wrapping things up. Kate and Liam understand that, to an extent."

"What about Johannah?"

Peter clasped his hands behind his back and shivered. "This is a very cold country. I never come here willingly. I prefer it much warmer."

"Will I know when my time with Johannah is over?"

Peter looked at him. "Yes." Again, nothing more.

Mickey pressed him. "When will it be?"

"I don't know."

Mickey's frustration extended beyond speech. Falling to his knees, his chin dropped to his chest and he closed his eyes. "I can't do this," he said. "I just can't." He felt Peter's presence beside him.

"I tell you that I don't know because it isn't my decision," the saint explained. "You will know because it is up to you to decide. When the time is right you will allow her to move beyond you to a place where she will walk alone."

"She's doing that now."

He felt the smile in Peter's voice. "No, my friend. You are still with her, caring for her, advising her and also holding her back."

"That isn't true.

"There is no timetable," Peter continued. "There is only to do what is right."

Mickey opened his eyes. Once again he was alone.

CHAPTER 40

Johannah

Johannah pulled the knickers, the nightgown and the two pairs of trousers her mother had picked out the other day from their packages and threw them in the laundry basket. Dolly would wear nothing new until it had been freshly washed. Once again Johannah was conscious of the amount of work even one more person in a household created. How quickly she'd adjusted to Mickey's absence, his clothes no longer hanging on the line, no marks on the stairs from his shoes, no wet towels on the floor or spots on the bathroom mirror he never remembered to clean off after brushing his teeth, circumstances so annoying when they happened and barely noticed when they stopped. How insignificant most of the normalcy of daily living was, not worth thinking about much less arguing over. Not that she'd ever argued with Mickey over his habits. Rather she'd steeped in simmering resentment wondering why he couldn't he pick up after himself? Between the two of them, she was the one needing to be up and about in the morning.

She couldn't imagine Jack Rafferty, a meticulous dresser having no wife, leaving wet towels on the floor or water marks on the tile. Quickly, she pushed the thought away. She had no business even wondering what his bathroom habits were. No one was perfect. Most likely he had a dreadful temper and took days to cool off. Maura's husband, Milo, was like that. He sulked forever, removing himself from all conversation, offering no affection, keeping himself coldly remote until his desperate wife threatened to throw his belongings out on the street unless he apologized immediately and became himself again. Sometimes it worked, most of the time it didn't. Maura would wait it out until Milo was ready.

Why did women put up with these things, Johannah wondered? Was her sex so desperate for love and companionship that they willingly accepted the miserable in order to ward of loneliness for as long as possible? Was self-doubt and insecurity preferable to being alone when not being alone inevitably led to coldness and hurt at least some of the time? Would the man who disappeared into the bathroom with the Victoria Secret Catalogue and made critical comments about his wife's aging figure support her lovingly while she recovered from a mastectomy? Would his impatience with her cautious map reading turn to understanding after her memory faded? Johannah didn't think so. In fact, her work experience proved it. Rarely did men look after their ailing wives. The reverse was far more typical. Women cared for their husbands, often with nothing more than a widow's pension to sustain them when their charges died. The worst tragedy was when the poor woman, finally out from under the drudgery of her role as caretaker, succumbed soon after her husband's demise.

Johannah was determined not to find herself in any of those situations. She'd managed to stay independent throughout her marriage and after, mostly because she kept her job. Mickey always had a healthy respect for her work. She'd wanted him to live to an old age, wanted them to retire together and travel to Spain and Portugal, Turkey and Morocco, colorful destinations where people had evolved into something brown, languid and exotic due to the benefits of a different kind of sun. But it was not to be. Mickey died young and unexpectedly, leaving her a house without a mortgage and no debt. She had her work and no financial problems. Life was, while not thrilling, predictable and occasionally rewarding. Due to luck and perseverance, she'd navigated well. All of which made her extremely wary of risking her emotional well-being on anyone, especially a stranger from Belfast who, despite his impressive resume, had no family, no home, no ties. Inherently, she felt there was something not quite healthy about a person with no roots.

Why, then, had she agreed to see him for the third time this week? It was a rhetorical question. Johannah always knew exactly why she did everything. Jack Rafferty flattered her and she was a woman in desperate need of flattering. He was an interesting conversationalist and he listened. Other than Maura, Johannah wasn't accustomed to people who listened. He wasn't a local man which meant that when her, or rather his, interest waned she wouldn't be seeing him on every street corner. Possibly the greatest draw was that he hadn't known her until now, a competent woman, in charge of her life. He hadn't known her as Mickey Enright's wife or for that matter Francie O'Shea's girlfriend. He didn't think of her as a mother or grandmother. She was a professional in a suit and heels, a woman who carried a briefcase and asked intelligent questions.

Johannah looked at her watch and sighed. There was just enough time to wash her hair before she dressed. He was taking her out to dinner. It occurred to her that a good amount of time was spent into doing oneself up to go out with a man. She'd forgotten that, the inconvenience of being single, the expectation that she would take time with her appearance. For the space of a second, she was conscious of a strong desire to curl up in her nightgown in front of the sitting room fire and read a book.

The West End was a restaurant located at the end of a row of buildings leading to Fenit Pier. Johannah would have enjoyed being there with her children, or Maura or even, as a last resort, her mother. Walking in with Jack Rafferty was another experience altogether.

Bridie Murphy, the hostess, held open the door for them. "Hello, Hannie, how are things?" She looked meaningfully at Jack.

Johannah chose to ignore the implied question and busied herself by taking off her coat. "Grand, and yourself?"

"Business is slow, but otherwise I can't complain. So many have closed up." She led them to their seats, set the menus on the table and looked at Jack. "The plaice is very good and it's fresh. I missed you at Mass today, Hannie."

"I went last night," Johannah replied. She knew what Bridie wanted but she was having none of it. There was no need to introduce Jack Rafferty to anyone. "How's the salmon?"

"Fresh as well. How is your mother getting on?"

"She's settling in. I'll tell her you asked after her."

Seconds passed. Bridie spoke again. "Can I offer either of you a drink to start with?"

Jack spoke for the first time. "Nothing for me, thanks, but I'd like to see the wine list."

"Right." Bridie rested one hand on her hip. "Would you like to look at it now?"

He smiled. "If it's convenient."

"Certainly it's convenient. This is a restaurant after all." She couldn't help herself. "You're not from the town are you?"

"No."

"Where did you say you come from?"

"I don't believe I said."

She took a minute to register his words. Finally it clicked. "Right. I'll bring the list straight away."

Johannah looked at her menu. "I've always liked salmon but I'll have it without the starter. Do you think, as a population, we eat too much?"

"I'm sorry, Johannah. I suppose I should have checked with you before booking a restaurant."

She smiled. "This is a lovely choice. It wouldn't have mattered anyway. Tralee is a small town and I've lived here all my life. I'm bound to know someone."

He looked relieved. "Then you don't mind?"

"Not at all. I think you handled her brilliantly."

"Will there be repercussions?"

"How do you mean?"

Bridie stopped at the table with the wine list. "We have a very nice white from South Africa and another from Chile."

Jack looked at the menu. "Are you having fish, Johannah?"

"I am."

He handed the list back to Bridie. "The California Pinot Noir, please."

Bridie was at her most professional. "Excellent choice."

Jack waited until she left. "Will you be the talk of the town because you were seen here with me?"

"Are you familiar with the term *nine days wonder*?

He frowned. "Is that how you see us?"

She was tempted to tell him she wasn't anticipating an *us* but it seemed especially rude sitting across from him in a lovely restaurant, contemplating a delicious meal. "I'm enjoying the evening," she said instead. "What I meant was that not even the worst scandals last beyond a week or two and the two of us sharing a meal certainly isn't that."

He laughed. "You're amazing, Johannah. Do you know that?"

"Thank you, but I have no idea what brought that on."

"You're much more polished than I expected. You hold your small town background in front of you as an excuse for a perceived lack of sophistication but you're plenty sophisticated."

"Really?" She looked surprised. "I wouldn't describe myself that way, but I'm accepting the compliment. Thank you."

Candlelight played across his features. Johannah was very conscious of his attractiveness, a combination of good genes and a lifetime of care. Why, then, was she feeling so detached as if she was Cinderella and midnight approached.

Bridie returned with the wine. "Would you like to taste it first?"

Jack shook his head. "Go ahead and pour. I'll risk it." He smiled at her. "I'll go with your suggestion and take the plaice. Johannah will have the salmon. We'll skip the starter."

"Potatoes and vegetables?"

"Yes."

"You won't be sorry. Enjoy the wine."

Johannah chuckled. "You've redeemed yourself. Now it will be all over town that you're a lovely person."

"The lovely person is sitting across from me."

"Jack—" She hesitated. "I don't—"

He waited.

"I'm not ready for what I think you want. I'm not accustomed to attention from a man. I've been widowed for just over a year and before that I was married for a lifetime."

He nodded. "I accept that, although I've been told attention is something women can get used to."

Was that laughter she heard in his voice? She frowned. "Are you taking me seriously?"

"Absolutely."

"I have no libido, whatsoever." There, she'd said it, forced the unmentionable words out of her mouth.

Briefly, mindful of their audience, he touched her hand. "I think you have some preconceived notions of men, Johannah. I'm not a boy. There's more to a relationship than sex. In fact, that alone indicates there is no relationship at all."

"Are you saying it's unnecessary?"

"Not at all," he said, smiling at Bridie as she set the plates of food in front of them.

"Can I get you anything else?"

"No, thank you," said Johannah. "Everything looks delicious."

Jack waited until she was well out of the way before resuming their conversation. "Sex is very necessary, but it doesn't come first and I'm willing to wait."

"For how long?"

"For as long as it takes."

Johannah chewed and swallowed a forkful of salmon. "What if it doesn't happen, ever?"

"Then we won't have that kind of relationship."

Her argument deflated, she stared at him, her eyes wide and round. "Why don't I believe you?"

"Probably because the last time you were in front of a potential relationship with a man, you were a child and all of your experience centered around a boy whose primary goal in life was to remove your knickers without benefit of marriage."

"Are you interested in marriage, Jack?"

He shrugged. "It hasn't come up."

"Somehow, I doubt that."

His eyebrows rose. "You have a wicked sense of humor, Mrs. Enright."

"I'm asking why you think this," she indicated the two of them, "is different."

"My primary goal is not to remove your knickers. I want to know you, Johannah. The rest will come later, if it's right."

Jack, intuitive enough to know when the subject was saturated, kept the rest of the conversation playful and interesting and Johannah enjoyed herself tremendously. There was a moment of tension when he walked her to the door, but it eased immediately when he kissed her lightly on the lips and said he would be in touch. She closed the door behind him feeling oddly bereft.

Her message machine alerted her that someone had called. She pressed the button and listened to Maura's voice telling her to call if it wasn't too late. Johannah looked at the clock and decided it was. Tomorrow would do just as well. She didn't want to talk with anyone just now. She wanted to run a bath, sit back in the bubble-filled tub and think about the evening.

Flipping on the main switch, she allowed fifteen minutes for the pipes to fill with hot water before filling the tub. Stripping off her clothes, she sank back into the steaming bath, closed her eyes and smiled. It was wonderful to have left youth behind, to be in the middle of her life, to no longer feel the desperate yearning associated with first love. Experience was so healing. Once she'd believed there was only one man for her and if she couldn't have him for herself, his voice, his smile, his eyes, his choice of phrase, she would wake with an ache in her heart for the rest of her days. How ridiculous she'd been. How quickly she'd adapted. Jack Rafferty was a lovely man and she would enjoy seeing him again. But there would be no drama, no hard choices this time. He'd given her a tremendous gift, the confidence to know she was desired. That knowledge put everything into a different perspective.

CHAPTER 42

Kate

Joan Connelly hung up the phone and leaned forward her elbows on her desk. I'll be sorry to see you go, Kate. I've really enjoyed working with you. We never did go to lunch. I guess we were both busy."

Kate smiled. "I know. It seemed like we had all the time in the world."

"I hope it's nothing anyone here has done."

"Not at all. Everyone here has been wonderful. I just need to move on." It was true. Everyone at the County Council offices was quite friendly.

"Maybe, when you come back to visit, we can get together." Joan laughed. "Wouldn't it be desperate if we became close friends after you moved to Dublin?"

"True." Kate continued to pack her personal belongings in the box. She was feeling quite strange.

The phone on Joan's desk rang. She picked it up. "Joan Connelly here. Yes, right away." She replaced the receiver and nodded at Kate. "Mr.

Halloran wants to see you in the conference room. I'm to come with you. He probably wants to be sure I'm caught up on your duties."

Kate packed Evan's photo, the last of her momentos, and sealed the box with tape. "That should do it." She smiled brightly. "Shall we go?"

Joan maintained a steady flow of conversation until they reached the conference room. Then she fell behind allowing Kate to pass in front of her. "After you," she said.

Kate opened the door and stepped inside. There was a hushed silence and then suddenly the room exploded in sound. "Surprise, Surprise," voices called out, crowding around, pulling her toward the long oval table and a very large cake decorated with pink roses, the words *good luck,* and her name spelled out in green letters.

Kate sank into the nearest chair. "My goodness," she said weakly. "I don't—, I didn't expect—, thank you, thank you, so very much." Then she covered her eyes with both hands and burst into tears.

Dolly

She sat in the garden just outside the solarium, deep in thought, her eyes closed against the rare sunlight warming the glass. Seamus sat at her feet, nose resting on his paws, his breathing even. Something important hovered on the edge of her consciousness but she couldn't call it up enough to get a closer look at it. She felt unsettled, almost uncomfortable, with a tension she'd never felt before and that was desperate considering the way life was now compared to when she was a child, the one bathroom outside with only a toilet, a sink in the kitchen and nine hungry children pressed together in a house the size of a postage stamp.

Johannah's house was lovely with its stone walls and brick facing, two chimneys, central heat, the gates opening to long green gardens. There were rooms for all of them, Kate and Liam, Evan, Johannah and even herself, although she resented having to live here. It wasn't that she didn't love them. They were her family after all. But she didn't want to be underfoot every day. She didn't always want to say good morning or share the newspaper or talk over tea. Some days she wanted to stay in bed past nine, wear her wrap until noon and go back to bed again. And then there was the food. Johannah was obsessed with food and the preparation of meals, not quite so much as Kate was, but still more than suited Dolly. Everything had to be healthy, whole meal and nonfat, or free-range and filled with Omega 3s, all things tasteless. What was the point of eating if food was tasteless?

Dolly preferred richness, whole milk in her tea, jelly with plenty of sugar, lovely soft white bread and real Kerry butter, golden and smooth, soothing on her tongue. Despite all of that, she didn't even weigh eight stone. These fat children walking around today with their sugarless drinks, their hamburgers and pizza were doomed. Good Kerry pork, fillets of beef and marbled lamb is what they should be eating, with plenty of spuds, parsnips and carrots.

In all fairness, Johannah was not a proponent of fast food and she was a fine cook, taking her time to put a lovely meal on the table. But outside of meals there was nothing in the refrigerator except yogurt and fruit and neither of those appealed to Dolly at all. She didn't want yogurt or apples with her tea. She wanted a proper crème cake, a vanilla or fruit scone with plenty of jam and butter, none of this Flora polyunsaturated stuff.

It wasn't just the food. Dolly missed her friends. They didn't stop in and visit the way they did in Kevin Barry's. The trek up to Ballyard was a deterrent to anyone over the age of sixty and Dolly's crowd was well over that. She wanted to go home but it looked like that was out of the question. A thought materialized in her mind. Perhaps she should go somewhere else, somewhere that catered to people her age. Quickly, before the idea was formed properly, she pushed it away. Those places were for old people. She wasn't old, at least not that old, not yet.

A shadow fell across the potted flowers beside her and a voice she recognized spoke. "Hello, Dolly."

She shaded her eyes. "Mickey, is it you? How lovely to see you. Sit down and I'll put the kettle on."

"Maybe later." He sat beside her. "How are you?"

She sighed. "I'm grand," she said automatically and then stopped. "No, I'm not. I don't like it here. I want to go home."

He smiled. "I know what you mean."

She considered him thoughtfully. "I imagine you do."

"Kevin Barry's is no longer possible."

She nodded. "I suppose I shall have to go into a facility."

He looked startled. "Hardly that."

"What else is there?"

"A Senior Citizen's Community would be a better choice, for now."

"For now?"

He looked up at the sky, a bright, cloudless blue, unusual for Ireland. "Your condition is manageable now, but you understand that it will get worse?"

"What condition are you referring to?"

"You forget things, Dolly," he explained gently. "Too often you're confused and frightened. No one should feel like that. Moving here with Hannie was a step, but she's not here during the day. Kate may be leaving soon and Liam needs a place of his own. You'll be alone. It's time to move on."

She opened her mouth, intending to contradict him and then stopped herself. He was right. The ugly truth was out and she had no argument. "I've seen those places," she said, her voice trembling. "I don't want to go."

"You're confusing a senior citizen's community with a nursing home. You won't be a prisoner, but there are other alternatives."

"How do you mean?"

He pulled his chair around to face her and took her hands in his. "It might be possible for you to return to your own home in Kevin Barry's if you agree to have someone stay with you, someone trained."

Her mouth thinned. "I don't want a stranger in my house."

"You could interview and find a woman to suit you. Wouldn't that be better than anything else we've already discussed?"

Dolly frowned and looked down at her lap. She didn't recall a discussion. Perhaps it wouldn't be so bad if she had a companion, someone to help her with the shopping and care of the house, someone she could count on to remember where everything was, someone to have lunch with in town. "I suppose so," she said slowly and looked up to meet his gaze, steady and reassuring, on her face. "I must have truly lost my mind, Mickey. I thought you died."

He smiled. "The thing is, Dolly, you haven't lost your mind at all."

She touched his cheek. "You feel real. Are you real, Mickey?"

"Yes."

A look of horror distorted her face. "You haven't come for me, have you, because I'm not at all ready."

"No, Dolly," he said gently. "You've some time left. I came back to sort things out with Johannah and the children, but I must leave soon."

Her relief was almost humorous. He would have laughed if he'd felt the least bit like laughing.

"It was kind of you to take time with me," she said formally.

He kissed her cheek. "You're my family. My wife is your daughter, my children your flesh and blood."

"You always were a good man, Mickey. I like—"she corrected herself, "liked you."

"I wasn't good enough, I'm afraid."

"Johannah misses you. We all miss you."

"I know that."

"I suppose I should tell Johannah that I've decided to hire someone to care for me."

"You're a strong woman, Dolly Little. I have faith in you."

"Shall I tell her about you?"

"As you wish."

"You're thinking she won't believe me."

"I doubt she will, but it doesn't really matter, does it?"

"No," she said after a minute. "It really doesn't."

"I'll leave you now, Dolly. Take care of yourself."

"Will I see you again?"

"You will, but not here, not in Tralee or even in Ireland." He squeezed her hand. "Does that frighten you?"

She thought a minute. "No. I'm relieved to know you'll be there to greet me."

He kissed her cheek. "I'll be seeing you."

"Slan Abhale, Mickey."

CHAPTER 43

Johannah

Maura poured herself a glass of wine, sat back in the chair, looked around Johannah's lovely garden and sighed. "It must be comforting having all this space and no one to hear when you flush the toilet."

"It is," Johannah agreed. "I've always been grateful that Mickey inherited this house."

"You've taken great care of it, Hannie. The stone work and the flowers give it just the right touch. I envy you."

"My mother wouldn't agree with you."

Maura frowned. "You sound as if you're insulted."

"I am, in a way."

"For heaven's sake, Hannie. She gave you a gift. She's moving back to her own house and leaving you in peace. It's what you wanted, your home back. Now that Kate and Liam are moving out, too, we should be drinking champagne."

"I suppose you're right." Johannah rubbed the etching on the globe of her glass. "I've become accustomed to having all of them here. I'll miss them, even my mother."

Maura chuckled. "Not for long, I guarantee it."

Johannah shook her head. "You're not the one coming home to an empty house."

"You won't be either if you play your cards right."

"How do you mean?"

"You've been about with Jack Rafferty for the better part of a month now. Didn't you tell me he was only staying

a week? I'm your best friend, Hannie. What's going on?"

Johannah leaned forward, propping her chin on her hand. Why wasn't she over the moon about Jack Rafferty? Once, he would have been everything she wanted, handsome, intelligent, sophisticated and clearly interested in her. "I'm not sure," she said honestly. "I can't put my finger on it. It's as if I'm waiting for something. I know he's staying on my behalf, that's obvious, although he's never said so which prevents me from telling him to move along."

"Why would you want to do that?" Maura was losing patience.

"There are no bells and whistles."

"Sorry?"

"You heard me. He doesn't excite me." Maura was staring at her, brown eyes wide and disbelieving. "Are you mad?"

Johannah laughed. "I know it sounds ridiculous."

"Hannie," Maura protested, "you're fifty-one years old. Bells and whistles are for children."

Johannah picked up her glass of wine for the first time. "This is lovely, isn't it? When Mickey was alive, I didn't drink at all, probably because he did so much of it."

"Do you know what I think?"

"Not really."

"I'm going to tell you anyway." She stopped, arrested. "What has Mickey's drinking got to do with anything?"

Johannah's cool green eyes rested on her friend's face. "I had bells and whistles with Mickey and I had bells and whistles with Francie. I'm capable of feeling bells and whistles. Without it, I can't imagine trying to make things work. How hard that must be."

"Maybe it isn't hard at all, if the person you choose doesn't have anything wrong with him."

"Don't be ridiculous. Eventually everyone is annoying. He'll bite his nails or become impatient or insist on the least expensive of a particular brand, or else the most expensive. He'll be pretentious or too blue collar or he'll resent my children and grandchildren. He'll want to go to the Bahamas instead of Paris and he'll be bothered because I spend so much time with you. No one is perfect, Maura. It's the bells and whistles that allow us to love someone despite all the imperfections."

"You're very particular. Do you know that?"

"Not at all," replied Johannah. "I love you and you're filled with imperfections."

"Hannie Enright! What a terrible thing to say." Curiosity won out. "What's wrong with me?"

"Let's see. Where shall I begin?" Johannah held up her fingers and began ticking them off. "You can eat until you're sick and never gain a pound. You never forget to write thank you cards. You say exactly what's on your mind without agonizing for days wondering if it's right or wrong. You have four children who are absolutely perfect and never forget your birthday. Your husband is alive and well and he adores you. Your hair curls naturally in all the right places and everyone loves you desperately."

Maura grinned. "You're right. I must be absolutely obnoxious. I can't imagine why you would want me for your friend. I know what your worry is, Johannah. You're afraid of making another mistake. Mind you, I don't think Mickey was a mistake, but you had your share of disappointments. I won't go into them now. It isn't kind to speak ill of the dead. I think you don't want to believe there could be a future with a perfectly acceptable man because you're afraid of being hurt if he doesn't meet your expectations of *the perfect* man. The really ironic part of all this is that you accept your friends, your co-workers and your blood for who they are, but you hold the men in your life to a higher standard." She stood and kissed Johannah on the cheek. "I'll take my imperfect self off now. Milo is waiting for his dinner. I'm assuming you'll be giving Mr. Rafferty the sack. Despite everything, I think you'll be sorry. Ring me when it's over and we'll take a long walk."

Johannah watched her until she passed through the gate and her car disappeared down the road.

Gathering up the glasses and the bottle, she walked through the sunroom into the kitchen, poured the wine remnants into the sink, threw the bottle into the recycler and began washing the glasses.

"Hi, Mom."

Surprised, she turned to see her daughter standing in the doorway. "Kate. I didn't hear the car. Where's Evan and your nan ?"

"They're coming. Dermot dropped us off. It's actually his car."

"Really." Johannah turned back to the sink. "I thought the two of you chose it together."

"You know what I mean." Kate walked into the kitchen and began filling the kettle. "Nan will be wanting a cup of tea."

"Did I hear my name?" Dolly appeared holding Evan's hand.

"I'm making tea, Nan. Sit down and I'll pour it in a flash. I'll pour yours, too, Mom."

Johannah shut the water off. "To what do I owe this honor, my entire family, except for Liam, home to have tea with me?"

"I found a place in Dublin."

"Already?" Johannah felt a sudden sick twisting of her stomach. "Where?"

"In Dublin 9. It's a lovely area."

"We're going to be Dubliners," Evan crowed.

Johannah left the dripping glasses on the counter and sat down beside her mother. "You're all leaving at once. I won't know what to do with myself."

"I doubt that," said Dolly. "You can't have been thrilled to have us all foisted on you."

"Believe it or not, I've grown accustomed to it," Johannah admitted. "I shall miss you."

Evan's smooth forehead creased. "Don't you want us to go, Nan?" He looked at his mother. "Can Nan come with us?"

"She won't want to do that, Evan," said Kate quickly. "Nan lives here. Her job is here, just as mine is in Dublin."

His lip quivered. "When shall we see her?"

Johannah held out her arms and he climbed into her lap. She buried her face into the folds of his sweet, sweaty neck. "I'll see you every month," she promised, "and I'll bring you something every time."

He stared at her solemnly, as if gauging the strength of her vow. Finally he nodded. "All right. I'll wait for you."

Kate looked stricken. "Are you terribly upset, Mom?"

"Good heavens, no," Johannah lied. "You've found a job in your field which isn't easy to do. You must live your life, Kate. I'm thrilled for you. Of course, I shall miss you, but Dublin isn't America or Australia, thank God. You'll be just around the corner."

Kate poured three cups of tea and sat down, smiling first at Dolly and then at her mother. Johannah was puzzled. Something wasn't right. Kate's voice was hollow and she looked as if she was trying very hard to convince everyone she was happy.

"I can't believe the luck I've had," she said. "The flat came up unexpectedly. I'd nearly given up hope of finding something so close to where I'll be working. It's a lovely Victorian with large rooms and two baths. The photos are beautiful."

Dolly looked perplexed. "When did you go to Dublin, Kate? We've been together all afternoon."

"On the Internet, Nan. It's called a virtual tour. Everyone does it these days."

Dolly pushed her tea away. "I've changed my mind about the tea." She looked around. "Where's Seamus?"

"He should be in the yard," replied Johannah.

"I'll check on him and then take a nap."

Evan squirmed out of Johannah's lap. "I want to see Seamus, too."

Kate frowned. "Oh, Evan, I don't think…"

"It's all right, Kate," said her grandmother. "You should know by now that Seamus won't hurt the boy."

"Seamus is my friend, Mommy," Evan explained. "Don't be afraid."

"I supposed you're right. If he hasn't savaged anyone yet, I suppose he's not going to."

"Don't forget the Costelloeees' dog," muttered Johannah, under her breath.

"I haven't lost my hearing," snapped Dolly, "and Seamus doesn't bite." She held out her hand. "Come with me, Evan."

The silence in the kitchen loomed overwhelmingly large. Johannah stared at the milky tea in her cup. The time was right. It was now or never. She bit her lip. "Katie," she began, "there's something I must tell you."

Kate looked at her mother. Her eyes sparkled and her lips curved up in a lovely smile. She was so happy. Johannah's heart sank. Was this the right time? Would there ever be a right time? "I don't think you'll like this very much," she began. "I don't feature well in this story but it must be said. All I ask is that you remember before I was your mother, I was a girl younger than you and, not too surprisingly, we weren't all that different in our preferences."

"What are you saying?"

Johannah could feel the acceleration of her heart. There was no easy or comfortable way to do this. Better to get it over with. She drew a long slow breath and began. "Years ago Francie O'Shea was every bit as appealing to me as his son is to you and I fell in love." She spoke quickly, anxious to get the words out and be finished with them. "He asked me to marry him. The banns were posted, but it turned out he didn't feel the same about me. He was seeing Kitty O'Connor at the same time and she turned up pregnant. Of course I couldn't marry him after that so I called it off. I'd always known

Mickey." She frowned. "We'd been friends for a long time. I suppose that's why I felt safe with him. That's how I justified my actions, that and the hurt and shame I felt with everyone knowing how it turned out for Francie and me." She looked over Kate's shoulder and deliberately focused on the photo she'd taken of a robin red breast bathing in the birdbath.

"The thing is," she continued, "I jumped right into a relationship with your father and soon, very soon, you were on the way." She met Kate's eyes for the first time since beginning her confession. "We got married right away. Do you know what I'm saying, Kate?"

For a long minute the only sound was the ticking of the mantle clock. Then Kate spoke. "I assume you mean that my dad married you not knowing if I was his daughter or Francie O'Shea's. I got that part. What I don't understand is why you waited until now to tell me this."

Johannah shrugged. "It seemed like the right time."

"Is that all?"

Johannah's eyes burned with the effort to hold back tears. "I'm terribly afraid you might be entertaining the idea of meeting Ritchie in Dublin."

Kate's question was unexpected. "Did you ever love Dad?"

Johannah replied wholeheartedly, without hesitation. "I adored him from the very beginning. I miss him every day."

Kate sighed, the hostility draining from her voice. "I should have asked you that sooner. It would have saved us both some anguish."

"How do you mean?"

"Dad told me all this a long time ago."

Johannah's eyes widened. "Why would he do that?"

"He knew I was interested in Ritchie. I suppose he thought it was the only effective way to nip it in the bud."

"Was it?"

"It served its purpose, I suppose, but it posed other problems. For a time, I was furious with you. I wanted to know who I was. Then DNA tests became accessible, my questions were answered and I grew up."

Something was missing, something important. Johannah needed a minute to think, to collect herself. "Are you still furious with me?"

Kate shook her head. "No, but then I suppose I always knew I was Mickey Enright's daughter." She looked at her mother. "Even if the test had turned out differently, I'd still be his daughter."

Johannah could barely breathe. When she spoke her voice sounded very far away. "How long ago was that?"

"Five or six years ago."

She released her breath. "Are you saying you knew—that your father knew, and that all this time I didn't?"

"Yes."

"Why would you keep something like that from me?"

"I didn't think you wanted to bring up the subject. It was my dad who told me, not you. There was never any question as to who my mother was. Proof of his paternity was a gift I gave to him, for raising me and loving me even though I might have been someone else's child although I think he always knew the truth. Liam and I are too much alike. I doubt he even considered the possibility that he wasn't my father and, honestly, I don't think it mattered to him at all. Apparently it meant more to you than I thought. I would never have brought this up if you hadn't started the conversation."

Johannah was furious. He'd known all along and he hadn't told her. Why? What did it mean?

Kate was still talking. "At least we were able to clear the air before I left."

"Where does that leave you and Ritchie O'Shea?"

"I told you that ended long ago. We aren't suited. Ritchie is one of those men who thinks he wants what he can't have. The truth is, he never thought of me that way at all." She finished her tea. "Are you planning dinner or shall I do it?"

"Don't worry about me," replied Johannah. "I'm not very hungry and there's something I have to do."

Kate looked at her curiously. "This hasn't upset you, has it, Mom? I mean, I'm grateful you didn't go away, have me and give me up to strangers. That took amazing courage. It's all water under the bridge anyway, isn't it? I mean, isn't that what Dad would say?"

Johannah's instinct was to placate, to settle her child, to reduce the guilt Kate must be feeling for keeping the secrets of one parent at the expense of the other. But she didn't because suddenly everything became dazzlingly clear. This time she would tell the truth and never mind what anyone thought. "Actually, Kate, it upsets me a great deal, but I'll get over it. I usually do." With that, she left the room, picked up her handbag from the hall stand and headed for the car.

CHAPTER 44

Kate

Evan sat across from his mother, staring at the row of letters on his paper, a perplexed look on his face. "What's the matter with it?" he asked.

"You've turned the letter around," Kate explained. "It goes like this." She demonstrated the proper method of printing an s and handed the pencil back to Evan. "Do you see the difference?"

"I like mine better," he pronounced.

"Yours is rather nice, but I'm afraid it isn't the way your teacher expects you to learn it. Shall we try another one?"

"You try another one."

Kate picked up the pencil. "One more and then it's your turn. After that, we have to pick up a prescription for Nan at the chemist and," she paused, "possibly stop in for an ice cream."

Evan immediately picked up his pencil and copied a row of perfect letters.

His mother laughed. "Nice work. Get your jacket and we'll be on our way in a flash. It's a lovely day for a walk."

Garvey's grocery was filled with usual crowd queued up at the check outs, the deli station, the off license that was no longer an off license but actually part of the store, and at the ice cream counter. Everywhere she looked, Kate recognized people she knew. Some merely nodded, others stopped to wish her well. She no longer wondered how information spread so quickly. Such was the way of a small town.

Sean Ryan leaned over the counter and winked at Evan. "What will you have, lad?"

"An ice cream with a flake, please."

"The boy knows what he wants, an ice cream with a flake. What about you, Kate? Will I make it two?"

"No, thanks, Sean. One will do it." She reached into her pocket for her coin purse. It wasn't there. Frowning, she reached into the other one and then into her back pockets. Not there either. The queue behind her was lengthening. Feeling the heat in her cheeks, she leaned forward. "Never mind, Sean. I must have left my purse at home. I've no money to pay for the ice cream. I'm sorry."

"Don't worry yourself, Katie. I wouldn't think of depriving the lad of his ice cream with a flake. Are you sure you won't have one as well? A free ice cream cone may be hard to find in Dublin."

Kate laughed. "Nonexistent."

Sean handed over two ice cream cones complete with chocolate flake biscuits. "Seriously, Katie. You'll be missed. I can't imagine what Tralee will be like without Katie Kelliher working her mischief. We'll miss you."

Once again tears welled up in her eyes. She blinked them back and busied herself with wrapping a napkin around Evan's cone. "I'll miss you, too, Sean. I'll miss everyone."

Back on the street, she took Evan's hand. "Shall we show your daddy how well you can write your letters?"

Evan's face lit up. "Yes."

Kelliher's Hardware was abuzz with activity just before closing. Maired was behind the register. Evan ran to her. "Hello, Nan. I learned a new letter today. Do you want me to show you?"

Mindful of the ice cream, Maired hugged him. "I certainly do. I'll ring your dad and he can watch as well." Pointedly ignoring Kate, she pressed the intercom switch and summoned Dermot from the back room.

He arrived immediately, smiled at Kate and swung Evan to his shoulder. "It's grand to see you both. Is everything all right?"

Kate swallowed. He really was quite good-looking, not sexy and dangerous in the Richie O'Shea way, but broad-shouldered, solid and reliable. "Evan wanted to show you his letters. He's mastered nearly all of them," Kate explained.

"Shall we go upstairs and find paper?"

"I'd like to see them, too, Dermot," his mother announced.

"All right. Find us a bit of paper and we'll put Evan through his paces."

Minutes later, with chocolate flake and the remains of vanilla ice cream smeared across his mouth and cheeks, Evan laboriously printed out two rows of credible letters, A through S.

Maired clapped her hands. "Brilliant, just brilliant."

Dermot grinned. "I'm proud of you, lad. Well done."

"Tomorrow, I'll learn T, and then all the rest. I'll show you all of them, every day."

Like a menacing cloud, silence descended over the three adults. Kate looked at Dermot, his friendly gray eyes and the new haircut. Most likely the credit went to the strange women sitting with him in Manor. She cleared her throat. "It's getting late. You'll be closing soon and we need to go."

"Kate." Dermot laid his hand on her arm. "There's something I want to show you. Do you have a minute?"

"Of course. Come along, Evan."

"If you wouldn't mind." Maired bit her lip. "Leave the lad with me while you visit. I don't get to Dublin very often."

Kate swallowed. She hadn't considered Maired but, of course, she would be one more casualty of their leaving. "Your mother hates me."

Dermot's hand found her elbow. "She doesn't hate you, Katie, not any more than you hate her. You're two different people. She can't see beyond what she's always known and she can't be blamed for being satisfied with what she has, just as you can't for wanting more. She's a bit jealous of you, you know, although she'd never admit it."

Kate stared at him. "You resented my wanting more."

"That was my mistake. I fell in love with you because of the kind of person that you are and then I wanted you to be content with the status quo." He shook his head, "No, with less than the status quo. Your friends were cashing in on the Celtic Tiger, buying land, building homes. I didn't pay enough attention to what you wanted, what you should have."

They were in the flat now, a flat much neater and more organized than the one Kate left months before. "You're not entirely to blame, Dermot. I made mistakes, too."

He picked up a long cylinder and unrolled it on the table. "This is what I wanted to show you."

"What is it?"

"A lot, two acres in all, with a rise here." He indicated with his hand where the slope elevated. "The view of the valley and the mountains is breathtaking and here, you can see the lights of the town after the sun sets."

"I don't understand."

"It's for you, Kate. For us. Look at this." He unrolled a set of blue prints. "These are tentative, of course, but the permit is for three thousand square feet, four bedrooms, three baths, a sitting room, large kitchen, laundry and dining room. Over here is an attached area for a commercial kitchen. You could start your own business. Liam said he would help with a business plan and a website. Just because we live here doesn't mean you can't expand with clients all over the country."

He'd done all this for her.

"I haven't settled on the details yet because I wanted you to help me design it." He stood back. "It's all here, if I can convince you to come back to me."

She couldn't look at him. "You want me to come back, after everything I've done."

"I'd want you back no matter what you'd done." He took her hands. "I love you, Kate. I always have. That won't change."

She had to ask. "Who was the woman I saw you sitting with at Manor?"

He looked puzzled. "What woman?"

"Blonde, attractive. I'm sure she's not from Tralee."

"I don't know who—"

"She was with you and Evan in the coffee shop at Manor the day I came back from Dublin."

His forehead cleared. "That's Evelyn Fleming. She's the estate agent I bought the site from."

The estate agent. Of course. Suddenly she was terribly ashamed. "I can't believe you did all of this for me."

"I hope it isn't too late." He lifted her chin, forcing her to look at him. "Kate. Tell me it isn't too late. Tell me you aren't going to Dublin with Ritchie O'Shea."

The tears flowed freely down her cheeks. "No, Dermot. It isn't too late, not if you still want me and I'll never go anywhere with Ritchie O'Shea."

"Thank God," he said, and held out his arms. "Thank God."

CHAPTER 45

Johannah

At first she was unsure of where to go but then it seemed sensible to head toward town and the spot where she'd met him in the first place. *The Daily Grind* was closed but she pulled into an empty spot on the street, turned off the engine and climbed out of the car determined to wait for as long as it took for him to show up. She knew he would. He always did.

Leaning against the window of the cafe, she propped herself up with one leg. If only she smoked. Smoking would pass the time. People seemed to enjoy their cigarettes. They endured pouring rain, extreme cold and eventual cardiac arrest just for a few puffs of tar and nicotine.

She felt his presence before she heard him. When he said her name she wasn't startled.

"Hello, Hannie."

Turning, she looked at him, wondering why it had taken her so long to recognize who he was. Her anger surged. She struggled to subdue it. "Hello."

"It's late for a latte, but you already knew that."

"Yes."

"So, what brings you here?"

"I think I should be asking that question, as well as a few others."

His thrust his hands into his pockets. "Such as?"

"Do you know that I don't even know your last name? What is your last name, Patrick?"

He hesitated before he spoke, his words cautious, a man finding his way, not sure of the path he should follow. "I'm not sure what you mean."

"You know exactly what I mean. Why did you do it?"

Watching the emotions play across his face, she knew the minute he understood and blushed at her own ignorance. How could she have overlooked the obvious? Every gesture, every movement was Mickey's. Now that she knew, everything fell into place and she was angry. "Why didn't you tell me?"

Minutes passed before he spoke. Finally, he answered. "When did you know?"

"Today. It was something Kate said, an expression that reminded me of you. Maybe I always knew."

"And you accepted it, not questioning your sanity or wondering how such a thing could be possible?"

"I believe in God."

"That doesn't explain anything."

"Of course it does," she said impatiently. "Life is full of miracles. I'm a social worker. I've taken courses in psychology. I've read Elizabeth Kubler-Ross. There are books filled with study after study about those who die and are brought back." She glared at him. "Do you think you're all that special?"

"Hannie." He laughed helplessly. "Why are you so angry?"

"You knew Kate was your daughter and you didn't think to tell me." She pointed at the spot in the center of her chest. "You struck a blow to my heart, Mickey Enright. You let me suffer and wonder. You have no idea of the guilt I carried. Did you do it on purpose? Were you so resentful that you couldn't put me at ease?" She turned to face him, her finger prodding his chest. "Wasn't it enough that I looked the other way and catered to every whim you ever had even when you came home without your paycheck and reeking of drink?" She was crying now. "Wasn't it enough that I loved you more than life itself and that I wanted to throw myself into the grave with you rather than live without you? How could you have kept silent? Didn't you know what it would have meant to me?"

He stared at her, opened his mouth and then closed it again. He reached for her hand. She let him take it. "I didn't know you felt that way, Hannie. Honestly, it had become so unimportant to me that I thought you felt the same. Kate was always my daughter, from the moment I felt her kick inside your womb. She asked me, you see. Apparently Francie told Ritchie and he told

Kate. It was important for her to know. I didn't even care about the results of the test. I didn't think you would either. So much time had passed. We had a life together, Hannie. We loved each other. All of that didn't matter."

Somewhere around the words, *Kate was always my daughter*, her anger began to fade. By the time he said, *I didn't even care about the results*, it had nearly disappeared. All that was important stood before her in the flesh, Mickey Enright, her husband. The trappings of the man who called himself Patrick had completely dissipated. He was all Mickey now, from the square, substantial height of him to the piercing blue of his eyes. She stared at him hungrily. "I can't believe I didn't know you from the beginning," she whispered. "I've wasted so much time."

"It wasn't supposed to be like that."

She clutched his hand tightly. "How it was supposed to be?"

"I was sent back here to straighten out a few unresolved matters."

"And did you?"

"Yes. I believe so, although my reasons for being here aren't the same as they were in the beginning." He frowned. "I feel different, lighter, more comfortable." He looked at her. "Have I changed?"

"Yes," she said slowly, her eyes moving across his face. "You're all Mickey now. There's none of Patrick left."

He touched her cheek. "I wasn't the best of husbands, Hannie. I know that now. But never doubt that you were my life. Always remember that."

Johannah felt the panic rise in her throat. "What's happening? Are you leaving?"

"That was always the plan," he explained gently. "Everyone leaves and I've been granted more time than most."

"But I'm not ready. I need more time. Please," she begged him, "everyone is leaving me." She clung to him. "There must be a way to ask for more time."

Slowly, his arms encircled her, crushing her against his chest. Seconds passed and then she felt it, warmth, beginning in the core of her, spreading out to her limbs, her fingers, toes and cheeks. She felt his breath on her face. "I want to come with you."

He laughed. "No, you don't. You want to be here for Liam's family. You want to share Kate's happiness and see Evan grow up. This is your time. Jump in, Hannie. Say yes to your life." He swallowed, cleared his throat and held her so he could look at her. "You are young. You will love again."

She shook her head. "No."

"Yes. You must. Do this for yourself. Live every moment and when your life is over, I'll be waiting for you."

Tears clung to her lashes. "You will?"

"I will."

"Promise me."

She felt his words, like the touch of a snowflake, and then the wind came out of nowhere, a rush of churning air that left her shaken and dazed. She closed her eyes and when she opened them again, he was gone.

Slowly, she walked back to her car, automatically inserting the key, pulling out on to the street, heading toward—where? Where did she want to go? Not home. She definitely didn't want to go home. Then with that flash of understanding that clarifies so much of what had previously been only a hazy premonition, she knew. Purpose sent energy surging through her body. She felt electrified in a way she hadn't since Mickey died. Checking her mirrors, she made a u-turn on Castle Street and turned right at the circle, past the park and the museum, turning into the Meadowlands Hotel carpark.

She was moving quickly now, locking her car, entering the lobby, waving at the clerk manning the desk. Purposefully, she chose the main corridor, the one with the larger suites, checking the numbers until she found what she wanted. She stared at the knocker, wondering where she would find the nerve to make her presence known, when the door opened.

Jack Rafferty's smile of delight reassured her. "Johannah, what a lovely surprise. I was just about to call you."

"Why?"

"I thought we might take a look at a house outside of town and then have dinner together."

"A house, outside of Tralee?"

"The owners won't be ready to leave until the end of next month," he explained. "I wanted to talk it over with you, to be sure you understand that I'm not trying to pressure you, but the thing is, we can't get to know each other if you're here and I'm not. I have a few things to take care of in London, but I'll be back when the house is ready. Is that all right with you, Johannah?"

She stared at him, speechless.

He laughed and stepped back. "This isn't the way I'd planned to ask you. Please, come in. We can't continue this conversation in the hall."

She held out her hand. "No," she said, finding her voice, speaking quickly so as not to lose her nerve. "I won't come in. I'm thrilled about the house, really. But I'd like to wait until you're settled before I see it, and I would like to have dinner with you except that nothing will be open that time of night." She stopped to breathe. "Why don't you stop by after you've seen the house and I'll have dinner ready for the two of us."

He didn't touch her. It wasn't necessary. "Really, Johannah?"

"Yes."

"Then I will gratefully accept your invitation."

CHAPTER 42

Mickey

This time the wind surrounded him gently, almost as if someone was leading the way, buffering him from the worst of it. When he opened his eyes, the myriad of greens nearly blinded him, lime-green hills, blue-green pines, yellow-green silage, emerald-green hedges, a land as richly green as Ireland was green except that a brilliant sun warmed the air and the sky hadn't a hint of cloud. "Where am I?" he said out loud.

Peter materialized before him. "You wanted green." He waved his arms. "Here it is."

"I'm finished," Mickey said.

"I know. You've done well."

"It wasn't easy."

"Worthy endeavors rarely are."

"How long will it be before I see them again?"

Peter shook his head. "I can't tell you that. Some you'll see before others. Time passes quickly here."

Mickey sighed. "Have I passed the test?"

"There's no test, lad. The only requirement for staying is that you believe."

"Are you saying I went through all of this for nothing?"

Peter looked outraged. "*Nothing*? You call your metamorphosis, *nothing*? You were a lout, Mickey Enright, self-serving and pitiful. Now you're a presentable specimen, quite satisfactory, in my opinion."

Mickey met the saint's dark, penetrating gaze. "You knew all the time that my reasons were selfish."

"Yes."

"Will Johannah be all right, with this Rafferty fellow?"

Peter hesitated. "I'm not supposed to do this—"

"Tell me."

"Under normal circumstances you would never have known about him. We don't allow that kind of thing. It confuses the bigger picture."

Mickey waited, sensing Peter would relent.

"You've done exceptionally well, with little direction." Peter stroked his chin. "I see no harm in giving you this small bit of information."

"I suppose we've all the time in the world."

"Don't get cocky with me," the saint warned, "or I won't tell you."

"I wouldn't think of it."

"She's a very intelligent woman, your wife. It's odd that she chose you, but she knows her own mind. You have no need to worry about Johannah." He rubbed his hands together as if dismissing the subject altogether. "Now, we must move on to other business."

"You're not serious. What more is there for me to do?"

Peter's hand reached out to rest on Mickey's shoulder. "That's the beauty of this place, lad. We are never finished with the good we can do. Come along with me."

AUTHOR BIO

Jeanette Baker is the award-winning author of sixteen novels, published by Pocket, Kensington and Mira Books, many of them set in the lush countryside of historical and contemporary Ireland where she lives and writes during the summer months. Her ancestors, the O'Flahertys, hail from Inishmore, the largest of the Aran Islands located off the coast of Galway. She takes great pride in the prayer posted by the English over the ancient city gates, 'From the wrath of the O'Flahertys, may the good Lord deliver us.'

Jeanette graduated from the University of California at Irvine and holds a Masters Degree in Education. For the remainder of the year, she teaches in Southern California, reads constantly, attempts to navigate the confusing world of Facebook and, more recently e-publishing, concocts creations from interesting cook books and enjoys the company of friends and her grown children. She is the RITA award-winning author of NELL. Please visit her website and blog at jeanettebaker.com and visit her on her Facebook page, Jeanette Baker – author.